About the Authors

Susan Stephens is passionate about writing books set in fabulous locations where an outstanding man comes to grips with a cool, feisty woman. Susan's hobbies include travel, reading, theatre, long walks, playing the piano, and she loves hearing from readers at her website. www.susanstephens.com

After leaving her convent school, **Miranda Lee** briefly studied the cello before moving to Sydney, where she embraced the emerging world of computers. Her career as a programmer ended after she married, had three daughters and bought a small acreage in a semi-rural community. She yearned to find a creative career from which she could earn money. When her sister suggested writing romances, it seemed like a good idea. She could do it at home, and it might even be fun! She never looked back.

Helen Brooks began writing in 1990 as she approached her 40th birthday! She realised her two teenage ambitions (writing a novel and learning to drive) had been lost amid babies and hectic family life, so set about resurrecting them. In her spare time, she enjoys sitting in her wonderfully therapeutic, rambling old garden in the sun with a glass of red wine (under the guise of resting while thinking of course). Helen lives in Northampton, England with her husband and family.

D1149592

Latin Lovers

Latin Lovers:
Spanish Sunsets

SUSAN STEPHENS

MIRANDA LEE

HELEN BROOKS

MILLS & BOON

All rights reserved including the right of reproduction in whole or in part in any form. This edition is published by arrangement with Harlequin Books S.A.

This is a work of fiction. Names, characters, places, locations and incidents are purely fictional and bear no relationship to any real life individuals, living or dead, or to any actual places, business establishments, locations, events or incidents. Any resemblance is entirely coincidental.

This book is sold subject to the condition that it shall not, by way of trade or otherwise, be lent, resold, hired out or otherwise circulated without the prior consent of the publisher in any form of binding or cover other than that in which it is published and without a similar condition including this condition being imposed on the subsequent purchaser.

® and TM are trademarks owned and used by the trademark owner and/or its licensee. Trademarks marked with ® are registered with the United Kingdom Patent Office and/or the Office for Harmonisation in the Internal Market and in other countries.

First Published in Great Britain 2021
by Mills & Boon, an imprint of HarperCollins*Publishers* Ltd,
1 London Bridge Street, London, SE1 9GF

www.harpercollins.co.uk

HarperCollins*Publishers*
1st Floor, Watermarque Building,
Ringsend Road, Dublin 4, Ireland

LATIN LOVERS: SPANISH SUNSETS © 2021 Harlequin Books S.A.

A Spanish Inheritance © 2003 Susan Stephens
The Blackmailed Bridegroom © 1999 Miranda Lee
A Spanish Affair © 2001 Helen Brooks

ISBN: 978-0-263-29966-3

MIX
Paper from
responsible sources

FSC
www.fsc.org

FSC™ C007454

This book is produced from independently certified FSC™ paper to ensure responsible forest management.

For more information visit: www.harpercollins.co.uk/green

Printed and bound in Spain
by CPI, Barcelona

A SPANISH
INHERITANCE

SUSAN STEPHENS

CHAPTER ONE

'THIS is a private beach.'

The deep Latin voice with its hint of censure brought the slender young woman scrambling to her feet. Struggling to fasten the top half of her bikini with eyes narrowed against the sun's glare, Annalisa drew herself up to her full height, only to find herself steering her gaze into the naked chest of a powerfully built man.

'I'm sorry,' she said automatically. So where was the notice saying this stretch of Menorcan sand was reserved for the use of arrogant Spanish males? 'I was just—'

'I gathered what you were doing,' he cut in.

'There's nothing to say this area is restricted,' Annalisa said, fighting to keep her gaze in check. She judged him to be in his mid-thirties. Black bathing shorts still wet from the sea clung to well-muscled thighs, while drops of water glistened on his bronzed, toned body. Her heart gave a jolt as she lifted her chin to take a proper look at his face. He had the most amazing eyes... Not just the colour, the shape, or even the fact that twin crescents of thick black lashes cast deep shadows across his chiselled cheekbones; they were simply the most expressive—

'Do you have signs in your garden back home?' he demanded, reclaiming her attention.

He spoke with all the quiet confidence of a man accustomed to respect, Annalisa thought as she took stock of her adversary.

'No, but my garden has a hedge around it...and a gate.'

To her surprise he almost smiled. 'Touché, Miss—?'

'Wilson. Annalisa Wilson,' Annalisa told him, feeling the need to cross her arms over her chest. It wasn't that his gaze ever left her face, and he certainly didn't try to crowd her like most men. But even standing a good few feet away he made her extremely nervous.

And now he smiled. But, instead of making her feel better, the flash of strong white teeth against his improbably handsome face made her feel more awkward than ever. Maybe it had more to do with the look in his eyes that suggested he knew a lot more than she did.

'Pleased to meet you, Annalisa. That is a beautiful and unusual name.'

'Thank you. My father was Spanish.'

'Really?'

Why that should amuse him she had no idea.

'Ramon di Crianza Perez,' he said, extending his hand in formal greeting.

As they connected she felt the strength in his fingers close around her, and instinctively snatched her hand away. 'I'm sorry if I'm trespassing. I'll go—'

'Go?' he queried sharply. 'How do you propose to do that?'

'I'll swim back the way I came…around the point,' she said, nodding towards a spine of rocks that divided the two beaches.

'The point!'

His incredulity stung her. 'Why not?'

'It's far too dangerous!'

'I think I can be the judge—' She held back the rest of the retort. Why on earth was she attempting to justify her actions to a complete stranger?

'You do?' His voice, like a whiplash, lacked all suggestion of Mediterranean charm, but his eyes still possessed the same infuriating sparkle that had captured her attention in the first place… It betrayed an interest that went far beyond a natural desire to protect his boundaries.

Staring back at him, Annalisa knew the fact she felt hot and edgy had nothing to do with the sun. 'Well, you swam here from that yacht,' she argued, glancing towards an impressive cruiser moored offshore. When his sardonic gaze licked over her she felt hotter still.

'You must consider yourself an exceptional athlete.'

'I swam for my school—'

'In a swimming pool?'

'Well, yes. But—'

'The Mediterranean is not a swimming pool, Annalisa.'

Was it really necessary to drawl her name like that? she wondered, conscious of the inadequate scraps of material struggling to contain her figure.

'These waters can be very dangerous,' he went on. 'The current by those rocks—'

'A strong swimmer—'

'Should have more respect for the ocean,' he countered evenly.

'I got here in one piece,' Annalisa muttered. But her defiance was being steadily eroded by this man's determined campaign of control.

She felt his brooding gaze rest on her face.

'Beginner's luck,' he said, holding up his hands to bring an end to the matter. 'Come. I will escort you off my property.'

Your property! So, they were to be neighbours, Annalisa thought, careful to keep her expression neutral as she digested this piece of information.

She panicked as he moved towards her, and backed up a step. 'I have to swim back. I don't have any dry clothes with me.'

He drew up short, and his assessing stare ran heat through every inch of her. 'I'm sure something can be found for you up at the house.'

His brazen inspection, together with his casual assumption that she would leap to do his bidding, sent storm waves pulsing through her. The sea was nothing in comparison to the danger on the shore, Annalisa thought as she tried to side-step her way out of trouble.

But his reflexes were razor-sharp and he blocked her path. 'My driver will take you wherever you want to go.'

'Look, I'm sure you mean to be kind—'

His impatient gesture sliced through the air. 'Kindness is not an issue. My only concern is to prevent you from making another mistake.'

I wasn't aware I'd made a first until I met you, Annalisa thought, watching his jaw tighten as if he couldn't quite believe one person could provoke so much aggravation in so short a time. 'I'll be fine,' she insisted firmly. 'It's an easy swim.'

'I don't have time for this,' he rapped, directing a level stare at her. 'And my invitation was not a suggestion,' he added pointedly. He turned abruptly to indicate a narrow track that cut a snaking path up the cliff.

The silent instruction made his autocratic air all the more intolerable. But with someone like Ramon Perez planted in the way Annalisa knew she had no alternative but to follow orders…for the moment.

Her mouth tightened angrily as she marched past him. But she was angrier at herself than with her forceful neighbour. There was just no excuse for going into battle unprepared. If she had only apologised for trespassing on his land, accepted his offer of some dry clothes and a lift home, the whole incident would have been over by now. Instead of which— Her stomach lurched as he strode ahead of her. Drinking in the wide spread of his shoulders and the taut power of a most agreeable back view, she was forced to concede that there were some things that made up for an attack of hurt pride.

It wasn't the climb that tightened Annalisa's stomach in knots, but the growing suspicion that with each step she was leaving the simple charm of the shoreline behind and entering some exclusive territory. The natural disorder of scrub and sand and pebbles gave way to steps that looked as if they had been swept recently, and the handrail had been painted in a shade that blended perfectly with the surroundings. This impression of affluence was only confirmed when they reached the top of the steep climb and a stout manservant, dressed from head to toe in a crisp white uniform, hurried forward.

Maybe he had been on sentry duty for hours, she mused, seeing the canary-yellow and white beach towels stacked on his outstretched arm.

Ramon acknowledged the man with a courteous nod. 'Please escort Miss Wilson to a guest room, Rodriguez. And see that she receives some refreshment before she leaves.' He swivelled round, appraising Annalisa at a glance. 'I'm sure Margarita will be able to find something suitable for you to wear.' And, swiping a towel off the pile, he draped it around her shoulders.

'Thank you,' Annalisa said, struggling to ignore the flash of sensation that rushed through her when his hand brushed her naked skin. She drew the towel tightly around her to ward off the cold hand of disappointment. He might be the most infuriating individual she had ever encountered, but he was also the most intriguing. And the way his voice had softened when he said 'Margarita' suggested this woman meant a great deal to him— Now she was being ridiculous! She'd only known him for five minutes and already her imagination was running riot!

He dipped his head briefly, signalling an end to the encounter. '*Adios*, Annalisa.'

Shading her eyes with her hand, Annalisa watched him power away towards an imposing white mansion. She felt sure that the home and lifestyle of Ramon di Crianza Perez were as different from her own as it was possible to imagine. But in some unaccountable way she felt the need to prove herself to her proud Menorcan neighbour.

A discreet cough distracted her. She turned and flashed a

quick smile at the manservant. But he had no time to waste on pleasantries. Having caught her attention, he was already making for the house, using short rapid strides that suggested he had far better things to do.

As she climbed the central marble staircase of the villa behind her surly guide, Annalisa shot some anxious glances at the closed doors. She felt sure everyone living in such a place would have to be as self-possessed as Ramon, and looking like a beached mermaid was not the best time to cannon into some elegant presence.

The grand house was completely silent. Maybe it was empty. But when the manservant opened a door leading off the first-floor landing, and showed her into a stunning room overlooking the sea, she knew there had to be someone in residence.

For bush telegraph read bush fire, Annalisa thought, spying the jug of freshly squeezed orange juice and the bowl of plump ripe figs. And an outfit had already been laid out on what looked very much like a priceless Louis Quinze *chaise longue*. The slim sofa was covered with the finest brocade in a delicate shade of powder blue, and its single arm was intricately carved and ornamented with gold leaf.

Margarita had a figure not dissimilar to her own, Annalisa realised as she picked up some sapphire silk Capri pants. A thrill ran through her as she read the label. She had never come close to wearing anything so exclusive. An ivory silk casual top by the same designer lay beside some flesh-toned underwear, still in the fuchsia-tinted tissue paper in which it had been packed in the boutique. The flimsy thong and bra were composed of so fine a fabric it brought the blood rushing to her cheeks. Margarita must be quite something, she thought, spotting some dainty cream leather mules lined up neatly on the floor.

Waiting until the door closed, Annalisa quickly stepped out of her damp bikini. There was a full-length cheval-glass in one corner of the room and it was too tempting not to steal a glimpse at herself as she dressed. Slipping into clothes like these was almost a sensual experience, like stepping into another world. But now what? she wondered, gazing around the fabulous room.

There wasn't long to wait before she found out. A tap on the door brought the answer. A young girl dressed in a maid's uniform stood waiting on the threshold.

'The car is outside when you are ready, Señorita Fuego Montoya,' she announced in halting English.

'Wilson. Señorita Wilson,' Annalisa corrected gently, smiling at her. 'But you can call me Annalisa if you like.'

'*Sí*, Señorita Fuego Montoya,' the young girl said, colouring up.

She doesn't understand, Annalisa realised, hoping the shock of hearing her late father's name wrongly applied to herself didn't show on her face.

'Are you ready, *señorita*?' the maid pressed, hovering uncertainly on the threshold.

'Yes. Thank you,' Annalisa said, reminding herself to add Spanish lessons to her list of things to do. 'And I'll return the clothes—'

'Oh, no, *señorita*,' the girl exclaimed, holding up her hands to emphasise the point. 'Señora Margarita intends you to keep them.'

'But I couldn't possibly,' Annalisa protested.

The maid shrugged, as if the generous gift was of no consequence. 'The *señora* has many such outfits, *señorita*.'

Wealth like this was hard to imagine... And yet she should try, Annalisa reminded herself. Quite out of the blue she had recently inherited a considerable chunk of land in Menorca, and even though she had precious little cash to throw around right now, if she sold the estate designer outfits like these would be well within her reach. 'I should still like to thank Señora—'

But the girl had already started towards the staircase, and

with a brief wave of her hand indicated that Annalisa should follow.

For just a beat Annalisa hesitated. If only her Spanish had been stronger she might have been able to ask the maid to arrange a brief meeting with Margarita. Then she could have explained her intrusion face to face, as well as thank her for the clothes. But for now she had no answer to the dilemma.

Annalisa frowned. Everything connected with Menorca seemed to have a dilemma attached to it as far as she was concerned. And the whole point in taking a sabbatical from the small law practice where she worked as a solicitor had been to resolve dilemmas, not create more. She had come to the island to uncover the truth about her Spanish father, not to involve herself in the lives of the island's super-rich. Her mission was to discover what had prompted an elderly Spanish grandee to leave a vast estate to her, when he had abandoned her mother the minute he discovered she was pregnant. And had never been heard from again as far as Annalisa knew.

During her mother's lifetime the relevant questions could not be asked. There had been an unspoken rule between them that strictly forbade all talk of the past. But her mother had died almost immediately after the news of Señor Fuego Montoya's death, prompting Annalisa to embark on her own quest.

So, here she was…feeling increasingly uncomfortable as she followed the maid down the sweeping marble staircase. The young girl's confusion over her name had caused the past and present to collide…and in the home of a man who might be as unprincipled as her father for all Annalisa knew. But thankfully she had the benefit of hindsight to guide her now…and better still there was no sign of her enigmatic neighbour.

Perhaps she had seen the last of him. And perhaps it was as well if she had. The chance to savour Margarita's dream existence for a short time had been a heady experience, but reality beckoned and Annalisa knew that she could not allow a distraction like Ramon Perez to get in her way.

Although it was a relatively short swim from one beach to another, the drive back to the *finca* took quite some time. One main arterial road stretched the length of the island, and each cove could only be reached by returning first to this highway. Annalisa tensed on the soft kidskin upholstery as the limousine bounced in and out of the ruts on the track down to her new home, and knew just enough Spanish to feel embarrassment when she caught the word *casucha* as the chauffeur muttered something under his breath. The *finca* might look like a hovel to him, but by the time she had finished with it—

'Thank you for the lift,' she said, managing to bite her tongue as he got out to open the door for her.

She really would have to do something about the approach if she wanted the property to achieve its full market value, she realised, gazing around. According to the estate agent there were already several offers on the table.

But even if some of the renovations were beyond her pocket, there was no harm in investing as much as she could afford in order to reap the maximum return when she came to sell.

When the limousine drove off she was enveloped from head to foot in a cloud of fine white dust. This served to point out the fact that the walls were crumbling, not to mention the roof, which in some areas was open to the sky. If she didn't sort that out before the rains came, the whole place would be flooded—that was if the infamous Tramuntana wind didn't lift it off first. But in spite of all the problems there was something very special about the mellow, honey-coloured stone.

Excited yelps diverted Annalisa's attention to one of the more forceful members of her ever-increasing menagerie. The welcome softened the worry lines that had been building up on her face all morning and replaced them with a smile. The ancient rag-tailed dog was so grateful for every second of her time that she had already adopted him, naming him Fudge for his colour. Along with Fudge, several cats, hens, and even a donkey had miraculously appeared on her doorstep, as if they accepted what she could not—that life on *finca* Fuego Montoya was about to resume.

They were more optimistic than she was, Annalisa thought, glancing around the cobbled courtyard at the daunting tasks that still lay ahead of her. Her immediate impression of the main house had been of overwhelming neglect. She had found it so dark and still the first time she'd walked through the curtains of dust motes suspended in the musty air. But somehow that hadn't put her off. And her determination had been rewarded.

Traces of what must once have been a fine family home had soon become apparent in the quality of the furniture, as well as the interesting collection of cobweb-festooned paintings. And then she had been filled with the urge to breathe life into it again—to fling open the shutters, to clean out every corner and polish the windows until the whole place gleamed and vibrated with life.

She didn't rest until each room was filled with the scent of beeswax and soap and flowers... But the outbuildings remained in a desperate state.

She closed her eyes briefly and drew a deep breath. Then, firming her lips, she opened them again. What she had started she would finish. So what if she had to learn to use a hammer and chisel? She had come a long way from her small solicitor's office in an undistinguished town in the north of England. Here the sun warmed her face and it felt good. Winter was barely over, but in Menorca she could already detect the scent of blossom on the air.

Having changed out of the delicious outfit into a pair of battered old shorts and a non-descript T-shirt, Annalisa headed down to the kitchen. Clearing a space on the rustic table, she prepared to write a brief letter of thanks to Señor and Señora Ramon di Crianza Perez. But even as she put pen to paper thoughts and impressions invaded her mind—and none of them was connected with the brief note she had planned. The truth was she was furious with herself. Somehow a married man had slipped beneath her guard, jolting something deep within her...something fundamental. Like an alarm going off in her heart, she acknowledged with dismay.

But she had seen her mother left embittered and had no intention of being lured along the same path. It was a bleak trail that led to nothing more than empty lives and worthless promises. With an impatient huff she forced her attention back to the blank sheet of paper on the table in front of her.

Willing the pen to move back and forth, she crafted the words that would convey her appreciation for the kindness of the Crianza Perez household and nothing more. Then, sealing the envelope, she propped it up next to the clock. She would post it on her next shopping trip to Mahon, the island's capital, and perhaps find some small token in an attempt to appease her formidable neighbour. But first things first; her legal representative on the island would be appearing in a little under an hour.

Taking a fresh sheet of paper, Annalisa began drawing up a list of subjects she wanted to discuss. It was only as she began framing the questions in her mind that a new possibility occurred to her...

'But, Señorita Wilson, you do not have the money to make the improvements you have just outlined. Why do you not accept the generous offer that has been made for *finca* Fuego Montoya and buy something more suitable for yourself?'

'I have decided not to sell.'

'Not to sell!'

Annalisa was certain the distinguished lawyer could not have looked more shocked if he'd tried. 'And that is my final decision,' she confirmed in a low, determined voice.

'But, no!' he insisted dramatically. 'This is impossible. How will you—?'

Annalisa could feel her patience evaporating. 'Don Alfonso,' she began firmly, 'I have always worked for my living and that is exactly how I intend to continue.'

'To work?' the silver-haired lawyer exclaimed in horror with a shrug that encompassed the world. 'But if you sell the *finca*, Señorita Wilson, you will never need to work again.'

'But I want to work,' Annalisa insisted stubbornly. 'And forgive me, Don Alfonso, but I thought *you* worked for me.'

'And so I do,' he insisted hotly. 'But it is my duty to tell you that if you were my daughter—'

'I am no one's daughter!' Annalisa's retorted sharply, regretting the words almost as soon as they shot out of her mouth.

'I understand that your father is dead, Señorita Wilson,' Don Alfonso reminded her solemnly.

And always has been to me, Annalisa thought bitterly as she fought to re-order her thoughts. 'I apologise, Don Alfonso,' she said, composing herself. 'Of course I will always be grateful to my father for entrusting me with the future of the *finca*.' Even if he never acknowledged me in his lifetime, she added silently to herself. 'I should not have raised my voice to you,' she admitted candidly. 'But you should know that I am quite determined to remain here. I intend to restore the house and all the ancillary buildings. Then I shall return the orange groves to a profitable working concern that will benefit everyone in the village.'

'The orange groves!' the elderly lawyer exclaimed in utter amazement. 'But what do you know about fruit production? Forgive me, Señorita Wilson,' he added, saving her the embarrassment of admitting the answer to that was nothing at all. 'I mean no offence.' Plucking a kingfisher-blue handkerchief out of his top pocket, he began dabbing away at imaginary moisture on his neck and high forehead, his concern all too evident.

'None taken,' Annalisa said evenly, wondering what on earth had prompted her insane proposition.

'But even if you were to proceed against my advice you cannot possibly take on such a task alone,' Don Alfonso insisted as he replaced the silk square in his pocket.

'Why? Because I'm a woman?'

He hesitated long enough for Annalisa to know she had struck a Latin nerve.

'You do not have sufficient money,' he insisted, bridging the controversial divide with sheer practicality.

'I can do many of the jobs myself. I shall seek advice in the village...and I am not afraid of hard work.'

'It is not the hard work that is my major concern—'

'And I'll find the money somehow.'

Don Alfonso looked unconvinced as he shook his head. 'I don't doubt your good intentions, Señorita Wilson.'

'Then what is your concern?' Annalisa demanded.

'The power and status of the family you have ranged yourself against may prove insurmountable,' he explained patiently. 'Please. Leave it a little while longer before you make a final decision to decline their generous offer.'

'But I have no intention of accepting any offers. And I don't need more time,' Annalisa insisted. 'My mind is made up, Don Alfonso.'

'I beg you to reconsider—'

'I cannot imagine why anyone could be so determined to buy up my land now when it has so clearly been neglected for years.'

'It was in your father's hands before he died,' Don Alfonso reminded her. 'No one knew why he insisted on hanging on to it. There were many offers during his lifetime—'

'Which he refused?'

'Yes, but—'

'As I shall,' she insisted, though quite where this sudden comradeship with the father who had abandoned her before she was born had come from she had no idea.

'And nothing I can say will dissuade you from this course of action?'

'That is correct.'

Don Alfonso made a bemused sound and then murmured distractedly, 'I cannot understand it...'

'And I cannot understand why you are allowing yourself to be influenced by anyone's interests other than mine.'

He looked offended, and when he spoke again it was in a conspiratorial whisper. 'We are talking about one of the most powerful families in all Spain, Señorita Wilson. Led by a man whom I should not wish to cross.' He shook his head in a grave show of disapproval.

Well, if that was meant to frighten her off it had missed its mark, Annalisa thought, firming her mouth. 'You may feel the need to abide by this man's dicta, Don Alfonso, I do not.'

'You can have no idea of what you are taking on.'

'So, tell me,' Annalisa challenged. 'Put a name to my opponent. We're not discussing some mythical villain, I presume?'

Her elderly advisor bowed his head in dignified acquiescence. 'No, Señorita Wilson. We are talking about an exceptional man with a mind like a steel trap and a will of iron. I fear you will find Ramon di Crianza Perez a most formidable adversary.'

Annalisa's wide mouth softened, images of sun-kissed flesh and rippling muscles uppermost in her mind.

Misreading her expression, Don Alfonso warned, 'It would be a mistake to underestimate Ramon Perez.'

'He's not such a monster,' she reflected absently.

'You know him!'

'I have—' Annalisa stopped, taking care over her choice

of words. 'I met Señor Perez briefly. He seemed perfectly civil—'

The lawyer's frown deepened. 'Forgive me, Señorita Wilson, but you are a young lady in her mid-twenties with limited experience—'

'I am a working woman with a law degree,' Annalisa returned sharply.

'You would be most unwise to take Ramon Perez lightly.'

I would be most unwise to take him at all, she reminded herself wryly. Apart from the knowledge that she would be playing well out of her league, Ramon Perez was a married man. 'I shall treat Señor Crianza Perez exactly as I would treat anyone else,' she said confidently.

Don Alfonso shook his head. 'I'm afraid that may not prove an effective tactic in this case.'

'Well, we will just have to find a way to make Señor Perez understand that *finca* Fuego Montoya is not up for sale, Don Alfonso. This is my home,' she said with a sweeping gesture. 'And I intend to stay here for the rest of my life.'

The lawyer sucked in a deep breath as he flagged up his defeat with his hands. 'So be it, Señorita Wilson. If those are your instructions—'

'They are, Don Alfonso,' Annalisa said firmly.

She was out in the yard when the low-slung black car screamed to a halt. Tossing back her wrist-thick ebony plait, Annalisa wiped her arm across her face as she waited for the dust cloud to settle. When she saw who was coming towards her she tensed. What on earth was Ramon Perez doing here? And why had she decided today of all days to emulate the local women by tucking her lightweight cotton skirt into her underwear while she worked?

Her mind revolved like a Catherine wheel, throwing off excuses…the hen hutches needed repairing…her shorts were drying on the line…

'Buenos días, señorita!' Ramon called out as he strode towards her, swiping the thick coating of limestone dust off his close-fitting jeans.

As he drew nearer she could see his sensuous mouth beginning to curve in the suspicion of a grin. And then he scanned her from head to foot.

'I like your outfit,' he commented approvingly.

Damn! Damn! Damn! Annalisa thought, wrenching her skirt free.

This was not the sort of meeting she had anticipated! She had instructed Don Alfonso to arrange something very different. Something cool and collected in the centre of town. In his shady, peaceful office—wearing suits, for goodness' sake!

'Thank you,' she said, hoping there was enough of a casual note in her voice to fool Ramon into believing she was as composed as he was. She smoothed the crumpled fabric to a modest length around her calves and plucked at the low-cut cotton top that had once been white. 'I bought it in the village.'

'I would never have guessed,' he murmured, turning away to study the various outbuildings before she had a chance to gauge his expression.

Even when the attention of those dark and disturbing eyes was deflected he had presence to spare, Annalisa thought, wishing she could relax.

'You have plenty of work ahead of you,' he called back to her. 'These barns don't look too safe. You mustn't think of housing animals.'

'I have no intention of doing so.' She wished she could keep the edginess out of her voice. But the sight of those strong tanned hands thrust into the pockets of his jeans—

He fielded her peppery response with a laconic, 'Forgive me, Annalisa. I am sure you will take every precaution. I did not mean to challenge your intentions.'

But his eyes said otherwise. They were watchful and

amused as he turned to face her while he raked his thick black hair into order.

'That's OK,' Annalisa lied, knowing her pale skin betrayed her feelings at the most inappropriate moments. 'So, why are you here, Señor Perez?'

A grin tugged at one corner of his mouth. 'I would have thought that was obvious.' When she didn't answer, he explained, 'To see you, of course.'

'Me?' He was viewing her discomfort with a worrying degree of interest, she thought.

He gave a brief nod. 'Don Alfonso came to see me on your behalf…to arrange a meeting. To discuss water rights.'

Annalisa tensed. He didn't need to say any more. The water was her Achilles' heel. If she was going to restore the orange groves, the closest source of fresh water ran across Ramon's land. 'In town. In his office,' she agreed quickly. 'Not here.'

'Why not here?'

She squared her shoulders, as if signalling her refusal to be drawn into a debate out of the hearing of her lawyer. 'What have you really come for, Señor Perez?'

Ramon dipped his head to bait her with his compelling stare. 'To make sure you got home safely.'

'Ah, yes,' Annalisa said awkwardly, realising she should have said something sooner. 'I can't thank you and Margarita enough—'

He brushed off her gratitude with a gesture. 'And to return this,' he said, uncurling one large fist to reveal her tiny bikini.

A sharp sound somewhere between a sigh and a groan escaped her lips as she stepped forward to take it from him. But as one looping bra strap fell over her fingers, he reeled her in with a snap of his wrist. For a long moment they both stood motionless. Then at last he murmured, 'Do you like playing games with me, Annalisa?'

Every tiny hair on her body stood erect as his warm

breath caressed her senses. She had no way of seeing the expression on his face. At that moment her eyes were level with the third button down on his shirt. Was he talking about the water rights...the sale of the *finca*? Or something else...something on a far more personal level? That possibility made her shake her head emphatically as she struggled to remain immune to the very masculine heat coming from him. It was a heat with very different properties from the scorching midday sun. It was a heat that beat at her senses with unrelenting purpose...

'Would you like to?' he growled, so close to her ear that she shivered involuntarily. And then, as if he had received the answer he was looking for, he laughed as if it was indeed just a game to him and let her go.

'I think it's you who is playing games,' Annalisa declared, struggling to hide the fact that she was very shaken indeed. 'But thank you anyway for returning my—'

'I was curious to see for myself the condition of the estate,' Ramon broke in, as if nothing unusual had passed between them.

How could he change pace as smoothly as that? Annalisa wondered, fighting for equilibrium as he moved away from her to stroll around the yard.

If Don Alfonso had wanted to remind her that Ramon Perez was unlike any other man she had ever met, he could not have orchestrated a better demonstration! And the fact that Ramon was forbidden fruit failed to stop her heart from careering around her chest—whilst apparently he was able to remain detached and totally in control.

Her mouth firmed into a determined line as she weighed him up. Just acknowledging the attraction she felt for him was enough to make her feel guilty. But guilt was an emotion that seemed to have bypassed Ramon Perez completely. To hell with gratitude! This was power play at its most refined. It was time to sharpen up her game and get her mind back in gear. The way he was prowling around her yard proved that this visit was nothing more than an excuse to take stock…to weigh up the opposition. But at least this was the sort of predator she could understand…and deal with. All Ramon Perez cared about was gauging how little he would need to pay to take the *finca* off her hands!

'Have you seen everything you came for now?' Annalisa demanded.

'For now,' he agreed. 'And I'm glad I came—'

'To evaluate the competition?' she supplied tersely.

He allowed the silence to hang between them for a few moments, and when he did speak his voice sounded mildly bemused. 'Competition, Annalisa?'

The challenge pierced her defences, releasing a flood of sensation into her tense frame. Too late to bite off her tongue! The damage was done. She had to tread a lot more carefully. Know your enemy… Don't reveal all your cards at once… As far as Ramon knew, she was just some small-town girl getting in his way…an easy target. Far better to leave it like that than to give him any advance warning of her plans…

Her plans? Annalisa's glance swept the ground as Ramon continued to study her. She had plenty of dreams…but no plans…not yet. They couldn't be formulated until she knew exactly what it would take to launch the orange groves as a commercial venture. The only thing she was sure about was that nothing could be accomplished without the fresh water that ran across Ramon's land.

Suddenly the enormity of the task she was taking on hit her square in the chest. The last thing she needed was to alert Ramon to the fact that everything hinged on him—or that where fruit production was concerned she was a complete novice. To have the slightest hope of allaying his suspicions she had to show more self-assurance, put everything back on a business footing—broach the subject of his water when his guard was down.

'Won't you come inside for a cooling drink?' she suggested briskly, heading off towards the house. But her heart was beating so hard she felt sure he would hear it. Perhaps he wouldn't follow. Self-assurance was all very well in theory!

But as she reached the heavy iron-studded front door she realised he was right behind her.

'I'd love a drink,' he murmured. 'If it's not too much trouble?'

'No trouble at all,' she said, trying to ignore the tingles of awareness spinning up and down her spine.

The moment she closed the door behind them she knew it was a mistake. Her hand was actually trembling when she lifted it away from the handle. Enclosed within four walls, Ramon's presence seemed to invade every nook and cranny. It was as if she was seeing the homely room for the first time—but through his eyes. On her way to the business end of the kitchen she managed to backhand a stack of documents into the bureau, plump a couple of cushions on the sofa and sweep up her mug and plate from breakfast, all without breaking stride.

'Don't go to any trouble on my account,' he drawled, when she discreetly removed the contents of the draining board and put them in the sink.

'I'm not. I—' Having given him the best she could manage in coolly composed faces, Annalisa found her gaze trapped by a pair of very dangerous black eyes…and it seemed a very long time indeed before he turned away to inhale deeply and appreciatively.

'You've certainly breathed fresh life into the old place.'

So he had visited the *finca* before. Probably as soon as her father died…looking around the place with a view to buy… And that, more than likely, was exactly what he was doing now! But in spite of every misgiving she was proud of the newly decorated interior. She had completed every bit herself and he was the first person to see the changes.

She had kept everything simple and in keeping with the

rustic setting. The kitchen floor was tiled in natural terracotta and she had placed a huge rug in shades of russet,
cream and slate blue in the centre of the room. There was
a wicker basket full of fruit on the scrubbed table, and another containing vegetables awaiting preparation by the
sink. She had dressed the windows with simple linen blinds
and a profusion of plants and herbs competed for space on
each window ledge.

He made a sound of approval as he turned full circle.
'Congratulations. I'm impressed.'

Praise indeed! She relaxed a little. 'What would you like
to drink?'

'Chilled water.'

While she was busy at the dresser, fetching tumblers, she
watched him out of the corner of her eye—roaming about
while he waited, running his hands along the walls and stopping occasionally to give them a sharp rap with his closed
fist. Her thoughts were in turmoil because…because he was
acting like a prospective purchaser, she decided hotly.

As his gaze tracked across the ceiling she heard him murmur thoughtfully, 'Structural improvements will have to be
made before next winter.'

'I have already come to that conclusion myself, Señor
Perez,' Annalisa heard herself snap as she held out the glass
of water.

The ghost of a smile was the only sign that he had registered her ruffled tone of voice. 'I am sure you have,' he
agreed pleasantly. 'Why don't you call me Ramon,
Annalisa? Señor Perez sounds so formal.'

Common sense screamed at her to keep the relationship
on a formal footing, but pride insisted they were equals.
Why not call him by his first name? He had no difficulty
using hers. But as she poured herself a glass of water
Annalisa realised her hands were still trembling. Ramon's
invasion of this, her private space, was far more unnerving
than she could ever have anticipated.

Avoiding eye contact as she shucked some ice into the glass, she drank deeply, relishing the cool sensation as it tracked through a body that was perilously overheated.

Waiting until she had come out of hiding from behind the glass, Ramon issued a reminder. 'It was you who called a meeting between us.'

'Yes,' Annalisa protested, 'but I don't propose to hold it here…now.'

The look he gave her suggested that Ramon Perez was a man who had never learned the meaning of the word no.

'OK,' he said without missing a beat. 'Let's make it dinner.'

CHAPTER TWO

'DINNER!'

'Don't sound so shocked,' Ramon insisted. 'I'm only suggesting a light meal...fresh fish...' Then he shrugged, adding as an afterthought, 'And perhaps a drop of champagne.'

'Don't you think it's a little early for celebrations?' Annalisa jumped in defensively. She might be eager to start discussions about water rights, but champagne made it all sound too much like a *fait accompli*—for him!

'We both have to eat,' he said matter-of-factly. 'If we do so together we can talk things through. Unless you have other plans, of course?'

She tried racking her brain for some excuse, but every brain cell was on strike. 'Well... No, I don't... But—'

'But?' Ramon queried, one sable brow raised in sardonic challenge.

How could he even ask? She steeled herself to ask the question. 'What about Margarita?'

He frowned. 'Margarita is in England at the moment. She was sorry to miss you at the house. She was packing. Well, Annalisa? What do you say?'

'Say?' she repeated, transfixed by the sight of his lean tanned fingers feathering an exploration over the tender surface of one of her plants.

'Dinner. Tonight,' he repeated, more sharply.

It would be a statement, not a question, she realised, if she didn't get her brain in gear fast. 'I don't think Margarita—'

'What the hell has Margarita got to do with this?' Ramon demanded impatiently.

'But she's your—'

27

'Margarita does not interest herself in my business affairs,' he cut in coolly.

Well, that she could believe after the way Don Alfonso reacted when she told him she intended to work. 'I'm not sure—'

'You're not sure?' Ramon said incredulously. 'I thought you would be as keen as I am to discuss the future of *finca* Fuego Montoya.'

Annalisa's heart-rate steadied fractionally. In the course of her work she dealt with just as many men as women. The fact that Ramon proposed to open negotiations over dinner was purely a convenience for both of them. He knew how busy she was at the *finca*, and there was no reason to suppose his working day was any less demanding.

'I need an answer,' he reminded her sharply. 'Or if you prefer we can leave it to our lawyers to draw up an agreement.'

He knew she would never agree to that. She was already far too committed to the *finca*. 'No, I prefer to handle this myself.'

His eyebrow quirked expressively. 'As you wish.'

His scrutiny made her uncomfortable at the best of times. Right now his flagrantly male presence shrank the room around them, giving her nowhere to look but straight up into his disturbingly lambent gaze.

She had to say something. Refusing his offer would make her look weak—hardly the best opening gambit. She held his gaze for a few moments, then agreed coolly, 'Before we involve our respective legal teams there's no harm in laying our cards on the table.'

'I couldn't agree more,' he said. 'We can do that over dinner, and once we come to an understanding we can instruct our lawyers.'

Annalisa's smile grew more confident. Now he was talking her language. Though whether her work as a newly qualified solicitor equipped her to do battle with Ramon Perez remained to be seen—even with all of Don Alfonso's years of experience to back her up. But, still, it would be better to have some idea of what she was up against. 'Dinner will be fine,' she said firmly.

'Good,' he said with a formal nod as he turned for the door. 'I'll pick you up around nine.'

'I'll look forward to it.'

She waited until the throaty roar of Ramon's sports car had died away before racing upstairs to change. There wasn't much point in entering discussions if she didn't have a clue how to make the best use of his water. And she had no intention of looking foolish. If only she hadn't been so busy making the *finca* attractive to prospective purchasers she might have paid more attention to the mechanics of fruit production. But what had started out as a short trip to lay the ghost of her Spanish father, sell his estates and return to England with enough money to set up her own legal practice, had suddenly mushroomed into something quite different. And now she had committed herself to the revival of the *finca*, she wasn't about to back down.

Plucking some clean clothes out of her wardrobe, she shrugged them on and hurried out. Chances were the same people who'd used to work at the *finca* still lived in the village. She would seek them out and ask for advice.

Standing beneath the creaking hand-painted sign of the local bodega, Annalisa groaned. The owner, Juan, spoke a crazy form of Spanglish, but somehow they managed to communicate. She had gone straight to him, knowing he was a mine of information. But now… She blew some strands of hair off her face as she pulled away from the wall. Her head was bursting with facts. Whether she would be able to marshal them in time for her meeting with Señor Perez…

'Pigs,' she murmured fiercely, distractedly, as she marched off down the narrow pavement. That was one thing Juan had been adamant about. Pigs snuffled up the fallen fruit and kept the ground clean once it had all been cleared and weeded.

She stopped outside the bakery, not really seeing the rows of delicious pastries and fat crusty loaves, her mind full of Juan's insistence that she clear out every single weed. She could have repeated his mantra by heart: weeds were the enemy; weeds drank all the water. And water… Annalisa's mouth tipped down at the corners as she remembered what else he had said. 'Feuds could last for generations where the precious *agua* was concerned.'

Didn't she know it! she thought with a sigh, seeking sanctuary in the bakery.

'*Señorita?*'

The vibrant woman behind the counter was the best possible advertisement for her fragrant assortment of freshly baked wares. Thrumming with vitality, she carried her weight lightly, and a dazzling flash of strong white teeth underscored the glow of genuine welcome in her attractive nut-brown eyes.

'I don't suppose…no,' Annalisa said, shaking her head as if to shake some sense back into it. The smiling shopkeeper probably wouldn't even understand her haphazard mix of Spanish and English, let alone know where she could lay her hands on some pigs.

'How can I help you, *señorita*? What about this?'

Annalisa's eyes cleared as she looked at the generous slice of moist chocolate cake the woman was holding out for her inspection. Tearing her gaze away from the delicious-looking treat, she exclaimed happily, 'You speak English!'

'Many years ago I worked in a household where English was spoken,' the woman agreed cheerfully. Then, taking another glance at Annalisa, she placed the cake on her scales. 'I recommend this when life gets on top of you. One bite and—' She smacked her lips together and shut her eyes in sublime concentration.

It took Annalisa about two seconds to decide that a few moments of bliss couldn't hurt. 'I'm sure you're right,' she said reaching for her purse. 'I'm Annalisa Wilson, by the way. I moved into the *finca* Fuego Montoya—'

'And I am Maria Teresa Gonzalez,' the cheerful assistant said placing the succulent portion of cake into a candyfloss-pink box. 'If you need anything else, *señorita*,' she insisted, deftly securing the container with a length of silver ribbon, 'please don't wait until you are worried. Come straight to me.'

'Well, as it happens...'

Maria Teresa was the answer to her prayers, Annalisa mused, feeling a rush of confidence as she put the finishing touches to her make-up that evening. Now she could meet Ramon with her head held high. Half an hour with Maria was as good as a year in the village. Pigs? No problem. A lusty cockerel to drill some life into her lethargic hens? He would be delivered tomorrow.

Better yet, Maria shared the bakery business with numerous relatives and could spare the time to help out at the *finca*. And, as if that wasn't enough, she knew every worker who had ever been employed at *finca* Fuego Montoya.

Oh, yes, Annalisa thought, taking a last look at herself in the mirror. Now she was ready for anything... *Even Ramon Perez?* a small but insistent voice in the back of her mind demanded. Narrowing her eyes, she answered back, 'Oh, yes. Especially him.'

Never, never again! Annalisa buried her head under the black satin pillows as she tried to convince herself. But the erotic reminders were everywhere... In the crumpled bedding, the evocative scent of him, and in the gentle swell of the waves as they rocked her in this, Ramon's cradle of seductive opulence.

OK, admit it, she thought, sitting bolt upright again. He

had set the bait and she had gobbled it up. Had she no pride, no scruples, no principles? And that was just on the personal front. The thought that she had slept with a married man filled her with horror enough, but who in their right mind slept with the opposition? A first-year law student would have shown more sense!

Dinner had sounded so harmless…so innocent. But dinner on Ramon's yacht was pleasure squared. Romantic, sensuous, seductive… It wasn't even as if he had made any secret of his wider intentions. As far as Ramon Perez was concerned there was no urgency. Even the sequence of events was irrelevant to him. But he would own *finca* Fuego Montoya…and take her to bed.

'What are you doing?'

Annalisa jumped guiltily and grabbed the sheet to cover herself as Ramon strolled back into the stateroom. Squeezing her eyes tightly shut until they burned as hot as her face, she sent desperate mind messages for him to leave. He was a married man—out of bounds, out of the question! Where was her common sense? Her sanity? As remorse bludgeoned her emotions she stretched out her long legs, searching for some cool spot to soothe her overheated senses. But she only succeeded in setting up some delicious after-shocks in a region of her body that insisted on responding to Ramon however hard she fought to remain detached.

'Get up.' His voice was sharp.

And was that contempt too?

'Look at me, Annalisa,' he warned when she only buried herself deeper under the sheets. 'This won't work.' And, crossing to the bed, he deftly flipped back the covers.

With an exclamation of alarm Annalisa snatched out a hand to grab them back, then realised that instead of being naked, as she had expected, she was in fact wearing the top half of a pair of rather elegant pyjamas. Clearly made for a man, in burgundy-coloured silk piped with black, they did an excellent job of preserving her modesty. With her vision partly obscured by tousled hair, she slowly raised her head.

Fresh from the shower, Ramon was wearing a dark grey impeccably tailored suit, which he had teamed with a crisp white shirt and a sober silk tie in shades of blue. Business uniform, she realised, vaguely recalling a phone call to Don Alfonso some time the previous evening to arrange a meeting in his office.

'What time is it?' she asked, trying desperately to instil some normality into the situation.

'That's better,' he said approvingly, seeing that she was at last making some effort to wake up.

There was amusement in his expression and, watching his lips, Annalisa found her mind wandering back—or rather stumbling back through a half-remembered tangle of impressions... Shock rippled through her when she thought what must have happened between them.

'You might want to drag your focus away from me and go and freshen up,' he suggested coolly.

It wasn't that easy, not when you had just spent the night together...and his arrogance pointed to there being another notch on his bedpost. But if that were the case would he not show some reaction? Even scorn would be better than nothing.

'The meeting with our legal teams is at eleven,' he said pointedly, 'and it is now—' he shot a glance at his wristwatch '—a little past ten o' clock.'

His commanding voice managed to convey any manner of things, but nothing of a personal nature. Mortified, Annalisa drew her knees up to her chin as he went on.

'As there is no time for you to return to the *finca*, I have taken the liberty of having a suitable outfit delivered to the yacht. I hope you will find it to your liking.' With a look he drew her attention to an Armani suit hanging inside an otherwise empty wardrobe.

Under anything approaching normal circumstances she

would have been ecstatic. But right now it was the final humiliation! No doubt this was his way of paying her off. Or maybe he was just cruelly underlining the fact that unwittingly she had been more suitably dressed for seduction than business the previous evening. The black slip-dress had seemed a good idea at the time, simple yet sophisticated. Her only nod towards frivolity had been a pair of high-heeled mules. And she had taken care to see that her unusually full breasts were safely concealed beneath a dove-grey cashmere shawl...

But in a sudden flashback she remembered the shoes going even before she embarked! She had taken them off to preserve the teak decks as they'd approached the gangplank, steadying herself with her hands planted tentatively on Ramon's arm... And as the white cruiser had slipped its moorings the sea breeze had plucked at the shawl until Ramon took it and handed it to a member of his uniformed crew.

Dinner had been set out on deck under a protective glass canopy. Just the two of them, waited on by men like shadows who had known just when to attend and when to disappear. As the sleek hull had sliced through a mirror-flat sea she had begun to sip the first glass of champagne...

'I think you'd better take a cold shower,' Ramon observed briskly.

Her dazed eyes transferred slowly to his face. 'What?'

'A cold shower,' he repeated patiently, as if trying to coax a child into action.

And, if she had wanted some reassurance of his intentions, there was not a hint of seduction on his face. Last night it had been the easiest thing in the world to adapt to Ramon's sybaritic lifestyle, but mornings were something else! Perhaps he would mellow over breakfast. The tone of his voice when he crossed the stateroom to fling open the curtains extinguished that hope.

'I'll have a tray of fruit juice and croissants brought to you.'

Hard to believe that dinner had placed her in such a hypnotic trance... How else could she explain how she had come to be leaning her head on his shoulder? Annalisa frowned as she tried to remember just when Ramon had removed his dinner jacket, opened the buttons on his shirt, turned back the cuffs, revealing strong, tanned arms shaded with dark hair? It was all so hazy...

'I'll run the shower for you,' he barked, interrupting her reverie with an impatient gesture. 'And then I'll wait for you on deck. If you care about the *finca* at all, you have exactly half an hour to get ready.'

She shook her head as she struggled to recall a single clear detail from the night before. She vaguely remembered leaning forward to reach for the champagne flute... somehow their fingers had touched. Then, removing the glass from her hand, Ramon had settled her back against the sofa—

'Annalisa! How can you expect to do business with me when you won't even get out of bed? I thought I told you to get up.'

'I'm sorry... I...I was thinking about last night—'

His expression was like a slap in the face. 'There's no time for that now.'

Stiffening her resolve, she sat up and confronted him. 'Didn't you enjoy yourself?'

'The meal was good,' he admitted impatiently.

'And the rest?' She watched as he mashed the door handle impatiently.

'The champagne was a good year—other than that I have no idea what you are talking about.'

Angrily she turned her back on him.

For a brief moment he remained silent and then he gave a short, virile laugh. 'Allow me to reassure you, Annalisa. If there had been anything else between us apart from a meal last night you would remember.'

'So, we didn't...?' Her glance flickered up to his face and away again.

'You are not accustomed to champagne,' he observed coolly. 'Do you think I would take advantage of you?'

She studied the stitching on the amethyst silk counterpane and made no reply.

'This is a very large boat,' he said dismissively. 'Let me reassure you that I slept alone. Now, get in the shower before I throw you over my shoulder and hose you down myself!'

During the meeting in Don Alfonso's dignified wood-panelled office it soon became clear that Ramon's legal team was picking holes in every suggestion made by the older man. Or perhaps it was just that he represented a different age and things had moved on, Annalisa thought, glancing around the table. The average age of Ramon's team couldn't have been more than thirty, and, boy, were they sharp. She was being forced to jump in constantly to defend her corner, knowing that many a fatal barb could be clothed in legalese.

The old adage, 'Why pay a dog and bark yourself?' sprang to her mind, but Don Alfonso had come highly recommended by... No. That was it. Don Alfonso had written to her stating that he had been one of her father's most trusted legal representatives. Everything about the bequest had come as such a bolt from the blue and she had had no reason to doubt him. However, the situation concerning agreed boundaries and water rights was far more complicated than she could ever have imagined...perhaps even beyond Don Alfonso's capabilities.

But with Ramon's gaze likely to fall on her at any moment it was the wrong time to admit that she had made so little enquiry into the details before jumping headlong into her new life. And after last night's fiasco she was determined to keep what little remained of her pride intact. She tensed as Ramon stopped the meeting with an imperative gesture.

Looking straight at her across the table, he said, 'I take it that Señorita Wilson has been fully apprised of every aspect of this dispute?'

Dispute? Annalisa looked questioningly at him and then at Don Alfonso. Out of respect for her mother's feelings she had made no enquiries whatever during her lifetime about the mysterious Spaniard who was her father, let alone any disputes that might have affected him. And Don Alfonso had volunteered no information beyond what she had requested.

Don Alfonso's warning glance urged her to let him speak for her as he rose to his feet. At once Ramon yielded the floor to the older man.

'Señorita Wilson would no doubt benefit from hearing your interpretation of the problems you both face,' Don Alfonso began vaguely.

So they shared some difficulty, Annalisa thought, wondering what it might be. She watched Ramon incline his head in gracious assent. She might have expected him to jump down Don Alfonso's throat for suggesting he suffered problems just like any ordinary mortal. But there was not so much as a flicker of impatience on his face. How attractive he was, she thought, relishing the chance to gaze at him without attracting curiosity as he rose to speak. What a tragedy to find herself ranged against him! And worse still to know he was spoken for...

'As Señorita Wilson is already aware,' Ramon began, his low, resonant voice commanding the whole room's attention, 'our fathers were partners. When my father died,' he added, directing his gaze straight at Annalisa, 'I inherited his share of the business.'

He paused, and that moment seemed like an eternity to Annalisa. She stared fixedly at a small knot of wood on the polished table while shockwaves pummelled her mind. She struggled to take in this latest breathtaking revelation. The only thing she had known about her Spanish father was that he had deserted her mother shortly before she was born. As far as she was aware they had never heard from him again. To discover that he had not only been a man of property, but had been involved in business with one of the most powerful families in Spain, was a staggering discovery... But why hadn't Don Alfonso mentioned this to her when he must have known? Feeling Ramon staring at her, she glanced up distractedly, but as his focus sharpened she looked away.

'On her twenty-fifth birthday,' he continued, 'Señorita Wilson discovered that she had inherited a large tract of land here in Menorca. Land that had been left in trust for her by her late father, Don Pedro di Fuego Montoya.'

A wave of emotion broke over Annalisa as Ramon mentioned her father's name. His voice contained such affection and respect. There had clearly been a bond between the two men, a bond that both thrilled and frightened her. It made Ramon Perez part of her life whether she liked it or not. And now all the men around the table were bowing their heads, as if they remembered her father quite differently from the way she had always imagined him. Her mother's refusal to talk about him had always led Annalisa to suppose that her absentee Spanish father must have caused some dreadful hurt. Wasn't his neglect proof enough of that?

She looked up again to hear Ramon say, 'This land was his to give freely. I have no dispute over title with Señorita Wilson.'

Don Alfonso made another discreet signal to silence Annalisa. 'You wish to purchase a piece of this land in order to advance your plans for development in the area?' he asked.

'That is correct,' Ramon agreed. 'I had imagined the new owner of the *finca* would be eager to sell. But that was before I met Señorita Wilson. Now I realise Señorita Wilson has plans of her own. However, in order for the orange groves to be restored to full production she will require a constant supply of fresh water: water that runs across my land.'

He stopped, his expression unfathomable. But Annalisa had heard enough. She sprang to her feet. 'I admit my intentions are still in the planning stage, but I can tell you two things: whatever difficulties are placed in my way, I intend to make my home in Menorca, and *finca* Fuego Montoya is not for sale.'

'Is the property viable?' one of Ramon's young lawyers asked doubtfully. 'Even forgetting the problem you will have obtaining sufficient fresh water for your commercial activities, I heard the house was in a terrible state.'

Emotionally, Annalisa was wrung out. Deciding to keep the *finca* had left her stranded on an island of uncertainty, where she was bombarded by facts and revelations and, worst of all, the scrutiny of a man who seemed capable of seeing beyond her professional façade to the vulnerable core beneath. Her glance flashed up as he began to speak again.

'You have not seen the *finca* recently,' he said, glancing first around the table and then back at her.

His eyes, Annalisa saw, had warmed past a point that was safe. And his voice when he spoke again wrapped around her like a comfort blanket, even though he directed his comments to everyone.

'Señorita Wilson has made many improvements already—'

Feeling an ominous pricking at the back of her eyes, she pulled herself together fast. Ramon as adversary was bad enough... Ramon back-pedalling out of concern for her feelings was really worrying.

'And Don Alfonso assures me that she has sufficient funds,' Ramon finished, with a 'so that's an end of it' shrug.

Then either Don Alfonso knew something she didn't, or

he had stretched the truth past breaking point, Annalisa thought uncomfortably as she sank back in her chair. When the sale went through for her modest home in England she might just be able to scrape together enough money to mend the roof, and perhaps even lay some sort of proper road to the property. But as for purchasing land from Ramon to secure irrigation for her fruit?

Picking up her pen, she stabbed at her notepad as if trying to pin down an idea. 'I will restore the orange groves to full production,' she insisted stubbornly, feeling her throat dry as she gave voice to her plans—plans that even she knew were ambitious to the point of being reckless. She had come to the island knowing nothing at all about agriculture, and even less about oranges. But she could learn... She would learn. 'It is my intention to live and work at the *finca*,' she went on, conscious that she had everyone's full attention now. 'And I mean to provide employment for as many of the local villagers as I can.'

Rapt faces stared up at her in frozen surprise, but only Ramon shifted slightly in his seat as he murmured, 'Bravo!'

'But the strip of coastline,' one of his team reminded him, clearing his throat to break the trance-like state of his companions. 'The strip you need to complete the marina, Señor Perez. Surely Señorita Wilson will not require a beach as part of her plans to re-establish the orange groves?'

Annalisa tensed. So that was Ramon's angle. So much for his concern...his kind words! She would be better off taking Don Alfonso's advice. At least he was honest! 'The coastline is not negotiable,' she said coldly.

'All things are negotiable,' Ramon argued amiably.

'My client has had a lot to take in,' Don Alfonso said, excusing her with a shrug. 'I should like a month to look into everything with Señorita Wilson. After which she may well reconsider how much of the land is necessary to her plans and how much is superfluous.' He gave another shrug as he looked around the table.

Every face swung to Ramon. He nodded briefly. 'That seems fair, Don Alfonso, but a lot can happen in the time you ask for, so I shall require weekly updates.'

'We'll see to it,' one of his lawyers said, making a note.

'No,' Ramon said quietly, planting both hands firmly on top of the table. 'I'm going to handle this myself.'

Annalisa silenced her gasp. And, staring around, she saw she was not alone in her surprise. The inscrutable faces of the lawyers had slipped just enough to prove that Ramon would normally delegate such an insignificant matter.

'This is a sensitive case,' he continued, as if that was explanation enough. 'And I am keen to achieve a settlement that will satisfy both Señorita Wilson and myself. After all,' he said wryly, 'it appears we are going to be neighbours whatever the outcome.'

Sensing the power and determination of her adversary, Annalisa tensed. It was as if a silken net had been cast by so skilled a hand she had barely felt it land on top of her...until it was too late. Swinging away from his knowing glance, she felt her heart thump ominously as Don Alfonso rose from the table. Directing his comments to Ramon, he inclined his head graciously.

'We are honoured to have your personal input, Señor Perez. I am sure we can reach an amicable agreement. If it is convenient to Señorita Wilson and yourself, I will arrange our first briefing for the same time, one week from today.'

Now it was Annalisa's turn to be the centre of attention, and again she felt Ramon watching her with that stillness she had already identified as his particular hallmark. 'That's fine with me,' she agreed in a voice that gave nothing away. What else could she say? She was in this to the finish and she had to keep track of Ramon's designs on her land...maybe even think up a way to barter some of her shoreline in exchange for his water...

As the meeting concluded the tension eased.

'Lunch?' Ramon said, directing the question straight at her.

It was the very last thing Annalisa had been expecting. She felt at a disadvantage from every point of view. She needed time to regroup, to recover… 'Oh, no,' she said quickly. 'I'm not even hungry.'

'Or thirsty?' he teased gently.

'I never drink in the middle of the day, Señor Perez.'

'You mean I can't even tempt you with a single glass of champagne?'

'Ah, now you make me wish I was joining you,' Don Alfonso said as he ushered them both out of the door.

'Lucky for you he didn't see that expression on your face,' Ramon said as he accompanied her across the street.

The touch of his hand on her arm even through two layers of fabric was electrifying. The knowledge that he was only being courteous should have filled her with relief, but shock came first and put a chill in her voice. 'I never want to hear the word champagne again.'

'That sounds like a challenge to me,' Ramon threatened softly.

'I'm serious.' But even Annalisa knew her words lacked conviction.

'For now,' Ramon murmured, increasing the pressure of his fingers enough to invade her body with warmth in a way that was both seductive and alarming. 'We'll stop off for something to eat on the way back to the *finca*.'

That was a really bad idea! She told him so.

'Why not? I'll drive you home.'

And then…? 'I can take a taxi,' Annalisa told him, willing her voice to stay firm.

'Why do that when you don't have to?'

She stopped and looked up at him. Was it that muscle working in his jaw, the smouldering amusement and confidence in his eyes, or the curve of his lips? Did it even matter? One thing she was sure about. There could be no such thing as a harmless friendship with a man like Ramon Perez.

'I'm going to take a taxi because you haven't been straight with me,' she said, for want of a better excuse. But even as she tried to free her arm from his grip he tightened his hold.

'What are you talking about now?' he asked, catching hold of her other arm and drawing her round in front of him.

The tang of warm clean male laced with sandalwood and musk was almost too much to bear. 'The shoreline...for your marina,' she said, whipping her head away from the evocative scent.

'The fresh water for your orange groves,' he countered lightly.

Annalisa gasped as he cupped her chin in one hand and brought her round to face him again. 'You didn't tell me about your plans for a marina,' she whispered, shutting her eyes tight as his fingers strayed beyond the sensitive area just behind her ear to mesh through her hair.

'And Don Alfonso didn't tell you that your father and I were partners...did he, Annalisa?' Ramon countered, releasing her abruptly.

She had been right to accept that intuitive warning. Ramon was a man that any woman would need an anaesthetic to resist. She took a moment or two to steady her nerves. 'I'm not sure... I—'

He cut in impatiently. 'And that's not the only piece of vital information he failed to give you. Is it, Annalisa?'

She shared his irritation at the incompetence of her lawyer, but a peculiar loyalty to someone who had once worked for her father prevailed. She wouldn't get rid of Don Alfonso. She would just have to mug up on Spanish law in her spare time. Spare time? That was a joke! 'Don Alfonso hasn't had a chance to fill me in on every detail,' she said casually, noting the look of suspicion in his eyes.

'You don't know much about your father, do you, Annalisa?' he pressed shrewdly.

'No, I—' She flicked her wrist in a gesture that suggested she didn't want to either, at this late stage.

'If you intend to live in his house…employ his workers…make your home in the village where he was born—'

'Surely the approach I take where that is concerned is up to me?'

'OK,' Ramon agreed. 'Perhaps it is too soon to revisit the past. But there's a lot to talk about besides that, and it won't hurt you to have lunch with me. You survived dinner—'

'Barely,' she reminded him quickly. And before she could stop it the hint of a smile warmed her eyes.

But Ramon appeared not to notice and only hummed a brief note of agreement before grabbing her arm to steer her across the street. 'I'm glad that's settled,' she heard him murmur as they wove their way through some ambling tourists.

His self-assurance jolted Annalisa out of her complacency. 'No!' she said, almost causing a pile-up as she stopped dead in her tracks.

'What's wrong now?'

Could a voice seduce you? she wondered, trying desperately to ground herself in the day-to-day bustle of the city street. 'I'm not sure we should.'

'Should what?'

His molten gaze was like liquid heat. It seemed to steal into every part of her. 'Be together when Margarita—' She felt her throat dry, attempted to swallow and gave up.

'This is work,' Ramon broke in impatiently. 'We've just had a business meeting. I need to eat. You need to eat.' He stared at her intently, as if daring her to argue.

She was being ridiculous. This was business—for both of them, Annalisa reminded herself, firming up her glance. And if she wanted to avoid making a fool of herself for a second time in twenty-four hours she should accept his invitation for what it was and stop running scared.

'This will just be a quick lunch with no champagne. Deal?' he demanded.

Taking her silence for assent, Ramon opened the door of his black Porsche and stood aside as he waited for her to climb in.

Mashing her lips together, Annalisa forced her feet to move. Right now running scared seemed not just the sensible option, but the only option. Then Ramon slammed the door and it was too late. She watched him stalk around to the driver's side. Confidence like his was…irresistible, she realised apprehensively.

Slipping the key into the ignition, he gunned the performance machine into life. 'That meeting has given me a real appetite.'

Me too, Annalisa agreed silently, acknowledging the powerful aura of the man beside her, an aura that had nowhere to go but around her, in the luxurious but compact interior.

'Would you like the roof down instead of air-conditioning?' he asked, turning to look at her.

'Do you read minds?'

'Sometimes,' he said with the hint of a smile.

Good intentions weren't nearly enough, she realised anxiously as waves of sensation coaxed her senses awake…and the steady thrum of pleasure was only intensified by the gentle but persistent vibration of the soft black kidskin seat that held her cradled in a firm and inescapable hold. A rogue shaft of arousal wrenched a sharper breath than usual from her. She knew Ramon heard it. He glanced across as if he knew exactly what she was thinking…feeling…

Determined to keep her mind on track, she began asking him about the marina as soon as they sat down at their spectacular harbour-front table.

He didn't answer straight away. Instead he took the

leather-backed menus from the waiter and arranged his long legs under the seat. 'Surely it is the responsibility of your legal advisor, Don Alfonso, to provide that information,' he said. His expression suggested that in spite of all his assurances he had not the slightest intention of discussing business matters over lunch.

Annalisa frowned, equally determined that they would. 'Well, I won't be held to ransom over the shoreline—by you or anyone else.'

'And I won't discuss the matter until we have both had something to eat,' he told her firmly. 'Shall I order for both of us?'

'I'm quite capable—'

'So I recall,' he said, summoning the waiter.

And that was how Annalisa came to be facing a mountain of food on one plate whilst Ramon picked at a selection of delicious-looking delicacies, both hot and cold, on any number of small plates and dishes.

'Would you like something?' he murmured, catching her glance. And before she could say no he had picked out the plumpest prawn and was feeding it to her.

When some juice escaped and trickled down her chin, he wiped it up with his hand and then lapped his fingers with his tongue before reaching for his napkin. 'Good?' he enquired softly, his eyes diffusing the simple question into countless possibilities.

'Very good,' Annalisa agreed hoarsely. 'Next time you can order for me.'

'Next time?' he challenged softly.

Well, there was still so much more she needed to discuss with him... Who was she trying to kid? An erotic heat was already stripping her mind of focus. She had to get away from him...from temptation. But he seemed in no hurry and ordered coffee for them both, exchanging pleasantries with the young waiter, who looked at Annalisa with naked interest until Ramon sent him on his way.

When he turned back to her Ramon's eyes had darkened to twin pools of compelling intensity. With a jolt, Annalisa realised he was well aware of the effect he was having on her. It was written all over his face. He controlled her responses. He was her jailer while she was imprisoned inside a dangerously sensitised body. Her nipples were swelling and straining against the fine white fabric of the blouse that had arrived with the Armani suit, and even the exquisite underwear only served to remind her that the most erotically charged place of all had the merest cobweb for protection. She might just as well have been naked under the precision tailoring.

Had he chosen the clothes himself? Did he find the outward show of severity arousing, knowing how little she wore beneath? If he restrained her first, and then very slowly peeled away all the puritanical layers to expose the flagrant evidence of her arousal, would he be pleased, or angry when he saw what a wanton she had become...how hot and moist, how swollen with desire? She stole a glance at his handsome, brooding face and moved convulsively in a hopeless attempt to ease the ache between her legs. But all it proved was that there was no cure and no relief...something she suspected Ramon knew only too well when she saw his thoughtful gaze resting on her face.

'I think we'd better go,' he said, breaking the spell. He settled his coffee cup into the saucer. 'There's something I'd like you to see.'

Annalisa started guiltily, as if she had been caught out in some dreadful act. But there was only purpose in his face, and that purpose was wildly at odds with her erotic fantasies.

'That is if you can spare another hour before I take you home?'

'I can spare the time.'

'Good,' he said looking at her keenly. 'I should be the

one—' He broke off as he stood aside to let her go past, and showed no inclination to explain himself further.

They got into the car and Ramon drove skilfully around the congested side streets until soon they were speeding along the main highway again. But he was taking her in the wrong direction for home. They were heading instead towards the north of the island, where the terrain became more rugged and the vegetation grew dense and lush.

Annalisa was on the verge of asking him where he was taking her, but something about the set of his jaw discouraged conversation. Along with his customary courtesy towards her she sensed a strange intensity; a determination to have her under his control for a little while longer.

CHAPTER THREE

By THE time Ramon pulled the Porsche to a halt the sky was a tapestry of rose-streaked viridian. In the dim half-light the trees at the side of the road cast smoky fingers across the dust-coated tarmac.

'This is as far as we can go by car,' he said, climbing out.

As he held the door for her Annalisa saw they had stopped beside a sandy track that snaked away into a shadowy wood.

'Are we close to the sea?'

'This path leads to the beach,' he confirmed, toeing off his loafers.

Annalisa was still wearing her high-heeled sandals from the night before, and following Ramon's lead she slipped them off. 'So. Where are you taking me?'

'You'll see,' he promised, turning as if to take her hand.

Not trusting herself, Annalisa tucked hers into her pockets.

Unperturbed, Ramon headed off in front of her. 'This is a rather unconventional expedition,' he admitted, calling back to her over his shoulder. 'But something tells me you're not ready to make a formal visit just yet.'

'A visit?' Annalisa queried, hurrying to catch up with him. 'A visit to whom?'

'You'll see.'

Finally the path opened out onto a small crescent-shaped beach. Where the forest yielded to sand a natural boundary had been created by a string of smooth boulders. Like beads in a giant's necklace, Annalisa thought as she followed Ramon across them.

49

'There,' he said, pointing away from the shoreline into the hills.

Following his gaze, Annalisa saw a large house that might have looked more at home in the Hollywood hills than on the brow of a hill in rural Menorca. It wasn't that the building lacked anything as far as she could see—far from it. But to Annalisa's eyes the stark lines of the modern construction with its austere regimented garden sat uncomfortably amidst the craggy limestone outcrops and luxuriant tumble of vegetation. 'This has to belong to a total control freak,' she murmured.

'Very observant of you,' Ramon commented, sounding pleased.

'You weren't meant to overhear,' she admitted. 'Who does it belong to?'

'It used to belong to your late father—'

'My father!' Why the idea should offend her to such a degree she had no idea. But it felt wrong, impossible—

'Are you going to allow me to explain?' Ramon demanded.

She swung around to see him settled back against a gnarled tree trunk with his arms folded as he stood watching her, shadows pointing up the extraordinary seductiveness of his sun-bronzed face. Was everything she had to learn about her father going to come from Ramon? She was caught between a desperate longing to know more and a fear of becoming emotionally entangled with a man who posed a very real danger to her...and whose motives were unclear.

But then they were distracted by the sight of a glamorous middle-aged woman strolling onto the terrace. Dressed for cocktails in a close-fitting red dress, she moved with great elegance, and her silver-blonde hair, swept into a chignon, was immaculate. 'Who's that?' Annalisa murmured.

Ramon came to stand beside her. 'That is Señora Fuego Montoya. Your father's widow.'

Annalisa froze. Everything she had learned about her father since arriving on the island had been chipping away at her contempt for him. But with this change of heart came strong passions…passions that had lain dormant until this moment. Her focus sharpened as she speared a glance at her stepmother and tried not to hate her. It was impossible to see clearly, but Annalisa guessed her shoes would match the dress exactly, as would her lipstick. Something about Señora Fuego Montoya suggested no fashion detail would be too small to escape her notice.

Ramon reached out to touch her arm in a gesture of support. 'Are you OK? You did know your father was married?' he asked gently.

Struggling to control her emotions, Annalisa pressed her hand to her mouth. Words were inadequate to describe her feelings, and it was a few moments before she could answer him. 'Yes—yes, of course,' she managed finally. She knew the stark facts only too well. But reality was proving to be far more of an ordeal than she had ever imagined.

His grip on her arm tightened a little. 'I think you've seen enough.'

She wrapped her arms around her waist in a defensive gesture. 'No. I'm OK… Honestly.'

'Come…come, Annalisa,' he said again, when still she didn't move.

'You said you'd explain,' she said, her glance fixed on the woman who had kept her father from her.

'In the car,' Ramon promised tersely.

His resolve swallowed up the last of her objections and she offered no resistance when he led her away.

But when they were both settled back inside the Porsche, Ramon only hugged the wheel and frowned.

'What's the matter?' Annalisa prompted.

The look he shot her was one of concern and incredulity. 'During the meeting today I began to suspect that you knew very little about your Spanish heritage,' he said. 'And now I wonder if you know anything at all.'

Annalisa felt her emotions building up like water behind a leaky dam. She wanted to trust him. And she longed to fill in the missing pieces of the jigsaw. But all her life the subject of her father had been taboo. How could she let down the drawbridge now? And it would be complete madness to let it down for Ramon. She knew nothing about him beyond the fact that he wanted her land…maybe a lot more besides. And he was married just as her father had been. Surely he didn't think she would make the same mistake as her mother?

'I'm right, aren't I?' he prompted.

'You certainly know more than I do,' she admitted carefully.

'I hope you feel you can ask me anything,' Ramon said gently. 'Speak to me at any time.'

Annalisa was sure any woman would jump at the chance to share confidences with Ramon Perez. But it was far too dangerous for her…and she had Don Alfonso to answer her questions. 'I appreciate you taking the time to show me my father's house—' She broke off as he made an incredulous sound.

'Your father never lived there. I'm sorry if I gave you that impression. He lived at the *finca*. And when he became ill…when the estates and the orange groves became too much for him…he moved into a small apartment in Mahon over our offices. He built the house I just showed you for his wife, Claudia—built it to her design, not his.' He stressed the name so there could be no mistake.

'I don't understand,' Annalisa admitted, shielding her eyes with her hand. 'I'm not even sure I want to.'

Ramon's lips formed a flat line of disbelief as he shook his head. 'Don't you want to breathe some life into your memories, Annalisa?'

'That's just it,' she said, finding it increasingly difficult to hold her feelings in check. 'I don't have any memories to breathe life into… Not of my father, at least.'

'Will you let me be the one to help you?'

Annalisa turned and gazed blindly into the darkness. Ramon Perez was the last person on earth she should choose for a confidant.

'You know, you look just like him,' he said softly. 'The same wonderful black hair, the same strong features—'

'Please. Stop it,' she warned in a tense whisper.

But Ramon was unaware of the tension building up inside her, and instead of letting up he gave a short, affectionate laugh. 'I would have known you anywhere, Annalisa...even before I learned how stubborn you were—'

'Stop it!' Her agonised shout was amplified in the silence, and the pain seemed to eddy around them long after the last sound wave had died away. 'Take me home. Please.'

Ramon made a move as if he would have liked to touch her...to reassure her...but then thought better of it. With a flick of his wrist he switched the engine on, released the handbrake and eased the powerful black car back onto the road.

Everything Ramon had said lingered in her mind...exerting a powerful fascination over her, Annalisa realised later as she sat gazing into her dressing table mirror. At least she was fleshing out the man to whom she owed her looks and temperament. Her mother had been a typical English rose, with fluffy blonde hair, fair complexion and pale green eyes. Only Annalisa's pale skin betrayed her share of Anglo-Saxon roots. For the rest she was wholly Spanish, with flashing eyes the colour of treacle and midnight-black hair. And, though she was tall with long slim legs, her figure was pure Mediterranean down to the last generous curve...

She had to see a photograph of her father. Call it pointless... Call it morbid curiosity... Or maybe she just hoped to see something in his eyes that would explain how he could abandon her mother to a lifetime of loneliness.

Just as she was trying to work out where to get such a

picture, the telephone shrilled. Her hand hovered over the receiver. It had to be Don Alfonso confirming the date of the next meeting.

'Annalisa?'

'Ramon!'

'Are you all right?'

Her heart had begun to race at the sound of his voice. Hearing his concern only trebled the pace. She hesitated, her mind a maelstrom of conflicting emotions. 'Why shouldn't I be?'

'I was worried about you.'

Her mind might have blanked, but her body responded instantly…eagerly.

'Are you still there?'

'I'm here.'

'Would you like me to come over?'

The pause was even longer now. 'Here?' she queried finally. The effect of his short deep laugh made her realise just how much she would like that…and how very dangerous it would be.

'Don't sound so shocked,' he warned. 'I just wanted to make sure that you were feeling all right after—'

'There's no need, Ramon,' she said quickly, before she could change her mind. 'I'm absolutely fine.'

'Well, if you're sure?'

Annalisa took a few deep breaths. She pictured him waiting for an answer…probably leaning back in some comfortable leather chair with his long legs crossed loosely one over the other as he toyed with the phone… It would be so easy to weaken. But no child of hers was going to be put through the torment of trying to put a face to its own father.

'I'm sure,' she said firmly. She felt her hearing had never been so acute as she strained to listen out for his response. But there was only silence at the other end of the line. 'I have to go,' she said into the vacuum. 'The animals need feeding.' This late at night? She grimaced. He would never fall for a pathetic excuse like that.

'Of course,' he said. 'So, we meet again in one week's time.'

As long as that—

'If you have any questions for me before then I would be delighted to answer them for you.'

But Ramon wasn't at the next weekly meeting at Don Alfonso's office, or the week after that. Of course it shouldn't have mattered, but it did. On the first occasion his lawyers gave no explanation for his absence and Annalisa felt she could not ask. When the second meeting came around she threw caution to the wind. And, having studied all the Spanish deeds to her property, she had just the excuse she needed.

She stood to address the room. 'I'm afraid I shall have to insist that Señor Perez attends the next meeting.'

At the word 'insist' his lawyers tensed.

Don Alfonso hurried to his feet. 'You can see my client's point of view,' he said, glancing at Annalisa. 'She is keen to bring this matter to closure.'

'Señor Perez is a very busy man,' one of Ramon's team pointed out.

The young lawyer's tone of voice got right up Annalisa's nose. 'And I am a very busy woman,' she said coldly. But it was her heart that needed answers and her heart that forced the pace. 'If Señor Perez fails to attend next week's meeting I shall assume he is no longer interested in acquiring any part of the shore.'

'But he is in England, Señorita Wilson,' the same lawyer informed her, lifting his shoulders in a shrug of indifference.

With Margarita, she thought, closing her eyes briefly.

'For the start of the race?' Don Alfonso both asked and confirmed, trading smiles around the table.

What race? Something else he had failed to inform her about? Annalisa wondered irritably.

Gathering her papers together, she pushed her chair back and stood up. 'Frankly, gentlemen, I don't care what he's doing. I see Señor Perez next week, or these negotiations are at an end.'

Annalisa felt pretty good about the stand she had made as she walked to the small run-around she had purchased. She felt even better as she drove speedily along the un-crowded highway and finally turned onto her own potholed lane. The sale of her house in England had finally gone through without a hitch, and she would use the money to improve the road. But that would almost clean her out. There might just be enough for one last splurge for herself, for when the going got tough—a reward for sticking by her principles and resisting the charms of Ramon.

'What the—?' Annalisa slammed to a halt in front of the *finca* and almost catapulted out of her seat. 'Stop! Stop that now!' she insisted frantically.

Swarming all over her roof, workmen were ripping up the few remaining tiles. They showed no sign of hearing her. Ladders leaned drunkenly against the uneven walls and puffs of old plaster and debris were falling all around like dirty snow. After standing there for just a few moments she felt her lustrous black hair was coated with an itchy grey crust.

Finally one of the men responded to her furious gestures and called down, 'Señor Perez's orders—'

Annalisa's emotions went up like a rocket. 'Señor Perez has no control here! How dare—?'

The man shrugged as he gave her a brown-toothed grin. 'You want we should leave it?'

'Yes! No!' Annalisa gazed around in desperation. Neatly stacked piles of brand-new roof tiles stood in one corner, whilst heaps of old tiles, now broken beyond hope of saving, littered the ground.

'Where is Señor Perez?' she demanded. 'No—' She flung up her hand to stop the man the moment she heard the words Inglaterra and Margarita. 'In England, at the race with Margarita,' she muttered fiercely, swinging around to consider what to do next.

'No, no, *señorita*,' another voice called from somewhere on the ruined roof. 'Señor Perez returned home today.'

'Right!' Annalisa said, tightening her mouth. 'Thank you very much,' she shouted. Swinging away from them, she ran back to the car.

'That's all right, Rodriguez. You can leave us,' Ramon Perez instructed his tight-lipped manservant. 'And, gentlemen,' he added, turning to the group of sober-suited men seated at the table with him, 'we will reconvene this meeting in one hour's time.'

One hour? Annalisa's brows lifted. He had been away for weeks, missed their meetings, played house with her home, and seriously expected to be rid of her within the hour?

'Annalisa,' Ramon said when they had all left the room. 'What an unexpected pleasure. What can I do for you?' As he spoke he eased his chair back and stood to confront her, his hawkish expression completely at odds with the courteous words.

Somehow the austere business suit only served to affirm his brutally male appeal, Annalisa realised, finding the effect on her resolve an added irritation. 'Don't try that power jag on me,' she warned. 'You've already done far too much for me already!'

'Really?' he murmured, turning to glance out of the window, but not before she caught the gleam of amusement in his dark eyes. 'How careless of me.'

'This isn't a joke, Ramon.'

'I can see that,' he said, turning so abruptly she jumped.

'No!' she warned, taking a step back when it looked as though he might come closer. 'I demand an explanation.'

'You demand?' he drawled, while his mouth curved in a long lazy smile.

'Yes, I—'

He held up his hands in an unexpected gesture of surrender. 'You have my apologies,' he said mildly, then spoiled the effect with his next observation. 'I should have realised how frustrating this must be for you.'

Frustrating! And now he was heading straight for her... 'I have no idea what you mean,' Annalisa flared, retreating a step only to find the door at her back.

He stopped short and shrugged. 'The waiting, of course.' And now his eyes were glinting with amusement. 'All these problems getting in the way,' he murmured, brushing a hand down the side of her face.

She jerked back. 'In the way of what, exactly?'

'Of an agreement being drawn up between us,' he clarified, moving away again.

Annalisa swallowed hard as she watched his lean, tanned fingers move to adjust his tie. It was so easy to fall under his spell...far too easy. Determinedly she rallied her wits. 'Really, Ramon. I must insist—'

'You must insist?' He looked at her with amused tolerance, as if she had lost her wits rather than rallied them. And then, advancing far enough to trap her against the door, he traced her full lips with one firm thumbpad.

As hard as she strained back there was nowhere to go. 'My roof—' she protested breathlessly, moving to protect her mouth with the back of her hand.

'Ah, yes,' he murmured, his amused glance straying to her hand. 'Your roof.'

The heat in her face went rampaging through her body. 'You're repairing it,' she gasped out.

With a sharp look he turned on his heels. 'Before it falls down.'

'It's not yours to repair!' Annalisa pointed out.

'Call it neighbourly concern, if it makes you feel better.'

'I can't afford to pay you back,' she admitted tensely. 'Not at the moment, anyway.'

'Have I asked for payment?'

'But you will want paying,' she chipped in, wishing her breathing would steady.

He swung around to face her again, fingering his stubble-darkened chin. 'Perhaps we could operate a barter system.'

The thought of how that roughened face would feel against her pink-flushed skin was disturbing...distracting... 'I won't be pushed into parting with any land before I am ready—'

'Stop jumping to conclusions, Annalisa. How do you know it's your land I'm talking about?'

'What else could it be?' The look he gave her threw her stimulated senses into turmoil. 'How can I possibly know what you're talking about when you can't be bothered to attend the meetings we arranged?' Her glance bounced off his eyes and landed on his lips.

'That was unfortunate, and I apologise. A family matter required my immediate attention. Family always comes before business as far as I am concerned, Annalisa. Margarita needed me—' He shrugged.

As an ice-cold hand grabbed her spine Annalisa's eyes flickered slightly—the only sign that she'd recognised his need to remind her that he had a wife.

'I promise you that I will definitely attend the next meeting.'

She managed a stiff nod.

A discreet tap on the door distracted them both.

'Come,' he called imperiously.

Rodriguez advanced a few steps into the room. 'You have a visitor, Señor Perez.' He glanced at Annalisa, then walked up to Ramon and whispered something in his ear.

Ramon's face hardened briefly. Turning to her again, he sighed. 'Forgive me, Annalisa. I'm afraid I shall have to continue this conversation some other time.'

'About the roof—'

'Let my men finish the job now they have started,' he suggested. 'We'll arrange payment the next time we meet. I assure you that my terms will be fair.' He cast her a long, assessing look from slanting umber eyes. 'The main thing is that you are safe and dry. I don't want you on my conscience.'

Annalisa kept her face neutral, but her heart was still reeling from his humiliating reminder about Margarita. As far as she could see Ramon Perez was singularly unburdened by conscience. 'Until our next meeting, Señor Perez.'

'Ramon,' he reminded her with a courteous dip of his head.

'Señor Perez,' Annalisa returned stiffly. And, sticking her chin in the air, she marched out of the room.

As she was crossing the hall Annalisa saw someone follow Rodriguez into the room where she had just left Ramon. There was something about the way the woman carried herself that reminded Annalisa of Señora Fuego Montoya. Even the snatch of a beautifully modulated voice was exactly as she had imagined it. Turning impulsively, she was sure she was right. But what was her father's widow doing with Ramon? Were they hatching something together? If so, it wouldn't just be a piece of beach that was up for grabs...it would be the whole estate!

As she ran down the front steps she weighed the evidence. Ramon had made sure she was heavily in debt to him. He missed meetings rather than commit to a deal. Could that be because he knew he could get for free what he allegedly wanted to buy? Was he simply playing for time? He was certainly unscrupulous enough. He knew she was drawn to him, a married man, yet did nothing to discourage her. In fact, she was sure now that he relished those times when he breached her outward composure. And as for Señora Fuego Montoya—her stepmother...?

Just forming the word in her mind made her feel doubly

vulnerable. Of course there would be resentment for a stepdaughter she had never met. A stepdaughter who had inherited vast tracts of land right over her head. It all made a horrible kind of sense. The son of her late father's business partner forming an unholy alliance with her father's widow...

Even the sight of her new red-pantiled roof failed to console her as she pulled into the yard at the *finca*. But she had to admit that the workmen had done an excellent job. Everything was neat and tidy, with not a hint of rubble to suggest the disruption there had been earlier. It was a quality job... but quality had its price.

She would cool her emotions with a quick swim. Hurrying into the house, Annalisa grabbed a bikini out of her bedroom drawer and quickly got changed. But even as she stripped off the Armani suit her stress levels increased. That had cost a fortune. Then there was the underwear, the silk blouse, and the first outfit from Margarita... She groaned. Ramon had reeled her in like a dazed fish. She would be paying off her debts to the Crianza Perez family for the rest of her life the way things were going.

By the time she made it down to the shore the sun was a huge orange ball balanced on the horizon. A light breeze had kicked up the waves so that they ran in truculent eddies around the rocks, tossing plumes of white foam into the soft evening air. Impatient to feel the soothing chill of deeper water, she plunged in and started to swim, embracing the waves with a reckless excitement as if the shock of the icy sea could really help soothe her overheated emotions.

As the familiar rhythm worked its magic she powered out, hard and fast, oblivious to the speed with which she was being carried away from the shore. Only when the ocean began swallowing more and more of the sun did she break stroke and start to head back. But the current was unforgiving. She trod water, her mind whirling frantically.

The only visible point of safety in a rapidly darkening sea was the sleek white roof of Ramon's cruiser; her only hope was to swim to it—to swim for her life... But she was tiring rapidly, and with every stroke the waves seemed to grow higher, rougher and faster, until choking on seawater, she battled for air.

And when she went under it wasn't her whole life that flashed before her eyes...just the same charismatic face that penetrated all her dreams. Feeling herself sinking lower, she kicked out weakly, in an attempt to break through the deadly ceiling so cruelly close to her head. But as the remorseless current tugged her sideways, her reaching arms achieved nothing more than a weak pass at a beam of moonlight that provided a slim shaft of light in the unremitting gloom.

Weakening fast, she barely registered the fact that a band of iron had snapped around her waist. But after Ramon brought her coughing and gasping to the surface she went rigid as a flood of expletives in Spanish exploded in her ear.

'Ramon!' she cried gratefully, trying to turn in his arms.

'Keep still, you little fool! Do you want to kill us both?' he rasped, kicking out strongly.

He was holding her so tightly she was almost more frightened by that than the thought of drowning. He was absolutely furious, she realised as she submitted to the indignity of being towed to shore like a piece of driftwood.

Yanking her from the water, he carried her to the beach—and when he saw she was all right he all but dropped her onto the sand at his feet. 'You little idiot!' he grated furiously. 'What the hell did you think you were doing?'

Spluttering helplessly, she retched violently in an attempt to expel the last of the sand and water from her lungs.

'I'm waiting, Annalisa.'

His voice was merciless, and when she was able to risk a glance at him she saw that every muscle and sinew betrayed the depths of his emotion. To make matters worse, he was dressed for dinner. Apart from the shoes he had obviously shed just before diving into the water, black trousers and a black silk shirt clung to his body like a second skin. Both were completely ruined. But it wasn't the loss of his clothes that concerned her most. 'I'm sorry,' she gasped at last. 'It's just that I'm unfamiliar with—'

'What?' he cut in harshly before she could say any more. 'Drowning?' And when she began to stutter an apology he hunkered down beside her, grabbing her shoulders in an unforgiving grasp to shake some sense into her. 'Let's keep it that way, shall we?'

Recoiling from the heat in his eyes, Annalisa hung her head as she nodded agreement.

But Ramon hadn't finished with her. He demanded her full attention. Seizing her chin, he forced her round to face him. 'No more swimming in the dark, *comprende*?'

'OK, OK.' He was very close…too close. She stiffened, ready to push him away…then relaxed. He had just saved her life…

'The sea knows no master, Annalisa,' he rapped starkly. 'The last time you did something foolish I warned you. Now I'm telling you. Don't ever swim in the sea on your own again.'

When he was satisfied her remorse was genuine Ramon stood up and tugged off his shirt. Exhausted as she was, Annalisa's senses sharpened as she took in the broad sweep of his shoulders and the taut muscles of his deeply tanned chest, along with the strength so clearly defined in his powerful arms. She looked away as he began to finger the buckle on his belt. Then, as he peeled off his sodden trousers, she instinctively whipped her head away, wrapping her arms across her chest and drawing her legs tightly underneath her.

'It's OK. You can look now,' he said.

She should have known he could not be trusted! She had seen him in bathing trunks before…but they had been designed for swimming. His close-fitting black silk underpants had not. She closed her eyes, as if that might help to obliterate an image already branded on her mind.

'Your little adventure seems to have temporarily rendered you speechless,' he observed sardonically. 'I think you'd better come out to the boat with me…dry off and get warm before you go into shock. I've got a dinghy moored just behind those rocks. You can have a hot shower…put on some dry clothes.'

He might have recovered, but she had some way to go. And it wasn't the close brush with drowning that was driving a battering ram through her composure.

'Come on,' he insisted. 'Before you catch a chill. The breeze is fierce tonight. That's one of the reasons you got into difficulties.'

Annalisa almost smiled. If only all her difficulties had been tied in to the weather she wouldn't be feeling half so worried. 'I'd rather go home,' she managed sensibly.

'That's not an option,' Ramon countered firmly. 'In your present state.'

'No, really. I'd rather.'

'And I'd rather you came with me,' he said decisively. 'I have plenty of towelling robes on board.'

'No. I'm sorry, but—'

'You will be.' Having put up with as much as he intended to, Ramon yanked her to her feet. 'You are proving to be a very troublesome neighbour, Annalisa Wilson.'

'And an expensive one,' she said, laughing nervously as his warmth stole through her.

'Have you eaten tonight?'

'No…' she admitted hesitantly.

'Then I'll see to that at the same time.'

'Oh, no… I—'

'I might as well finish the job.'

She knew from experience that it would be better to give in gracefully…to the offer of a meal and some dry clothes at least. She glanced up through lashes clotted with sea-water. 'You saved my life... How can I ever—?'

He cut brusquely through the commendation. 'You can thank me by never taking risks like that again.'

'I've never swum so late before,' she admitted.

'You could have been killed! *Madre de Dios!*' Ramon exclaimed, frightening her with his vehemence.

'I'm sorry. I can't understand what—'

'Neither can I understand,' Ramon broke in passionately, 'how the Annalisa Wilson I hear about in the village could do something like this!'

So they were talking about her in the village...and, worse still, Ramon was aware of the rumours. 'What have you heard about me?' she asked, dreading the answer. Her skills as a fruit-grower wouldn't bear much scrutiny.

'Señorita Wilson's self-sufficiency, her intelligence, her common sense... Common sense?' he exploded. 'For goodness' sake!'

It was a few moments before she realised he was teasing her. And, despite her misgivings, she liked the feeling. She liked it a lot.

Without warning he grabbed hold of her. 'Are you acting in this crazy fashion because of me?'

'Don't be so ridiculous!' she protested, trying to ignore the fact that they were both practically naked.

He let the silence hang between them for a while, and then released her. 'You're shivering. Hardly surprising after the shock you've had. We'd better go.'

Back in her own bed, Annalisa sat hugging her knees. Fudge lay across her feet and she could hear the cats patrolling outside the door.

This was not the finale anyone else might have expected to Ramon's dramatic rescue...and anyone else might have been more successful than she had been in getting answers to the questions buzzing around her head. Questions that

Ramon could have answered for her after her shower on his boat…or during the meal that had followed.

But after what had happened she had been subdued and he had been… She frowned as she hunted for the right words. Very considerate? Very considerate should have suited her down to the ground. At least she only had a serious case of embarrassment to deal with along with another item of clothing—this time a bathrobe to add to her growing collection of booty from the Crianza Perez household. But the more she saw Ramon, the more…

The telephone was almost a welcome interruption on the route her thoughts were taking. But she sucked in a breath fast when she heard his voice.

'I'm just calling to make sure you're all right.'

Maybe it was just a casual enquiry, but she could hear more than concern. There was warmth…and a smile.

'I'm really sorry about what happened tonight,' she said frankly, trying to corral the conversation into a safe area. 'Thank you for everything you've done for me…and for telephoning.'

'Why are you still awake? You should be asleep…resting after what happened.'

He was trying to sound stern, and now it was Annalisa's turn to smile. 'I was asleep until you called—'

'Liar,' he retorted softly.

She had never been struck by the intimacy of the telephone before, but the familiarity of his challenge launched a firebolt through her veins.

'Don't ever do that to me again,' he said, in a voice barely above a whisper.

'I'm really sorry about your clothes…' She heard her own voice soften in response.

'Damn the clothes. You—'

'Are a pain in the backside. I know,' she broke in awkwardly, trying to force a joke out of a situation that was rapidly spiralling into a danger zone.

'No. I was going to say,' Ramon corrected her firmly, 'that you are unique.'

Telling herself not to read anything into it—after all, everyone was unique—she said solemnly, 'I promise not to do anything so stupid again.'

He gave a soft laugh. 'Does that mean you're agreeing I'm right for once?'

'About this, perhaps.'

'This is not a laughing matter,' he warned gently. 'How could we hold our meetings if one of us is missing?'

'I managed very well on my own for the past couple of meetings,' she said, holding her breath to see how he would respond.

'Very well?'

'OK, so maybe they were a bit one-sided.'

His laugh ran through her like warm honey.

'I have apologised for my absence already,' he said cutting off her thoughts.

'I know.'

'Not sufficiently, perhaps,' he argued pensively.

'No?'

'No. In fact, I will have to take you for dinner tomorrow evening to make up for the oversight.'

'And what if I decline?'

'You won't.'

A thrill ran through her. So much for being a new woman! Remembering Margarita she voiced a caveat, 'As long as I have a reasonably early night.'

'I'm sure I can build that into my plans.'

'I'll look forward to it, then.'

'So will I,' Ramon said softly. 'Goodnight, Annalisa... Sweet dreams.'

'Goodnight, Ramon,' she whispered, and then realised she was still nursing the receiver in her hands long after the line had gone dead.

CHAPTER FOUR

ANNALISA woke with a start. And then a second yodelling screech revealed why, after a fitful night, she had suddenly been returned to full consciousness.

'Damn bird!' she groaned, casting a look at the clock. It wasn't even five o'clock yet, but the strutting general of the chicken run was rising earlier each morning—a sure sign that spring had arrived. Even with the pillow clamped firmly over her head, his shrill alarm continued to demand her attention.

Throwing the pillow aside, she yawned, stretched and sighed as she thought of the evening that lay ahead with Ramon. This time she wouldn't mess up. No champagne, no troublesome outfits and definitely no midnight swims!

After feeding the animals and clearing up the house she planned to visit the new health spa that had just opened in Mahon and buy something to wear. It was a rare treat, but she had kept some money back to buck her up when the going got tough—and after what had happened last night this was definitely the right moment! And she wanted to look sophisticated—to throw Señor Perez off balance. She was quite determined that when Ramon next saw her he would be amazed by her new image.

By the time Annalisa made it to the yard the sun was already bathing the terracotta cobbles in a soft coral glow. At first she had been surprised to discover how quickly dawn could chase away the sultry Menorcan night. There was no lingering grey half-light as she was accustomed to in England. Each morning began early and at full tilt, and she found she liked it better that way.

'You'd make delicious soup,' she teased the cockerel,

casting some seed on the ground for him. But he knew her better than that, and only crowed a little louder to join his voice to the neighbourhood chorus.

Drawn by the sweeter sound of the birds roosting in her orange groves, Annalisa walked away from him across the yard to a point where she could survey a wide sweep of her property. She still hadn't quite come to terms with the fact that everything she could see as far as the mist-shrouded hills in the distance belonged to her.

Putting down the basket of feed, she climbed the first few bars of the wooden gate that divided the agricultural land from the yard and rested her head on her arms. Fresh green leaves were beginning to show on the twisted black branches of the orange trees and a light breeze carried across the fields, bringing the delicate perfume of thyme and wild myrtle to overlay the last musky scents of the Mediterranean night.

'Heaven,' she murmured, gazing around. It was hard to believe such perfection existed.

'Oh, yes,' Annalisa was telling the young girl at the beauty salon confidently. 'I can quite easily leave everything for a few hours. The animals have been fed, the house is tidy and the orange groves look after themselves.'

She laughed happily. It was far more important to be relaxed and in control for tonight, she thought, watching the stripes of shimmering pink gradually turn her well-buffed toenails into shell-like perfection. She wriggled her toes contentedly as the beautician finished her work. Next came the seaweed treatment. Annalisa had no idea what that entailed, but it promised miracles for the skin as well as relaxation for the mind. Perfect!

As she drove home Annalisa was smiling contentedly. She had gone straight from the beauty salon to buy a new dress. White, simple in design, and extremely chic, it had had a price tag to match. But that didn't matter—not today. Today was a special day. A day for taking control of her life and for spoiling herself. She doubted that she had ever been so well groomed. There was not one inch of her that had not been brushed, buffed, plucked or polished. And mood wise, having been painted from neck to ankle in thick green goo and then baked in a foil blanket before finally being hosed down with an icy cold power jet, she was ready for anything…or so she thought.

She had hardly stopped the car before she flung herself out of it.

'Hey! What are you doing?' Her voice sounded hoarse in her ears and she completely forgot the fact that she was dressed ready to go out.

Sprinting towards the wooden gate, she didn't wait to open it and snagged her dress as she scrambled over the top. Stumbling through the tangled shrubbery, she tripped several times as she struggled to negotiate a treacherous carpet of recently cut tree branches…so many branches! Not caring that her new shoes were getting scuffed, or that the elegant white dress was already smeared with dirt and ripped in several places, she hurried to the clearing where she had spotted the intruder.

Her arms and legs were quickly covered in scratches and weals, but nothing mattered—nothing except stopping the carnage. Almost beyond speech, she could only fling wide her arms in a failed attempt to encompass the devastation and gasp, 'What have you done?'

The man she was confronting had a face as gnarled and as brown as the tree branch he was clinging to. *'Buenos tardes, señorita!'* he said, clearly oblivious to her distress. And, brandishing a battered greasy hat in the air, he embroidered the greeting with a tobacco-stained, gap-toothed grin.

Annalisa's mouth formed a circle of despair as she stared

up at him. Wearing an assortment of clothes that might have been handed down through the generations and had certainly never been washed, the wiry vandal wore a garland of cutting tools around his waist and a bright, inquisitive expression in his raisin-black eyes.

'So you are the daughter of Don Pedro,' he called out in heavily accented English, tapping his chest. 'I am Enrique Caradonda.'

'Never mind who you are,' Annalisa retorted sharply. 'I think you'd better explain what you're doing here…and this!' She gestured fiercely at the piles of branches littering the ground. All that was left of her beautiful orchard as far as she could see was a forest of leafless skeletons.

'I am working,' Enrique declared with an affronted shrug. 'Señor Perez—'

At the sound of Ramon's name Annalisa uttered a sharp angry sound and ordered Enrique Caradonda out of the tree.

'Sí, señorita,' Enrique agreed amiably. 'The light will soon be fading. I'll come back tomorrow.'

'You'll do no such—'

But Enrique had already swung to the ground and was quickly swallowed up in the deepening shadows as he hurried back to the village.

Slowly turning in a circle, Annalisa felt a sob rising in her throat. She was so quick to trust…too quick. How could anyone, especially Ramon, do this to her? Was he really so impatient for progress on the proposed site for his marina? If he thought he could drive her away by pulling a stunt like this he was badly mistaken. The property was hers to develop as she chose.

She drew a ragged breath and tried to confirm the extent of the damage. The trees would never recover in time to crop. And if she had nothing to sell how could she possibly keep afloat financially for another year? To rub salt in the wound it had happened while she was at the beauty salon, congratulating herself on how well things were going! Her grubby hands balled into fists. Ramon Perez was about to get the biggest tongue-lashing of his life!

As her old car bounced along the lane there were lots of ominous creaks and crunches, but nothing could distract Annalisa from keeping the accelerator pedal flat to the floor. As she landed with one particularly bone-crunching jolt the car stalled and refused to start again. Then, when she finally got it going, an ominous grinding noise accompanied her the rest of the way to Ramon's.

'Good,' she muttered fiercely, seeing his unmistakable rangy figure poised beside the Porsche. He was obviously on the point of setting out to pick her up. Well, she had saved him the trouble! Stamping her foot down on the brake, she managed to slew to a halt a hair's breadth away from his car. And then she almost fell out of the door in her rush to apprehend him.

But he moved a lot faster than she did and, executing a clean leap past her, dived into the driver's seat she had just vacated. Wrenching on the handbrake, he called through the open door, 'I think you forgot something.'

She clamped her angry mouth shut as he climbed out again and watched him shoot a wry glance at the driver's door that refused to close until his third and most vigorous attempt.

'No damage done,' he said, patting the roof of her bargain basement car.

'Save your condescension and the sarcasm,' Annalisa warned. 'I've got something to say to you.'

'But there will be plenty of chance to talk over dinner,' he reminded her in an infuriating drawl, his eyes glinting with amusement as he looked her up and down. 'Is mud art the latest fashion, or have I missed something?'

'No,' she said clamping her hand over her bare thigh. 'And I don't know how you have the nerve to mention dinner.'

'Wasn't that what we arranged?' he said mildly. 'Dinner seems a perfectly reasonable topic of conversation to me.'

'Well, that's because you haven't seen what I've seen.'

'Clearly,' he agreed, shooting a sideways look at her.

She would find some way to extinguish that smile in his eyes. Planting her hands on her hips, she glared. 'Don't pretend you have no idea what I'm talking—'

'What *are* you talking about?' he demanded, cutting over her with brutal force. 'What exactly am I being accused of now?'

As he prowled closer she threw up her arms to ward him off, but again he was far too quick for her. 'Let go of me!' Annalisa protested, shaking her arm in a fruitless attempt to throw him off. His hold only tightened.

'Oh, no,' Ramon told her in a tightly controlled voice. 'You don't get away so easily. You have to take responsibility for your accusations as well as your actions, Señorita Wilson. We're taking this inside.'

'I'm not setting one foot inside your house,' she said furiously, tugging back.

His short laugh left her in no doubt as to the outcome. 'This is my territory and I make the decisions here.' And, sweeping her up in one arm, he carried her into the house. Shouldering open the door to a large airy salon, he dropped her down on a cream leather sofa. 'Explain.'

'OK!' she said, springing up again.

'Whoa!' he exclaimed, raising his hands in mock alarm. 'Let's talk about this calmly. I can see that you're upset—'

'Understatement of the year! My trees are destroyed—' She had no money to replace them but he didn't need to know that. 'And you expect me to be calm!'

'Here. Wipe your face,' he said, dangling a spotless white handkerchief in front of her eyes.

She hadn't even realised that she was crying, thanks to the battering her emotions had taken, and it wasn't anything to do with the vandal in the orange groves, she thought, avoiding his fingers as if they were red-hot.

'Let me,' Ramon suggested. 'You look like you've fallen head-first into a bucket of mud. I'm sure you'll feel better when you've had a chance to talk about it,' he murmured, removing from her hands the fine lawn handkerchief she was twisting into a rope of string. Shaking it out, he began to work on the worst of the smudges.

'There's no need,' Annalisa insisted, squaring her shoulders. Predictably, he ignored her. She tried pulling the handkerchief away from him but he only moved in closer, forcing her to push against his chest...and then her fingers softened and eased into a caress. Horrified, she snatched her hands away. 'You can't get out of this,' she flared, badly shaken. 'I want an explanation.'

'Then we're both going to get what we want if you come and sit down and we discuss things reasonably,' he countered.

But there was an edge to his sensible words that betrayed a very male interest in her lapse.

'So,' he began when they were both seated across a table made of some pale wood, 'what's your problem, Annalisa?'

'You,' she began honestly. And you can take that smile you're trying so hard to hide off your face right now, she thought, squaring up to him. 'Water rights, marina, and now my orange trees,' she ticked off briskly.

'Orange trees?' he demanded. 'What am I supposed to have done to your orange trees?'

Annalisa gave a short, incredulous laugh. 'If you saw them you wouldn't need to ask.'

'I'd like that very much, as it happens.'

The speed of his capitulation threw her for a moment. 'OK,' she said. 'What about right now.'

'Why not?' His expressive lips curved in a wry smile of assent. But there was a lot more going on behind his eyes as he stood up and indicated that she should too.

'When we get to the *finca* you'll see why I'm so upset,' she promised.

'Mud-fights?'

She stopped dead, feeling his gaze on her back. 'Don't tease me, Ramon. This is serious.'

'Well, I can't see anything that a nice warm bath won't cure,' he said in a deep, sultry tone that made her bristle defensively.

'You might change your mind when—'

'I doubt it,' he cut in. 'When you're all cleaned up you can make a list of your demands and I promise to consider each one of them in turn. Come on, I'll drive,' he added. 'The sooner we get to the *finca*, the sooner we can get all this straightened out.'

Lifting her chin, Annalisa walked straight past him.

He glanced at her car when they got outside. 'I'll get someone to look at that for you.'

'There's no need—'

'You're not taking that vehicle off my property until I'm certain it's safe,' he said bluntly. 'Get in,' he ordered when she hesitated beside his car. 'I don't have all day.'

'There,' Annalisa declared dramatically, standing back so that Ramon could have a clear view of her ruined orchard.

'Who did this?' he said, looking around.

'Enrique Caradonda.' She watched him relax. 'And don't pretend you don't know who that is, because Enrique told me that you sent him.'

'I asked Enrique if he would consider paying you a visit,' Ramon corrected evenly. 'No one commands Enrique Caradonda. He's almost a legend.'

'What?' Annalisa burst out. 'For destroying perfectly good fruit trees?'

'No,' Ramon said, going on to explain, 'Enrique is the best tree surgeon on the island. He is always in demand— particularly now, in the spring.'

'But there was nothing wrong with my trees that a little care and attention couldn't put right.'

'They might have looked all right to your untrained eye, but years of neglect were masking disease in some and a serious lack of pruning in all of them,' he informed her. 'If I could have warned you he was coming I would have done so, but Enrique is a law unto himself.'

'There should be a law against him,' Annalisa muttered as she viewed the devastation. 'So,' she said, 'having organised this chaos, how do you intend to put it right?'

Levelling a hooded stare at her, he hummed in consideration. 'Dinner?' he suggested, raising his upswept ebony eyebrows a fraction.

'Dinner!' It would take more than a meal to make up for this, Annalisa thought as her glance swept over the orchard again.

He threw her a challenging look. 'Would you rather I got some glue and we spent the evening sticking branches back on?'

'It's not funny, Ramon!'

'The hungrier I am the less funny I become,' he warned.

Dusk was falling quickly. Annalisa glanced impatiently at her wristwatch. 'What time are we expected at the restaurant?' It made her mad to admit it, but Ramon was right; the damage was already done. If she went ahead with dinner she could pin him down over some form of reparation for the damage.

'We can eat whenever we want to,' he said.

Did that mean dinner on his boat? She felt herself heating up. Of course it did. He wouldn't want to risk being seen with her in public, would he?

'Plenty of time for you to take that bath,' he said, allowing his gaze to track over her slowly.

She felt her body responding as his perceptive stare lingered on her breasts, where mud streaks drew attention to her generous cleavage. 'Why don't we just call it off?' she suggested huskily, remembering that he didn't want to be with her in private either unless she made herself present-able for him.

'No chance,' he said, shaking his head very slowly as he continued his leisurely appraisal. 'I'd like to cover all your grievances while they're still fresh in your mind.'

The orchard was the least of those right now, Annalisa acknowledged as she fought to control her breathing.

'The bath will give you time to calm down,' he went on, but the dark humour in his eyes told her he knew how un-likely that was. 'You don't want to miss the chance to get everything off your chest, do you, Annalisa?'

His gently chiding tone was far too provocative, Annalisa realised as she fought to keep her mind on her battle plan. 'All right,' she agreed. 'That suits me fine. But I'll make supper.' That fixed him! On Ramon's boat she was subject to his will. In her own home she dictated the terms.

'Sounds good,' he murmured. 'I'll even soap your back.'

'This is purely a business meeting,' she reminded him quickly. 'And I have a perfectly good loofah.'

His knowing look slid effortlessly into something ap-proaching innocence. 'If you change your mind—'

If she prepared a simple meal she could say what she had to say and be safely tucked up in bed before midnight, Annalisa thought, holding his stare.

'Shall we go?' Ramon suggested.

'I'm ready,' she said. 'The sooner we start, the sooner we can sort out the problem.'

The corners of his mouth tugged down wryly. 'I'm sure we can. Whether now is the right time—'

The bath at the *finca* was a marvellous cast iron affair that could comfortably accommodate a family of four. Having treated herself a selection of expensive products at the beauty salon, Annalisa added a good splash of scented bath oil before reaching across to turn off the taps. 'Judged to perfection,' she murmured. But while the flow of water from the hot tap responded at once, the cold tap wouldn't budge. The choice was flood the floor or— 'Ramon! Can you give me a hand here? Quickly!'

She had left him sprawled on the sofa in the front room, chilling out to some music, but he reached her in seconds, bursting through the door.

'Are you all right?' he said, anxiously scanning the room.

Annalisa stood back and pointed to the tap. 'I can't turn it off.'

'The tap?' Ramon said, as if he had been expecting a collapsed ceiling at least. Moving in front of her, he applied brute strength to the problem.

'Brilliant!' Annalisa exclaimed. 'But your shirt's all wet,' she observed when he straightened up again.

'Then I'd better take it off and you can dry it for me,' he said with a grin.

Before she could argue he was stripped to the waist. Moving fast, he grabbed her arm and reached for the zip on the back of her dress. 'Just in case this gets stuck too, I'd better see to it while I'm here,' he whispered against her neck. His warm breath sent shivers round her shoulders that spread all too fast.

'Are you cold, Annalisa?' he demanded softly, knowingly.

'Cold? No!' she protested, trembling and laughing at the same time. But the touch of his naked chest against her arm was having a cataclysmic effect on her senses. 'A little tired, maybe…'

'You should take a good long soak in the bath,' Ramon advised huskily, his warm hand lingering on the soft swell of her buttocks where the zip fastener ended.

But just as her will-power was faltering he pulled away.

'*Dios!* You're covered in scratches,' he said. 'Where's your antiseptic?'

'In that cupboard over the washbasin,' Annalisa said, holding her dress together as best she could.

Fishing around, Ramon pulled out a small bottle and some cotton wool. Unscrewing the top, he sniffed and grimaced. 'If you're not stinking of this when you come down I'll send you straight back again.'

'Thank you,' Annalisa said, snatching it out of his hand. Who said romance was dead?

Why didn't it help that she had nothing to regret? Annalisa mused as she put away the last of the dishes. The meal had lasted for hours, and then they had talked on for hours after that. Ramon had been a revelation…even if the business issues had been somewhat overlooked. She hadn't realised before just how badly she had been missing the simple art of conversation. Except that where Ramon was concerned of course, nothing was simple.

And now it was dawn and she was alone again. She had made him a hastily prepared breakfast—freshly laid eggs whipped up with melted butter and lightly cooked…

She swerved from the sink to dash away some tears, her emotions at odds with the mundane household tasks. Taking a few steadying breaths, she went back to finish the chores. There was no comfort in them, but at least there was some semblance of normality in the routine. But when that was done there was nowhere left to go but back to the moment when the dream that perhaps they could be friends after all had been laid bare for the sham it was. The hammering on the front door had been the start of it—she had already been halfway off her chair when Ramon stopped her.

'It's four o' clock in the morning,' he cautioned. 'You stay here. I'll go and see who it is.'

In the end they both went. But when he opened the front door, and she peered around his back, Ramon's chauffeur was standing on the doorstep. And the expression on his face made it clear what he thought they had been doing. His eyes were flint-hard as they flicked over her, then he cut her out, speaking to Ramon in rapid Spanish. Annalisa could not grasp every word. But she felt sure he wanted her to pick up the name Margarita, as well as the Spanish word for airport.

After a clipped response Ramon shut the door and, turning towards her, said, 'I'm sorry, Annalisa. I have to go.'

'Go?' Of course he had to go. What a fool she was! What right did she have to keep him? Ramon was a married man. His wife needed him. It was that simple.

He glanced at his wristwatch and frowned. 'Would you mind if I took a quick shower?'

'No...no, that's fine. You'll find some clean towels in the bathroom cupboard.'

He caught hold of her arms. 'I need one more favour.'

'Which is?'

'Could you rustle up some breakfast?'

He took her fixed stare for agreement, and as she watched him sprint up the stairs she knew that in his own mind Ramon had already left. He couldn't wait to get back to his real life...to Margarita.

And so she had made him breakfast, squeezing oranges in silence, cooking eggs, brewing coffee... But she had got a peck on the cheek, as well as a swift kiss on both hands for payment, Annalisa reminded herself wryly. Wrecked by a rushed, 'Sorry. Have to go. Plane lands in fifteen minutes.'

'You mustn't be late,' she had agreed, holding the door open.

The last she'd seen of him was a brief wave, almost a salute, as the sleek limousine swept out of her yard, heading at speed towards the highway.

Was this what she wanted? Stolen time? She thought about her mother's plight and reason answered the question for her. Though how she would harden her heart sufficiently to think of Ramon only in terms of business she had no idea.

CHAPTER FIVE

I WILL drown if I stay here, Annalisa thought, trying to shake herself out of the doldrums as she stepped out of the front door of the *finca* later that morning. And it won't be the sea that kills me... Ramon wasn't her friend and couldn't be her lover. The sooner she got those facts through her head the better.

But just because she felt bad that didn't mean the animals' routine could be disrupted. And at least Fudge was his usual carefree self. Even while she went through the motions of feeding chickens and setting things straight in the yard he sprang around her feet like a puppy, trying to look as cute as his lopsided face would allow. He could do everything but speak, she thought, dredging up a thin smile as she watched him dash to the path that led to the beach and then race back again to bark excitedly at her.

'All right. I give in,' she said finally. 'But you will have to wait until I get changed.'

Running upstairs to her room, she quickly crossed to the chest underneath the window where she kept her swimwear. As she dragged off her top it grazed her nipples. Just thinking about Ramon had plunged her into a state of arousal, she realised with a bitter half-laugh. Some joke! Her mind on one track, her body on a detour. It seemed as if each erotic zone had Ramon's personal brand on it whether she liked it or not. An early-morning swim in the freezing cold water would sort that out, she decided, impatiently snatching up a bikini and wrap from the drawer.

Fudge was waiting for her when she arrived in the yard, his excitement evident in the tense way he held himself and the erect set of his tail. As soon as Annalisa called out he scampered off down the path in front of her, yapping with triumph. Scooping up the bright red ball she had bought for him in the village, she broke into an easy jog behind him. Ramon's warning about swimming alone did briefly cross her mind when she was forced to slow at the cliff-edge. But Ramon wasn't here. And this was still her beach…her life.

Scrambling down to the shore, she threw the ball as hard as she could, her tension easing into a smile as she watched the old dog race after it. When he caught up at last he executed an exaggerated pounce and then looked back at her for approval, wagging his tail furiously before trotting back with his head held high.

The game could have gone on much longer, but Annalisa was growing restless. 'That's it,' she said finally, untying her wrap. The sea beckoned. Palest sage edged with a white lace frill, it was mirror-flat except for the treacherous spine between the two properties where the rocks broke the surface. It promised a cooling swim…a soothing swim. And she had learned her lesson. She would stay away from the point. Shading her eyes with her hand, she plotted her course.

The faithful old dog scampered after her as far as the shallows, but the breaking waves soon provided him with an alternative playmate and he made no attempt to follow her when she continued out to sea.

Swimming warily, she trod water occasionally to test the current. If she stayed well away from the rocks it was quite possible to swim over to Ramon's beach in complete safety. There was no logic in doing so, but some inner demon drove her on. She had no idea what she meant to do when she got there… Sneak up to the house? Spy on him?

She had barely rounded the point when her feet hit the bottom. Standing up, she waded the last few yards to the shore. She was just smoothing her hair back from her face when she heard voices. They seemed to be coming closer. A kind of fearful excitement gripped her as she looked around for somewhere to hide. A little way up the cliff and away from the path that led from Ramon's house there was a jumble of huge boulders. They offered the perfect cover.

Taking care to swish sand over her footprints, she turned and ran quickly through the shallows. Scrambling up the rocks as fast as she could, she slid into a deep crevasse from where she had a perfect view of the beach.

At first she saw only the child. A chubby toddler tanned the colour of nutmeg, wearing a vivid green bandanna on her halo of black curls. She couldn't have been more than three years old. A smile softened Annalisa's face as she watched the little girl skip along the beach. But a couple followed close on her heels.

They walked along arm in arm, moulded into each other and chatting with the easy familiarity of long acquaintance. She felt sure her heart would stop. The woman was almost as tall as Ramon, slender and with masses of wavy black hair caught up in a style that managed to be both casual and chic. She wore a sleeveless calf-length dress in cream-coloured linen and trailed a large-brimmed straw hat in her free hand. Her feet were bare and—

Annalisa turned away, unable to watch any longer. *Margarita*, she thought. Shame lodged in her throat like a fist. And Ramon had a daughter too... The pain was unendurable. For a moment she just shut her eyes, hoping it was all a bad dream. But then she heard the child call out and instinctively looked up again. Ramon had the little girl's arms locked in his hands and was swinging her off the ground... Round and round she went, her shrill laughter bouncing off the rocks, while Margarita stood by watching her with her hands clasped together in pleasure.

The happy tableau was like a dagger in Annalisa's heart. She would never consign Ramon's child to the same fate she had endured—a mother grown bitter from neglect and a father she hardly knew... And if Ramon chose to stay with Margarita...? If? He would. She only had to look at the two of them together to know that.

She sucked in a deep breath, as if she was trying to store

the salty tang of the seashore in her memory, and took a last look around at the fine white sand and the gently lapping sea, already turning a deeper shade of jade. It was all so beautiful, and she had almost called it home. But that had been a fantasy, a hopeless dream that was already in the past. Home was a small town in England. She would put the *finca* on the market in the morning.

As experiments went, her time in Menorca had been a disaster, Annalisa thought, putting the phone down. And now she could not even make a success of rehoming Fudge and the rest of her menagerie.

The only bright spot in the whole nightmarish fiasco was the estate agent. He had nearly bitten her hand off when she'd rung him to tell him the *finca* was for sale. And Don Alfonso had endorsed her decision with exactly the level of enthusiasm that she had anticipated. It had been clear from the start that Ramon and his legal team had completely overwhelmed him. He was glad to be out of it. She had never really stood a chance.

Oblivious to the storm clouds brewing on his own horizon, Fudge was busy worrying the loose strap on her sandals. He cocked an ear and looked up at her expectantly.

'Sorry, Fudge. I'll take you to the village tomorrow and see if I can tempt anyone.' Annalisa's mouth turned down as she petted him. Looking at it brutally, who would want to take on an elderly, ugly dog? Another idea occurred to her and she smiled into his rheumy brown eyes. 'OK, so how do you fancy exchanging fenceposts for lampposts?' It would take some time to sort out a pet passport for him. But if she could find someone trustworthy to take him on...someone she could liase with to make sure that his transfer complied with the regulations...to see he got all his jabs and tests and the microchip...why not? When the *finca* was sold she would be able to afford to fly Fudge back to live with her in England.

She jumped at the sound of hammering on the front door.

It sounded like every raid she had ever seen on a screen. She half expected a call of, Open up! Police!

'All right, I'm coming,' she yelled as the thunderous attack continued.

Flinging open the door, she gasped, 'Ramon!' and tried to shut it in his face.

But he was too quick for her and held it firm with the heel of his fist. Hoisting her half off the ground, he slammed the door shut behind them.

'What do you think you're doing?' she demanded, squirming frantically as she struggled to free herself.

'What do I think *I'm* doing?' Ramon grated, backing her up against the wall. 'What the hell do you think *you're* doing, don't you mean?'

The look on his face was enough to send anyone running for cover, but after seeing him with Margarita, Annalisa was determined to stand her ground. 'Get out!' she raged, with every bit of venom she could muster.

'I can see that would suit you,' he snapped, holding her upper arms fast. 'But I'm not going anywhere until you tell me what's going on.'

'Meaning?'

'Meaning I received a very interesting phone call when I got back home.'

'Really?' she said, turning her face away from a pair of blazing eyes.

'Yes,' he snarled, snatching hold of her chin and turning her back to face him. 'An agent in town tried to sell me *finca* Fuego Montoya.'

Annalisa made a bitter sound. 'Well, excuse me, Ramon! But wasn't that exactly what you wanted?' She saw a muscle in his jaw work as he held his temper in check.

'What?' he rapped incredulously. 'You think I want some random salesman calling to tell me that you want to sell the *finca*? Are you mad? You didn't think to speak to me about it first?'

'It's my property,' she pointed out sharply. 'I can do what I like with it.'

His glare lanced through her. 'I'm really sorry you feel like that,' he said steadily. 'And I'm also disappointed that it doesn't seem to matter to you that I had to learn about this from a complete stranger.'

Suddenly she felt sick and uncertain. He sounded sincere. A host of doubts battered her mind. But still she made a dismissive sound. 'Surely it came as a pleasant surprise for you.'

'What does this mean, Annalisa?' Ramon demanded, staring deep into her eyes as if trying to root out her deepest thoughts.

'What does it mean?' She could feel her face heating up and she couldn't stop now. 'Surely that's obvious?'

A cold anger was brewing in his eyes. 'Well, not to me,' he grated.

She squared her shoulders. She had to force closure. End it now. 'It means that I have had enough of Menorca. I am going back home.'

'*This* is your home!' Ramon exploded.

'No,' Annalisa argued, fighting to keep her voice steady. 'This *was* my home. For a few foolish, misguided weeks.'

Ramon shook his head slowly with an obvious lack of comprehension. 'You were doing so well—'

'Oh, thank you.' Tolerating the fact that you're a married man, do you mean? she wondered, frantically fighting to put her thoughts into words. 'Considering all the obstacles you put in my path—'

'Obstacles?' Ramon exclaimed incredulously, swiping a hand over the back of his neck. 'What the hell are you talking about. If you want obstacles, I'll—'

'Fortunately I won't be staying long enough,' Annalisa cut in coldly.

'Fortunate indeed,' he agreed.

They stood facing each other tensely until Ramon broke

the angry silence. 'So why didn't you sell the place as soon as you arrived on the island?'

'Because I really thought I could make a go of it,' she flared. 'And I would have done if you hadn't stooped to using tactics—'

'I stooped? I'm not going to allow you to get away with that, Annalisa.'

'OK,' she said holding up her hands. 'So let's go through the facts one by one: you carry out building works at the *finca* without my consent, knowing that I have no money to pay you back, you insist that I accept clothes, from Margarita and from yourself, knowing that I have no money to pay you back, you employ a vandal called Enrique to chop down my orange groves, the only possible source of income I might ever have to pay you back—'

'I do *what*?'

'Don't come the innocent with me, Ramon.'

His face radiated anger, but his voice was tightly controlled. 'I'm sorry. I was under the misapprehension that I was helping you.'

Her stomach clenched as she hardened her eyes. 'I'd like you to leave.'

'Perhaps I should.'

His fury was like a coiled spring. It showed in every tendon, every muscle; Annalisa had never seen anything like it and backed away from him instinctively as he made for the door.

'I'll make you a fair offer for the *finca*,' he flung back over his shoulder.

In spite of everything that had happened between them, she believed him.

When Ramon had gone, Annalisa felt completely numb. It was a long time before she was ready to make the phone calls necessary if she was to find someone to take care of all the animals until the *finca* was sold.

The best news of all came when Maria Teresa agreed to taking on the responsibility of Fudge's proposed transfer to

England. 'You might be an ugly mutt,' Annalisa told him fondly when he came to lie across her feet, 'but everyone loves you.'

When all the loose ends were tied up she devoted the rest of the afternoon to packing up her few belongings. There were still a couple of days to go before she left the island, and when she left she would give everything Ramon had ever given to her back to him. She folded the beautiful clothes carefully with tissue paper, and then put them into some decent carrier bags. She would ask the taxi driver to deliver them after he dropped her at the airport.

Her last few hours on the island flew by at breakneck speed, and before she knew where she was Annalisa found herself dragging the last of her suitcases up to the front door.

Fudge would soon be living with Maria Teresa. She would drop him off on the way to the airport. She sighed as she looked down at him. Was she doing the right thing? Would he take to suburban life? No beaches...no sea to play in... She turned as she heard a car draw up and took down his lead from the door.

'It's only the taxi, Fudge,' she said, wondering why he didn't leap around as he normally did when a walk was in prospect. But instead of being wildly excited, the old dog was poised stiffly by the door with his nose rammed into a small gap at the base. 'Come on,' she murmured as she tried to ease him away. But, having set up a rumbling persistent growl, Fudge refused to budge.

Opening the door carefully, so he was forced to back away, Annalisa stiffened too as every antagonistic bone in her body went on full alert.

'You don't know me, but—' a woman's voice spoke.

But I do know you, Annalisa thought, hiding her shock as she surveyed her father's widow.

'I'm afraid I'm about to leave—' she started. Instinctively she glanced down the lane. There was still no sign of her transport. Curiosity and outright antipathy did battle in her mind until curiosity won. 'But my taxi's not here yet. Won't you come in?'

Elegantly clad in soft shades of peach, and carrying a waft of some exclusive scent about her, Claudia di Fuego Montoya looked around as she walked past Annalisa into the main living room. 'My word,' she exclaimed in a melodious if faintly patronising voice, 'I heard the rumours, but I never imagined for one moment—'

'That I would make my home here?' Annalisa prompted softly.

'Well, yes. I suppose that's what I mean. But this is really very nice,' Claudia Montoya admitted as she peered about the room.

'Would you like to sit down?' Annalisa suggested.

The older woman hesitated, her limpid gaze embracing everything including the suitcases. 'I can see this is not a convenient moment.'

'There will be no convenient moment,' Annalisa said truthfully. 'In fact, Señora Montoya, I am leaving Menorca…for good.'

'Oh, dear. I had thought—'

Her regret was about as genuine as a pawnbroker's pity, Annalisa thought, gesturing towards an easy chair set by the window. 'Yes?' she enquired politely.

'Well,' Señora Montoya began, 'before you arrived I had thought to buy the *finca*—' She left the sentence unfinished and reached one hand into the air in an almost balletic pose, as if trying to snag the right phrase.

'For a song?' Annalisa supplied.

'That's putting it rather too bluntly, my dear.'

'The time for niceties has gone, don't you think?' Annalisa returned evenly. 'I came here to claim my inheritance only to find myself ranged against Ramon Perez. And, forgive me, Señora Fuego Montoya, but now it seems that I am about to leave at the point where you identify yourself as yet another rival for this land.' From the look on her face

Annalisa guessed that no one had ever spoken to her father's glamorous widow in quite such a direct manner.

'I admit I was thrown by what I heard about developments here,' Señora Montoya admitted. 'And also by talk of you restoring the orange groves.'

Now her tone was distinctly patronising.

'At least we are being honest with each other,' Annalisa returned dryly.

The older woman's shoulders eased into an elegant shrug.

'Would you care for a drink?' Annalisa suggested, more out of politeness than any real desire to prolong the encounter.

'No. I don't think so. There's hardly time, is there?' Claudia Montoya rose gracefully to her feet. 'But there is just one more thing.'

'Yes?'

'Do I take it that the rumours are true? The *finca* is back on the market?'

'That is correct,' Annalisa said, noting the gleam of triumph that even thickly applied mascara couldn't hope to conceal.

'Then it only remains for me to wish you, *bon voyage*, my dear. And as for the future...well, every—'

'Success?'

'Yes. Yes, of course,' Señora Montoya agreed. That's exactly what I mean. I wish you every success, my dear. Oh, and I'm sure you have already received an offer for the *finca* from Ramon Perez,' she said casually, as if it was just an afterthought, 'but, whatever he offers, I would like to think we could offer more.'

Annalisa frowned. 'We?'

She fluttered her hand. 'What I'm trying to say is that I will better any offer he might make...whatever that offer might be. You do understand?'

'I think we understand each other,' Annalisa replied pleasantly. 'Though I have to say I had no idea that orange groves in such a state as mine could provoke such wide-spread interest.'

'Oh, it's not the orange groves, dear. It's the shoreline we want.' Her voice was now openly patronising, as if Annalisa could not be expected to know about such things.

'The shoreline?'

'I'll have my lawyer get in touch with you,' she said, brushing off the detail. 'And just remember: whatever Ramon Perez offers, we'll do something a little better for you.'

'Oh, I'll remember,' Annalisa said coolly. 'Goodnight, Señora Fuego Montoya.'

There was not a jot of warmth coming from the woman, in spite of all her fine words, Annalisa thought as she ushered her stepmother out of the house. Her first impressions had been spot on. Señora Montoya was no friend. She didn't give so much as a backward glance before climbing into her expensive little red sports car. Mission accomplished, Annalisa guessed, closing the door and leaning back against it with a sigh of relief. The woman probably couldn't believe her luck now she had established that the *finca* was definitely back on the market.

Smoothing her hands down the front of the simple sun-bleached two-piece she had chosen to travel in, Annalisa gave a thin smile.

Compared with Señora Fuego Montoya's designer outfit, her clothes felt shabby. Since her disaster with the white dress she hadn't had a chance to go shopping. Señora Montoya clearly didn't have her marked down as a challenge. Neither did Ramon. No wonder he thought he could use her for target practice whenever he was bored.

Curiosity drew her to the window and she watched for a few moments until Claudia Montoya's car disappeared down the lane. Then, turning away, she shot a wry glance at her canine defender. 'You can stop growling now, Fudge. She's gone.'

The airport at Mahon was clean and modern, and lacked the hectic confusion of many a larger facility. Annalisa was on her way to the check-in desk when, seeing the woman who lay in her path, she suddenly drew up short. Then pulling herself together, she marched forward determinedly. She would just have to make a wide curving detour around the attractive woman shifting from foot to elegantly clad foot.

'Annalisa?'

Annalisa stopped dead in her tracks. Her back tingled with the knowledge that Margarita was right behind her. She turned around slowly and they stared at each other.

Margarita was even more beautiful than she had guessed from seeing her at a distance. Her thick glossy black hair was gathered back loosely and held in place by a wisp of chiffon. She wore a loose-fitting jade silk two-piece with a natural flair that owed nothing to the artifice employed by Claudia Montoya. Her make-up consisted of nothing more than a slick of ruby gloss to accentuate the curve of her lips and a suggestion of grey shadow on her doe-brown eyes.

Her expression showed natural curiosity, as well as relief that her wait was over—nothing more. It flashed into Annalisa's mind that Margarita didn't have a clue about Ramon's extra-marital activities... But if that was the case what was she doing here?

Margarita broke the silence first. 'Have you time for coffee?' she asked in a lightly accented voice.

'Well, my flight—'

'Doesn't leave for almost two hours,' Margarita reasoned, making it difficult for Annalisa to refuse without appearing rude.

'I have to check in.'

'I'll help you.' Without waiting for an answer, Margarita took the passport and travel documents from her hand and walked along to a desk that seemed to be out of use. Several young men rushed to her assistance.

'There. That's done,' she said, coming back to hand the

empty envelope and passport to Annalisa. 'Shall we find that drink?'

Annalisa's legal training took over that part of her brain that was still able to function. It was better to hear what the other side had to say before you opened your mouth. That way you didn't reveal anything they didn't know. But against all her instincts for self-preservation came the realisation that she had already warmed to Margarita.

'How did you know I'd be here?' Annalisa said when they had both settled into a discreet booth in the self-service café.

'Maria Teresa told me,' Margarita replied with a quick smile. 'She thinks a lot of you,' she added. 'They all do.'

'They?'

'The villagers,' Margarita explained. 'They can see what you are trying to do. Your father was a wonderful man. And now they see that you mean to carry on his legacy—' She broke off and reached out to touch Annalisa's arm. 'I'm sorry. Did I say something to upset you?'

'No,' Annalisa said softly. She was the one who was sorry. 'I had hoped to make a go of things here—' There was an air of closure about the remark. It was both a commitment for herself and a silent promise to Margarita.

Margarita's expression changed from empathy to concern. 'You can't mean you're leaving the island for good?'

'It just didn't work out.' Annalisa spread her hands in a helpless gesture. How could she explain? Their gazes glanced off each other and she realised that under different circumstances they might have been friends.

'That's not what I heard,' Margarita argued, reaching across the table to touch her hand. 'No one here can understand why you are going back to England. Surely they are mistaken? Surely this is just a visit?'

'No,' Annalisa said flatly as she drained the last dregs of coffee. 'What you've heard is true. I am leaving for good.'

'Would it change your mind if I told you that all the villagers who used to work for your father are planning to gather at the *finca* this afternoon to show their support for you?'

'Their support—'

'They want to work for you, Annalisa…for nothing to start with, if they have to. They will put in a few hours each evening to get the estate running again and then—'

'I can't let them do that.'

'Why not? If that's what they want—'

'No!' Annalisa said sharply, covering her ears in an instinctive gesture. 'It's too late for that.'

This time Margarita would not be put off, and taking both Annalisa's hands in her own she drew them down to the table, keeping a firm hold. 'Please, Annalisa. They deserve this chance. Even if you won't reconsider for your own sake, think of them. They begged me to come here to try and change your mind.'

Her innocent plea settled around Annalisa's heart like a band of thorns, but her answer was a slow shake of her head.

'If you won't come back for them, then at least come back for Ramon.'

Even her astonished expression failed to deflect Margarita.

'He's devastated,' she carried on in a tense whisper. 'But he's so proud—'

Snatching her hands away, Annalisa stumbled to her feet. 'You don't understand. I can't—' She made a clumsy attempt at pushing the table back and only succeeded in banging it hard into Margarita's leg. 'Oh! I'm sorry! I'm so sorry!'

Making a dismissive sound, Margarita reached for Annalisa's wrist. 'Then sit down again and listen to me.'

Annalisa held back, then gave in. 'You're right. It's time I was honest with you.'

'Good,' Margarita said with a smile of encouragement. 'Come and sit down again. Happiness is such a fragile condition, Annalisa. We must never waste an opportunity to preserve it.'

'I'll get some more coffee first.' Annalisa was desperate to regroup her thoughts before she caused any more damage in Margarita's life.

Returning with a selection of pastries and two cups of coffee, she cautiously restarted the conversation, 'You want to talk to me about Ramon?'

'Let me tell you about my husband,' Margarita began, spreading her fingers wide as if she didn't quite know where to begin. 'He is quixotic…and a little arrogant.' She made a rueful gesture, as if to say that was only to be expected. 'And of course he is very passionate—' She broke off and laughed self-consciously, her face reddening at the revelation. 'I suppose you have guessed that by the way I talk about him. But we have loved each other since we were children.' She stopped and smiled, reaching out a hand to touch Annalisa's arm. 'Don't look so alarmed. I'm sorry if I'm embarrassing you. I know we've only just met, but I feel as if we could be friends.'

Annalisa lowered her gaze as she smiled. Was it possible to feel any worse?

'Separations between us are inevitable,' Margarita continued, unaware of the effect her words were having, 'but it could be so different for you, Annalisa. I have no right to ask this of you, but I'm going to anyway—for all our sakes, please don't go back to England.'

Annalisa shook her head adamantly. 'I must.'

Margarita stirred the froth in her coffee cup as silence hung between them. 'Then you're making a terrible mistake,' she said at last.

'How can you of all people say that?' Annalisa demanded incredulously.

Margarita's slender shoulders lifted in an elegant shrug. 'I know everything from Ramon.'

'He told you what, exactly?'

Margarita leaned towards her. 'He is in love with you, Annalisa.'

'I'm sorry—'

'Sorry? Why are you sorry?' Margarita exclaimed, biting down on one of the sugar-coated pastries.

'Your daughter—'

Margarita's eyes softened to liquid gold as she wiped the crumbs from her lips with a paper napkin. 'What does my little Aurelia have to do with this?'

Were relationships taken so lightly amongst the super-rich? Annalisa wondered, knowing it would never do for her. 'I'm sorry, Margarita, but I really must catch this flight—'

'Then I'm sorry for Ramon,' Margarita said. 'And I'm sorry for myself too. I get very lonely—' She broke off, waving her hand with embarrassment as she began fishing in her handbag, tears chasing down her cheeks.

'Surely your husband—'

Margarita shook her head dumbly as she dabbed at her face with a tissue. 'When he's with me I am the happiest woman on earth. But he is away so much… And now I'm pregnant again—' Her voice broke into a sob.

Annalisa felt as if someone was putting her insides through a shredder. 'Surely that's a good thing?' she managed tightly.

'Good?' Margarita exclaimed passionately. She settled back in her chair again and nodded. 'Of course, you're right. It is wonderful news. But I want to share everything with him—' And, mistaking Annalisa's expression for incomprehension, she added, 'Don't you see, Annalisa? I will have had the baby by the time he gets back.'

'Ramon is going away?'

'Ramon?'

Annalisa raised her voice, desperately seeking clarification. 'You have told him about the baby?'

'Of course I have told him.'

The confirmation was like a blow to her heart. 'Then—'

Margarita grabbed her hand. 'You can make him understand how it feels for a woman, Annalisa. He would listen to you—'

'No! Really! I don't think I—'

'But you must,' Margarita insisted, talking over her. 'I know Ramon cares passionately about the race, but—' Her gaze ran wildly around the café and then settled back square on Annalisa's face. 'You're my last hope,' she cried pitifully.

'The race?' Annalisa probed. However bad her own position, she couldn't just sit there and say nothing. And something was starting to rattle the bars of her memory bank.

'Yachting...the round-the-world race,' Margarita prompted, as if everyone knew about such things. 'It's got to stop,' she hurried on. 'And if Ramon says it must, it will. You must speak to him for me. I don't want my babies growing up wondering who is their father—'

'Hold on,' Annalisa cut in. She was beginning to feel she was trying to find her way through a very thick fog. 'You think it would help if I spoke to Ramon?'

'I know it would,' Margarita declared in a passionate whisper, taking hold of her hand.

'But what would I say to him?'

Margarita's eyes held her gaze in a bright, intense stare. 'Just tell him that I feel as he does...that I love as he loves... Tell him to stop his brother racing yachts all over the goddamned world! Tell Ramon that Luis must stay home now, with his wife and babies!'

CHAPTER SIX

SHE was pleased to be going home, but terrified too, Annalisa thought as she sat beside Margarita in Ramon's limousine. Margarita had made everything easy for her at the airport with just a flashing smile and a couple of flicks of her fine-boned wrist. But it would take a lot longer for Annalisa to recover her composure.

The thought of seeing Ramon again was tying her stomach up in knots. She had misjudged him so badly. But she would have to try put all personal thoughts to one side if the *finca* was to be saved…and, whatever Margarita said, after their last encounter he probably wouldn't want anything else to do with her.

'We'll soon be there.'

Annalisa peered out of the limousine's tinted window as Margarita distracted her. They were just coming up to the turn-off for the *finca*.

'Close your eyes,' Margarita insisted as the chauffeur slowed to negotiate the pot-holed lane.

'Why?'

'You'll soon see. Just close them,' she insisted. 'There! Now you can look!' she exclaimed.

They had pulled to a halt in the yard and, opening her eyes, Annalisa climbed out quickly. As she looked around she shook her head in bewilderment. 'I don't understand—'

'Welcome to the famous orange groves of Finca Fuego Montoya, Señorita Annalisa,' Margarita proclaimed with a mock bow.

Annalisa gasped. Small groups of men were busy painting and repairing the outbuildings, and in the orchard she could see a lot more people weeding and clearing and generally collecting up all the detritus of neglect. Half the village seemed to be busy with some task or other. She turned to show her delight to Margarita. 'I can't believe it. This is fantastic—'

'Look at this!' Margarita interrupted, grabbing her hand.

Turning, Annalisa saw two men carrying a beehive under the direction of Maria Teresa, who had Fudge trotting at her heels. The minute he saw Annalisa he pelted across to her, yelping in ecstasy.

Maria Teresa stopped in her tracks. 'You came back!'

With a smile and a shrug, Annalisa cocked her head as she peered at the domed white structure. 'What do we need that for?'

'Bees,' Maria Teresa said, turning to chide the two men for almost running it into her.

'Bees?' Annalisa repeated blankly.

'They say bees are the cupids of the orchard,' Maria Teresa insisted, 'because without them the blossom is no use. And without the blossom...' She shrugged.

'I would never have thought of it,' Annalisa admitted. 'How can I thank you? All of you?' she said, turning full circle to include everyone within earshot.

'By employing us and our families when your orchards start producing,' Maria Teresa declared pragmatically.

'But I can't pay you.'

'You have eggs. You have chickens. You have a donkey we can borrow,' Maria Teresa argued. 'And soon you will have oranges. Plenty of oranges.'

Annalisa grimaced. 'I don't think so,' she said with a rueful glance towards the orchard. 'Enrique has been here.'

'Exactly, *señorita*!' Maria Teresa said, beaming at her. 'Enrique has been here. There will be plenty of oranges. Just you wait and see.'

'Is she right?' Annalisa said, turning to Margarita.

'Maria Teresa is always right. Ask anyone,' Margarita replied with a smile.

Annalisa pulled a face as she sighed. 'I did. I asked Ramon. I didn't believe him when he said it would help. I didn't believe him about Enrique...or about anything else.'

'I know,' Margarita said gently touching her arm. 'But when he gets back you can explain.'

'Back?' Surprise and disappointment hit her at the same moment. 'You mean he's left the island?'

'He left before I knew what the villagers meant to do. He came to pick me up from the airport because Luis asked him to. He said he had something important to do. Then he took the jet and left. As soon as I realised you were serious about leaving I had to come and find you.'

'I'm so glad you did,' Annalisa said, feeling all the resolve she had thought lost flood back into her veins. 'Do you know where he went?'

'Who knows, with Ramon?' Margarita said with a shrug. 'Business, perhaps. But he has business interests all over the world. Maybe it was just a short trip,' she added hopefully. 'Maybe he will be home tonight. Claudia has called a gathering this evening. She must surely have invited Ramon. Perhaps you should be there,' she added mischievously. 'I believe it is to discuss the purchase of *finca* Fuego Montoya.'

'To rig the sale, you mean?' Annalisa guessed.

'I wouldn't put anything past her,' Margarita agreed. 'Claudia knows all the interested parties, so fixing the price shouldn't be too difficult for her. You'll come, of course?'

'I wouldn't miss it for the world.'

'I hope Ramon will be there for you,' Margarita said gently.

Annalisa's stress levels rocketed. She ached to see him again, particularly now, after everything Margarita had told her. But setting things straight between them was sure to be difficult. Just thinking about him leaving the island for destinations unknown at the controls of his own private jet showed how little she really knew about him.

* * *

Ramon was not at Claudia Montoya's home that evening. And at first Annalisa thought she knew no one—until she spotted Don Alfonso. He hid his surprise well when he saw her—almost as well as Claudia Montoya had managed to do…

'I can't imagine why you're surprised to see Don Alfonso, dear,' Claudia exclaimed, towing her across the patio by the arm. 'He was your father's most trusted lieutenant…and I was married to your father for a good many years.'

Good had nothing to do with it, Annalisa thought as she made a sound of acknowledgement and forced a smile. What on earth had possessed her to walk into the lion's den? But it was too late now. Don Alfonso was already stepping forward to greet her.

'Annalisa! You have decided not to leave us after all. How fortuitous it is to find you here.'

'Really?'

'But of course,' he said, directing a glance at Claudia Montoya. 'We have gathered to discuss the purchase of the *finca*—'

'Don't you mean the sale of the *finca*?' Annalisa suggested acerbically. 'You are still acting for me, as far as I am aware.'

'Of course, of course,' Don Alfonso agreed. 'A mere slip of the tongue.'

'The family as well as all the other interested parties wanted a meeting to discuss the matter,' Claudia confided as her glance darted between the two of them.

'The family?' Annalisa queried. 'I don't see Ramon Perez here, or his brother Luis. And I don't believe I received an invitation either,' she added pointedly. 'Yet I think I can safely call myself an interested party.'

Claudia's voice was stiff with affront. 'But I called round—don't you remember?'

'I don't remember you mentioning anything about this.'

Her stepmother's rapidly diminishing smile dissolved completely. 'How was I supposed to know you would change your mind and decide to stay? Oh, look!' she said, her voice suddenly brimful with syrup. 'Here's Margarita!'

'Where's Ramon, Claudia?' Margarita demanded, cutting straight through the bull. 'Didn't you tell him about this evening?'

Annalisa looked at her new friend with renewed interest. Margarita was shaping up to be a lot more than a pretty face. Suddenly Claudia Montoya seemed suspiciously uncomfortable.

'Snacks anyone?' she called, snatching a tray of canapés from one of her uniformed maids.

Don Alfonso took her place, sidling up to Annalisa as if he had private matters to discuss. Taking the hint, Margarita made herself scarce with a half-wave to suggest she would be around if needed.

'I have to confess I am surprised to see you here,' Don Alfonso said as soon as Margarita was out of earshot.

'But surely you must be glad that I decided to stay,' Annalisa countered smoothly. 'I would have been completely unaware of this meeting, for one thing. And as it has been called to discuss the disposal of Finca Fuego Montoya…' She looked at him pointedly.

'Yes, yes,' Don Alfonso agreed, studying the amber liquid in his cut crystal glass. 'But I am afraid I have some very bad news for you.'

'Really?' she said, finding it increasingly difficult to hide her poor opinion of him.

'You can't imagine how relieved I am to be able to explain this to you in person—'

'Get on with it, Don Alfonso,' Annalisa suggested. Her patience with him was running out. Why hadn't she seen through his artificial old world charm before? Keeping her so badly informed could not be construed as acting in her best interests. He was either totally incompetent or heavily embroiled in some form of shady deal with Claudia Montoya. She watched as he settled his glass on the top of an ornate console table.

'The *finca* has accumulated many debts over many years, Señorita Wilson.'

'But my father had money—'

'Tied up elsewhere.' He spread his hands wide. 'Where, exactly, no one knows. I am afraid I cannot hold off the creditors any longer.'

There was not one iota of emotion in his voice, Annalisa realised with irritation. He wasn't even going to put up a fight. 'No matter,' she said determinedly. 'I have people who will work side by side with me.'

'My dear young lady, you are missing the point.'

'Oh, really?' Annalisa said coolly. She was determined not to allow anyone else to patronise her... or cloud the issue by making her angry, she warned herself. First she had to find out everything he knew.

'Unless you can raise sufficient funds by the end of the month,' he continued, 'the banks will call in their loans and the *finca* will be turned over to its creditors... and sold.'

For a song to Claudia Montoya? Over my dead body! Annalisa thought furiously.

'Annalisa—'

She turned distractedly to see Margarita dabbing at her forehead with one hand and swinging her wrap weakly in the other.

'Do you mind if we go?' she said. 'I feel a little faint.'

Annalisa's brain clicked into overdrive. The baby! 'Of course I don't mind. Are you all right?'

'I will be as soon as I get out of here,' Margarita murmured, taking her arm in a surprisingly firm grip.

Don Alfonso bowed to them, but not before Annalisa had spotted the shrewd calculation going on behind his eyes. If he was in league with Claudia Montoya, the sight of her cosying up to Margarita could only be bad news for the two of them.

'I'm sorry about that,' Margarita said as soon as they got outside. 'But if I had stayed there a moment longer I know I would have done someone an injury.'

'You think they fixed the meeting for tonight, knowing Ramon was away?'

Margarita nodded as she opened the door to Ramon's limousine. 'Of course. Where is that driver?' she said, gazing around distractedly. 'He's never here when you need him.'

'He's probably getting something to eat,' Annalisa said reassuringly. 'We can wait—'

'No. We can't,' Margarita broke in. 'You couldn't have known half those people, but I can assure you they weren't connected with any legitimate business on the island. They're not really interested in robbing you of your inheritance. It's just a means to an end. They're out to ruin Ramon.'

'But you were invited,' Annalisa pointed out.

'And I'm sure that had them quaking in their boots,' Margarita said with a self-deprecating laugh. 'I was only there to provide window-dressing. These men are such chauvinists, Annalisa. You have no idea. Claudia might be their ringleader, but none of them see me as any type of threat—' She broke off as Ramon's chauffeur slipped into his seat. 'We need to get in touch with Ramon fast,' she whispered in Annalisa's ear. 'Before Claudia can do him any more harm. The villa, please!' she said, addressing the driver in Spanish.

'My father must have known what Claudia was like,' Annalisa insisted, steadying herself on the seat as the chauffeur sped onto the highway.

Margarita cut her off with a derisive snort. 'Your father was too honourable for his own good. And because of that he wasted his whole life trying to keep that greedy bitch from ruining him.'

Her bluntness forced a small rueful smile from Annalisa. 'Is Don Alfonso involved?'

'Your father sent Don Alfonso packing years ago,' Margarita informed her scathingly. 'Everyone was surprised when he turned up again working for you…but it was hardly our place to advise you.'

Annalisa groaned softly and shook her head. She couldn't believe she had walked blindfold into such a can of worms. But there might still be chance to retrieve something. 'Don Alfonso said the banks are about to foreclose.'

'What exactly did he say?' Margarita demanded.

'He said I was broke.'

Margarita frowned. 'I can't believe that's the case. Your father was a very rich man. He must have left you some money.'

'Believe it,' Annalisa insisted. 'My mother never had any money. When I sold the house in England there was just enough to carry out a few repairs on the *finca* and treat myself to a day out. Nothing more.'

Margarita shook her head as they turned off the main road and started dodging potholes. 'It just doesn't make sense. I wish I knew how to contact Ramon. He would know what to do.'

'Well, he isn't here, so I'll just have to sort it out myself,' Annalisa pointed out reasonably.

'If we could find him I know he would help,' Margarita argued.

'How?'

'He could lend you the money.'

'That's not an option,' Annalisa said firmly. 'I would never borrow money from Ramon. The two of you have done more than enough for me already.'

'I've done nothing yet,' Margarita said dismissively. 'But there is something I could do for you.'

'What?'

'I could get your airline ticket changed.'

'Why bother?'

'Presumably your mother had a solicitor in England?'

'Yes,' Annalisa agreed, 'of course she did. But don't you think I've talked to him? I can assure you there is no secret stash of money waiting for me there.'

'You don't know that for sure,' Margarita persisted stubbornly.

'I do. My mother left everything to me. There are just a few stocks and shares waiting to be sold.'

'I think you should go back to England,' Margarita said. 'Make another appointment with the lawyer. Find out how many stocks and shares.'

'What are you trying to say, Margarita?'

'It's just a hunch. And while you're there telephone every five-star hotel within a twenty-mile radius—'

'I can't afford to stay—'

'Not you, silly. Ramon.'

'Ramon,' Annalisa murmured. On cue her heart started to thunder. 'Do you think—?'

'I don't know what to think,' Margarita said frankly. 'And I don't want to raise your hopes. But after what I saw at the *finca*…all those people putting their trust in you…and then seeing the sharks circling at Claudia's. You have to keep up your investigations, Annalisa, until every single possibility has been exhausted.'

As the plane levelled off Annalisa opened the buff-coloured envelope that had been waiting for her at the airport. She blinked as she read the contents through again. She had never seen so many noughts in her life. And the offer for the *finca* had come from—Claudia Fuego Montoya.

She stuffed the letter back into the envelope and then stuck them both into the rubbish bin at her side. There wasn't enough money in the world to tempt her to sell the *finca*. There had to be a way to save it and she wasn't about to give up without a fight.

It seemed odd, coming back to her hometown and feeling like a stranger. But all her friends were married and scattered. She had no relatives, and the tiny house where she'd used to live with her mother had new occupants... She couldn't resist walking down the old road, and smiled when she saw the children playing in the front garden that seemed to have grown so much smaller than she remembered. She stood watching for a moment and then, burying her head deeper into her jacket, she hurried on.

Officially it was spring, but there was a sharp north wind and, catching sight of a bus, Annalisa hurried across the road. The appointment with her mother's solicitor was later that afternoon and she had already checked into a small bed and breakfast establishment just off the high road. Paying the fare, she steadied herself as the bus jolted forward. It was quite a change from Ramon's limousine. But if it took her to someone who could help her save the *finca* it was the best transport on earth.

She stopped dead in her tracks and tucked her chin even deeper inside her jacket. Her heart was racing so fast she could hardly breathe. Even cloaked in a long navy blue cashmere coat, the tall figure was unmistakable. She turned around to catch her breath, hoping he hadn't seen her yet. She needed time to think, to prepare—

'Annalisa!'

Pulling her jacket collar higher around her face, she started walking towards him.

'You look frozen.' Instinctively his hands went to her shoulders and he rubbed as if to coax some warmth into her.

'I'm fine.' But his touch only accelerated her tremors.

'Like hell,' Ramon argued. 'Come on, I'll get you a coffee...warm you up.'

'Why are you here?' As she stared up into Ramon's handsome, familiar face, all she could think about was Margarita saying he loved her...and that now, instead of feeling ashamed, she could revel in the honey warmth of desire as it trickled through her veins.

'I might ask you the same question,' he drawled, the customary amusement glowing behind the intelligence in his shrewd dark eyes.

'This is my hometown,' she murmured, feeling as if her lips were already swelling in response to his hooded appraisal.

'Believe it or not, you don't need a permit to come here,' Ramon countered softly, the curve of his sensuous mouth directing a bolt of lightning to her senses.

'You haven't answered my question yet,' she reminded him in a low, challenging voice.

'Where are you staying?' he demanded.

'Answer my question first,' Annalisa insisted.

Ramon did—with an amused look and then silence.

'You really are the most infuriating individual.'

'So I'm told,' he agreed. 'So, where are you staying?'

With a look of exasperation she gave in. 'At the Elm Tree.'

He thought for a moment. 'Never heard of it.'

Hardly surprising, Annalisa thought. The simple accommodation was more likely to be rated in meteors than stars.

'Let's go back to my place,' he suggested.

'Actually, I can't,' she said, reminding herself why she was there. 'I have an appointment with my solicitor.'

'Patterson?' he queried. 'I'd like you to see someone else.'

'How do you know the name of my mother's solicitor?'

'Don't be so naïve,' Ramon insisted. 'What do you think it takes to stay ahead in business?'

'I don't see the connection between my mother's solicitor and your business,' she said suspiciously.

'Like I said, Annalisa,' he murmured, 'Don't be so naïve.'

'Don't you know how unethical it is for Patterson to discuss my business with you?' she said, hardly knowing whether to be more concerned about his interest in her private life or the subtext in his eyes.

'Don't be so defensive. I might know his name, but I wouldn't expect him to divulge any secrets—'

'So how did you know when I would be here?' Annalisa cut in.

'Patterson's secretary was less discreet,' he admitted, in a way that made Annalisa picture the secretary's rush to be as accommodating as possible.

'So, who is this other lawyer?' she demanded.

'He's a barrister. Would you like me to take you to see him?'

'No, thank you,' she said, determined to play it cool. 'I'm sure that Mr Patterson will tell me everything I need to know.'

'Well, if you encounter any difficulties—'

'I won't,' Annalisa said confidently. But just as she was about to move past him something in his eyes held her back. 'Why are you here, Ramon? Surely Finca Fuego Montoya is a very small project on the scale of your usual business?'

'I'm committing no crime,' he said obliquely.

Annalisa's keen gaze tacked around his face, searching for clues. 'Are you seriously telling me you couldn't find a lawyer closer to home?'

She couldn't help noticing how his eyes crinkled attractively at the corners when he smiled—she tore her gaze away. Ramon kept a whole legal team on his payroll. So what was he playing at?

'I don't have anyone working for me who had the right qualities to take on a case like this,' he said.

Pressing her lips together, Annalisa narrowed her eyes. Was she going to call him a liar? It was hard to think straight when Ramon was standing right in front of her.

'Well, if you'll excuse me,' she said evenly, 'my appointment is in five minutes—'

'I'll wait for you.'

'If you like.' She could only hope she sounded calmer than she felt. Her heart rate was right off the scale. 'I'd better go. I don't want to be late.'

As he gave her a courteous half-bow Annalisa was left with the identical feeling she had experienced when they first met…that he knew a whole lot more than she did…and about far too many things.

CHAPTER SEVEN

'YOU mean there's nothing?'

'I mean there's not enough to furnish you with sufficient funds to save the *finca*. I'm very sorry, Miss Wilson.'

Annalisa swallowed and looked at her hands folded neatly in her lap, then up again into the concerned, bespectacled face of her mother's lawyer. 'Well, thank you, Mr Patterson, for being so frank with me.'

'I only wish I had better news for you.'

'I always knew it was a long shot,' she said, sighing. 'But I had to try.'

'As I understand it,' the solicitor continued in a more positive tone of voice, 'if you sell the *finca* you will be a very wealthy young woman.'

Annalisa laughed mirthlessly. 'That's true. But I had hoped…' She sighed again.

'I know,' Patterson said sympathetically. 'Life seems to give with one hand and take away with the other. I see cases like this all the time.'

'I'm sure you do,' Annalisa said, her face relaxing into a smile. 'And I really have nothing to complain about. As you said, I will have enough money to come back here and set up my own law practice.'

'Something tells me that's not what you had set your heart on.'

'You'd be right,' she admitted.

'If you'll take a little advice from me…?'

'Of course.' What had she got to lose?

'Follow your heart,' he said.

Annalisa eyes sharpened with surprise. She had expected

111

another dose of sound common sense, not some romantic notion from her mother's legal advisor.

'I can see you're surprised,' he said. 'But believe me, Miss Wilson, I see far too many people trapped in a life they don't want because they missed their window of opportunity. That window has opened for you. Don't walk past it until you're sure there's no other way.'

'Thank you, Mr Patterson,' Annalisa said, smiling as she got to her feet and extended her hand. 'If my dream survives this harsh brush with reality, you'll be the first to know.'

'I'll be waiting to hear,' he said, taking her hand in a firm grip. 'And I have a good feeling about this.'

Annalisa blew sceptically through her lips as she went down the narrow flight of stairs that led from Mr Patterson's office to the street. Since when had solicitors become optimists?

'There you are,' she said, walking over to where Ramon was standing beside his car.

'Did you think I'd desert you?' he demanded, opening the passenger door for her. 'How did your meeting go?'

'It ended on an optimistic note,' she said honestly.

'I'm pleased for you,' Ramon said, drawing the large saloon smoothly away from the kerb.

'Nice car.'

'Not bad. How long do you plan to stay?'

'How long do *you* plan to stay?' she countered, smiling— but she should have known better.

'As long as it takes. Hungry?'

She hadn't thought about it up to now, but— 'Yes. Starving, actually.'

'Good. Me too.'

Being with him made her feel warm and safe, and as the indicator made a mellow ticking sound she stared out of the window to see where he was taking her. He turned into a long curving driveway, and now she could see what looked like a stately home coming into view. 'Is this yours?' she asked in surprise.

He shrugged non-committally. 'Not yet. But it's a rather good hotel. There's an excellent restaurant,' he added as he stopped in front of an impressive sweep of steps. 'And you can use my room to freshen up.'

That jolted Annalisa out of her complacency. 'I'm sure the ladies' room will be fine,' she said quickly. A visit to his room was not on the agenda. She had to keep a clear head until she knew what he was up to. 'Are you sure I'll be all right dressed like this?' She peered down at the simple grey suit and plain white sweater she was wearing underneath a heavy wool jacket. Perfect for a visit to a solicitor's office, but a bit understated for a swanky hotel.

'You'll be fine,' Ramon said, brushing off her concern like any man who preferred the contents to the package. 'I'm happy to eat in my suite, if you'd prefer. But something tells me you'd be more relaxed in the restaurant.'

He'd got that right! So why was she trembling? She had eaten lunch with him before…and dinner…

Before she could say anything he opened his window as a young man in a smart bottle-green uniform walked over to them.

'Would you like me to park your car, sir?'

'Thank you,' Ramon said, climbing out and handing him the keys. 'Annalisa?' he said, coming around to open the door for her.

Stepping out, Annalisa gazed up the steps towards the impressive entrance, and then turned to look behind her at gardens laid out like a chessboard. 'I'm definitely not dressed for this.'

'You look perfect to me,' he said, catching hold of her hand. 'And, just to make sure you don't disappear, I'm going to hold onto you.'

He wasn't married, so it was all right to take his hand, she reminded herself—only to snatch it away again when she remembered that he was still a formidable business adversary.

'Relax,' he murmured, guiding her up the steps.

She had to force herself to try. There was no reason to suppose he had come to England for anything other than perfectly straightforward reasons. He probably intended to buy the hotel. But there was nothing remotely straightforward about the touch of his hand…it was electrifying.

The huge arched oak entrance doors led directly into a discreetly lit womb-warm lobby. The carpets were the kind you sank into, in various shades of red, and provided a mellow counterpoint to the carved wood panelling. Oil paintings lined the walls and there was a grand piano under the curve of the stairs. The glint of crystal and newly polished brass was the only ornament she could see apart from the profusion of fresh flowers in strategically placed vases.

'Do you like it?' Ramon asked when he had collected his key.

'From what I've seen so far, I love it,' Annalisa said honestly.

'I may add this to my portfolio of luxury hideaways,' he confided as he steered her towards the restaurant entrance. 'Luigi?' he called over a red corded rope.

A man in his middle fifties, wearing the immaculate uniform of a *maître d'*, hurried forward from the hushed depths of the sumptuous room. Seeing Ramon, he came across to unhook the rope with a flourish.

'Signor Crianza Perez!' he exclaimed in a flourish of Italian-accented English. 'What may I do for you?'

'A discreet table for two.'

'Certainly, *signore*. And for the beautiful *signorina*, a red rose, I think.'

'Twenty,' Ramon said casually.

The suave Italian didn't miss a beat. '*Certamente, signore*. Delivered to your suite?'

'To the table,' Ramon said, shooting Annalisa an amused glance.

'That's really not necessary—' Annalisa began.

'Once again, Annalisa,' Ramon informed her darkly, 'you find yourself on my territory. And, once again, here I make the rules.'

They were sharing private jokes?

'And the ladies' room is where?' she said, in case he thought he was getting it all his own way. 'I'd like to freshen up.'

'To the right of the reception desk, *signorina*,' Luigi said with a curious glance at Ramon.

When the menus arrived, Ramon waved them away. 'Feed us, Luigi. Give me a taste of the kitchen.'

'*Certamente*, Signor Perez.'

The smile on Luigi's face couldn't have been any wider without doing serious damage to his dentures, Annalisa thought. And if their table had been attracting attention before, it was nothing to the interest shown now, as dish after dish of delectable *antipasto* began to arrive.

A vast bouquet of red roses had been expertly arranged in a vase placed on a stand beside them, and if she felt something of a mouse in her businesslike outfit, Ramon looked stunning. His dazzling film star looks and black designer suit with its scarlet lining set him apart from every other man in the place. To say he was causing something of a sensation was an understatement, she thought, noticing how many of the young waitresses found an excuse to bring something to their table.

So far there had been no further clues as to what had brought either of them to England, until finally he said, 'There's someone else I'd like you to visit tomorrow.'

'Ramon, before you tell me, I must warn you—' He looked amused. She stopped. 'I mean it, Ramon. Are you going to listen to me or not?'

'Not.'

'But I—' She should be warning herself, not him, Annalisa realised as his gaze gradually darkened into something sensual and predatory.

'You want to warn me about Claudia,' he said softly, dipping his head to stare into her eyes. 'Right?'

'Well I—'

'I already know,' he said. 'It's all in hand. Don't worry. Leave it all to me.'

'But what about—'

'Margarita? I trust my brother to do what is right.'

'The *finca*—'

'Can wait,' he cut in firmly. 'Whereas I can't,' he said, maintaining eye contact until he was certain her frustration had shifted onto another track.

'There's more,' she admitted hoarsely.

His eyebrows rose infinitesimally.

'I…I owe you an apology.'

'For what?'

'For misjudging you.' He wasn't going to make it easy for her, Annalisa thought as she watched amusement start to tease the corners of his beautifully shaped lips.

'Go on.'

'I thought you were married—' her throat dried completely '—to Margarita.'

He appeared to think about this for a moment. 'Anything else?'

'Well, there's Enrique—stop it, Ramon!'

'What am I doing?'

'Stop looking at me like that.'

'I like looking at you.'

'But you like teasing me even better. Admit it.'

'Guilty.'

Her heartbeat seemed to have taken over the whole of her body now, and as she tried to meet his eyes with confidence she felt sure he would see the vibrations thundering through her. 'Well, I'm sorry, but—'

'I accept your gracious apology.' He cut over her smoothly. 'Now before we go any further down this road, can we return to what I was saying?'

'What—?'

'I want you to see another lawyer.'

Her sigh of relief was almost audible. Now she knew how a fish felt when it was thrown back into the water! 'Well, I've got the outfit,' she said, feeling confident enough to risk a joke at her own expense.

'It's a date, then,' Ramon said, leaning across the table to feed her a plump chocolate-tipped strawberry.

The way he sucked the chocolate off his fingers held her spellbound. Everything he did was so sexy…and so thorough. She could feel herself responding…softening…and had to force herself out of the trance when he broke eye contact to wipe his fingers on his starched white napkin. But even that was bewitching, when his long tanned fingers were so supple and strong— She started guiltily when she realised that he had put the napkin down and for the last few moments had been staring at her.

'I really can't eat another thing,' she protested when he pointed to the fruit.

'It's a shame to waste them,' he murmured, picking one up while his gaze remained fixed on her mouth.

As some of the juice escaped onto his finger she watched as he licked it away…and then she realised that even her breathing had fallen in time with his tongue—

'Champagne?' he suggested softly, meeting her gaze.

'I've had a bottle of chilled Krug delivered to your suite, Signor Perez,' Luigi anticipated, looking pleased with himself.

Ramon looked across the table at her, waiting for an answer.

'I don't think so,' Annalisa protested weakly.

'Ah, but *signorina*, I have also arranged for some delicious sweetmeats from my own region of Italy to accompany the champagne…and some freshly ground coffee from the Blue Mountains in Jamaica.'

'Thank you, Luigi,' Ramon murmured, his gaze never leaving her face for a moment.

'You're all as bad as each other,' Annalisa said in an attempt to break the spell when Luigi had swaggered back to the kitchen.

'Who's bad?' Ramon demanded softly.

'Men,' she managed, finding it hard to look away.

'Don't you like being spoiled?'

'I wouldn't know.'

'Then may I suggest you lower your guard a little and try something new for a change?' And, reaching across the table, he took hold of her hand. Slowly, languorously, he began stroking her fingers one at a time.

It was possessive and erotic, and made her feel as if she was the only thing in the world that mattered to him. 'I would like that champagne now,' she murmured. 'If I'm not too late…'

His lips curved in understanding. He stood with the grace of a panther, grasping both her hands to bring her in front of him.

They made it to his room—just.

Kicking the door shut behind them, Ramon fell back against it, dragging her to him. Sliding her fingers up the front of his jacket, Annalisa had the buttons open and the jacket off his shoulders before his lips had a chance to close over her mouth. Even as he dragged the breath from her lungs with his first kiss she was working on his shirt buttons, fingers flying, while her own clothes added to the heap on the floor.

Swinging her into his arms, he crashed onto the bed, stripping the covers away and wrapping one of her legs around him at the same time. She felt the hard corded muscles of his belly rubbing against her and climaxed suddenly, violently, gasping out his name in shock. But he held her fast until her breathing steadied, and when he felt her gradually softening against him he dipped his head to her breast.

'I can see I have a lot of work to do,' he chided contentedly.

'Meaning?' she demanded softly, lacing her fingers through his hair to increase the pressure a little.

'Meaning...' He lifted his head reluctantly. 'You are deliciously untutored in the art of love. A skill I shall take the greatest pleasure in teaching you.'

'And you are so arrogant—'

But he wanted to kiss her again...kiss her until she thought they would melt together. And when his tongue plundered her mouth, retreating slowly in an unmistakable prelude to the moment when he would answer all her needs, she gave freely, urgently, pleading for more.

'We've got all night,' Ramon reminded her softly, holding her still. 'I want to take my time...enjoy you slowly. No,' he said firmly as he softened his grip and she went to slip beneath the sheet. 'On top...here...so I can look at you.' And then, very steadily and firmly, his hands followed the same scorching trail set by his eyes down the length of her blush-pink quivering body. 'You are beautiful... *magnifico*,' he said, slipping into his own language as he feasted his eyes on her breasts.

Annalisa could only answer with a soft moan as he sank down to suck one painfully erect nipple into his mouth. Meshing her fingers through his thick black hair, she encouraged him while she floated on a cloud of sensation. And when he moved to take the other he still attended to the first tender nipple, with his thumb and forefinger, until she thought she would go mad under his skilful stimulation.

He was everything...everything she had dreamed of and so much more. But as he gauged her state of arousal and shifted position again, lodging himself between her thighs, she sucked in a sharp, involuntary breath.

He stopped immediately and pulled her against him,

stroking his hand down the length of her back as he nuzzled his face against her cheek and neck. 'What's wrong, *querida*?'

'Nothing,' Annalisa whispered against his mouth, curling up defensively when he rolled away from her.

'Come here,' he murmured after a few seconds. 'Come to me.'

She wanted to…she wanted to so badly.

Ramon made the decision for her, drawing her into his arms and bathing her eyes, her nose and her cheeks with kisses. And then he murmured, 'What are you frightened of, Annalisa?'

'I'm not—'

But he didn't believe her…and he changed the pace of his lovemaking completely, soothing her with kisses so tender she felt teardrops come to balance on her silky lashes. When he saw them, Ramon licked them away, laughing softly and deeply in a way that made her smile. And while he quietened her his hands worked their magic…so light and gentle she could have broken away at any time.

'Is that better?' he murmured when his hand moved down over the soft swell of her belly, seeking the core of her sensation. And when he parted her plump swollen lips to stroke gently and persistently she answered his question with a small sound of longing as she offered up her face for his kiss.

'There's no need to be frightened,' he murmured when he pulled away. 'You're very, very wet…and I will be gentle…until you ask for more,' he added wickedly, moving to nibble on her bottom lip.

His voice aroused her, his caresses seduced her, and his stroking fingers knew just where to touch…and how and when.

'Relax for me, *querida*,' he said, opening her thighs wider and cupping his hands underneath, to lift her until she could wrap her legs around him.

Annalisa gasped as she felt him huge and hard against her belly, and then he moved steadily down between her legs so that there was a new and even more seductive touch stroking her...one that was long and warm and firm. But as he allowed the tip to catch inside her she braced herself instinctively, and he felt it, so that instead of consummating their lovemaking he pulled away.

'I told you there was no need to be frightened,' he chastised softly, moving back to repeat the delicious torment.

It was like nothing Annalisa had ever known or felt before. She had never imagined that anyone could be so skilled, so patient, so good at reading her responses. Instead of tensing each time he slipped a little way inside her now she wanted more, but it was Ramon's turn to hold back. 'Not yet,' he murmured regretfully when she begged him. 'Not for a long time yet, *querida*,' he whispered, even when she held her thighs open for him and moved sinuously beneath him.

But as he drove the ghosts of the past from her mind Ramon finally saw his victory mirrored in her eyes, and thrust into her fully with a growl of triumph.

Early the next morning Ramon had to attend the first in a series of business meetings to discuss the possibility of buying the hotel. But he insisted they have breakfast together first...in the dining room.

Sitting across the table from him, dressed demurely in her plain suit, Annalisa found the whole situation both seductive and amusing. There was a current racing between them now that surely the whole room must be aware of, she thought, glancing around.

Each move seemed to contain an intimate significance, whether it was passing a milk jug so that their fingers touched, or reaching for the condiments so that her arm brushed his. And when their glances met and lingered there was a new knowledge, a new bond, that said she had given him more than her body—she had given him her trust…her respect. In return he had given her the confidence to move forward into the future…perhaps the most precious gift of all, she mused, feeling a rush of warmth flood through her as he glanced up and smiled at her.

'I thought of something to entertain you while I am in my meeting,' he murmured confidentially, leaning towards her. 'While you were in the shower I ordered some new clothes for you. I knew you would be feeling uncomfortable without anything fresh to change into. They should have arrived in the room by now.'

'Ramon, you shouldn't—'

'It gives me pleasure to buy you things,' he said simply. 'I hope it will give you as much pleasure trying them on as it will give me when I take them off again.'

She sucked in a fast breath as she felt her face fire up, and cast a self-conscious glance at their fellow diners. 'You won't be long?' she murmured.

Ramon's arched brows rose a little as his eyes darkened. 'I will be as fast as I can be. Depend on it.'

He was as true as his word.

Annalisa had barely finished folding up the reams of tissue paper and stacking the discarded carrier bags in a neat pile by the bin when Ramon returned to the room. Judging by the look on his face, the meeting seemed to have gone well.

'You look beautiful,' he said, when she showed off the new dress to him.

'You really are too generous. I don't know what to say—'

'Don't say anything,' he growled. 'Just come here.'

'Ramon… Ramon,' Annalisa protested softly. 'You said something about meeting another lawyer—'

'Not now,' he said, running his hands over every curve and plane of her body. 'Is that water I can hear running?'

'Yes,' she managed to gasp as she pressed into him and felt how hard he was. Already he had trained her senses to respond to him…business was forgotten as he backed her towards the bathroom door. 'So, making love all night wasn't enough for you,' she teased softly as he left her for a moment to slip off his suit jacket and loosen his tie.

His answer was in his eyes. Dipping down to switch off the taps in the huge marble-framed Jacuzzi, he straightened up again and softly called her to him. And now his kisses were deep and possessive as she strained towards him, and it took only the smallest movement for him to ease the dress from her shoulders. It pooled around her ankles, leaving her naked apart from a slip of white lace that served for a bra and an even flimsier thong.

'If you're going to be as aroused as this, I'll have to buy a bigger size,' he murmured as he stared appreciatively at her engorged nipples, thrusting urgently against the fine lace bra. His stare was bold and challenging as it tracked slowly down over her breasts and on to where the dark shadow between her thighs provided a stark contrast to the snowy-white strip of lace.

And then his fingers were looping through the sides of the thong and his lips were closing over hers. She cried out and gasped for breath as his mouth tracked down, but he ignored her protests and sucked hard on the first nipple. The feeling was intense to the point of pain, and when his tongue forced the taut lacy fibres of her bra against the already tender flesh he was forced to support her weight as her legs weakened beneath her. Without pause he moved from one over-sensitive tip to the next, until she heard a sound of moaning, pleading, and realised it was her own voice, begging him shamelessly not to stop.

He gave her what she needed, with his lips and his teeth and the rasp of his tongue. And when at last he lifted his head to fix her with his bold and knowing stare it was only to give him the chance to unhook the fastening on her bra. Now it was Ramon's turn to draw a sharp, excited breath as the full beauty of her breasts was revealed. And holding her gaze, so she could watch his satisfaction, he cupped them in his hands, weighing them appreciatively as he mercilessly chafed each jutting pink nipple with his firm thumbpads.

'No. No more,' Annalisa pleaded breathlessly. 'I can't take any more—'

'You submit?'

'Never!'

Ignoring her, he began feathering kisses against her mouth, and as his stubble scraped her neck she groaned and moved to help him, until she felt the thong slide free and fall at her feet.

'Look, Annalisa,' he said, tugging off his shirt and then whipping her round so that she had to stare at their reflections in the large mirror over the bath, partly obscured by steam. It was as if discretion was attempting to cast a veil of secrecy around them, and they were a seductive sight: one towering over the other with a hand clasped possessively over the smaller form's slightly raised buttocks.

'It seems a shame to waste that bath,' he said in a fierce whisper as he glanced down.

'It's not a bath I want,' Annalisa answered, moving against him.

When Ramon laughed it was a low and seductive rumble of sound. 'I'm in control here,' he whispered, reaching out a hand to clear a portion of the glass. He took her chin in his fist, forcing her to face the mirror again. 'And first you have to be soaped all over...'

'Can we start now?' she whispered, pressing her hips into him.

'Not so fast,' he warned, moving away.

She bit down on the soft swell of her bottom lip as she narrowed her eyes and gazed at him warily.

Finally he appeared to relent. 'OK,' he agreed sternly, loosening his belt.

She watched entranced as he moved to draw the heavy

blinds across the window. 'Light those candles,' he said, pointing to the thick creamy white pillars installed in brass holders around the room. 'And switch off the lights.'

She did as he asked and in a few moments the bright artificial light was replaced by the flickering glow of a dozen or more scented candles.

'That's much better,' Ramon murmured, holding out his hands to her. 'Now, come here.'

She obeyed, her eyes fixed on his. Keeping her locked in his gaze, Ramon slowly eased his suit trousers down over his lean hips. Her fast intake of breath sounded above the seductive murmur of the bathwater, bouncing off the walls as the tension rose between them like the heat in a sauna. Adrenalin raced through her veins as he stood naked before her with all the assurance of some priapic warrior. And then slowly…almost lazily…he reached out and drew her close.

Tipping her chin so that she had to meet his gaze, he swung her into his arms and lowered her down carefully into the warm soapsuds. Joining her, he drew her back into his arms again, and now his kiss was long and slow, his hands sliding through her hair in a caress that stole away every thought in her mind but him. As she scored the broad expanse of his shoulders with her fingertips and arched against him his kiss grew hotter in reply, his tongue clashing against hers until daggers of desire brought her bucking against him. Reaching down to take him in her hands, she trembled at what she found, and trembled still more with the need to have him inside her.

They moved quickly, reversing positions as he brought her round to sit over him. His hands were firm on her buttocks as he guided her, teased her, held her back until, understanding that she was almost beyond control, he lowered her down, entering her slowly, only to lift her again at the same steady pace. She was all sensation, all compliance, all need as he continued to direct her movements. And when he relaxed his hold she slid as he had taught her, inch by inch, while Ramon rested against the end of the tub with his head thrown back and his arms stretched out along the sides.

But when she heard his soft, knowing laugh she started moving at her own pace, faster and faster, grabbing at his powerful shoulders for support while her head went back and her mouth opened to suck in the breath she needed to carry her through to release. And then he brought her back into his embrace again, stroking and kissing and murmuring to her in his own language as she shuddered through the last violent spasms in the safety of his arms.

'And I haven't even washed you yet,' he murmured, his lips nuzzling her ear.

'Mmm?' Annalisa answered contentedly, turning a little in his arms.

'Pass me the sponge,' he instructed.

And she rested between his powerful thighs with her head leaning against his chest while he soaped her all over.

'Am I clean enough now?' she asked huskily.

'For now,' Ramon said, smiling as he squeezed out the sponge and tossed it back onto the shelf.

'What are we going to do for the rest of the day?' she murmured, snuggling into him.

He lifted her away from him so that he could stand up. 'Unfortunately I have business meetings scheduled...as do you, tomorrow,' he said when he saw her face. 'But I have extended my stay here for another night and I have made several bookings so that you can test the beauty salon for me. I take it that is agreeable to you?'

Annalisa smiled back as she held out her hand for a towel. 'You think of everything.'

'I try to,' he confirmed. 'Come here and let me dry you, and then I can prepare for my meeting.'

'"For love's sake, kiss me once again!"'

Stirring sleepily in Ramon's arms, Annalisa reached up

to stroke his neck, his cheek...his lips. What a wonderful way to meet the new day. His voice was like chocolate, rich and deep, as it seeped into the furthest reaches of her drowsy mind to coax her to full wakefulness. 'No. Don't stop there,' she purred against his lips. 'I want more.'

'Your wish is my command,' he murmured, brushing her lips with the lightest touch before taking full possession of her mouth again. His tongue plunged deep and retreated slowly, his message unmistakable now.

'That's not what I meant,' Annalisa whispered when he lifted his head to level a burning gaze on her face.

'You're complaining?'

'No,' she admitted softly, linking her hands behind his neck to bring him back to her. And this time the kiss was long and slow as the rhythm of his tongue reflected and induced her seductive responses. But as his touch became firmer and seemed about to answer all her needs he broke away. She knew now that exercising control over her responses intensified his pleasure as well as her own—a thought confirmed when she saw that the harsh masculinity in his face had grown brooding and sensual. She trembled as he began to feather kisses along her neck and shoulders. There was a tantalising lack of haste before he traced steadily down towards her breasts...and it took almost more will-power than she possessed to place her hands on his shoulders and push him away. 'First you have to finish what you were saying when you woke me.'

'Can you wait that long?'

Annalisa's wide mouth curved in a smile. 'No,' she admitted huskily. 'So talk fast.'

'You can't hurry Ben Jonson,' Ramon argued with a sigh as he turned back to her breasts. 'Who would think these could bring such pleasure...and in so many ways?' he murmured, lifting his head to level a darkly amused stare at her.

'Ramon,' Annalisa groaned in complaint, fighting to keep in touch with reason as his teeth toyed lightly with her nipple.

He broke off long enough to look at her. 'You want me to stop?'

'Just long enough to finish that quotation…if you can,' she challenged in a broken whisper, the words melting into a long shuddering sigh as his lips moved down over her belly. And when his tongue began lapping the top of her thighs she grabbed hold of him, ploughing her fingers through his ebony hair. 'I've changed my mind. Don't stop.'

But Ramon was enjoying her arousal too much. 'You don't care for Jacobean dramatists?'

'I love them…I love them!' Anything to have him back where he belonged. 'So finish the quotation! And be quick!' she urged. She knew he was playing with her…controlling the pace of their lovemaking… Well, two could play at that game! Somehow she managed to sit up. 'So when did you become interested in literature?' she said, clearing her throat to give him the idea that this could turn into a very long discussion indeed.

His sensuous mouth edged into a teasing curve. 'Let's just say I've had an extremely wide-reaching education.'

'You can say that again, she thought. 'So…finish the quotation.'

Ramon made a seductive sound deep in his chest. 'How dare I refuse?' His winged brows rose in a lazy gesture of compliance. '"For love's sake, kiss me once again! I long, and should not beg in vain—"'

'You? Beg—?'

He cut her off decisively this time, his tongue plunging into the moist warmth of her mouth while his hands brought her round easily beneath him. 'Who's begging now, Señorita Wilson?' he husked fiercely in her ear as he eased her thighs apart and lodged himself between them.

'"For love's sake"?' Annalisa challenged ironically as she fought to control her breathing.

He paused, suspended over her. 'Are you frightened of love, Annalisa?'

'I'm not afraid of anything.'

Lowering himself to her side, Ramon looked her straight in the eyes. 'You don't need to pretend with me, *querida*. We're all frightened of something.'

The intensity in his gaze threatened to bounce their relationship onto a whole new level. A rush of sensation carried fear in place of passion. She moved restlessly in his arms even as he tried to reassure her. There were so many unanswered questions…and, yes, she was frightened—of commitment, pledges…love. Love was fragile, unpredictable. She didn't know if she had the courage to expose herself to the hurt that came with it.

'I promise I'll never hurt you,' Ramon said, more gently than she'd ever heard him speak before.

'You promise?' Annalisa demanded softly, stroking her finger across his lips. 'And what if you break that promise? Why should I take that risk?'

He caressed her face and kissed her eyes. Then, sifting her silky black hair through his fingers, he murmured, 'If you never take a risk, you'll never know.'

At that moment she believed him and, reaching up her hands to him, she drew him close. 'For love's sake?'

'For love's sake,' he confirmed, kissing her deeply, tenderly, seductively.

Annalisa found he had ordered room service while she was in the shower.

'Champagne!' she said accusingly.

'Buck's Fizz,' Ramon corrected, slanting her a look as he lifted the glass jug of freshly squeezed orange juice.

'But if I'm to see a lawyer this morning—'

'That's later. First there's another important matter I want to discuss with you.' He tightened the belt of his towelling robe before settling into an easy chair.

'Since when do we drink champagne before a meeting?' she challenged, raising the glass to her lips. Surely business could wait just a little longer?

'Take a seat,' he said, raising his glass. 'To us.'

Sitting on the edge of her chair, Annalisa took a sip. The champagne was delicious, and his toast had her heart thundering into a gallop…but the tone of his voice put a brake on her excitement. It was so businesslike; *too* businesslike. She put the glass down again on the small table between them.

'I'm thinking…partnership,' Ramon said making a steeple of his fingers as he waited for her reaction.

'Partnership?'

'Why not?'

'Professional, you mean?'

'No. Permanent. Marriage is for life as far as I'm concerned,' he said as he poured them both another drink.

'Is that a proposal?' Annalisa demanded incredulously as he placed the glass in her hand.

'What do you think?'

He was so objective, so cold and calculating, she felt ice trickle in to replace the spark of confidence he had worked so hard to instil.

'Marriage between us makes a lot of sense.'

'Sense!' She almost choked on her drink.

'Yes,' he said evenly. 'To me…to your father.'

'My father's dead!'

'Surely you can see that he hoped you would make your home in Menorca?'

'Well, yes, perhaps I can now. But—'

'Maybe he hoped for a lot more than that.'

'Meaning?'

'Maybe his last wish was that we should be together.'

A whole slew of possibilities churned around in her mind… Perhaps Ramon had tried to buy the *finca* from her father and been refused…the daughter had proved a far easier target…just seduce her and— She felt physically sick just thinking about it. 'I never imagined you'd sink to using tactics like this.'

'Tactics?' Ramon demanded sharply. 'Your father thought of me as his son. He trusted me. And he loved you.'

The breath exploded out of Annalisa's mouth in a sound of utter disbelief. 'Well, he had a funny way of showing it.'

'You're wrong—'

'So, tell me the truth about my father, Ramon,' she challenged angrily.

He looked at her steadily for a few moments. 'When your father and mother first met, his relationship with Claudia was over. He considered himself free to marry. And that was his intention…'

She heard the hesitation in his voice. The pause told her he was trying to phrase some unpalatable truth to make it acceptable to her. 'Go on,' she prompted.

'Then Claudia told him she was pregnant.'

'And that's supposed to make me feel better?' Annalisa demanded incredulously. 'Knowing he got two women pregnant around the same time?'

'But Claudia wasn't pregnant,' Ramon went on calmly. 'She sacrificed everyone's happiness when she tricked your father into marriage. She didn't even want a baby. She just wanted his money.'

'But my mother *was* pregnant,' Annalisa said bitterly. 'With me. And he abandoned us both.'

Ramon shook his head. 'No. His code of honour would never have allowed it. I know he would have provided for you.'

'Well, sadly, that's where your story unravels,' she broke in. 'There never has been any money.'

'I'm sure you're wrong. But, whatever the outcome for your fortunes, marriage to me—'

'Save your breath!' Did he really think she would follow in Claudia's footsteps and marry for money?

'Try looking at things calmly, logically. There's attraction between us—'

'Sex?'

'Don't say that!' he warned. 'It's a great deal more than that as far as I'm concerned. You have everything I need. And I have—'

'Too much,' Annalisa interrupted coldly. 'You don't need me to add to your trophies. You don't even need to buy my land at a fair price. You can just wait until I go broke.' And then something else occurred to her. 'Or is that what this meeting with another lawyer is about? Signing contracts, Ramon? Take me to bed and it's a done deal—is that what you think?'

His eyes were little more than blazing arrow-slits of pent-up fury. 'Why don't you just sit down, calm down, and listen to me?'

'Listen to you? I've listened to you for long enough!'

'Why can't you trust me, Annalisa?' The question started in a shout and ended in a whisper, as if some giant fist had coiled around his guts and yanked it out of him. 'I thought we were close—'

'And I thought you wanted me for my own sake and not for my land.'

'What are you talking about?' he demanded angrily.

'Your marriage proposal is nothing more than a cynical attempt to manipulate my feelings so that you get the land for your marina!' She made an angry sound, as if enlightenment had truly struck this time. 'If I sell on the open market someone else might beat you to it—my father's widow, for instance!' She gazed up at him accusingly. 'You really think I'm for sale, don't you? You think you can take advantage of me because you have all the money in the world and I have nothing! Nothing except that stupid piece of sand! What you want, Ramon, is a merger, not a marriage!'

'You have no idea what I want,' he said calmly. 'You've made that abundantly clear.' And then without warning he came towards her and backed her up against the door.

'Don't come any closer,' she warned, knowing he could turn her anger into passion in an instant. 'Do you really think I'll do anything you say just because we slept together?'

'We slept together?' he said, spitting out each word as if it was too bitter to keep in his mouth. 'Is that what we did?' And when she didn't reply he straightened up with a sharp gust of exasperation and turned away. 'Think what the hell you like, Annalisa! I've got nothing left to say to you.'

CHAPTER EIGHT

BY THE time she finished in the bathroom Ramon was gone. Annalisa tiptoed across the sitting room, but the silence was absolute. The suite was empty, with not a sign of him ever having been there. And she didn't even know the name of the lawyer he had arranged for her to see. But the lonely ache in the pit of her stomach had no connection with her inheritance, let alone lawyers.

And then she saw it. Leaning against the clock on the mantelpiece. With a sharp cry of relief she crossed the room and snatched up the small cream business card. In Ramon's handwriting she read, *Michael Delaney, Barrister at Law, Chaucer House 11.30 a.m. Wednesday 23rd.* Glancing at her watch, she firmed her mouth. If she hurried she could still make the appointment.

She was shown straight into an imposing book-lined office. The rotund gentleman advancing from behind a vast and cluttered desk reminded her of a clean-shaven Father Christmas.

'Ah, Miss Wilson. What a pleasure to meet you. Michael Delaney at your service. Won't you take a seat?' he invited, ushering her towards a well-worn leather chair. 'Tea? Coffee? Something a little stronger?' he demanded eagerly.

'Oh, no, thank you. It's a little early—'

'Perhaps not when you hear what I have to tell you,' he said, beaming over the top of his wire-rimmed spectacles.

Her tentative smile faded. Not more bad news!

'Don't look so worried, young lady. I hear you're a lawyer turned agriculturist.' He sat down across the desk from her and rubbed his hands together as if the idea delighted him.

134

'Perhaps it was a little rash—'

'Nonsense! Nonsense!' he said, growing more expansive with each exclamation. 'Don't you think I'd exchange this dusty old office for a chance to get out in the fresh air—?' He broke off, inhaling theatrically to make his point.

'There's a lot to be said for dusty old offices,' Annalisa said, her eyes fixed on his framed certificates banked across one wall.

'Courage! Courage, Miss Wilson,' he insisted with a wave of his hand. 'Now, then. I have it here somewhere.'

'What...what do you have?' Annalisa prompted anxiously.

He stopped what he was doing and cocked his head to one side. 'Are you telling me that Señor Crianza di Perez didn't tell you why he had arranged this visit?'

'He didn't tell me anything,' Annalisa confessed, omitting to add that she hadn't given him much of a chance.

'Ah,' the lawyer said, plucking at his lips with his fingertips. 'I had imagined... No matter! No matter! Yes! Here it is!' he exclaimed triumphantly, plunging in his hand like a conjurer to extract a slim file from the midst of the muddle.

'What is it?' Annalisa said curiously.

'What is it?' He turned it over thoughtfully in his hands. 'This is the codicil to your mother's will, Miss Wilson.'

'But shouldn't that have been kept by Mr Patterson?'

'Strictly speaking this is an unofficial document...a letter, if you like, left in my keeping—'

'By my mother?'

'Correct.'

Her heart-rate picked up. 'Shall we open it?'

'Good idea! Good idea!' Tipping out a single envelope, he picked up a bone-handled paperknife and neatly slit the top. Scanning the letter inside, his face became still. 'Ah, yes. I see. All is as I had imagined. It's quite clear...quite clear.'

'What's clear?' Annalisa asked, dreading his answer.

He smiled, his twinkling eyes barely visible above his ballooning cheeks. 'You are an heiress, Miss Wilson. And of some considerable worth...just as Señor Perez said—'

'Ramon knew!'

'He suspected something,' the lawyer said carefully. 'He insisted there should be some treasure at the end of your rainbow. And now I shall have to congratulate him, both on his perspicacity and his persistence in winkling me out. After all, you didn't leave a forwarding address when you sold the house in England, did you, Miss Wilson?'

'That's right, I didn't,' Annalisa agreed slowly. Shakily she rose to her feet. 'So he wasn't trying to buy me—'

'Buy you? Buy you!' Michael Delaney exclaimed, slapping the table as if it was the funniest thing he had ever heard. 'I can assure you, Miss Wilson, that Señor Crianza Perez's only motive in coming to see me was to ensure that you received your inheritance in full.'

Annalisa shook her head stubbornly. 'I still don't understand. My father never gave my mother a penny—'

'He gave her far more than a penny,' the elderly lawyer argued kindly. 'There was money for you and for your mother so that she would never have to worry.'

'But we didn't have any money,' Annalisa insisted. 'How can this be true?'

'I tell you it is true,' he said. 'It's all in here. See for yourself,' he offered, passing the letter over to her. 'Your mother chose not to touch any of your father's money. She saved all of it for you—' He broke off and looked at Annalisa anxiously. 'Would you care for that drink now?'

So much had changed, Annalisa thought as the huge jet eased off the runway. Now she was not only the owner of a huge estate, but had the funds to restore it as she wanted. It was like standing outside the secret garden, holding the key to the door. But her mind was still spinning with unanswered questions—about her parents, and above all about Ramon. Without him it might have taken years for Michael Delaney to track her down…by which time the *finca* would have become nothing more than a distant memory. Had he done all this because he wanted an equal partnership, a merger, just as she had suggested?

That seemed the most rational explanation… But rational explanations were not enough to plug the hollow in her heart.

The low-slanting rays of early morning sunshine looked as if they had been finger-painted by a child across the pellucid sea, and suddenly Annalisa couldn't wait to get out of the taxi. 'Would you drop me here?' she said, leaning forward in her seat.

'Here, *señorita*?'

'It's not far now to the *finca*.'

The taxi driver shrugged, but pulled over as she'd asked.

Climbing out, Annalisa asked him to take the luggage on for her, knowing that Maria Teresa would have been up at dawn to feed the animals. 'Here,' she said, pushing a generous amount over the fare into his hand, 'I'll walk from here.'

The taxi was quickly lost to sight on the meandering lane, but Annalisa made no move to follow. Standing motionless, she drew deeply on the herb-scented air. Then, shading her eyes with both hands, she looked beyond the intricate dry-stone wall to where the fields stretched up into the pine-clad hills. At the highest point stony fingers of talayotts and taulas pointed to the sky. These mysterious monoliths of a distant Bronze Age stood as monuments to the generations before her who had cared for the land. But no one could own the majesty of the cliffs, she reminded herself, or the deserted sugar-sand beach where a drifting film of mist still hovered tenaciously.

She turned at the sound of muffled hoof-beats. It was hard

to be sure where the sound was coming from until she saw
the horse and rider streaking down the valley towards her.
The horse was black and his tail streamed behind him like
a banner as he galloped, his neck outstretched full-tilt with
his rider crouched low across his back. And then she gasped.
'Ramon!'

Taking the wall in his stride, Ramon brought the horse
round in a sharp turn and then reined him in to a wild-eyed,
snorting halt in front of her.

'Welcome back, Annalisa!'

But there was more challenge than welcome in his eye,
and certainly no warmth in his face. Annalisa made herself
stand unflinching as the horse raked the ground with his
ironclad hooves. But when suddenly he reared up and
punched the air she started back.

'Don't worry. I've got him,' Ramon rasped as he urged
him down.

'How did you know I'd be here?' she said fighting to stay
calm.

'Lucky guess?' he suggested sardonically.

The only luck about it was the fact that Ramon Perez was
such a force on the island everyone wanted to keep him
informed of anything that might interest him, Annalisa
thought, raising her eyebrows in a show of disbelief. He
would have known the instant she set foot on Menorcan soil.

'Things went well for you in England.'

He knew that too. 'Yes. Thank you for—'

He flicked the reins on his horse's neck and straightened
up as if he was impatient to go. 'That's good,' he said,
brushing off her attempt to thank him.

She stared at his strong hands, wanting to forget how they
felt when they were caressing her. But she would never
forget, she realised as the hollow place inside her grew.
Searching his face, she saw his mouth was hard and firm.
And his eyes...those eyes that she remembered so vividly,
dark liquid eyes that burned with desire for her...were hard

and stony as they stared straight back. 'It went better than I had any right to expect,' she blurted out, suddenly desperate to keep him there.

'I'm pleased for you,' he grated, battling with his impatient mount. 'We have to go. He's bored,' he added, to her consternation. Did that mean he was too? 'Don't look so alarmed,' he said misreading her expression. 'I would never let him harm you.'

'I'm not alarmed,' Annalisa lied coolly. But seeing the magnificent horse reduced to something quivering and quiescent in the grip of Ramon's powerful thighs wasn't exactly a soothing sight. And Ramon, with his billowing traditional shirt slit almost to the waist and hide chaps flapping loose over his handcrafted boots, looked more like a wild Spanish gypsy than an international tycoon. And she... looked like a travel-weary tourist! 'You just startled me,' she said.

'Then both Dardo and I apologise,' Ramon said sardonically, bowing low over the stallion's sweat-slicked withers.

'Dardo?'

'It means dart,' he explained, adjusting his grip. 'The name on his pedigree is grander, of course—Black Diamond Cupid's Dart.'

'That's quite a name,' Annalisa agreed, wondering which was safer—looking the horse in the eye, or Ramon.

'Well, he has quite a responsibility—don't you, boy?' Ramon said, giving his mount a vigorous slap on the neck as he spoke to him. 'Dardo is the most valuable of all my stallions at stud.'

'I see...'

'He's had enough,' Ramon said, easing the great horse round in a circle.

At first she didn't understand. But when he held the stallion at a prancing halt in front of her Annalisa's pulse took flight. 'Oh, no—I'll be fine.' Ramon was riding bareback, with just a bridle to control what looked to her like a mountain of over-excited and extremely unpredictable muscle, and if he thought for one moment—

'Are you scared?' he challenged.

'Of course not,' she shot back. 'I've done a lot of riding—'

'Like your swimming?'

As she flashed him a look, a picture of her riding school hacks crept into her mind.

'Nothing to say?'

'Plenty,' she said, levelling a long cool stare at him. 'But first I'd like to continue my walk, if you don't mind.'

'But I do mind,' he assured her. 'Don't you trust me, Annalisa?'

He was looking for a lot more than an endorsement of his riding prowess, she thought as she met his dark, challenging stare. And, whatever machiavellian schemes he had up his sleeve for her where business was concerned, she wouldn't have found the money without him...

As she took a step closer the stallion blew a gale down his nose and stared at her boldly through fierce brown orbs. She took another step, then stopped when he lifted his head to gust a long whinnying sigh, his pliant lips rolling back over his large ivory teeth.

'Ahh,' Ramon sighed sardonically. 'He likes you.'

Oh, really? Annalisa thought, locking eyes with the hard-hearted brigand on Dardo's back.

'But he's impatient,' he murmured. 'And so am I!'

The next step was her last. As the stallion surged forward Ramon hoisted her off the ground and settled her in front of him in one seamless move.

'Relax. Relax!' he rasped, his arm a steel band around her waist.

'How can I?' Annalisa wailed, wondering how she came to be balanced on the horse at all as it launched itself over the wall and thundered across the field.

'Lean into me,' Ramon breathed against her ear. 'Don't

fight it. Wrap your hands round his mane. Like this,' he encouraged, his strong fingers directing her movements. 'That's better,' he said approvingly. 'Now we can go faster!'

'No!'

But Ramon was harder to curb than his stallion, and his passion infected her. Only moments later she was begging him to go faster. He only reined in when they came up to the stone arch that marked the entrance to the *finca*.

'That was—' Annalisa exhaled deeply and sagged, lost for words.

'Almost as good as sex? Or just very good, but not that good?'

If there had been any warmth at all in his voice she might have responded, but instead she pulled away as he moved to lift her down.

'Not had enough yet?' he murmured, wheeling the horse around.

There wasn't much choice—she was under his control for now, Annalisa realised, tightening her grip on the mane as she made a futile attempt to distance herself from Ramon's warm body.

'Lean against me,' he ordered. 'You'll hurt him, sitting so far forward—or is there some reason why you can't?'

'You haven't shaved,' she said primly.

His familiar laugh ran a bolt of sensation through parts already rubbed tender by the horse.

'I don't remember you complaining before.'

'Where are you taking me?' she said, struggling to remain immune to his potent masculinity.

'They're your orchards,' he said, reining in to point over the fence. 'You should know.'

Annalisa stared in amazement. In the few weeks since Enrique had wreaked havoc with his radical surgery it seemed that a miracle had occurred. 'I don't understand,' she murmured.

Lush green foliage cloaked every branch, and half the

village seemed to be busily employed clearing and digging, clipping and spraying.

'That's because all your life you have lived fifteen hundred cooler miles north,' Ramon said. 'Here in Menorca everything happens much faster.'

There could be no safe comment on that, she thought.

'So you see, Annalisa,' he went on. 'You should have had more faith. All it took was some sunshine, dung—'

'How romantic,' she murmured under her breath.

'I thought you'd be pleased,' he said mildly.

'Anything else apart from dung?' Annalisa demanded suspiciously.

'Sunshine.'

'And?' she pushed, levelling a cool amber gaze on him.

His beautifully shaped lips tugged down at each side. 'Rather a lot of water.'

'From where, exactly?'

'Why don't I show you?' he suggested, nudging the horse into a turn. A few strides further along he showed her where trenches had been dug around the trees. 'Until a proper pipe can be laid underground we have cobbled together this arrangement,' he said.

'We?'

'The water can only come from one source.'

'You,' she said coldly.

'Of course,' he agreed. 'Would you like to see what else has been done while you were away?'

Her mind was in turmoil. He couldn't just march in and take over the running of her property each time she was away... But on the other hand, thanks to his water, the orchards were thriving. 'Of course I'm interested,' she said.

Swinging his leg over the stallion, Ramon jumped to the ground. 'Here,' he said, holding Dardo steady as he reached up to help her down.

She hesitated a moment, then slid into his arms. Pulling away quickly, she tried to concentrate on what he was saying.

'A galvanised pipe runs from my well down the length of your orchard. A series of hoses are connected to the pipe, so each evening we can irrigate a certain number of trees. As more channels are dug so more water can be supplied.'

'And what is this going to cost me?'

'I'm sure you will be able to satisfy all my demands.'

'I hope you're right,' Annalisa murmured, weighing up the huge storage tank that now stood in place of a rickety old barn. If it was a case of Just hand over your shoreline in return for everything that had been done, he was in for a big disappointment.

'*Eh! Señorita!*'

'Enrique!' Annalisa exclaimed with pleasure. 'The trees... it's a miracle!'

Baring his gums, the wily old villager lifted his shoulders in an expansive shrug. '*El bon sol y agua!*'

'Just the good sun and water,' Ramon translated.

'I know,' Annalisa said, watching Enrique's pleasure when Ramon clapped the old man on the shoulder.

'Nothing would have been possible without your expertise, Enrique,' he said.

And Ramon's water, she thought.

As Enrique returned to his work she turned to Ramon and said frankly, 'It was nice of you to give him all the credit.'

'I am nice,' Ramon insisted, his dark eyes brewing up a storm as he gazed at her lips. 'Given half a chance...'

As their eyes met her senses surged beyond the point where reason could dictate caution.

'Welcome back, *señorita!*'

Snapping out of the trance, Annalisa turned to see Maria Teresa hurrying across the yard with a basket over her arm. Well, she did have thirteen children back home. She could hardly expect her to stay on indefinitely.

'Fudge has been fed. Don't let him fool you. See you tomorrow.'

'Goodbye, Maria Teresa…and thank you.'

'Dardo has earned a rest too,' Ramon murmured, slapping his stallion's neck.

'Why don't you turn him out in the field?'

'OK. I'll just go and wipe him down…find him a drink.'

'Would you like a drink?' Well, it was only polite.

He paused and looked at her. Suddenly the small distance between them seemed part of them both. 'That would be good,' he said, still holding her gaze.

As she watched him lead Dardo across the yard Annalisa could feel the familiar honey-sweet lethargy stealing over her limbs.

But the languor was ruptured the moment she opened the door and a small tornado hurled himself at her legs. With an exclamation of pleasure she knelt to fuss over the old dog. But Fudge was so confident of his hold over her affections that he seized his opportunity to scoot past her and scamper away towards the orchards. No doubt there would be plenty of lunch packs to share there, she mused wryly.

'So, Annalisa—'

Her hand flew to her throat as Ramon walked into the house, ducking his head to avoid the garlands of herbs Maria Teresa had installed over the door.

'I'm sorry,' he said softly. 'I didn't mean to startle you.'

'I'm always on edge after a long journey,' she lied.

'Coffee?' he suggested, strolling over towards the range. 'Make yourself at home.'

'OK,' he agreed, reaching for a jar of coffee beans from the shelf.

Her eyes fixed on his easy movements. Half new man, half unreconstructed male—most women would be drooling… OK, she *was* drooling.

'You can help me if you like,' he suggested, without turning around.

An offer to make coffee should come without any extras, she thought, trying to will her heart to slow down. 'You seem to have everything under control.'

He set the water to boil on the range. 'Come here,' he insisted softly.

It wouldn't hurt to find the mugs for him.

The moment she was within reach Ramon seized her waist and had her on the counter in front of him. She was still gasping with shock when he parted her legs with his hip and moved in close. His hands slid over her buttocks, cupping, controlling. A sound of pleasure and surprise escaped her lips as his large buckle chafed her and she heard him laugh...just a rumble of satisfaction down low in his chest. Ramon was all male, she thought weakly as his mouth brushed hers with a light and tantalising touch.

'You missed me,' he said. A statement not a question. And then his tongue drove her lips apart and he pressed hard against her, his body so big, so muscular and unyielding as he brought her into his arms. She groaned as sensation streamed through her body, erotic and extreme... The scent of him was curling around her, warm and evocative, the seductive lines of his hard frame beneath her hands. She heard herself moan and then beg as her fingers scored his back.

'Gatito!' he exclaimed softly. But it seemed to please him, for he only teased her more, whispering suggestions that made her writhe in his arms. Then, banding one arm around her, he allowed his fingers to trace the pulsing mound of her femininity beneath the fine lace thong, playing her skilfully and judging her responses while he murmured encouragement until she was all feeling, all passion, all need... And then, finding her hot and wet, he dragged off the scrap of lace and plunged his fingers in deep, so that she arched against him.

'No,' he said sternly when she clung to him, crying out with pleasure. 'This is not enough for me, *querida.*' And she reached down, exhaling fast as she fumbled with his buckle and then took him in her hands.

Parting her legs wide, she wrapped them around him, clutching him with her thighs, leaning back and offering, waiting until with a last searing glance he drove deep inside her and set up a seductive rhythm of long slow strokes. Their gazes locked, reflecting, intensifying each other's pleasure, until with a last shuddering cry Annalisa felt him tip her over the edge of reason into a moment so intense, so violent and uncontrolled, he had to use all his strength to keep her beneath him. But then he moved as she wanted him to, and made sure that it was all over, and she lay trembling in his arms before surrendering to the thought-robbing pleasure of his own savage release.

When at last he lifted her down they stood entwined for a while in silent communication.

'That was—'

He put his finger over her lips. 'I want to stay here...I want to spend the night with you.'

She lifted her chin, but he cut off her questions with kisses that were tender now, tender and searching.

And when he broke away at last it was Annalisa's turn to silence him. And, finding his hand, she linked her fingers through his, led him across the room and took him upstairs.

Maria Teresa had placed a terracotta bowl of country flowers in the hearth of the old stone fireplace and their subtle scent perfumed the air. The shutters had been left open a crack so that the bed was a haven of shade streaked with pale streamers of sunlight.

There was no rush now, just clothes pooling at their feet, eyes meeting, holding, trusting. Nothing existed beyond his warm touch and her eager responses. Lips brushing his chest, whispered sighs, sweet murmurings of love, one thought, one desire... The desire she felt only with him.

And then he was moulding her to him, and his hands grew firm as they explored her body. He found her breasts first with his lips and then his tongue, and now it was his turn to drag in a fast involuntary breath. Supporting her weight over one arm, he slipped his hand between her legs and, hearing her moan, carried her to the bed. Wrapping her legs around him, he made a seamless transition from one welcome invasion to another fuller and more complete assault.

Again their hunger overtook them, so that there was no finesse: none possible and none sought. They moved fiercely together, Annalisa held firm between thighs of steel as she called out his name and shuddered repeatedly in his arms while he kissed her slowly and deeply, brushing her hair back from her damp face with long, tender strokes.

As she faced herself in the bathroom mirror Annalisa saw a puzzled reflection staring back at her. She knew Ramon was still asleep, his long, sun-bronzed limbs sprawled in casual contentment across her bed. She was at a loss to identify exactly what had changed. There was no physical cause she could pin down, just a great and compelling stillness inside her that seemed to demand recognition.

'Is everything all right?'

'Ramon! You startled me.' As his arms looped around her waist she rested back with an easy familiarity she had never found with him before.

'You'll catch cold,' he murmured, reaching out one hand to grab her robe from its hook on the door. 'What are you doing in here on your own?'

'I'm not on my own,' Annalisa pointed out, nestling into him.

'Not now,' he agreed, brushing away her thick curtain of hair to kiss her neck. 'Nor ever again, *querida*. But you haven't answered my question. And you know what that means…'

'Do I?' His kisses roused her senses so easily.

'It means I have to make you tell me what's troubling you,' he murmured against her lips.

'I can't wait—'

'No,' he warned softly, pulling his head back. 'I saw something in your face just now. There's something wrong. And you must tell me what it is.'

How can I do that when I don't know? Annalisa wondered.

'Is it your father?' Ramon suggested, wrapping a towel around his waist.

'He meant a lot to you,' she observed gently, relieved to have the chance to concentrate on something safer than the impenetrable sensations she had no key to unlock.

'You only had to ask,' he chided when he saw the sadness in her eyes.

'I was wrong to misjudge him so badly. He sent money all those years—'

'Don't punish yourself. You weren't to know.'

'And my mother never spent a penny of it...and he left me the *finca*—' She broke off and her voice was choked with emotion when she spoke again. 'I can't believe I didn't trust him—'

'Trust takes time, Annalisa,' Ramon said. 'You didn't have any time with your father, and your mother was too heartbroken to explain. But somehow I'm going to prove to you that trust is possible—however long it takes.'

'But—'

'What do I have to do to keep you quiet?' he demanded softly. And without waiting for an answer, he swung her into his arms and carried her back to the bedroom.

CHAPTER NINE

'Do YOU mind if I take a look around up here while you take your bath?'

'Of course not,' Annalisa said. She had nothing to hide. 'But be warned—the only bedroom that I've done anything with is this one.'

'Why aren't you using the master bedroom?'

He didn't need to know that as soon as she'd realised it had been her father's room she had shut the door and never opened it again. 'No reason. I just preferred the view from this room... It's smaller...and should be easier to keep warm in the winter...'

His brows knit together. 'You're not in England now,' he pointed out. 'Surely when the hot nights come you would be more comfortable in a larger room?' He didn't press it when she stayed silent. 'Sure you don't mind?' he said, making for the door.

'Go right ahead,' she said, swinging out of bed.

She had finished her bath by the time Ramon came back to the bedroom.

'Look at this,' he said, sitting beside her on the bed.

As she took the faded photograph from him her heart began to thunder. 'Where did you find it?'

'In the main bedroom. Aren't you going to look at it?' She held the piece of dimpled card tighter, as if touch was all it took to reveal the images contained on the faded print.

'I'm surprised you didn't see it sooner. It was lying right on top of that old carved chest.'

As if someone had intended her to find it... 'I've been so busy I haven't had time to search every inch—'

'You don't have to explain,' Ramon said. 'You do know who it is?'

Of course she did. Her hands dropped to her lap, still clutching the photograph. The laughing girl was her mother—a much younger version, but unmistakable. The man with his arm around her, smiling into her eyes, was— She let out a small cry and thrust the photograph back at Ramon. 'I don't want to see it. Take it away.'

'But that's your father,' Ramon said gently. 'I was hoping to find something like this…to prove to you—' He sighed heavily when he saw that her face was set and distant. 'Look, Annalisa, you can see for yourself how much they loved each other.'

'I don't need to see proof of what he felt for my mother!' she exclaimed. 'I lived with the results of that love every day.' Confusion was churning around inside her. If her father had loved her mother so much, where had it all gone wrong? 'I'll always be thankful for the money…for the *finca*. But I can never forget what my mother went through…the poverty, the bitterness—'

'Stop it, Annalisa,' Ramon insisted fiercely. 'I won't let you do this to yourself.'

'Why not? Because it's true? Because it would suit you very well if I went down the same path as my mother?'

His silence was absolute. In a single heartbeat his eyes turned to stone. 'I thought we were long past that.'

'What?' Annalisa demanded, throwing her arms wide in a gesture of distress and frustration and anger.

'The point where you insult me by suggesting I can't be trusted,' he said coldly, standing up and moving away from her.

'I'm not suggesting anything. I'm stating facts as I see them.'

'But that's the trouble, Annalisa. The facts as you see them have nothing to do with the truth.'

'So what *is* the truth? Pregnant woman discarded by

Spanish grandee awarded generous pension? How are you going to clean that up for me, Ramon?'

'Life is never as straightforward as you seem to think it should be,' he said. 'Get your head out of the textbooks, Annalisa. Take a look around at real life, real people, real problems... You find me some nice straightforward situations and then I'll concede you've got a point.'

'And what about our "situation"?' she said, stressing the word to emphasise the ambiguity of their relationship. 'How would you describe that?'

'What do you mean?'

'What if *I'm* pregnant?' The words shot out of her mouth without making contact with her brain. It was instinct, sheer instinct, and terror at what he might say if he ever gave that possibility some thought.

Ramon went very still. 'Are you pregnant?' he asked softly.

'I don't know... No! I just had to know how you'd react if—'

His hands shot up to cradle his head, and then swept down again in an angry gesture of denial. 'Stop it, Annalisa,' he warned. 'I thought we had a better understanding than this—'

Her short contemptuous sound cut him off. 'An understanding? Is that what we have?'

'You know what I mean,' he insisted angrily. 'You know how I feel—'

'Oh, do I?' Annalisa demanded as she shot to her feet. 'And how would I know that, exactly?'

'Haven't I proved my feelings for you with everything I do?'

'I don't know,' she said, feeling her chest constrict as ghosts from the past refused to let her see past her own insecurities. 'You haven't mentioned love once.'

Briefly he looked shaken. 'You want a sonnet a day?'

'I want—' Annalisa began angrily. Then, breaking away,

she rushed to the bathroom before he could see that she was crying. 'I don't know what I want!'

'That's right. Run away,' she heard him shout after her.

She stopped by the door, her hand on the wall, steadying herself. 'I'm not running anywhere, Ramon. I'm here to stay. Get used to it.'

When she emerged some time later the bedroom was empty. Standing uncertainly in the centre of the room, Annalisa waited, listening. She felt some of the tension ease when she heard Ramon moving about downstairs. But then it returned again when she thought how much she wanted him...but not on any terms. She owed him so much, but that didn't mean she had to adopt his views on the past, or accept a role on the sidelines of his life.

She put off drying her hair and dressed quickly in a pair of decent shorts and a short-sleeved shirt.

Wearing just his jeans and a close-fitting top, Ramon had made himself comfortable in one of her easy chairs. Holding a mug of coffee in one hand, he was reading the local paper with his long legs stretched out and his bare feet resting against Fudge's back. He looked up. His expression was as uncompromising as her own.

This was never going to be easy, Annalisa realised. They were both strong. Both equally determined they were right. 'Lunch?'

'Coffee's fine.'

'Can I get you something else?' she said, crossing to help herself from the pot.

'I have to get back.'

'Of course.' She tried not to let it matter.

'Why don't you come with me?'

She managed not to choke—just. The casual invitation flew in the face of all her suspicions. If this was a game of chess she was in check. 'OK. Why not?'

'Ten minutes suit you?' he said, shooting a glance at his watch. 'I've sent for the car.'

'Fine,' she agreed evenly.

'Someone will collect the horse while we're gone.'

'Should I ask Maria Teresa to see to Fudge?'

'It wouldn't hurt.'

'Am I all right dressed like this?'

'Yes.'

'Do I need anything?'

'Only you can answer that, Annalisa,' Ramon said as he got up to put his mug in the sink.

His distance was like a reproof. Was this his way of punishing her for stepping over the mark…for demanding too much of him? She felt her emotions shift gear as frustration and anger gathered in her throat. There were two ways to answer the challenge: she could lose control again, or accept that the type of relationship Ramon wanted cut both ways; you surrendered nothing, you gained nothing. 'I'll just make that call,' she said.

Stepping over the threshold of Ramon's home was very different from her first visit. This time Rodriguez bowed to her as he opened the door.

'I've got a few calls to make,' Ramon said as they stood side by side in the hall. 'Take a look around while you wait.'

'You're sure—?'

'I had the run of your place. I'll only be a few minutes. Make yourself at home. Please show Señorita Wilson into the library,' he said, turning to Rodriguez. 'There are plenty of interesting early volumes in there for you to root through,' he said, turning back to her. 'First editions… Ben Jonson…' The look on her face drew an ironic half-smile from him. 'See you in a minute,' he said quietly.

And then she was following Rodriguez into a large airy room overlooking the sea. It didn't look much like a library.

'The air-conditioning is not working in the library, Señorita Wilson,' Rodriguez explained. 'But you will be equally comfortable in here. Ring for me if you need anything,' he added, pointing to an ivory velvet pull-cord in one corner of the room.

Was he joking? No, he wasn't, Annalisa realised when she walked across and examined the length of thick plaited cord hanging in a corner. It disappeared through an opening in the ceiling and obviously rang through to some other part of the house.

She gazed around... Where to start? It was a great opportunity—temptation with a license, a chance to discover what Ramon's home revealed about him.

Quality, comfort, but no clutter, she thought as she prowled about. Marble floors covered with priceless Aubusson rugs in shades of rose, peach and ochre. She skirted those and continued with her appraisal in another area.

Vast picture windows dressed with nothing more than pale wood shutters, folded back at present. Two blue and white man-height Chinese vases either side of a baronial-size stone fireplace... A profusion of fresh flowers cascading out of one mammoth vase on top of a stone plinth... Ivory-coloured sofas punctuated with jewel-coloured silk cushions—a suggestion of exotic allure amidst all the restraint... Very Ramon, she decided, smiling faintly. Then, just when she had begun to think that all the room lacked was a personal touch, she spied a clutch of silver-framed photographs arranged on top of a rosewood desk.

There were several striking shots of Ramon and another man she took to be his brother. Standing easily together, their arms draped loosely across each other's shoulders, they stood on the deck of a boat...a racing yacht, she corrected herself after studying the picture more closely. Almost as handsome as Ramon, Luis appeared to be a few years younger. And where Ramon's hair was pitch-black, Luis's was a warm, sun-streaked tawny brown. A consequence of his addiction to sailing, she decided, taking another look. His eyes were penetrating too, but a fierce green rather than smouldering amber-brown. No wonder Margarita was in love with him. He was stunning. And they looked so happy together in their wedding photograph...

There were studio portraits of Margarita and Aurelia, along with several family groups just as she might have expected. And behind this most recent group of photographs stood an older collection of prints. Some were black and white, some sepia. Annalisa presumed they showed distant ancestors of the Crianza Perez family. Her glance was just sweeping over them when Ramon strode into the room.

'What are you doing in here?'

In the space of a heartbeat he was standing next to her.

'I'm sorry,' Annalisa began, but he waved his hand impatiently and steered her away from the desk.

'The calls took longer than I anticipated,' he explained.

'That's all right. I've been looking at your photographs.'

'The photographs?'

'You. Your brother...Margarita, Aurelia... They're all so good.'

'Why didn't you go into the library as I suggested?'

'Rodriguez said the air-conditioning wasn't working in there,' Annalisa explained, wondering about his short incomprehensible outburst in Spanish. She could understand how crucial the air-conditioning system would be as the weather grew hotter. Even a house as large as his would be stifling without it.

'There's something you need to know,' Ramon said.

His expression frightened her. 'Now?'

He answered by propelling her towards some double doors that led onto a veranda overlooking the sea.

'This is so beautiful,' Annalisa murmured distractedly, moving away from him. Resting her hands lightly on the cool stone rail, she felt as if she could happily gaze out at the timeless beauty for ever...prolonging the moment of blissful ignorance indefinitely! She felt intuitively that whatever Ramon had to say wasn't good.

'The photographs,' he began, coming to stand beside her. 'I should have been with you—' He broke off with an exclamation of impatience and swiped a hand across his forehead.

Angry with her, or for her? She couldn't tell. 'Is it so important?' she said, pulling back from the balustrade. 'They're only photographs.'

'It is important…very important.'

'Why?' Annalisa demanded softly, not sure whether she was ready to hear his answer.

'Understand first,' he began, 'that I use this house as a convenience. This is not a home. There are few personal touches here…apart from those photographs.'

'I had noticed—'

He put his hand on her arm, urging her to hear him out. 'This is serious, Annalisa. I want you to believe me when I tell you that I have had no reason to look at any of those photographs or even think about them for years…until I met you.'

'And now?' she said apprehensively.

'I'll show you.' His hand was on her back, compelling, relentlessly driving her forward.

They walked back inside and Ramon took her over to the desk. He didn't intend to prolong the agony with meaningless platitudes. He simply picked out one of the silver-framed photographs and gave it to her.

'Who is this?' she said, but in her heart she already knew. The black and white photograph showed three people: Don Pedro di Fuego Montoya stood in the centre, with two beautiful young women either side of him. Claudia was one; her mother was the other. Vaguely Annalisa became aware that Ramon's arm had moved to circle her shoulder. 'What does this mean?' she asked, turning her face up to him.

'Your mother was employed by Claudia's father,' he said, prising the photograph out of her hands and returning it to the desk.

She frowned and gave her head a shake, as if trying to release the memories locked inside. 'I know she worked here on the island... I know that's how she met my father... I never knew the details—'

'I'll tell you everything I know.'

'Please,' she said, resting her hand on his arm almost as if she was reassuring him now. She needed to know more...everything.

'Claudia's father was highly respected on the island. He came from old money. He was a widower, bringing up his daughter alone. He indulged her every whim. But an aristocratic lifestyle costs a lot of money and puts none in the bank.'

'He went broke?'

'Yes,' Ramon confirmed. 'But that didn't stop him spending money on Claudia...her education, her clothes...'

'And my mother?'

'Claudia met your mother when she was at school in England.'

Comprehension dawned in Annalisa's eyes. 'My grandfather was a teacher.'

'Claudia and your mother became friends. Your mother returned to the island as Claudia's paid companion.'

'Her companion?' Annalisa said with surprise, glancing at the photograph again. 'My mother never mentioned Claudia once.'

'Hardly surprising,' Ramon murmured dryly. 'They spent holidays together, almost always over here...for the freedom as well as the weather.'

'I can see why,' Annalisa murmured as she remembered her loveable but rather authoritarian grandfather. She couldn't imagine anything getting past him.

'As soon as Claudia began to appreciate the financial predicament her father was in, she began to cast her eye around to find something...someone...who could bail her out.'

'And Don Pedro—'

'Was certainly rich enough,' Ramon confirmed. 'But Don Pedro di Fuego Montoya was in love with your mother.'

Annalisa passed a hand across her brow as she worked the rest out for herself.

'I'm sorry. I wish I hadn't had to tell you this,' Ramon said gently.

Annalisa lifted her chin. 'I'm only glad that someone has told me the truth at last. Thank you.'

Ramon stared at her intently for a moment. 'You're sure?'

'And I'm glad it was you,' she added softly.

'Then I'm glad it was me,' he said.

She was glad. Ramon had made her face up to the past instead of living in its shadow. She would always be grateful to him for that.

'Would you like to see the rest of the house?'

She smiled her assent. An impersonal tour would buy her the time to adjust she so badly needed.

'I'm keen to see what you think,' he said, leading the way out of the room, 'because my plan is to make this house the centrepiece of my development.'

'You mean you wouldn't live here any more?'

'That's right,' he said. 'When Margarita and Luis move into their own place this house will be far too big for me.'

'So you'd turn it into a hotel?'

He confirmed her deduction. 'Very select. Twenty bedrooms to begin with, all *en suite*…every sports facility you could imagine—'

'Including a marina?'

His eyes slanted in wry agreement.

'And you would live where, exactly?'

'I've got my eye on a few desirable properties in the country.'

'A few?'

'One in particular.'

The amused challenge in his stare met the growing comprehension in Annalisa's eyes. 'The *finca* is not for sale,' she said flatly.

'Did I say I wanted to buy it?'

'You've seen something similar?' she guessed.

'Having seen what you've achieved with the interior of Finca Fuego Montoya, I have to confess that I am attracted to that style of property.'

'A rural retreat?'

'A home,' Ramon corrected softly. 'You have no idea how envious I am,' he said, holding her gaze.

Was he serious? 'I could help you do something similar when you find a suitable property.'

'Would you do that for me?'

'I'd be happy to do that for you.' She had the feeling she was hearing everything and learning nothing about his true intentions, but her enthusiasm spilled over. 'I really enjoyed working on the interior of the *finca*... I'd love to have the chance to do something like that again.'

'I've been hoping you would take an active part in the design and development of my hotel complex.'

'You're offering me a job?' she said in surprise.

'Why not? You won't be able to practise law here in Menorca. And I imagine that once the *finca* is fully operational you will soon be looking for fresh challenges.'

His regard for her work on the *finca* seemed genuine enough, and her mind *was* stuffed with ideas... But he was only offering her a job, Annalisa reminded herself—hardly a dream proposition. Yet right now it suited her just fine. 'I'd love to,' she confirmed briskly. 'When do I start?'

The sickness began the next day.

'Señorita Wilson, are you OK?' Maria Teresa called as she came hurrying across the yard.

When the bucket of feed had fallen from her hands Annalisa had hoped no one had noticed. But now she was slumped against the gate with Maria Teresa's arm around her waist to hold her up. 'Fine... I'm fine,' she said weakly, pulling away only to sway backwards again.

'Let me get you back to the house,' Maria Teresa insisted firmly. 'You need to take more rest or you will weaken the baby.'

'Baby!' Annalisa exclaimed, struggling to right herself. 'What on earth are you talking about, Maria Teresa?'

'Señorita Wilson...' The capable housekeeper sighed patiently. 'I have had thirteen babies. I know.' She tapped her nose. Then, looking concerned, she added in a conspiratorial whisper, 'Señor Perez...does he know?'

'No! And you mustn't tell him,' Annalisa insisted.

'But of course, Señorita Wilson,' Maria Teresa agreed solemnly. 'You must do that.'

Ramon had to know. There could be no putting this issue on the backburner. She wouldn't be able to hide the pregnancy from him for ever, Annalisa reasoned as she drew up outside his house.

The manservant Rodriguez seemed to have anticipated her visit and stood waiting for her beside the open door.

'Good morning, Rodriguez.' She couldn't believe her voice sounded so calm. 'Is Señor Perez at home?'

'He is at the office in Mahon, *señorita*. But I believe he won't be long, if you would care to wait?'

'Thank you. I will,' she said, walking past him into the hall.

'You can wait in here,' Rodriguez murmured, showing her into the same room as before—the room with the photographs. 'I'll have some coffee brought to you.'

'No,' Annalisa called before Rodriguez had a chance to leave. 'Don't go.' She was determined to lay each ghost in turn...permanently.

'Can I do something else for you?'

Annalisa thought she detected a cool edge to his voice. 'Yes,' she said candidly. 'Why do you always show me into this room, Rodriguez?'

He looked at her blankly. 'I have no idea what you mean, Señorita Wilson.'

'Really?' Annalisa said pleasantly. She walked across to the rosewood desk and picked up the photograph of her mother. 'I understand old loyalties more than you might suppose, Rodriguez,' she said, turning around to face him, 'but you should know that there are no surprises for me here.' She held the photo frame towards him. 'Señor Perez has explained everything to me...about my mother,' she said, using sufficient emphasis to ensure there could be no mistake.

A mixture of emotions flashed across the manservant's face, but almost immediately he resumed his customary professional mask. 'Shall I bring the coffee now, *señorita*?'

'Thank you, Rodriguez.'

As Annalisa returned the frame carefully to its place their eyes met briefly in a glance of mutual understanding, and then with a low bow Rodriguez left the room, closing the door softly behind him.

Annalisa sighed with relief as his footsteps disappeared. Whether the remaining ghosts agreed to be laid so easily remained to be seen. But for now the past could wait. She had the future on her mind and that had to come first.

'Annalisa!'

Ramon didn't just walk into a room, he charged it with electricity, she realised, springing to her feet.

'Rodriguez is looking after you?' he demanded, shooting her a keen stare.

'Very well,' she confirmed. 'Shall I call for some fresh coffee?'

'Don't bother,' he said, tossing his jacket onto a chair as he dropped onto the sofa. 'What brings you here?'

They were meeting later for dinner, to discuss her appointment to his team, so no wonder he was surprised to see her. 'I have to talk to you.'

'Talk away.'

'Ramon, this is serious.'

'So come over here,' he said, patting the sofa, 'and tell me what's on your mind.'

'I don't want you to think I'm here because I expect anything—'

'What's happened?' he said, leaping up. 'What is it, Annalisa? Something at the *finca*? Tell me,' he insisted, moving towards her.

'I will if you just give me chance.'

'OK, OK,' he said, lashing a strong hand through his hair as he stared at her with concern.

'I'm having a baby...our baby.' She froze as he just stared at her. Somehow she forced the words out again.

'I heard you the first time,' he said, shaking his head as if he couldn't quite believe the evidence of his own ears.

'Don't worry,' Annalisa said quickly. 'This doesn't change a thing. I can still work on your project and I don't expect anything from you. I've got plenty of money—'

'Money! What the hell does money have to do with this?' Ramon demanded passionately. 'And as for not changing anything...a baby changes everything!' His grip on her arms was fierce; the look in his eyes was no less intense. 'You're sure about this?'

'According to Maria Teresa—'

His grip softened and she watched his lips tilt at the corners. 'I should have known,' he murmured. 'But this is the most wonderful news...isn't it?' he demanded softly, tipping her chin with one hand so that she was forced to look into his eyes. 'You must be the happiest—' He frowned as he read her expression. 'You're not happy, are you, Annalisa?'

'I'm frightened—' She stopped. That wasn't what she meant. And he knew it too.

'You? Frightened?' Ramon chided gently, allowing his fingers to wander into her hair. He turned her gently to face him again and dipped his head until their eyes were on a level. 'That doesn't sound like you, *querida*.'

She had never seen such emotion in his eyes…such tenderness, such intimacy and warmth. 'OK. Not frightened. I know I can manage—'

'Manage?' His brows knit together as he studied her face. 'On my own.'

He seemed stunned for a few moments, then in a low, tense voice he said, 'Is that what you want, Annalisa?'

As he let her go she shook her head, confusion sliding into vehemence. 'I only know that if my mother had thought things through sooner she might have been better prepared when my father abandoned—'

His sharp curse cut her off and his keen gaze fastened on her face as his fingers cupped her chin and forced her round to look at him. 'Let the past go before it ruins your life too!'

'How can I forget?'

'Remember the past by all means. But learn from it, build on it—'

'What? Use it to hone my parenting skills?'

'Don't be so cynical,' he insisted. 'You'll be a great mother.'

'And how do you come to that conclusion?'

'I only have to look at what you've done with the *finca*—'

'What? Filled a few plant pots and cleaned out—' She stopped. Everything he said was designed to prepare her to face the challenge of bringing up their child alone.

'You've not only made a home for yourself and every stray animal within walking distance,' Ramon insisted, oblivious to the effect his words were having, 'you've resurrected dozens of jobs for the villagers, giving the young people reason to stay here instead of heading for the mainland first chance they get.'

Her face twisted with pain as he said everything but the words she needed to hear. 'I don't see what that has to do with—'

He grabbed hold of her arm and brought his face very close to hers to say fiercely, 'Don't underestimate your worth, Annalisa. You've got guts and compassion and you're not afraid of hard work. If that doesn't match the job description—'

She tore her arm out of his grasp. 'I only did what had to be done—'

'And your father gave you that chance,' Ramon insisted fiercely. 'That's why he refused to sell the *finca*...why he left it to you. He wanted you to have financial independence as well as the freedom of choice he never had. It was his way of letting you know that he cared...that he never forgot you...that he always loved you—'

'Don't!' she warned, feeling his passion stoking her own raw emotions.

But he wouldn't let her turn away. 'Don't run away from your feelings, Annalisa. This time it is too important. You will pass on everything you create at the *finca* to our child...your father's grandchild.'

His voice was so eloquent...so full of need... At that moment Annalisa thought that if he had been asking her to take down the *finca* and rebuild it brick by brick she would have found it easier than confronting the savage intensity in his face.

'Everything has come full circle, Annalisa,' he said, more gently now. 'Don't let the past steal away your chance of happiness. Not now that you have everything to live for.'

But what part would Ramon play in her future...the future of their child? He had talked about everything, but not that. Annalisa's gaze sharpened as she listened. If she was to build on the past, go forward as he suggested, she would need to arm herself with facts, not emotion. 'I fully intend to pass on the *finca* to my child, as you suggest,' she said, forcing steel into her voice. 'And that is exactly why I don't intend to allow my beautiful beach to form part of any hotel complex.'

He eased his grip as he stood back. 'I can understand that.'

'So—?'

'We will come to an arrangement,' he said distractedly.

'And the water?'

His impatience showed clearly in his broad-shouldered shrug. 'Will form part of that agreement. Must we talk business—?'

'Oh, yes,' she cut in coolly. 'Now that I'm about to become a mother I have to think about the future security of my baby.'

'Our baby,' he reminded her quietly. And when her chin shot up he added wryly, 'Just don't forget to feel as well as think, Annalisa. And if you need anything…anything at all—'

'Do I still have that job?'

He gave her a bemused look as he nodded agreement. 'Of course you do. For as long as you want.'

She tossed him a thin smile as she walked out of the room. She had achieved her aim. But his tacit agreement that she would bring up their child alone was a pyrrhic victory that could bring nothing but sadness. His offer of a job only made things worse. She was fated to be with him now…but in the wrong role. Being the lawyer she was, her argument was strong—too strong. She had argued her way out of everything she wanted and replaced it with nothing but a hollow prize.

CHAPTER TEN

ANNALISA stared at the telephone accusingly. Since leaving Ramon's house the previous day he had rung her four times to discuss a point in the contract his lawyers were preparing. He was prepared to let her continue using his water for a peppercorn rent if she reconsidered her position on the shoreline. A small patch of beach out of sight from her favourite spot didn't seem a high price to pay for the success of the *finca*—but not once had he suggested meeting up to talk it through.

As her hand hovered over the receiver she felt her eyes fill with tears and dashed them away impatiently. Even if the survival of the *finca* depended on his co-operation, parenting was different. She could manage that perfectly well on her own.

Typically, the phone cut out as she picked it up, and she was reduced to pacing up and down the room as she forced herself to concentrate on the safer topic of hotel accommodation. Apart from all the standard rooms they would need a family suite, an owner's suite...a bridal suite. Clenching her fists, she stopped and went to stare aimlessly out the window just as an unmistakable black car swept into the yard. Jolted into action, she raced around in a panic, checking and straightening. Pausing to pluck a brush out of her shoulder bag, she snatched it through her hair. But before she could finish the door flew open and Ramon walked in.

'Are you all right?' he demanded, striding across the room.

Her throat dried as she felt the tension in his hands. 'Of course I'm all right.'

'You didn't answer the phone.'

'That was you?'

'Of course,' he said impatiently.

'Are you here to check out the shore? The water supply?'

'Sometimes,' he said, glaring down at her, 'I really do despair.'

'Why? I—'

His hands moved fast, as if he would have liked to seize her and shake her, but he stopped himself midway. 'Let's get out of here,' he murmured, and his touch was gentle as he steered her towards the door.

'I still find all this hard to believe,' Annalisa admitted as they dodged a couple of wheelbarrows full of trimmings.

'You had the vision,' Ramon pointed out, yanking her out of the way when it became clear that a race was in progress between some young boys from the village.

'But without your water—'

'A perfect partnership?'

The amusement in his voice made it hard for her to concentrate on talking business. She was thankful when they reached the big yellow trailer where most of the activity was taking place. 'I've only just been able to start paying everyone,' she said as they dodged some flying trimmings.

'But that never stopped them coming to work, right?' Ramon prompted.

Guard down, she turned to him. 'I'm not used to such—'

'Trust?'

The look he gave her was both provocative and challenging.

Raising her chin determinedly, she said, 'Will you call everyone together for me, so that I can explain about back pay?' She was determined to keep the exchange on a professional level. 'I want to make it clear that I'm going to compensate everyone for all the days they—'

'Señorita...señorita!'

'Maria Teresa!' Annalisa said, swinging round in surprise. 'I thought you left ages ago.'

'First, Señorita Wilson, I have this to give to you.'

'A present for me? You really shouldn't,' Annalisa said self-consciously as Maria Teresa pressed a package into her hands.

'Aren't you going to open it?' Ramon murmured diplomatically. 'Everyone's waiting.'

'Of course.' Annalisa glanced around self-consciously, realising she had suddenly become the centre of attention. She tugged the string off the brown paper package and her eyes widened as she examined the contents. 'But this is—' She had been about to say exquisite. But as she shook out the fine lawn shirt she could see that it was far too big for her. Hastily folding the sides inwards, to make it appear several sizes smaller, she held it up. 'It's really lovely…beautiful. Thank you, Maria Teresa.' And, grabbing hold of her, Annalisa landed a kiss either side of her beaming nut-brown face.

'No, no, Señorita Wilson! Not like that,' Maria Teresa protested, shaking her finger in mock-reproach. And, taking the shirt out of Annalisa's hands, she stretched up on tiptoes to spread it across Ramon's chest. 'Like this!'

'I don't understand,' Annalisa whispered to him. 'Is it a gift for you?'

'It is a Menorcan wedding shirt,' he informed her dryly as he executed a formal bow to Maria Teresa.

'A what?'

Putting his hand on Annalisa's shoulder, Ramon turned her slightly to murmur discreetly, 'She has given you a traditional shirt—the type a Spaniard might wear at his wedding. And look,' he said, pointing to a gap in the black silk stitching. 'She's left some of the embroidery for you to finish.'

'I don't understand—'

'Just thank her,' Ramon prompted softly. 'She must have been working on this for weeks.'

'But what will I do with it?'

'Put it in your bottom drawer. You do have one?'

'Surprisingly, no.'

'Perhaps you should start one.'

Acutely aware that their whispering had gone on long enough, Annalisa pulled herself together. 'Thank you,' she said, smiling as she turned to Maria Teresa. 'It is a truly beautiful gift and one I will treasure always.'

'It's not a museum piece,' Ramon cautioned. 'You're supposed to put it to use.'

'Doubtless I will,' she said. 'If I ever marry.'

'I've left some stitching for you to finish, *señorita*,' Maria Teresa said with a broad wink as she hustled between the two of them. 'To bring you good luck...and many, many children!'

Remembering Maria Teresa had thirteen, Annalisa reminded herself to go steady on the stitching.

'Will you examine the well now, Señor Perez?' Maria Teresa demanded, gazing around anxiously at the waiting villagers.

'Yes,' he said, shooting a glance at Annalisa.

'A well! That really is more than I deserve!'

The look Ramon slanted at her suggested she might be right.

'It will be an attractive feature in the courtyard, as well as performing a practical function,' he said.

'When did this happen?' she said incredulously when they turned a corner and she saw what the villagers had built for her.

'Is it a good surprise?' he murmured.

'How did you keep it hidden from me?'

'Camouflaged with trimmings...think of it as a gift.'

'Another gift,' she said, remembering the shirt. 'I really can't accept anything for myself until everyone knows about the back pay.'

'Don't worry,' Ramon said, holding up his hands. A hush fell as he began to speak, then one or two people interrupted.

'What are they saying?' Annalisa demanded anxiously as she watched the negative gestures amongst the villagers.

'No one is prepared to accept back pay,' he translated for her.

'But they must—'

'You can't force them to take the money,' he pointed out. 'They say the success of the *finca* is reward enough. They are pleased to have this opportunity to repay your father's generosity.'

Annalisa's mouth opened and shut again. She was running out of arguments, running out of ghosts... Turning round to include everyone in her reply, she said, '*Gracias... le agradecen cada uno—*'

'I'm impressed,' Ramon growled. 'You're a quick study.'

'I have a good teacher.'

'And you're a great student,' he said in a soft drawl that made her feel warm all over.

Then Maria Teresa intruded unwittingly as she cried excitedly, 'And now the well, Señorita Wilson.'

As the crowd parted Annalisa clapped her hands with delight. 'It's lovely! Thank you all so much! And, thank you, Ramon!' Throwing her arms around his waist, she hugged him impulsively. But the warm, hard feel of him was dangerously seductive, and as a cheer went up she ricocheted back in time to hear his mellow voice.

'*Maria Teresa—el honor es el tuyo.*'

Grabbing her by the wrist, Maria Teresa pointed to the sturdy black handle.

'What?' Annalisa mouthed to Ramon.

'You have to draw the first bucket of water,' he said, lacing his explanation with a slow-burning smile. 'For good luck.'

But the handle turned far too easily. 'Is it dry?' she whispered anxiously to Ramon.

The corners of his mouth tugged down, as if there could be a problem. 'I'm sure there's something down there,' he said, frowning as he leaned over to peer into the well shaft.

'But if the bucket's empty—'

He straightened up and speared a look at her. 'Break the mould, Annalisa. Take a chance.'

The timbre of his voice was low and challenging. She lobbed the dare straight back. 'OK. If you're so confident, come here and help me.'

'My pleasure,' he said, moving through the crowd.

An expectant hush dropped like a blanket around them as he placed his hands over hers. As they began to turn the handle together shouts of *'Arriba! Arriba!'* grew around them, until the bucket burst into the sunlight and jiggled between them on its tough hemp rope.

Grabbing hold of it, Ramon brandished it in the air to even louder cheers.

'I told you,' Annalisa said, plucking at his arm. 'There isn't any water.'

'And I say you're wrong,' he insisted fiercely. 'About that and a great many other things.'

'Let me see,' she insisted. The silence now was tense and expectant. What if the bucket was dry? What if Ramon's system had failed? Annalisa couldn't bear to think about it, and, flashing an anxious glance at Ramon, she dipped her hand in. There was nothing except maybe an inch of water sloshing about in the bottom. Pressing her lips together, she shook her head.

'Check again,' Ramon growled softly.

'I have checked,' she shot back tensely. 'There's barely enough for two coffees—'

'I had something stronger than coffee in mind.' He flashed her a grin.

'This is hardly a time for celebration,' Annalisa pointed out, shooting anxious glances at the waiting villagers.

'So you still don't trust me?'

'What on earth has that got to do with—?'

'Get your hand back in there,' he ordered, grasping her wrist.

With a frown she tried again. There was something at the bottom...

'Don't give up,' he warned.

She froze suddenly and, drawing her hand out, stared straight into Ramon's eyes. 'Is this a joke?'

'I'm not laughing.'

'So what is it?' she demanded hotly.

'What the hell do you think it is?'

Her hand closed around the ring. 'A rather large emerald-cut diamond?' she managed faintly.

'Correct,' Ramon confirmed. 'Give it to me.'

As she handed it over to him sunlight refracted through the stone, shooting rainbow colours through the blue-white diamond. 'I've never seen anything like it...' she murmured.

'I should hope not,' he said dryly.

'Who is it for?'

'The mother of my child.' Selecting her ring finger, he stared deep into her eyes. 'For the mother of my child,' he repeated steadily, 'and—' he put a finger over her lips so she was forced to let him finish '—the woman I love.'

He turned briefly to acknowledge the cheers of the villagers, but when he turned back to her only Annalisa saw the passion in his eyes. *'Annalisa, tu me hara el honor de acordar hacer mi esposa?'*

'I think I can answer that in Spanish.'

'I'm waiting,' he warned softly.

'Sí, mi amor,' she breathed against his lips.

Her wedding dress was the first thing Annalisa saw when she woke up. A gauzy mist of the finest white lace ruffled by the breeze coming through the partly opened shutters. And on a similar blue silk padded hanger hung the boned bodice and fine lawn petticoat that were to be worn beneath the transparent overdress. Ramon had flown her to Paris to find it, and now the most beautiful dress in the world belonged to her.

She had planned everything down to the last detail. And now this matchless summer morning heralded the most perfect day...her wedding day.

She stretched luxuriously as she contemplated the pleasure-filled agenda. There was nothing left to do but bathe, step into the dress and wait for the antique barouche Ramon had arranged to take her to the tiny village church.

The clatter of horses' hooves made her swing around to look at the clock. The carriage was supposed to arrive at midday, and it wasn't yet nine.

Leaping out of bed, she hurried to the window. Perfectly matched Andalucian mares stood patiently in front of a highly polished open carriage. She could only see the crown of the driver's wide-brimmed black felt hat…he didn't respond when she leaned over the balcony and called to him.

Dressing quickly in a pair of faded jeans and an old T-shirt, Annalisa slid her feet into a pair of flip-flops and raced out of the bedroom.

'No one's here yet,' she said, shading her eyes as she hurried across the yard. Her first proper sight of the carriage made it hard to contain her excitement. And the horses had been groomed to glossy perfection, their long manes falling in silken waves over their ebony withers. 'Won't you come inside?' she suggested, coming round so she could talk to the driver properly. 'Let me make you some breakfast. You can wait in the house while I get ready—'

Her torrent of words dried up when he turned to stare. The expression on the face of Ramon's chauffeur was as disdainful as ever. The shock of seeing who it was unsettled Annalisa, but she had no intention of allowing anything to spoil her day. 'It's still very early. If you want to untack the horses they can go in the small paddock.'

'The carriage is to be decorated, *señorita*,' he said coldly. 'The horses too—'

'Well, at least take them to wait in the shade,' she said firmly.

'As you wish.'

'There's a water trough under that rattan canopy.'

She couldn't help wondering about the man's discontent. Ramon treated all his staff with the same courtesy and consideration, whatever their position in his household. She judged the chauffeur to be in his middle fifties, with the physique of a much younger man. But his face was always pleated into the same sour expression, as if there wasn't enough happiness in his life to iron out the creases. Marking it down as another project to work on once she was married, Annalisa turned back to the house.

While she was soaking in the bath she smiled as she listened to the activity building in the yard. Maria Teresa had arrived and was bustling around in the kitchen. The reception was to be held at the *finca*, and as the orange groves had just yielded their best ever crop of first-class fruit the occasion had suddenly been transformed into a double celebration.

She had chosen to share the day with the villagers rather than opting for a grander ceremony at the cathedral in Mahon. Her love for Ramon needed no elaborate endorsement. It was enough to have Margarita as her attendant and little Aurelia to scatter petals. She closed her eyes as she tried to picture her own child, Ramon's child...

Climbing out of the bath, she snatched up a fluffy towel and padded barefoot to the head of the stairs. 'Maria Teresa...can you come and help me dress?' But before she received a reply she heard a knock at the front door. 'That's probably Señor Perez's chauffeur,' she called down. 'Will you see to him first? Make sure he has everything he wants.'

She waited for Maria Teresa to call back. But after a few minutes there was still no sign of her. Quickly putting on the underskirt, Annalisa couldn't resist a twirl in front of the mirror before going to the door to call again.

'May I help?'

Ice ran through her veins. Claudia was supposed to have left the island. Ramon had parted with a huge sum of money to make sure of it...and to acquire the ancient fishing rights belonging to Claudia that cut across both their beaches. Annalisa gasped as she turned to stare. 'Where did you get that?' The diamond necklace her stepmother had slipped over her head had only been delivered late the previous evening. It was Ramon's wedding gift.

Claudia answered with a faint smile.

'Give it to me,' Annalisa insisted, tensely holding out her hand.

Pausing in front of the mirror to admire the reflection of the glittering stones against her own neck, Claudia sneered, 'I'm not sure I will.'

To see her mother's tormentor toying with Ramon's precious wedding gift infuriated Annalisa. 'You agreed to leave the island,' she said tightly.

Raising a soft manicured hand, Claudia wafted the agreement away. 'I'm entitled to second thoughts, just as you are. Perhaps I didn't ask enough for the fishing rights...perhaps this will appease me. It is very beautiful—'

'But it's not yours,' Annalisa pointed out icily.

'You're very direct...too direct.'

'If you mean I tell the truth, I'd agree with you,' Annalisa said, skirting warily round her stepmother. 'Give it back to me. Now.'

With a scowl, Claudia tossed the necklace onto the dressing table as if it was a worthless bauble. 'Shouldn't you be getting ready? You don't want to miss your wedding.'

'And you don't want to miss your flight,' Annalisa retorted. 'I'll call Maria Teresa to see you out.'

'I have dismissed her.'

'You had no right—'

'Don't you dare presume to tell me what my rights are! At least your mother knew her place.'

'Yes. You made sure of that,' Annalisa interrupted coldly. 'But I'm not my mother. And I'm asking you to leave.'

'Señora Fuego Montoya is not ready to go.' Ramon's chauffeur was standing in the doorway.

'What are you looking so surprised about?' Claudia demanded triumphantly.

'I thought Don Alfonso...' Annalisa stopped as everything fell into place.

'Don Alfonso!' Claudia exclaimed derisively. 'What? That old has-been? Surely you couldn't imagine that Don Alfonso and I—?'

At least Don Alfonso was a gentleman, Annalisa thought, straightening her shoulders as she levelled a steady gaze at the pair of them. 'I'm sorry to disappoint you, but this is a very busy time for me.'

'*Was* a busy time,' Claudia said, examining her red-painted talons. 'Everyone's left for the church...everyone but you.'

'Maria Teresa would never leave without me,' Annalisa said confidently.

'Maria Teresa does what I tell her,' Claudia said. 'Her family has served mine for generations. And she has been working for you for...how long?'

'I can't believe she would—'

'Not so sure of yourself now, are you?' Claudia cut in coldly.

'But Ramon—'

'Is waiting at the church, with a smile on those arrogant lips of his—waiting for his bride.' Annalisa's stepmother paused to allow the impact of what she was about to say reach its target before continuing. 'But when you sign over your share of the fishing rights he has just purchased from me, Señor Ramon di Crianza Perez will be reduced to begging on the streets.'

Annalisa's short harsh laugh startled them. 'You really don't know anything about Ramon...or me, do you Claudia?'

'Just sign this and we'll be on our way,' her stepmother suggested, taking a step forward and brandishing an official-looking document at Annalisa. Following her lead, the chauffeur also came a menacing step closer.

'Not a chance,' Annalisa informed them both coldly.

As Claudia lurched forward, Annalisa darted past and went racing down the stairs. Tearing through the kitchen, she burst into the yard. Blinded momentarily by the brilliant sunlight, she stopped abruptly. But then, hearing heels rattling across the kitchen tiles, she sped off again.

Her bridal shoes held her back, but their dainty ankle straps would take precious time to release—time she didn't have. Scrambling up the path, she had almost reached the cliff-edge when she heard the sound of hysterical yapping—unmistakable yapping. She stopped short, panting for breath, and swung around to scan the rocks in an attempt to find Fudge. And then she saw him—a small barrel of loyalty, attempting to keep Claudia and her lover at bay. Sensing Annalisa's abrupt halt, the old dog turned to look at her. Wagging his tail uncertainly, he came trotting after her. It seemed to Annalisa then that the whole scene played out in slow motion as Claudia dipped down to pick up the red ball and took aim...

It smacked against the rocks and Fudge stopped to watch, his head lifting and falling as he followed its hypnotic progress. It bounced once, twice, and then disappeared completely down a jagged gap—with the old dog careering after it.

'Better get down there after him before he drowns,' Claudia called across to Annalisa. 'Oh, and don't worry about signing this.' She waved the contract at her. 'I'll just take the necklace instead.'

Annalisa could only ball her hands into impotent fists as she watched them go. Ramon's chauffeur must have worked for Claudia's father at one time, she thought, furious with herself for not thinking of it sooner. She channelled her mind determinedly to the present. 'Don't worry, Fudge. I'm coming!'

But even as she was scrambling over the rocks with her underskirt scrunched up around her waist she managed a fierce smile. Claudia belonged to the past. Ramon and their child were the future.

Annalisa inched her hand cautiously through the rusted grille to feel around and realised that Fudge had blundered into some sort of underground cellar. When he had fallen he'd dislodged the cover. The hinges were so stiff it took all her strength to lift it, by which time her hands were cut and her nails smashed to smithereens. Lowering herself down gingerly, she found a foothold on some treacherous steps. Blunted by slime into more of a slope, they made the rescue of the old dog doubly perilous.

Just when she made out his luminous brown eyes she heard an ominous clang as the cover slammed shut again. And then she noticed the basement was flooding with sea-water. If she didn't take care she'd slide straight down and they'd both be trapped. Hardly stopping to think, she began to unhook her sturdily constructed couture bodice. Tugging it off, she unfastened the straps on her white satin shoes. Using the heels to scrape away at the build-up of moss and lichen, she made a reasonably flat surface, laid the bodice down and stepped onto it. The cover yielded easily now she had a firm foothold, and she made a bundle of the bodice, putting it on the ground to wedge the grille open if it should fall again.

Fudge's howls told her he was getting tired. Waves were sweeping into the cellar and at any moment he could be lost. She needed a rope…something to attach to his collar to bring him back up the steps. Casting around desperately in the gloom, her eyes lit upon her sodden petticoat. The lace edge was perfect for what she had in mind. Ripping the pearl-strewn trimming off its filmy lawn base, she twisted it into a rope and tested it.

'Perfect,' she murmured with satisfaction.

Taking her time over each step, she slowly descended into the cellar and knelt down in the murky water next to the shivering dog.

'Annalisa! Annalisa! Thank God! What on earth are you doing?'

'Ramon!' Rocketing back on her haunches, Annalisa stared up at the circle of sunlight above her head. 'Fudge fell down…' She watched as he quickly discarded his short formal jacket and tugged off the traditional wedding shirt embroidered with the black silk into which she had so painstakingly added the last few stitches.

'How is he? Is he hurt?' he called.

'No. He's fine,' she called back. 'I've got him here with me.'

'Stay exactly where you are,' Ramon instructed. 'Don't move.'

'How did you find us?'

'Maria Teresa,' he explained shortly, lowering himself in. Testing the steps, he chose to swing over the side, clinging on by his hands and then dropping into the water beside her. He dragged Annalisa into his arms. 'She ran all the way to the church to find me, poor woman. As soon as she told me what had happened I went to find you.' He stopped, burying his face in her hair. 'I didn't know what had happened to you…I was so frightened.'

'You—frightened?' But when she pulled back and saw the depth of the pain in his eyes she linked her fingers behind his neck and softened against him.

'*Dios!* If they had hurt you!' he exclaimed. He threw his head back in anguish. 'How cunning they were…waiting until everyone had left for the church…shooing everyone off…trying to trick Maria Teresa. All to get you alone.' He cursed again, a short, violent outburst. 'I've been out of my mind with worry. Half of our guests are out scouring the countryside.' His eyes devoured her as if he would never trust himself to let her out of his sight again. And then he saw the state she was in—covered in mud and slime and completely naked except for a badly ripped, near-transparent underskirt and a very tiny thong. 'Something blue, I presume?' he murmured huskily.

'You guessed,' Annalisa agreed, rubbing against his naked chest.

'Later,' he promised, pulling away reluctantly. 'We have a very important appointment to keep first.' And, putting

Fudge under one arm, he wrapped his other firmly around Annalisa's waist and helped them both up the steps.

'Is this Claudia's work?' he demanded when they were out.

'She threw the ball; Fudge followed,' Annalisa said, collapsing onto a sliver of damp sand between the rocks. 'She wanted me to sign—'

'You didn't?'

'She took the necklace instead.'

He hunkered down beside her and drew her into his arms. 'I'm sorry, *querida*. I know how you loved it. But a necklace can be replaced. You can't.'

'I knew Claudia hated me, but I never thought—'

'When she found out where all your father's money had gone, on top of him leaving the *finca* to you, it was the last straw,' Ramon said, holding her tight. 'Then when Don Alfonso refused to co-operate with her scheming she brought in her lover, Rafael. And he had been my chauffeur for—'

She saw his stunning dark eyes narrow at the thought of the betrayal by a member of his own staff. 'But why did she need Rafael?'

'Presumably to try some strong-arm tactics on you if her bullying didn't work.'

'Your chauffeur was a pussycat in comparison to Claudia,' Annalisa said, nestling against him.

'Who knows what depths they might have sunk to when you refused to sign?' he warned. 'If they hadn't decided that the necklace was more portable than a hostage—'

'A hostage!'

'Well, I've made no secret of the way I feel about you,' he said. 'You're worth far more to me than everything I own. The whole world knows it.'

'Why didn't you get rid of your chauffeur before?'

'I didn't know what he was up to until now. And when I first employed him—'

'Go on.'

'This is a small island, Annalisa. He couldn't find work when Claudia's father died...he came to me.'

'So, you didn't know about the two of them?'

'And neither did your father, I suspect.'

'Of course,' Annalisa murmured as the last piece of the jigsaw fell into place. 'I should have known.'

For a few moments Ramon just held her. Then Fudge's bark distracted them both.

'There he goes,' Ramon said, as without so much as a lick of gratitude the old dog leapt away from them and shot off towards the *finca*.

'You're covered in sand,' Annalisa said, enjoying the view as Ramon stretched his cramped limbs and relaxed onto his back.

'And you're covered in mud,' he reminded her, cupping her breasts in his hands. As she gasped with pleasure he lifted his head and began to suck each outthrust, dirt-smudged nipple clean. And then, tugging her over him, he meshed his fingers through her thick dark hair and brought her down for his kisses, penetrating her mouth with the unmistakable rhythm that always flooded her nerve-endings with fire.

She felt his erection jutting against her belly and tightened her thighs. 'Is there time?' she demanded huskily.

'Sadly, our guests are waiting,' Ramon reminded her, though it failed to stop him slipping his hand underneath her. '*Dios*, you're wet,' he murmured as his searching fingers found the fine fabric stretched tight between her thighs. His lips tilted down in pretended regret as he withdrew his hand, but she knew the teasing foreplay was only preparation for their wedding night.

'Here,' he said reaching out to grab the filthy bodice. 'Cover yourself up, *querida*, before I lose control. We can't keep our guests waiting for ever.' And flashing her a grin he sprang to his feet.

* * *

Maria Teresa had been looking out for them, and she rushed from the *finca* the moment they entered the yard. She insisted on enveloping Annalisa in her own black lace shawl.

'Come, *señorita*…quick, quick!'

Releasing her into safe hands, Ramon left her to thank everyone who had manned the search parties.

Annalisa found the *finca* full of excited women. They whisked her straight upstairs, where she found a warm fragrant bath waiting for her. Then later, as she was rooting through her wardrobe to find something to wear, she heard a tap at the door.

'Yes?' she said distractedly, as she held up a turquoise floor-length dress in fine, flower-sprigged voile.

Poking her head into the room, Maria Teresa smiled. But when she saw what Annalisa was doing she shook her head vehemently. 'No, no, Señorita Wilson. We have brought you something special to wear.'

Annalisa hesitated, then, seeing all the other women standing behind Maria Teresa, she beckoned them in.

With an urgent gesture Maria Teresa summoned two young girls into the room. They carried between them the most exquisite gown Annalisa had ever seen. In heavy silk the colour of clotted cream, every inch of the figure-hugging sheath was intricately embroidered with tiny bugle beads that shimmered subtly like moonbeams on a lake. 'It's absolutely stunning,' Annalisa breathed. But, knowing it had to be someone's treasured possession, she shook her head. 'I couldn't possibly wear it.'

'But *señorita*,' Maria Teresa began, 'the dress was your mother's. She would want you to wear it.'

'But my mother—' Annalisa stopped, swallowed, and started again. 'My mother never owned anything so…'

'It was to have been her wedding dress, Señorita Wilson. For her marriage to your father, Don Pedro,' Maria Teresa said gently.

Annalisa froze, her thoughts in confusion, while Maria Teresa chivvied everyone out of the room. Before they left the two girls reverently laid the dress on top of Annalisa's smooth white bedspread.

When the door had shut quietly behind them Maria Teresa continued her explanation. 'Before Claudia told your father she was pregnant he bought this dress for your mother to wear at their wedding. It has never been out of the beautiful box…or even out of the tissue paper…before today.'

Annalisa stared at it again. Her mother's hopes for the future had been invested in the ravishing gown. The pleasure of wearing it should have been hers. She leaned forward, wistfully tracing the beautiful fabric with her finger. Ramon had told her to build on the past… 'Will you help me to put it on?' she said, turning to Maria Teresa.

On Maria Teresa's signal everyone trooped back into the bedroom.

Annalisa turned to face them. 'Do I look all right?'

'All right?' Maria Teresa scoffed. 'You look beautiful, Señorita Wilson.'

Another woman stepped forward to place a crown of orange blossom on Annalisa's hair, while someone added a mantilla of ivory lace to float bewitchingly around her shoulders.

'Thank you,' Annalisa exclaimed, grasping hold of as many hands as she could reach. 'You saved my wedding.'

'You saved the *finca*,' Maria Teresa countered, shooing her out of the door.

Annalisa had expected to find Ramon at the church, but when Maria Teresa opened the door of the *finca*, he was there waiting for her in the courtyard. Dressed as a proud Castilian, and mounted on his prancing ebony stallion, his eyes grew stormy with passion when he caught sight of her in her wedding dress for the first time.

Annalisa watched, mesmerised, as slowly he removed his broad-brimmed black hat and bowed low over Dardo's sleek withers. But as her gaze strayed to the powerful thighs that held the stallion so firmly beneath him her breath caught in her throat to think of the moment when she would feel their steely pressure. And then she saw the barouche, decked out with bridal wreaths and ribbons. Even the gentle Andalucian mares had garlands of blossom looped through their bridles. And in place of the sour-faced chauffeur—

'Enrique is ready!' the impish tree surgeon declared, stabbing the air with his own battered traditional black hat.

'Ready, Señorita Fuego Montoya?' Maria Teresa demanded, reverting to the name everyone on the island believed was Annalisa's due.

'Ready,' Annalisa confirmed, gazing up at Ramon.

As she settled herself down onto the bank of white satin cushions their gazes locked. And in that moment she knew that she trusted him with all her heart and more… She trusted him with the life of their child.

'Le adoro, Annalisa.'

And as she heard his impassioned murmur reach her across the courtyard, Annalisa's hand strayed to mould the gentle swelling of her belly.

She knew then that the power of Ramon's love was more telling than words, and infinitely more precious than diamonds.

THE BLACKMAILED
BRIDEGROOM

MIRANDA LEE

CHAPTER ONE

THE jumbo jet was twenty minutes late setting down at Mascot Airport, but Antonio was one of the first to alight. The head of Fortune Productions, European Division, didn't look as if he'd been on a gruelling twenty-two-hour flight from London to Sydney. His superb grey suit was sleek and uncrumpled. His thick jet-black hair was slicked back from a freshly shaven face. His dark eyes were clear and rested.

The advantage of flying first class.

Not that Antonio Scarlatti had always travelled first class. He knew what it was like to do it tough. He knew what it was like to travel long hauls cramped in steerage, with wall-to-wall passengers and little chance of sleep, then have people look down their nose at him at the other end, when his suit had been wrinkled and his job far less prestigious than the one he now held.

Antonio had no intention of ever going back to that existence. He'd made it to the top, and the top was where he was going to stay. The world was for the winners. And the wealthy. At the age of thirty-four, he was finally both.

The company limousine was waiting in its usual spot, the engine idling at the ready. Antonio opened the back door and slid into its air-conditioned comfort.

'Morning, Jim,' he addressed the chauffeur.

'Mornin', Tone.'

Antonio smiled. He was back in Australia all right. In London, and all over Europe, he was always addressed

5

by his drivers as 'Mr Scarlatti'. But that wasn't the way down under, especially after an acquaintance of some time.

Antonio leant back against the plush leather seat with a deeply relaxing sigh. It was good to be home and off the merry-go-round for a fortnight's break. His contract stated he could fly home for two weeks rest and recuperation every three months, a necessity since he worked seven days a week when on the job. Being in charge of selling and promoting Fortune Productions' extensive list of television programmes to the hundreds of stations and cable networks all over Europe was a challenging job.

'Straight home, Jim,' he said, and closed his eyes. He'd bought himself a luxury serviced apartment overlooking the harbour bridge a couple of years back, and couldn't wait to immerse himself in its privacy and comfort. The last few days had been a nightmare of negotiations and never-ending meetings. Antonio needed some peace and quiet.

'No can do, Tone,' the chauffeur returned as he eased the lengthy car past the long line of taxis which had queued up to meet the flight from London. 'The boss wants you to join him for breakfast.'

Antonio's eyes opened on a low groan. He hoped it wasn't one of those media circus breakfasts Conrad was always getting invited to and which he occasionally attended. Antonio couldn't stand them at the best of times. 'Where, for pity's sake?' came his irritable query.

'The Taj Mahal.'

'Thank God,' Antonio muttered.

The Taj Mahal was Jim's nickname for Conrad Fortune's residence at Darling Point. It was an apt term. The place was over the top with its grandeur and opulence, a monolithic mansion sprawled across an acre of some of the most expensive land in Sydney's exclusive Eastern suburbs.

What the house lacked in taste, it made up for in sheer size. The façade had more columns than the Colosseum, the foyer more marble than the British Museum, and Romanesque statues and ornate fountains dominated the front landscaping. The sloping backyard was more low key, terraced to incorporate the solar-heated swimming pool and two rebound ace tennis courts.

Antonio thought the place ostentatious in the extreme. But it *was* impressive, no doubt about that. Socialites grovelled to be included on the lists for Conrad's celebrated parties. Magazines and television programmes clamoured to photograph beyond the high-security walls which enclosed the property.

Not Conrad's television programmes, of course. They knew better.

'You wouldn't have any idea what he wants me for, Jim, would you?' Antonio probed.

'Nope.' A man of few words, Jim.

Antonio decided not to speculate. Time would tell, he supposed.

Fifteen minutes later, the limousine slid to a smooth halt in front of the grand front steps, and this time Jim did the honours with the door.

'You won't be needing that,' he advised when Antonio went to pick up his laptop.

Antonio shot the chauffeur a sharp look. So he *did* have some idea of what was up. And clearly it wasn't a business matter.

Curiouser and curiouser.

The housekeeper answered the door. Evelyn was in her late forties, and very homely, as were all of Conrad's

female employees. No fool, was Conrad. He'd been
stung once, by an ambitious and beautiful maid, and had
no intention of harbouring any females under his roof
who might present him with unwise temptations.
Although now rising seventy, Conrad was still very interested in the opposite sex, as evidenced by the three
mistresses he kept. One here in Sydney, one in Paris and
one in the Bahamas.

Evelyn had been Conrad's housekeeper now for over
a decade. She was efficient and reliable. More impor-
tantly, she knew how to keep her mouth shut to the
press.

'Conrad's expecting you,' she told Antonio straight
away. 'He's in the morning room.'

The morning room overlooked the terrace, which
overlooked the pool. The floor-to-ceiling windows faced
north-east, and captured the sun all year round. On a
winter morning, the room was a dream. In summer, the
air-conditioning had a tough job preventing the place
from turning into a hothouse. Spring found it coolish,
especially since the sun was only just rising at six-thirty.

Conrad was sitting at the huge glass oval table in the
centre of the conservatory-style room, wrapped in a thick
navy bathrobe. Despite his age, he still had a full head
of hair—a magnificent silvery grey—and piercing blue
eyes. They flicked up at Antonio's entrance, and raked
him from head to toe, disconcerting Antonio for a moment. Why on earth was Conrad looking him over like
that, as though he'd come to audition for one of his soap
operas? What was going on here?

'Sit down, Antonio,' Conrad ordered. 'Take a load off
your feet and have some decent coffee for a change.' He
picked up the coffee pot and poured an extra mugful of
steaming brown liquid.

'What's the problem?' Antonio asked as he sat down and pulled the coffee towards him.

His employer gave him another long, considering look over the table, and Antonio's gut tightened further. He knew, without being told, that he wasn't going to like what Conrad had to say.

'Paige has come home again,' came the abrupt announcement.

Antonio almost said, So? What's new?

Conrad's wild and wilful daughter had been running away from home regularly since she was seventeen. She turned up again regularly too, every year or so. But no sooner had she returned than she'd be off again, saying she was going to share a flat with some girlfriends. But only once had this been the case. Usually, when the private investigator's report came in several weeks later, her flatmate was male and good-looking, invariably an artist or a musician. Paige seemed to like creativeness. Not one of them had denied sharing more with Paige than the cooking.

At first, Conrad had worried Paige might be exploited for her money. A whole family could have lived comfortably on his only child's generous monthly allowance! But perversely, from the day she'd first left home, Paige had never touched a cent of the thousands deposited in her bank account every month. When Conrad had found out his money was being donated to the RSPCA, and that Paige was working to support herself, he'd stopped the allowance altogether.

'Let her work, if that's what she wants to do!' he'd raged to Antonio, but would still cringe when he learnt that she was working as a waitress in some café, or behind the bar in a club or pub.

His worst nightmare, however, was that Paige would

fall pregnant to one of her live-in boyfriends and then bring the baby home with her. Conrad was not large on babies. Which gave Antonio an idea.

'She's not pregnant, is she?' he asked.

'No, but she's going to come to a sticky end, that girl, unless I do something about it. Do you realise she turns twenty-three next week?'

Antonio was surprised. How the years had flown!

'I would imagine you've tried everything,' he said sincerely. Most girls would give their eye-teeth for what Paige had once had. A lovely home. Designer clothes. An allowance fit for a princess, if she'd wanted to claim it. If none of that was enough to keep her happy, and at home, then Lord knows what was!

'Not…everything,' Conrad said slowly, and he set those penetrating blue eyes on Antonio again. 'There's one thing I haven't tried.'

'And what's that?'

'Marriage,' he pronounced. 'To a man who could control her.'

Antonio couldn't help it. He laughed. 'You think Paige would marry a man of your choice?'

'Of course not. I was thinking of a man of *her* choice. Namely, you, Antonio.'

'*Me?*' Antonio was floored.

'Yes, you. Don't pretend, Antonio. I know exactly what happened just before Paige ran away from home that first time. The first thing Lew did when I put him on the job of tracing her was to question all the staff here at Fortune Hall. Did you think that little incident by the pool between you and my daughter hadn't been overheard?'

When Antonio opened his mouth to explain, Conrad waved it shut.

'Please don't bother to defend your actions,' he swept on. 'You have nothing to answer for. You did exactly the right thing. How were you to know that the silly little fool would take your rejection so badly and run off with her broken heart?'

'Her heart wasn't broken,' Antonio contested heatedly. 'She took up with the next fellow soon enough!'

'A girl rarely forgets her first love.'

'I was *never* her love, first or otherwise!'

Hell, he hadn't even kissed the girl. He'd been polite to her when she'd been at home on holiday from boarding school, making small talk when their paths had crossed. Hard not to run into her when he'd been living at Fortune Hall in his position as Conrad's personal assistant, his first job with the company. No one had been more surprised than him when she'd thrown herself into his arms that day by the pool and declared her undying love and devotion.

Antonio hadn't taken advantage of her schoolgirl crush, despite acknowledging she was a serious temptation to any man, especially dressed as she'd been that day, in a minute pink bikini. On top of that, Antonio was always physically attracted to blond women. He especially liked tall, slender blond women, with big blue eyes, high, full breasts and a waist his hands could span.

His hands had spanned Paige's waist that day, as he'd reluctantly put her aside, then told her in no uncertain terms that he didn't return her feelings and that he thought of her as a silly little girl.

Not strictly true, of course. He'd thought of her as a silly *big* girl, extremely beautiful and extraordinarily sexy. Some evenings, when she'd been home from school and she'd come down to dinner in one of those tight, short low-cut little dresses she'd favoured, he'd been glad to be sitting at a table with a serviette covering his lap. If Paige had been any other man's daughter things might have turned out differently by the pool that day. But Antonio had had no intention of losing a second job because of the boss's daughter. No way!

Perhaps his rejection *had* been a little rough. Paige's obvious humiliation and tears had caused him pangs of guilt for a while, especially when she'd run away instead of returning to school, not sitting for her final exams into the bargain.

He'd got over his guilt soon enough, however, when Lew, Conrad's personal private investigator, had found her less than a month later, living on a remote North Coast beach with some surfing bum a good few years older than herself. Since the shack they'd been sharing only had one bedroom, it wasn't difficult to conclude their relationship had been far from platonic. She certainly hadn't denied it when Antonio himself had travelled all the way up there and tried to bring her back at Conrad's request.

Antonio's male ego had been dented by her indifferent reaction to his arrival on her doorstep, but any lingering concern for the girl had been well and truly dispelled once he'd seen for himself what sort of life she'd chosen to live.

Paige was trouble, in his opinion, an opinion reinforced every time their paths crossed, which thankfully wasn't often. The last time he'd seen her had been at Conrad's Christmas party the previous year. She'd sashayed downstairs, wearing a short strapless red dress which might have ended up around a less shapely females' ankles, so precariously had it been perched. To his eternal irritation and frustration, Antonio had found himself wanting to sweep her back up the stairs, rip that infernal scrap of red satin from her body and ravage her senseless upon the first available bed. Or floor. Or whatever.

Instead, he'd had to forcibly keep his eyes away from Paige's luscious young flesh, pretending to be enraptured by his date, a female lawyer on Fortune Productions' payroll. To his discredit, Antonio had shamelessly used the woman—both at the party and later—to sate the dark desires Paige had evoked.

Not that she'd minded. As it had turned out, she'd liked her sex a little rough, and without strings.

He hadn't seen Paige since that night, and tried not to think of her at all these days. But he was certainly thinking of her now.

'You can't be serious about this, Conrad,' he said disbelievingly.

'I'm very serious.'

'It's a crazy idea!'

'Why? She *was* in love with you once, whether you like it or not. And that was before you developed into the man you are today. Do you think I haven't noticed the way women react to you? You could make any woman fall in love with you. A girl like Paige should be a cinch.'

'But I don't *want* Paige to fall in love with me,' he pointed out icily. 'And I don't want to marry her.' Her, least of all, he thought angrily.

'Why?'

Antonio did not feel like explaining that he'd been in love very deeply once, with the daughter of his previous boss. He'd thought Lauren had loved him as much as he'd loved her. But when push had come to shove she hadn't been prepared to actually marry an Italian migrant with a questionable background and nothing to his name but his modest salary as a wine salesman. She'd just been slumming for a while, before moving on from her cosy, cushy life as a rich man's daughter to the cosy, cushy life of a rich's man's wife.

He'd stupidly turned up at her house on the night of her engagement party and made a big scene. Naturally, he'd been given the sack, with no references. It had been several months before he'd been able to get another job, during which he'd practically had to eat the paint off the walls. When Conrad had hired him to be his assistant and interpreter he'd been eternally grateful, even though he suspected he'd been the only applicant who could speak the five languages Conrad required during his business trips overseas.

Antonio had worked his guts out to get where he was today. He had no intention of giving it up for anyone, or of sharing his life with the same sort of silly, selfish, shallow creature who'd once almost destroyed him.

'When and if I marry, Conrad,' he said with cold fury, 'it will be because I'm so much in love that I couldn't bear not to.' Which was about as likely as Conrad himself breasting the altar once more.

When his boss said nothing to this, Antonio's black eyes narrowed. 'If I don't agree with this plan of yours, is it going to cost me my job?'

'No, of course not!' Conrad denied expansively. 'What kind of man do you take me for?'

Antonio hesitated to say. But you didn't get to be one of the richest men in Australia by being full of the milk of human kindness. Over the six years in Conrad's employ, Antonio had gleaned a lot of information about his boss.

Conrad had started out with nothing, as the son of penniless Polish migrants, changing his name from

Fortuneski to Fortune and getting in on the ground floor with television in Australia when it had started, in the fifties, working behind the camera at first before forming his own production company and buying the Australian rights to a successful American game show. It had made him his first million. More game shows had followed, and more millions. Then, in the late sixties, he'd tried one of the first soaps made in Australia, an outrageously sexy series which had made its name with scandalous storylines. Serious millions had begun to roll in, and Fortune Productions had never looked back. Neither had its ambitious bachelor owner.

Conrad had lived and breathed his work, and had had no intention of getting married. But then, in his mid-forties, Conrad had made the mistake of giving his then housekeeper *carte blanche* to hire and fire staff, and she'd taken on Paige's mother to serve at table. During a misguided interlude after a rather lengthy and boozy dinner party, Paige had been conceived.

Once presented with the reality of a child-to-be, Conrad had done the right thing and married the woman. He'd been hoping for a son and heir to take over the business. Instead, Paige had been born.

It had not been a happy union, and when his wife of one year had run off to America with a salesman, Conrad hadn't been shattered. Antonio imagined that his boss also hadn't lost much sleep over the news, a few years later, that his errant wife had been found dead in a New York hotel room of a drug overdose.

He was not a sentimental man.

'I'm planning on retiring at the end of the year,' Conrad went on now, snapping Antonio back to the matter at hand. 'I'll be moving permanently to my home in the Bahamas. When I do, the position of CEO of Fortune

Productions will become vacant. I intend to promote you, Antonio,' he said, and Antonio sucked in a sharp breath. 'But only if you're my son-in-law at the time,' Conrad finished.

Antonio exhaled with a rush. 'Damn and blast it, Conrad, that's blackmail!'

'No. That's good business. Who better to look after one's interests but family? You, as a born and bred Italian, should appreciate that.'

Antonio kept his temper with difficulty. 'And if I refuse?' he bit out.

'I'll make the same offer to Brock Masters. I imagine he could handle both jobs almost as well.'

Antonio gritted his teeth. Brock Masters was head of the North American Division. Publicly, he was all capped teeth and false charm, in Antonio's opinion. Handsome as Satan, but privately he had the morals of the Marquis de Sade.

'He'll ruin the company,' Antonio warned. 'And he'll destroy your daughter,' he added as an afterthought.

'If you think that, Antonio,' Conrad said smoothly, 'you know what to do.'

'You're a ruthless devil, do you know that?'

'Takes one to know one.'

'Yet you want me to marry your daughter!'

'She needs a real man for a change. One who will keep her on her toes in order to keep him. And one who can give her what she keeps looking for.'

'Which is?'

'What all women want. Love, of course.'

'For pity's sake, Conrad, you know darned well I don't love her.'

Conrad shrugged. 'What's love but an illusion anyway? Just tell Paige you love her. The silly little fool won't know the difference, as long as the sex is good. And the sex *will* be good, I'm sure. The way the ladies chase after you—even after one short evening in your bed—speaks volumes for your abilities in that department.'

Antonio stared at the man. He almost felt sorry for Paige, having such a cold-blooded bastard for a parent. He could not understand how a father could do such a thing to his daughter.

Still, Antonio was not a fool. He knew if he knocked Conrad back on this he was finished at Fortune Productions. Brock Masters hated his guts. Antonio supposed he could quit and find another job with a rival company, settle back and watch the rot set in at Fortune Productions. It would serve Conrad right if he did just that.

But pride in a job well done—and in the company— would not let him seriously consider such an action. And then there was the added image of Paige, being seduced, corrupted and destroyed by an amoral, cocaine-snorting pervert.

Antonio's stomach turned over. A silly little fool she might be, but she didn't deserve that.

'Under the circumstances,' he said, in that coolly ruthless voice which emerged when he was cornered, 'I will expect something in writing.'

Conrad beamed. 'But of course, Antonio. I'll have it ready for you when you come to dinner here tonight.'

Antonio frowned. 'Tonight?'

'I thought the sooner you got started the better. After all, you have to be back in London in a fortnight. A whirlwind romance is just what the doctor ordered. I see no reason why Paige shouldn't travel back with you, once she's wearing your engagement ring.'

'You expect her to agree to marry me in two short weeks?'

'You've negotiated more difficult contracts in much faster time, Antonio. Speaking of contracts, the day you marry Paige you will have your contract as CEO of Fortune Productions, plus I will give you the deeds to this house as a wedding present.'

'No, thank you, Conrad. The contract will do. I wouldn't want to live here.' Even if he could tolerate the space, he didn't want to be surrounded by Conrad's extra ears.

Conrad smiled. 'I had a feeling you'd say that. Shall we expect you around seven-thirty, then?'

'Are you sure Paige will still be here?' Antonio commented caustically.

'I should think so. Her latest boyfriend gave her quite a scare.'

'Oh?'

'He hit her.'

Antonio was surprised at how angry this news made him. There again, violence against women had always pushed savage buttons in him. 'I gather you know this charmer's name and address?' he ground out.

'Actually, no, I don't.'

'But you *always* know where Paige is living and who with!'

Conrad sighed. 'I stopped putting Lew on the job this past year. I just couldn't take it any more. I have no idea what she's been up to since January. Paige rang me out of the blue last night around one, and asked if Jim could come and pick her up at Central Station. She sounded scared, which, as you know, isn't like Paige at all. But the penny dropped once I saw the big bruise on her face.

She wouldn't tell me anything when I asked her last night. But maybe she'll tell you.'

'Maybe.' If she did, Antonio was going to teach the creep a lesson he wouldn't forget in a hurry!

Still, it had only been a question of time before Paige became mixed up with a really unsavoury type. The girl never could see the risks she was taking in living with men she didn't really know. She had no common sense, and no appreciation of the consequences of her actions. She'd be the perfect victim for the likes of Brock Masters!

Possibly there were excuses for her many and potentially dangerous relationships—Antonio was beginning to appreciate there'd been little enough warmth and affection here at home—but one would have thought she'd have learned by now. Almost twenty-three, and she was still looking for love in all the wrong places!

Well, she certainly won't find it with you, either, came the coldly cynical thought.

'You know, Conrad,' he said with a sardonic twist of his mouth. 'Has it occurred to you that Paige might say no to marriage, whether she falls in love with me or not?'

'It did cross my mind. If needs be, I suggest you use a method as old as time.'

'And what's that?'

'Get her pregnant.'

Antonio's eyes widened.

'I'm sure you won't find such a task beyond you,' his boss drawled. 'I gather the Wilding girl had to have a little operation before she could become engaged to the Jansen millions. Which was understandable. She couldn't risk a black-eyed baby born to a blond, blue-eyed father, could she?'

Antonio momentarily went white. Lauren had been *pregnant* when she'd run home to Daddy? She'd aborted *his* child, just to marry money?

'You really know how to strike below the belt, Conrad,' he said bitterly. 'How long have you known about my relationship with Lauren?'

'From the start. Do you honestly think I would employ a man to be my personal assistant and to live in my home if I hadn't had him thoroughly checked out? Forget the Wilding girl, Antonio. She was a fool, and so was her father. I know a good man when I see one. Marry my daughter, and you'll never regret it.'

Now *that*, Antonio conceded ruefully, was a matter of opinion.

Rising from his chair, he set a cool black gaze upon his future father-in-law and stretched out his hand. 'It's a deal.'

Conrad took, then pumped his hand. 'Splendid, my boy. Splendid. I knew you'd make the right decision. See you tonight, around seven-thirty. We'll have a celebratory drink together before dinner.'

Antonio said nothing to that, just spun on his heels and strode towards the doorway.

Evelyn barely had time to retreat hastily from where she'd been listening to every single word.

CHAPTER TWO

PAIGE woke mid-afternoon and just lay there for a while, staring up at the bedroom ceiling, thinking.

Home again.

If you could call this wretched house a home, that was.

The word *home* normally conjured up feelings of peace and warmth. It was where you could be yourself; where you were most relaxed; where you felt loved and accepted.

But home had never been like that for Paige. Fortune Hall was a cold, heartless place which evoked nothing in her but feelings of failure and inadequacy, of being unwanted and unloved, of being unsure of who she was or what she wanted out of life.

Only once had Paige momentarily been happy in this house: the year when Antonio Scarlatti had first come to Fortune Hall to live.

The memory of their first meeting was indelibly imprinted on her brain. It had been her last year in high school, and she'd caught the train home for the Easter break, feeling miserable when her father had said he couldn't possibly meet her at Central.

'Just catch a taxi home, Paige,' had been his offhand and impatient words on the telephone the night before. 'It's not as though it's far. I can't leave an important meeting for such a silly little thing.'

Such a silly little thing! That was what she was to him. A silly little thing. It was what she'd always been to him. A nuisance. An inconvenience. He'd never loved her, or made time for her. Not once.

Paige had stepped off the train at Central, no longer expecting to be met, so she'd been startled when a dark-haired, dashingly handsome young man had approached her and introduced himself as her father's new personal assistant, Antonio Scarlatti. She vaguely remembered thinking he didn't have an Italian accent at all, but that he had the most riveting eyes. Black and penetrating and incredibly sexy.

'Your father mentioned your arrival by train today,' he'd added, while those eyes held hers. 'I didn't think it right for you to make your way home all by yourself, so I told him it would be my pleasure to meet you. Come...' And he'd cupped her elbow with a gallant hand.

She'd been captivated from that moment.

Captivated and completely infatuated.

By the time he'd driven her through the gates of Fortune Hall, her racing heart had succumbed to a hero worship which had banished every other male idol whom her love-starved teenage heart had gathered over the previous few years. Her favourite music and movie stars were nothing compared to Antonio Scarlatti.

By the end of the two-week break she'd centred a thousand romantic hopes and dreams around him, crying her devastation when the holiday had ended all too swiftly. During the next term at school she'd spent long hours every day, imagining and fantasising all sorts of exciting scenarios with her handsome Italian at centre stage, till she'd begun to believe her own fantasies, turning each simple smile he'd given her into evidence that he was as secretly enamoured with her as she was with him.

Her schoolwork had suffered for her daydreaming,

and the comments on her report card had been none too impressive to bring home at the end of term: *Paige would do a lot better if only she would concentrate! Paige is an intelligent girl but her mind doesn't seem to be on her work!*

Which it hadn't been. Yet what a wonderful term it had been! What secret pleasures she'd hugged to herself, thinking about her beautiful Antonio all the time, weaving all sorts of fanciful dreams around him.

Her next holiday at home had seemed to cement all those dreams. The things he carefully hadn't said. Those secretive but scorching glances he'd bestowed on her across the dinner table. The way he'd held her slightly longer than necessary the day they'd run into each other on the stairs. The inordinate time he'd taken to help her find a book in the library one evening.

Paige had been sure he was just waiting till she finished school that year before he showed his hand. By then she would be eighteen, and a woman!

In her mind, they would eventually get married and have half a dozen babies, beautiful, black-eyed children who adored their mother and father and were so very happy, wrapped in the type of warm cocoon of family love that she'd never experienced herself, but she'd vowed to give *her* children.

By the time she'd come home again in September she'd become totally obsessed with him, her rather romantic feelings taking a more physical turn when she'd spotted him swimming in the pool the first morning of her holiday. She'd watched him from her bedroom window while he'd done lap after impressive lap, her eyes widening when he'd climbed out and just stood there as he towelled himself down, wearing only the briefest of black swimming costumes.

There had been something decidedly animal in his powerful physique, with its deeply olive skin and light covering of dark body hair, plus the way he was drying himself, with rough, rubbing strokes. Paige had gobbled him up with her eyes while the sexuality simmering deep within her feelings surfaced, stark and startling in its raw and naked need. Suddenly, she'd craved more than his love. She'd craved the man, and that part of him which made him a man, her galloping heart seizing up with shock at the explicitness of her desire.

When he'd looked up and spied her watching him at the window she'd nearly died, her face flushing wildly. He'd stared back at her for a few seconds, before whirling away and striding off inside the pool house.

Paige hadn't needed another sign.

Suddenly, she couldn't wait to finish school, or for him to say something. She had to speak up first. But when she'd gone in search of him after breakfast it had been to find her father and his assistant had left on a business trip. They would not be back for a week. It had been the longest week of Paige's life, only made bearable by the heart to hearts she'd had with Brad, her oldest and closest friend.

By the time Antonio had come back she'd been dying to talk to him, breathless and emboldened by the surety of his love.

Oddly enough, Paige could no longer recall exactly what she'd said to him. Or what he'd said back. The only words which lived on in her memory were his calling her a silly little girl. They remained very clear, as did the overwhelming wave of humiliation which had accompanied them.

Suffice to accept that it had been the most awful moment of her life.

Paige found it ironic that she didn't rate what had happened last night to be nearly as awful. Jed might have hurt her physically, and he'd frightened her enough into coming home, but he didn't have the power to hurt her where the hurt never healed. How could he, when she didn't love him?

Her right hand lifted to push her hair back behind her ear before gingerly touching the tender swelling just below her temple. Pity the blow hadn't knocked some sense into her, she thought bitterly.

Still being in love with Antonio was insane. She could see that. But recognising the stupidity of her feelings seemed to make no difference.

Brad had talked her out of her 'infatuation' for a while, had made her temporarily believe it was nothing but a schoolgirl crush, a romantic obsession which had nothing to do with reality.

'You don't even know the man,' he'd reasoned with her during the dark days after Antonio's visit to the beach-house. 'Your love's a figment of your romantic teenage imagination, conjured up because you need someone to love, and to love you back. But it's not real, Paige. It's a destructive self-indulgence to keep harbouring such a one-sided obsession. Let it go, love. Let *him* go.'

So she had, for a while, and eventually she'd settled for a different sort of love with Brad than the one she'd dreamt of in Antonio's arms.

Still, looking back, she did not regret it. Brad had been kind to her. Kind and understanding and undemanding. He'd taught her a lot about the sort of person she was, made her see that she was very intelligent, despite not having done too well at school. He'd even encouraged her to go to the local tech and finish her schooling, which she had. She might still have been with him if one stormy afternoon and an unforgiving sea hadn't ended their carefree and easygoing co-existence.

She'd stayed on at the beach-house for a few weeks. Brad had always paid the rent ahead in three-month lots. But in the end loneliness—and curiosity, perhaps—had sent her back home to Sydney, to Fortune Hall, her father, and Antonio.

A *big* mistake.

For nothing had changed.

Nothing.

She hadn't been able to get out of the place fast enough, answering an ad in the paper to share a flat with two other girls and taking the first job she could get, waitressing in a coffee house on Circular Quay.

Another big mistake. Not the job. She'd rather liked waitressing, enjoying the contact with tourists and people always on the go. Paige had soon found, however, that sharing accommodation with other girls was hazardous in the extreme, unless you looked like the back of a bus. Unfortunately, Paige's long blond hair, pretty face and striking figure had caused all sorts of troubles with the other girls' boyfriends, who hadn't been able to keep their eyes and hands off. After one extremely unpleasant encounter—and a disbelieving flatmate—Paige had found herself out on the street with nowhere to go except home once more.

This time Antonio had no longer been in residence, thanks to a promotion and a new apartment of his own somewhere.

Perversely, Paige had been disappointed. Had she become addicted to the emotional turmoil the sight of her unrequited love caused?

Possibly, because after leaving home again, to live

with two male flatmates who had been closet gays and had caused her no trouble at all, she'd still deliberately returned at Christmas—and every Christmas after that— for no other reason than that was the season her father entertained a lot, with dinner parties and other larger parties, to which Antonio was always invited.

She had seen him a few times, but he'd invariably ignored her, or just said a few polite words before turning his attention elsewhere, usually to some woman. Paige knew he had lots of women—she'd made a point of questioning a few of the staff at home about his dating activities. Not Evelyn, of course. But the cook, the maids, and Jim, the chauffeur.

Paige consoled herself with the thought that there never seemed to be anyone special, anyone who lasted. On top of that, she'd never experienced the agony of actually seeing him in action with a woman...till last year's big Christmas Eve party.

Paige had turned twenty-two the previous October, and believed she'd never looked better. Her skin had been lightly tanned, and her long honey-blond hair fell halfway down her back in one smooth shiny curtain. She'd come downstairs, dressed in a very sexy strapless red dress, hoping against hope that this time Antonio might see that she was at last a woman, not a silly little girl.

Antonio had just arrived with a date, a striking and sophisticated creature of thirty-something who had still made Paige feel like a little girl by comparison. His gaze had skated over her—and her revealing dress—with nothing but barely held irritation.

Never had the futility of her feelings been hammered home so strongly as that evening, when she'd watched him turn from her to dance attendance on his date, never once giving Paige a second glance. Each touch of his hand on the woman's arm had been like a dagger in Paige's heart. Each drink he'd given her. Each dance.

But the *coup de grâce* had come when Paige came across them kissing on the terrace—if 'kissing' was the appropriate word to describe what they'd been doing. For it hadn't just been their mouths which were locked, but their whole bodies. Moulded and melded together in the most erotic fashion, one of Antonio's legs jammed hard between the woman's, one of hers lifting to run sinuously up and down his thigh.

Paige was sure she'd cried out in pain, but nothing short of an atomic bomb exploding would have disturbed their passionate clinch. No one but the most naive could not imagine how their evening would end, or that Antonio wouldn't be the most unforgettable of lovers.

But then, Paige had already known he would be.

It was that same intense, all-consuming passion she'd thought she'd found in Jed. Only this time it had been directed at *her*, not some other woman. She'd been so flattered by Jed's pursuit of her. Flattered, yet disastrously deluded.

Paige winced as she touched the bruise once more.

She was about to go into the bathroom and inspect the damage more closely when there was a knock on her bedroom door.

'Who is it?' she asked agitatedly. Not her father again. Oh, please not him. He'd harangued her for ages last night, wanting to know what had happened, who had done this to her, what was his name, and his address? Had she been living with him? Was he her boyfriend, her lover? What had she done to make him hit her? She must have done something!

Dismay had kept her silent, and defiant, as usual.

She'd speared her father with a coldly contemptuous gaze before finally escaping to her room, only to fall onto the bed and cry herself to sleep. But now she was conscious again, and the transitory peace of oblivion was no longer hers.

'It's Evelyn. I've brought you up a tray.'

The door swung open before Paige could say another word, and in swept Evelyn. She was dressed in the same sort of bleak black dress she practically always wore, as though it were required uniform for a housekeeper. Paige noticed that she'd put on more weight this past year. Her cheeks had become jowly, and her already small eyes looked smaller within her pudgy face.

'Your father said you were not to be allowed to skip meals while you're here this time,' Evelyn pronounced haughtily as she placed the tray on the bedside table. 'He expects to hear that you've eaten every bite. And he expects to see you downstairs for dinner tonight as well. Right on eight. In a dress,' she added, throwing a derisive glance over Paige's jeans.

'I didn't bring any dresses with me,' Paige said, already regretting her decision to come home, despite not having any other real alternative this time. She needed the safety and security Fortune Hall provided, for she suspected Jed was not going to take her leaving him lightly.

'Don't be ridiculous, Paige,' came the sneering retort. 'You left a whole wardrobe full of clothes behind when you first left home. I moved them all into the guest room next door when I thought you weren't coming back and this room needed a thorough spring clean. There's plenty of dresses among them.'

'For pity's sake, Evelyn,' Paige pointed out wearily,

'you can't expect me to wear the same clothes I wore at seventeen.'

'Why not? I seem to recall you spent all that year buying and wearing clothes that were way too old for you. On top of that,' Evelyn added drily, 'if there's one thing I've learned since working for the rich and famous, it's that designer clothes don't date all that much. I'm sure you'll find something among them that'll do. It's not as though you've put on any weight. You're as skinny as ever.'

Evelyn had always made comments about her weight and Paige hated it. She was a tall girl, and naturally slim. But one could hardly call her 'skinny'.

'Whatever you say, Evelyn.' She was too tired of spirit to argue. And what did it really matter?

Evelyn went to leave, then stopped, peering closely at Paige's face. 'That's a nasty bruise you've got there, dear,' she said, with a malicious glint in those beady eyes of hers. 'Walk into a door?'

'Something like that.'

'You should watch where you're going, or one day you might really get hurt.' And, with an expression which implied such a prospect would please her no end, Evelyn exited the room, deliberately leaving the door open behind her.

Sighing, Paige rose and closed the door before returning to see what Evelyn had brought her to eat. Two huge club sandwiches, stuffed with mayonnaise. A piece of cream-filled cake big enough to feed an army, and a huge chocolate milkshake.

Paige knew she wouldn't be able to consume that amount, let alone such rich food. But she didn't dare leave any behind. Evelyn would report back to her father, who would lecture her on everything from anorexia to ingratitude. Defiance always had its price around Fortune Hall.

If only Blackie were still alive, she thought wistfully as she flushed half of the food down the toilet. That dog had been the perfect garbage disposal.

Paige's heart turned over as she thought of her long-deceased pet. As dogs went, Blackie had been exceedingly ugly: a flea-bitten mongrel Paige had rescued from the pound after they'd put his photograph in the Sunday papers. Her father had been furious when she'd bought him and brought him home. Blackie had almost been as old as she was. Seven to her nine. Her father had declared him a health hazard because he was recovering from mange. He'd told her that if she returned him he would get her a proper pup, a poodle with a pedigree and papers.

But she'd dug her heels in—the forerunner of future rebellions—and said stubbornly that she wasn't taking Blackie back to die and that she'd look after him herself, using her weekly allowance. He'd cost her a small fortune in vet bills, but she'd managed. Dog and girl had been inseparable till that dreadful day when she'd had to leave for boarding school. The housekeeper had promised to look after him, but when Paige had come back on her first home weekend, a month later, Evelyn had been installed as the new housekeeper and Blackie was declared dead, supposedly run over by a car. She'd never quite believed this story, but could never prove otherwise.

Paige had vowed to get herself another dog one day. But she never had. It was hard to risk one's heart a second time after being so badly hurt, she'd found. Very hard.

With half the food flushed away, and the rest reluctantly stuffed down into her fragile-feeling stomach, Paige went along to the next room to review the dresses that had appealed to her seventeen-year-old taste.

She shook her head over most of them. If ever she needed evidence of her schoolgirl obsession with Antonio, it was in the collection of clothes before her. Never had she seen such an array of painfully provocative purchases: all designed to flaunt her body, and all, as Evelyn had pointed out, way too old for a seventeen-year-old.

No wonder Antonio had stared at her across the dinner table when she'd come down dressed in those. Any living, breathing man would have given her a second glance. Paige was not ignorant of her physical attractions. She'd had them thrown in her face often enough in the past few years.

Her hand ran along the hangers, searching for something—*anything*—which was suitable for a simple dinner with her father. She bypassed everything which was too short, too clingy, or too low-cut.

Her eye finally landed on a cornflower-blue trouser suit which she'd never actually worn at all, come to think of it. She'd bought it at one of those end-of-season sales because the saleslady had raved about her in it. But when she'd got it home Paige had childishly thought it far too simple and plain.

Now, she liked its elegant simplicity very much. And blue always looked good on her, with her fair hair and blue eyes. But it wasn't a dress, was it? Too bad, she decided mutinously, and tugged the hanger out.

Fortunately, the left-behind shoes didn't present any choice problem at all. Paige had been five-nine by the time she was fourteen, so she'd never bought too high a heel, not even during her Antonio-mad year.

Selecting a pair of open-toed cream shoes with a low-ish heel, she returned to her room, where she stripped down to her undies and tried on the trouser suit. The reflection in the full-length cheval mirror in the corner brought an instant frown. Dear heaven, but she looked terribly busty! Bras did that to her in some clothes. Taking off the cardigan-style top, she removed her bra, then slid the silky cardigan back on, doing up the three small pearl buttons and having another look.

Much, much better. Her breasts looked smaller for having settled lower and wider apart on her chest, and there wasn't an in-your-face cleavage filling the deep V-neckline. There were no ugly bra lines, either, to mar the way the silky top smoothly outlined her bust before falling loosely to her hips. The trousers had a similar cut, fitting snugly around her hips before falling straight down to her ankles in softer folds. It was a very wearable and comfortable outfit which would fit a wide variety of occasions. She really must remember to take it with her when she next left.

Whenever that would be...

Paige hadn't just lost the roof over her head last night. She'd lost her clothes as well. Which was a pity. She'd spent quite a bit putting together a decent work wardrobe to go with her new career direction.

If only she'd dared go back into Jed's bedroom and get her set of keys before sneaking out of the place. If she had, she'd be able to slip into the building—and the apartment—while Jed was at work.

Paige sighed. She could hardly see herself showing up while Jed was home, and politely asking permission to come up and get the rest of her clothes. Better she cut her losses and just disappeared.

Maybe it was time to head interstate. Maybe up north

to Queensland, where there were plenty of holiday re-
sorts, and plenty of jobs going for an attractive girl with
a wide range of working experience.

A move to Queensland, however, would require
money for her fare and some new clothes. She had some
savings, but would need every cent to set herself up in
a flat. Bond money and such. Her father would give her
money if she asked, Paige knew. He might even resume
putting that obscene monthly allowance into her bank
account, if she begged.

Frankly, she was tempted. All she had to do was eat
humble pie and tell her father he was the greatest.

But then she would have nothing left, would she? No
self-respect. No independence. No pride.

She had to find some other way out of the hell-hole
she'd dug for herself this time. Maybe she could stay
here for a while, and get a job which had a uniform and
gradually put together a wardrobe. She supposed she
could bear Evelyn and her father for a few weeks. And
at least she had one decent interview outfit!

Paige stripped off again and headed for the bathroom.
Time to have a long, relaxing bath. Time to pretend she
hadn't totally stuffed up her life once more. Time to
transport herself to a world where the man she was with
would never dream of raising his hand to her, where the
rings on her left hand spoke of love and commitment,
and the babies they made together would never know
the hurt and unhappiness which had marred her own
childhood.

When at her lowest, Paige always kept herself sane
by wallowing in just such a fantasy world. So she lay
there for ages beneath the lavender-scented bubble bath
she'd found in the vanity and conjured up old faces, old
dreams, and old desires. Time flew by, and if, eventually,

tears rolled down Paige's cheeks, her soul had still been strangely soothed by her imaginings.

At five to eight that evening, Paige carried her softened and perfumed body slowly down the huge sweeping staircase, crossed the cavernous foyer, with its domed, chandeliered ceiling, and entered the huge living area which led into the smaller and more elegant room where her father always had pre-dinner drinks. He did this for half an hour before every meal, regardless of whether he had visitors or not. Paige never joined him, partly because she didn't like to drink on an empty stomach, but mainly because she didn't like to give her father the opportunity to hurt her. When he drank, he developed a sarcastic tongue.

Given that it was a Monday, Paige assumed he would be alone. So when she opened the door which led into the drawing room she was startled to see that wasn't the case at all.

No...*startled* did not adequately describe her reaction to the sight of an elegantly attired Antonio, sitting in one of the armchairs which flanked the fireplace, a crystal flute of champagne in his hands. *Stunned* better described her instant state of mind. Stunned and sickened.

Antonio was the last man in the world she wanted to see again, especially tonight, with the mark of another man's contempt for her glowering angrily on her cheekbone.

CHAPTER THREE

FOR a few fraught, fragile moments, Paige just stared at Antonio. Hard not to when the sight of him had always made her heart hammer madly against her ribs.

This time was no different, except that her head began whirling angrily at the same time. Why hadn't Evelyn warned her Antonio would be here for dinner? She must have known he was coming.

The answer was obvious, and cruel.

Because she didn't want you to be prepared. She wanted you to stumble in here and make a fool of yourself, as you always do in Antonio's presence.

Paige knew there wasn't anything that happened around Fortune Hall which Evelyn wasn't privy to. What the housekeeper didn't come to know by virtue of her position she found out through slyness and stealth. Over the years, Paige had caught the woman eavesdropping more than once, especially on the telephone. Her omission to mention Antonio's presence at dinner could only have had a malicious intent, which meant the hateful woman was aware of Paige's feelings for Antonio.

Pride came to the rescue, as did some hard-won experience. Maybe she was getting used to handling the emotional devastation seeing Antonio always caused her. Or was it that at last she was beginning to grow up?

'Why, hello, Antonio,' she said casually as she strolled into the room and over towards the drinks cabinet in the corner. 'You startled me there for a moment. No one said anything about you being here tonight.

36

You're looking well,' she added, somewhat tongue-in-cheek. *Well* was not a word one would use to describe Antonio. It was far too insipid for his brand of raw physical impact.

Tonight, he was looking exceptionally sexy all in black, his fine woollen suit given a casual look by being teamed with a black crew-necked top rather than his usual shirt and tie. The outfit seemed to intensify his dark colouring and brooding sex appeal, a fact which certainly didn't escape Paige's poor, pathetic heart.

'I was thinking the same of you, actually,' he returned silkily. 'Considering…'

She laughed, sliding a mocking glance over her shoulder at him. 'You mean for someone who's boyfriend has just beaten her up?' Paige had found over the last few years that being mealy-mouthed and defensive around Fortune Hall only brought more looks and lectures on the way she was living her life. Better to face any sticky situation head-on, with a suitably defiant façade.

'Paige, for pity's sake!' her father protested.

'*Pity*, Father?' she scoffed as she swept the bottle of champagne from the ice bucket and poured herself a glass. Suddenly, drinking on an empty stomach was not only desirable but imperative!

'Now that's a word I've not heard often in this house,' she muttered, and turned back round, the crystal flute cupped firmly in her hands, her knuckles white in the effort to stop them from shaking. 'So what have you been drinking to with this very expensive champagne? I can't imagine its your health. You'll both still be taking the television world by storm when I'm six foot under.'

Her gaze swept over the two men, who stared back at her with perfect poker faces, telling her nothing, and everything. 'Oh, I see,' she said drily. 'It's a secret, is it? Something to do with business. Something silly little girls like me couldn't possibly understand, or shouldn't know.'

Paige was surprised to see her spiked sarcasm brought a wry smile to Antonio's beautifully shaped mouth. 'Not at all,' he said. 'I'm sure your father wouldn't mind your knowing.'

Did Antonio see the warning glance her father shot him? If he did, he ignored it.

'We're celebrating a forthcoming and hopefully desirable merger,' he went on smoothly, his black eyes glittering with some secret amusement. Or was it suppressed anger? One could never quite tell with Antonio. 'Unfortunately, negotiations are at too early and too delicate a stage to supply you with more details right now.'

'How delightfully vague!' she exclaimed, rolling her eyes at him. She should have known Antonio wouldn't cross her father. He knew what side his bread was buttered on.

Not that Antonio was easily cast in the role of flunkey. He was far too strong-willed and opinionated to be a mindless yes-man. She'd heard him disagree with her father more than once when it came to business.

But she was still piqued that he felt he could play with words around her. It was so patronising. And so like the treatment she'd always received around Fortune Hall. If she'd been born a boy she would have been drawn into their world of negotiations and deals, not excluded, then cynically condescended to!

Her eyes flashed as she lifted her glass in a mock toast. 'To the forthcoming and hopefully...what kind of merger did you say it was, Antonio?'

'Desirable,' he said quietly, and that inscrutable black gaze of his ran slowly over her from head to toe.

Paige's heart tripped, then stopped altogether when those eyes began to travel back up her body even more slowly, lingering on the swells and dips of her female form, leaving them burning in his wake. He inspected her mouth for what felt like an interminable length of time, forcing her lips to fall apart and drag in some much needed air for her starving lungs.

Now his eyes lifted to hers, holding them in a hard and merciless gaze which was as blatantly sexual as it was chillingly cold.

She quivered. All over. Inside and out.

It was the most erotic thing which had ever happened to her.

Her heart began to race, an uncomfortable heat suffusing her skin.

Paige did the only thing she could think of to survive the moment. She quaffed back the chilled champagne she was holding. The whole lot.

Unfortunately, her ragged breathing sent some down the wrong way and she began to choke.

Antonio was beside her in a flash, slapping her firmly between the shoulders. The champagne came flying back up and sprayed out from her mouth, most of it falling to the carpet but some dribbling down her front.

'Try to breathe slowly and evenly,' Antonio advised, once she'd stopped choking to death.

She tried, but it was almost impossible with him standing so close to her, then perfectly impossible when Antonio drew a snow-white handkerchief from his trouser pocket and started wiping down her top where the champagne had stained it, stroking the handkerchief down over the swell of her right breast, working his way closer and closer to her hardening nipple. As he drew dangerously close she felt her flesh tighten even further in anticipation of his touch, craving the contact, practically begging for it.

Paige sucked in sharply when the handkerchief finally slid over the tautened peak, her head spinning wildly. He did it again. Then again.

Confusion flung her eyes wide to search his. Was he being deliberately cruel? Did he have any idea what he was doing to her? She dared not believe this was real, but when their eyes met Paige was stunned to see he was as enthralled as she was by what he was doing.

The handkerchief came to rest over the traitorous peak, hiding it from sight. 'Do you want to go upstairs and change?' he asked her in a low, thickened voice.

'I...I don't have anything to change into,' came her shaky reply, and Antonio frowned.

'There's no *time* to change,' Conrad snapped irritably, from where he'd risen and was moving towards the now open dining room door. 'Dinner's ready to be served.'

'Why don't you have anything to change into?' Antonio asked in a disconcertingly gentle tone as he led her still shaken self to her place at the table. 'Or don't you want to tell me?'

Suddenly, she *did* want to tell him. Suddenly, he wasn't the disapproving, remote, unattainable man he'd become over the years. He was more like that other Antonio Scarlatti, the one who'd kindly met her train that day, and started her obsession with him.

Was one of her futile dreams in danger of coming true? Had Antonio finally seen her tonight as a grown-up woman, and not a silly little girl?

'Later,' she whispered to him when he pulled her seat out for her.

His breath was warm against her ear as he scooped

her chair under her. 'I'll look forward to it,' he murmured, and she quivered helplessly.

Dinner was agony. And ecstasy. One minute she would be smiling and sparkling at him, then doubts would besiege her and she'd fall worriedly silent. Why now? she agonised. Why tonight? Did her father have anything to do with this? Had he ordered Antonio to be nice to her?

No, no, that couldn't be it, she decided at long last. If Antonio's ambitions lay in that direction, he would not have waited this long to pursue her. No, he was genuinely attracted to her tonight. She could feel it. There was a predatory glitter in his eyes, eyes which didn't stop looking at her. Paige knew what it was like to be the object of a man's sexual interest, and she could feel Antonio's desire hitting her in waves.

He wanted to make love to her.

The thought was breathtaking. And compellingly exciting.

It was only a sexual thing, of course. Paige was not naive enough to think anything else. Antonio was a man of the world, a confirmed bachelor type whose commitment was to the company. His bed-partners were transitory, and replaceable, like her father's. According to the staff at Fortune Hall, Antonio hadn't brought the same woman to dinner, or a party there, in all the years of his employ. If Paige let him seduce her, he would promise her nothing but passing pleasures, followed by the ultimate in pains.

But, oh…those passing pleasures…

Paige could barely begin to imagine them.

The ultimate in pains, however, she *could* imagine.

She groaned a silent groan. She'd have to be crazy to set herself up for that!

'Paige!' her father snapped. 'Evelyn's asking you if you want some dessert. What's the matter with you tonight, girl? One minute chattering away sixty to the dozen, the next off in some dream world!'

Her blue eyes cleared to see the hated housekeeper smirking at her from her position at her father's shoulder.

'No dessert, thank you,' Paige said stiffly, while she struggled to suppress the overwhelmingly negative feelings the woman always evoked in her.

'You're not becoming anorexic again, are you?' her father demanded, exasperation in his voice.

'I was *never* anorexic!' she defended hotly. 'I have no idea where you ever got such an idea,' she finished, whilst looking daggers at Evelyn.

The housekeeper's beady eyes didn't move an inch.

'Then prove it by having some apple crumble!' her father insisted. 'Bring Paige a large helping, Evelyn. With plenty of cream.'

A helpless fury flooded Paige as the housekeeper swanned off with a triumphant expression on her face. If Antonio hadn't been at the table she would have left the room. Instead, she was stuck there, feeling belittled and foolish. She could not bear to look over at Antonio, afraid to see his earlier attraction for her had faded because she was being treated like a difficult and wayward child.

'The reason Paige probably turned dessert down, Conrad,' Antonio said, and Paige's eyes snapped up to stare across the table at him, 'is because she promised to have supper with me later. I should have said no to dessert as well.'

Paige was as amazed as her father by this announcement. She'd only agreed to *talk* to Antonio later. Nothing more. But she wasn't about to say anything. Not now.

'You and Paige are having supper together?' her father challenged. *'Tonight?'*

Antonio didn't look at all concerned by his employer's tone of disapproval. 'I trust you have no objection to that?' he returned, an icy counter-challenge in his voice.

Paige was mesmerised by the exchange.

'No, no, I suppose not. It's just that…well…I'm surprised, that's all.'

No more than herself, Paige thought dazedly.

'You only flew into town this morning,' her father went on a little testily. 'I would have thought you'd be too tired to go out.'

'I slept on the plane,' Antonio explained coolly. 'I'm only home for two weeks, as you know. Terrible to waste my holiday sleeping it away, don't you think? There are much better ways to spend one's leisure time. What say you, Paige? Should we make our escape now, before Evelyn returns and force-feeds us both?'

Paige didn't need any encouragement. She was on her feet in a flash. Too late, however. Evelyn was already coming into the room, carrying a tray of desserts towards the table.

Paige hesitated. Not so Antonio, who strode around the table towards her.

'Our apologies, Evelyn,' he said smoothly as he took Paige's elbow and steered her towards the doorway. 'Paige and I are going out and haven't time for dessert right now.'

Paige expected the woman to look put out. Instead, she smiled oh, so sweetly at them both as they passed.

'That's quite all right, Antonio. Dessert will keep. It's nice to see you and Paige are friends at long last.'

Paige's mouth dropped open at Evelyn's hypocrisy. There was no level to which that woman would not stoop!

'Don't wait up, Conrad,' Antonio called back, with a nonchalant glance over his shoulder. 'And don't worry. Your daughter will be perfectly safe in my hands.'

CHAPTER FOUR

ANTONIO almost laughed at the expression on Conrad's face. It seemed it was one thing to callously blackmail an employee into bedding and wedding your wayward daughter, quite another to witness the process first hand.

Antonio suspected his employer might be having second thoughts.

But it was too late now. The wheels had been set in motion, and Antonio meant to see the journey through to the bitter end.

'My car's outside,' he told Paige as he urged her across the living room floor towards the foyer.

She nodded, but said nothing, which was fine by him. He wanted to get her out of the house as quickly as possible. No way did he want Conrad trying to stop things now, just because he'd had a momentary flutter of conscience, or because the reality of an illegitimate Italian peasant seducing his daughter stuck in his throat.

Actually, Antonio found this evening's events perverse in the extreme. He'd fumed all day over being backed into such a corner, arriving for drinks and dinner tonight in a smouldering state of black fury. Only the thought of Brock Masters being handed the job which *he'd* worked so darned hard for had stopped Antonio from throwing the cold-blooded bargain back in Conrad's face.

But the moment he'd set eyes on Paige this evening, looking surprisingly elegant and incredibly sexy, his male hormones had kicked in, and Antonio had decided a man's fate could be worse than having such a delectable creature as his wife for a while.

But only for a while.

Antonio had no intention of staying married to the girl. Which was one little loophole his employer hadn't thought of. Nowhere did the promissory letter in Antonio's pocket say he would lose his job as CEO if he divorced Paige. He would make sure that the contract he signed on his wedding day was irretrievable and unbreakable, no matter what!

Of course, that still left the problem of getting Paige to marry him in the first place. Antonio had no doubt he could get the girl into bed with him in no time. Dear Lord, she *was* a push-over where the opposite sex was concerned. He'd only had to make eye contact with her a few times tonight, and she'd been his for the taking.

Admittedly, she exuded a pretty powerful chemistry of her own. Once those big blue eyes had clamped on to his, he'd found it difficult to keep his mind—and his body—on track. When he'd been wiping down that top of hers he'd almost forgotten who was seducing whom.

But getting the man-mad Paige into bed was a far cry from getting her to agree to marry him. She hadn't married any of her other lovers, had she? Why should he be any different? It was naive of Conrad to think a school-girl crush was the same as being seriously in love. Antonio doubted Paige had ever been seriously in love in her life.

Get her pregnant had been Conrad's ruthless suggestion. Antonio wondered if his boss was still so keen on *that* idea.

Antonio didn't fancy it at all, though he could see it might become his final option. He would certainly try the whirlwind romance bit first. And plenty of sex. Oh, yes, definitely plenty of sex. Hell, he hadn't been this turned on in years!

But the bottom line was Paige had a mind of her own, a stubborn, rebellious, changeable mind, and she obviously had a low boredom threshold when it came to the men in her life. She'd promised *him* undying love and devotion once, a promise which had lasted all of a week or two. Loyal wife material she was not.

But marry her he would, by hook or by crook!

His hand tightened on her arm and she threw him a look which almost stopped him in his tracks.

For never had Antonio seen such vulnerability in a woman's eyes. Or such sweet gratitude.

His gaze dropped to the ugly bruise on her cheek, and that sometimes awkward conscience of his raised its infernal interfering head. How could he ruthlessly seduce her later tonight when she was looking at him as though he were a hero, rescuing her from the villains of this world? Couldn't she see that *he* was the villain this time?

But, damn it all, what was the alternative? Leave her to Brock 'Marquis de Sade' Masters? Compared to Masters, he *was* a hero.

Besides, it wasn't as though he was going to hurt the girl. He was going to be very nice to her, make beautiful love to her, tell her he loved her.

Lie to her, you mean, came the brutal voice of honesty.

'Antonio?' Conrad called from the dining room, his voice gruff. 'Antonio! Are you still there by any chance?'

Antonio hesitated, but Paige left him to run over to the security panel behind the front door. 'Hurry,' she urged as she punched in the gate code.

His black Jaguar was waiting, like Lochinvar's trusty

steed. They dashed down the steps and dived into their respective seats as one, slamming the car doors behind them and tugging on their seat belts.

'Don't stop for anything,' his breathtakingly beautiful and stunningly sexy passenger advised as he gunned the engine.

'Don't worry,' Antonio muttered, his body making his decision for him. 'I won't.'

The car screeched off, gravel spraying out behind them. The die was cast. There was no going back.

CHAPTER FIVE

PAIGE'S heart accelerated with the car as it sped around the circular drive and shot through the gates. The tyres squealed when they hit the road at an angle, but Antonio corrected the small skid and pointed the Jaguar towards the city centre.

'You can let go of the seat belt now,' he said, with dry amusement in his voice, and Paige saw she was indeed gripping it across her chest, as a child might grip the security bar on one of those wild fairground rides.

But in truth that was how she felt, as though she'd jumped onto a runaway rollercoaster which was in danger of hurtling out of control.

'What do you think Father wanted you for?' she asked breathlessly.

'Probably something to do with business. It can wait,' he pronounced, with a confidence Paige could not help but admire.

There again, there was so much to admire about Antonio. And she wasn't just talking about his looks, although he was still one of the handsomest men she'd ever met. Antonio was an enigma, in a way. A man of contradictions. Privately passionate, Paige had no doubt. But with a public and professional self-possession she could only envy. If only she had half as much control over her own emotions. And her life.

This last thought brought her back to earth with a jolt. What *was* she doing here with Antonio, letting her feelings for him run away with her common sense again, agreeing to a date which could only have one motivation and one ending?

That was a part of Antonio which wasn't so admirable. His treatment of women. He never let a woman into his life, except briefly, and then only on a superficial sexual level.

Which was probably why her father hadn't liked their going off together at this hour of the night. No doubt he knew exactly how Antonio's supper dates usually ended, and, whilst Paige didn't believe her father gave a damn about Antonio's personal morals, he probably didn't like to see his own daughter being used in such a fashion. It wasn't a matter of parental caring—when had her father ever really cared about her?—but male ego. Her father was always going on about her making a fool of herself over men, simply because he was afraid her behaviour might somehow reflect on him. He was probably worrying it might be awkward to face Antonio at the office in future, knowing the other man had *known* his daughter.

Known…

Paige's throat thickened at the thought.

The Bible had a way of saying something which sounded like a euphemism, but which was, in fact, incredibly explicit. If she went to bed with Antonio, he would know her as no man had ever known her before. For, although she wasn't a physical virgin, she was still very much an emotional virgin. She'd never given her all to a man, had she? Never given her heart and soul along with her body.

But she would with Antonio, wouldn't she?

How could she not?

And when she did, what would he see? What would he *know*?

'Father seemed a little worried about our going out together,' she choked out, echoing her own inner misgivings.

'He'll get used to the idea.'

Paige blinked, then turned her head slowly to stare at Antonio. 'What...what do you mean?'

'Exactly that. Recognising that one's daughter is finally a grown woman is hard for most fathers. Even yours, Paige.'

'He's always thought of me as a silly little girl,' she said bitterly. 'As did you, Antonio.'

'Never!' he denied.

Shock was mixed with confusion. 'How can you *say* that?'

He shrugged. 'Quite easily. Because it's true.'

She shook her head vehemently. 'That's not what you said to me that day by the pool. And it's not what's been in your eyes every time we've met since then.'

'Ah, but Paige, you should never try to read a man's eyes. It's his body language you must learn to take note of. Believe me when I say I've never thought of you as anything but the most irritatingly attractive female.'

'Irritating?'

'Well, of course! How would you expect a lowly employee to view the boss's beautiful daughter, especially when she was only seventeen? No matter how I felt about you that day by the pool, I couldn't in all conscience do anything about it, could I?'

Paige's breath caught. 'Are you saying you *did* feel something?'

He flashed her the sexiest of smiles. 'Let's just say I was eternally grateful there was a towel between us.'

Paige's heart fell. Sex. That was what he was talking about. That was all he'd felt for her. That was all *most* men felt for her. She should have known better than to hope for anything more, even for a second.

'I'm sure you didn't suffer for too long,' she bit out. 'A man like you would never be wanting for that kind of company.'

'Nor a girl like you,' he retaliated, the counter-attack not sitting well with her.

As usual, when hurt, Paige laughed, then went on the offensive. 'How right you are! But be fair, Antonio, I haven't been seventeen for quite some time.'

His black eyes flicked her way, glittering and hard as they raked over her. 'Your father mentioned you turn twenty-three next week. What day, exactly?'

'Wednesday.'

'We'll have to do something special for you.'

Paige stiffened. If by *we* he meant he was going to talk her father into having Evelyn organise some ghastly party, then he could think again!

'Unless you've already got plans, of course?'

'No,' she said coldly. 'No plans.' But there would be no party!

'The boyfriend isn't going to be forgiven?'

The insensitive question infuriated Paige. 'Are you serious? You think I'd go back to some man who did this to me?' And she pushed her hair back behind her ear to show him the full extent of the bruise.

To give him credit, his eyes *did* show something this time. Although their expression conveyed more anger than sympathy.

'I should hope not,' he grated out. 'But women have been known to return to violent situations. God knows why!'

'Perhaps they have nowhere else to go.'

'Don't give me that, Paige. That's just an excuse.

There's always somewhere else to go. Women are their own worst enemies sometimes.'

'What would *you* know about being a woman, or what it's like to be female and afraid? It's easy for you to make snap judgements from behind your six-foot frame and macho muscles.'

'If you say so,' he remarked drily. 'I really don't wish to discuss this subject other than to find out who did that to you. And don't even *consider* defending him, Paige.'

'I won't. But, frankly, it's none of your business, just as it was none of my father's business.'

'I beg to differ. Men like your bullying boyfriend make the rest of my sex look bad. They can't be allowed to get away with thinking they can beat up their girl-friends, no matter what she does or says to provoke him.'

'He didn't beat me up. He only hit me once.'

'Once is enough. If you'd stayed, the next time it would have been worse.'

'Why do you think I left?' she snapped.

'So what set him off?' Antonio persisted. 'What *did* you do?'

'It wasn't what I did,' she muttered. 'But what I *didn't* do.'

'Meaning?'

Her stomach churned as she looked over at the man who was behind it all. How blissfully unaware he was, sitting there, probably thinking he was helping her. Yet, really, he was to blame. For everything.

Perhaps he was right to say that women were their own worst enemies. They often loved stupidly, without sufficient reason and without hope.

Suddenly, the urge to fling the truth at him was acute. And she almost did. But at the last moment she let her love for him lie hidden within her words.

'Jed had just had sex with me,' she said baldly instead. 'But I hadn't enjoyed it. He took it badly, and personally. He accused me of not loving him, of wanting some other man instead. When I didn't deny it, he lost his temper and hit me.'

Antonio was deathly silent for several excruciating seconds while the car stopped at a set of red lights, the engine idling like some snarling animal, poised and ready to pounce.

The man behind the wheel seemed just as tense. Paige gained the impression her confession had angered him. Yet, when he spoke, his voice was icy cool.

'That was a dangerous thing to do, Paige. A man's ego can be very fragile.'

'Only *some* men's, Antonio.'

His dark eyes narrowed on her. 'Did you provoke him like that because he was disappointing in bed and you wanted to end your relationship?'

She shrugged. 'What can I say? I realised I couldn't bear to have him touch me again, so I let him believe what he wanted to believe.'

'So there *isn't* some secret love, waiting in the wings to become your next conquest?'

'None but you, Antonio,' came her dry but perversely true comment.

His laugh carried just the right amount of return cynicism, letting her know that he hadn't twigged to the truth at all. The lights turned green and the car leapt forward, leaving Paige to live with the consequences of what she'd just done.

No doubt Antonio now thought she was a promiscuous little piece, going from man to man, moving on as soon as her lover began to bore her in bed. Little did he know that Jed was the first man she'd slept with since

Brad, all those years ago. Or that last night had been their first time together.

Still, perhaps it was better that Antonio thought she was a woman of the world, whose heart was rarely involved in her various dalliances. That way, if tonight ended as she suspected it might, she could pretend to be unaffected afterwards, and whenever she ran into him in the future.

Her eyes suddenly cleared to find they were crossing the bridge and heading towards the north side of the harbour.

'Where are you taking me?' she asked abruptly.

'Where would you like me to take you?'

'I thought we were going to supper somewhere. I imagined some place in the city.'

'I've decided to head for my apartment instead,' he returned, without missing a beat. 'It's only a couple of minutes from the city, and has several advantages over a nightclub. Firstly, it has free parking. Secondly, a view *par excellence*, not to mention a complete range of in-house services. I thought it would be very pleasant to complete supper on our own private balcony overlooking the harbour.'

'I'm sure it would.' After which, it was just a short stroll inside and into the bedroom. No doubt Antonio thought *that* the best advantage of all!

Paige tried to find the strength to tell him, no, she preferred somewhere far more public. But the devil was in her ear, along with her own traitorous weakness for the man.

Turn him down tonight and you might never have another chance. He's home on holiday, and wants a woman for the night. Maybe even for the whole fortnight! Fate threw you into his path this evening, Paige, and finally he noticed *you* were a woman.

Cynicism added that there had to be dozens of women in Sydney he could date instead, who would do admirably—women who would drop everything to be with him. He wouldn't suffer if she turned him down. And he wouldn't be alone. Men like Antonio were never alone when they didn't want to be.

Could she bear the knowledge that he was somewhere in Sydney, making love to some other woman when it could have been her? Could she lie in bed at night and sleep, craving him?

The simple answer was no. She could not.

'Is it far to your apartment?'

Antonio could hear the sexual tension in her voice and felt his own flesh prickle alarmingly.

He almost felt sorrow for the fellow she'd walked out on last night. No doubt he was crazy about her, and thought his feelings had been returned. Antonio could see the scenario now: Paige coldly turning from her lover while her body was still hot from his lovemaking and cruelly telling him he wasn't up to par.

Women like her could drive a man crazy. They wound a man up, promising so much with their eyes and their body language, not to mention their sheer physical beauty. It was criminal for Mother Nature to give one woman so many attributes.

Conrad's daughter was sheer feminine perfection, with not a single flaw visible to the eye. Her face was classically lovely, with fine bone structure and symmetrical features. Her forehead was high and wide, as were her eyes: big blue eyes with long, curling lashes. Her nose was narrow and straight, its slightly uptilted end bringing attention to the full mouth beneath. Her even, white teeth might have been due to good dentistry, but, if so, the dentist had done an excellent job. Her smile was as dazzling as the rest of her.

Of course, it was the rest of her which had often unravelled Antonio, and which was unravelling him at this moment. He could not wait to wallow in the lush sensuality of her body. To spread her hair out over his pillow, to bury his mouth in her breasts, to feel her legs entwine themselves around him as he sank deeper and deeper inside her.

Not long now, he told himself as he turned off the expressway and headed towards his apartment. The twenty-storey building was situated at the end of a cul-de-sac at Milson's Point, with the back of the block facing the harbour.

Antonio was only two streets away when his car phone buzzed. Scowling impatience, he pulled the Jag over to the curb to answer, snatching the receiver up and snarling, 'Scarlatti,' down the line at the same time. Truly, there were times when he would like to consign mobile phones to the bottom of the harbour!

'Conrad, here,' his employer replied curtly, startling Antonio. 'Don't let Paige know it's me on the line. Just wanted to call and let you know I was only putting on an act earlier tonight. Knowing Paige, it seemed a good ploy not to seem too keen about you two being together. Do you see what I mean?'

'Yes,' Antonio muttered. 'I see.' Talk about devious!

'How are things going? Are you taking her back to your place?'

Antonio practically ground his teeth. If Conrad was expecting a blow by blow account of his daughter's seduction then he was going to be very disappointed.

'Yes. Thank you for that information,' he said. 'Must go,' he added, and slammed the phone down.

'Who was that?' Paige asked. 'Or shouldn't I ask?'

Be damned if he was going to lie to her!

'Your father.'

'What did he want?'

'Just passing on something he considered important. You know your father.'

'Oh, yes,' she sighed. 'Business comes first. Always.'

Her head turned away to stare through the passenger window as he drove off, but the moment he turned into his street she suddenly sat forward in the seat, her head whipping back round. When the Jaguar shot down the short street and straight onto the ramp which led down to the underground car park beneath the apartment block, Antonio felt her eyes boring into him.

'Is this some kind of sick joke, Antonio?'

A quick glance sidewards showed unexpected alarm in her eyes. Frowning, he moved his eyes frontwards to safely negotiate the tricky circular driveway which wound its way down to the car park. Once there, he swiftly angled the Jaguar into one of his two private spots and switched off the engine. He was about to ask Paige what on earth she was talking about when she swept on, her face flushed and undeniably furious.

'I can't believe you would do something like this. Oh, I dare say Father's behind it. That was what that call was all about, wasn't it? He had that creep of a detective of his find out Jed's name and address. It's no more than I'd expected of him, but not you, Antonio! I didn't think *you'd* be involved in something this underhand. For pity's sake, if Father was determined to confront Jed about what happened last night, then so be it! But to trick me into coming here with you by pretending to ask me out is beyond the pale! I'm not going up to Jed's with you, so don't think you can make me!' she threw at him, her voice shaking with emotion.

It didn't take long for the penny to drop, and when it did Antonio experienced a rush of emotion himself. 'Are you saying the man who hit you lives here as well?'

Her eyes grew wide upon him. 'Are *you* saying you *really* live in this building?'

'I own one of the two penthouse apartments.'

She paled, then laughed. 'You've got to be joking!'

'Do I look like I'm joking?'

'No...' She began shaking her head, as though she could hardly believe it.

Antonio was also having a hard job believing it. Now he knew the identity of Paige's lover, and where he lived.

Jed, she'd called him.

Jed was not a common name. The man who owned the other penthouse apartment was Jed Waltham, a successful Sydney stockbroker. Antonio had naturally met him a few times, since they shared the same lift, and the pool on the roof. In his early thirties, Waltham was darkly good-looking, and had an ego you couldn't climb over.

'How long have you been living with Jed Waltham?' he asked, trying to come to terms with his feelings at actually knowing Paige's errant lover. It was one thing to scornfully imagine her cohabiting with some ne'er-do-well in a fleabitten flat in some grotty suburb. Quite another to picture her in a luxury penthouse, in a luxury bed, beneath the likes of Jed Waltham.

'You...you *know* Jed?' she asked, disbelief still in her eyes.

'Not to any great degree. But naturally we've met in the lift a few times, and around the pool once or twice.'

Her frown carried genuine puzzlement. 'The pool?'

'You didn't ever use the pool on the roof?'

'I...no... I...I only moved in with Jed yesterday.'

Stupidly, Antonio felt relief at this news. But he hadn't liked the thought of her being there with Jed Waltham while he'd been right next door.

'Had you been lovers long before that?'

'We...we'd been going out for a while,' she hedged, which could have meant anything.

'Where did you meet?'

'At work.'

Now it was Antonio's turn to frown with genuine puzzlement. Paige gave him a dry look.

'I see Father *hasn't* been having that flunkey of his follow me around lately. I thought he'd stopped, but I wasn't sure.' Paige inhaled, then exhaled a weary sigh. 'Frankly, I'm surprised Father bothered for so long. He doesn't give a fig for me.'

Antonio supposed the man *did* care about Paige, in his own weird way, but it was hardly the kind of caring a daughter would appreciate. Once again, a certain sympathy for the girl undermined Antonio's determination to keep his mind focused on what he had to do. But, damn it all, she was beginning to stir things in him. And not just the obvious.

His own sigh carried a whole host of feelings, none of which he was comfortable with.

'You don't have to feel badly for me, Antonio,' she said ruefully, and his eyes jerked round to stare at her. 'I've long come to terms with my father's non-existent feelings for me.'

Once again, Antonio began to feel sorry for her, which

annoyed him. Seduction, not sympathy, was his aim here. 'You didn't answer my question,' he snapped.

'Which one was that?'

'About how you met Waltham?'

'Oh, that one. Well, as I said, we met at work. I was doing a few weeks as a temp at his firm. And before you ask I did a night course at tech during the first six months of this year. I finally decided I couldn't spend the rest of my life as a waitress. I needed a job where I could make more money than to just make ends meet. So I learnt word processing, and other secretarial duties, then signed up at one of those agencies which find you work. They suggested that I start out as a temp. Because of my looks, they said I was a cert for a reception job. When the receptionist at Waltham & Coates went on maternity leave for three months, I applied for and got the job.'

Antonio was surprised, and quietly impressed. It seemed she *had* started growing up after all. 'When did you start there?'

'The tenth of July. I finished up last Friday.'

'And moved in with the boss two days later,' he mused aloud. In *that* she hadn't changed. There always had to be some man in her life, didn't there?

'Which moves us into the territory of questions I'm *not* going to answer,' she said, with a defiant toss of her head. 'I repeat, my relationship with Jed is none of your business, Antonio. Let's just say I thought he loved me. But a man doesn't do this to the woman he loves, does he?' And she held her hair back again, for him to see the evidence of Waltham's violence.

Antonio's stomach tightened as he stared at the bruise, which had become darker and uglier since he'd last looked. Any empathy he might have momentarily felt for Paige's ex-lover disappeared as he glanced from her physically damaged face into her emotionally damaged eyes.

'You're quite right,' he ground out. 'Nothing justifies that. Come on, Paige. Get out of the car. We're going upstairs.'

CHAPTER SIX

PAIGE froze, her back pressed against the leather, her hands gripping the seat belt once more, lest Antonio forcibly undo it and drag her out. 'No! I'm not going up there. You can't make me!'

'I'm not taking you up to Waltham's apartment. I'm taking you up to mine. Then *I'm* going over to Waltham's.'

'But…but what for?' she asked shakily.

'To get back your clothes, for one thing. And to have a quiet little word,' he added, in the kind of low, coolly civilised voice she imagined a clever hitman might use to lure his prey to their deaths.

A shiver ran down her spine as she realised Antonio didn't want a *quiet word* with Jed. He wanted to beat him to a pulp. The vengeful part of Paige wanted him to do just that. But her softer, more sympathetic side knew she'd seriously provoked Jed by not responding or co-operating with him, and then in not denying his accusations.

Not that those things justified hitting her.

'I can't let you do that, Antonio,' she said, almost regretfully.

'Do what?' he asked.

'You *know* what. You're going to pulverise Jed. I can see it in your eyes.'

'You can read me that well? My poker face must be slipping. But so what if I want to teach Waltham a lesson he won't forget? Are you saying you don't want me to, that you still care about the creep?'

'No. But I do care about *you*.' Her eyes remained steady on his, despite her heart fluttering wildly inside. 'I don't want you having to answer to some assault charge because of me. I would really appreciate your getting my clothes. But for the rest…I would much prefer you left well enough alone, and came back to me safe and sound.'

Antonio didn't know if he felt triumphant or troubled. Nothing was going as planned. The Paige who'd always irritated him to death was now engaging far more than his carnal desires. He wanted to know more about her, wanted to put the pieces of her puzzle together.

What was real and what had he presumed? Was she shallow and silly, or sensitive and misunderstood? Was she genuinely promiscuous, or a love-starved woman, desperate to find some real affection from any man?

Antonio noted that most of her lovers had been some years older then herself. Perhaps she was looking for a father figure. Perhaps her never-ending bed-hopping was the result of a quest to find the sort of love she'd never had from Conrad.

Antonio appreciated that everyone who'd ever been emotionally neglected as a child craved love as one would crave a drug. He himself had once been needy in that regard. He'd thought he'd found the answer to his need in Lauren, lavishing all the love he'd had to give on her. But he'd been as deluded by Lauren as Paige had obviously been by Waltham.

He wished he knew *exactly* what had happened last night. He could not imagine a man like Waltham being an inadequate lover. If he *was* unsatisfactory in bed, then why had Paige moved in with him in the first place?

Unfortunately, Paige was not going to give him any details. She'd been adamant about that.

Whatever, Waltham was about to wish he hadn't struck Conrad Fortune's daughter.

Antonio had never told his neighbour what he did for a living, other than to make some casual remark about being in business. He always kept a low profile, media-wise, letting Conrad have all the limelight. Antonio wasn't into that kind of thing. He valued his privacy too much. Consequently, he could give his position at Fortune Productions any slant he wanted.

'Did Waltham know you were Conrad Fortune's daughter?' he asked abruptly.

'Heavens, no. I never tell anyone that! I'm not stupid, you know.'

'Stupid?'

'Aside from the security angle, I like to be liked for myself, thank you very much, not because I'm a rich man's daughter.'

Antonio found it ironic that her being a rich man's daughter had always been an obstacle in *his* liking her. Before tonight, that was. Tonight he was finding he liked Paige a lot. Far too much, actually. He would have preferred keeping his feelings for her firmly on a lust basis. Lust he was comfortable with. Lust he could handle.

'Are you coming up?' he said a touch sharply. 'Or are you going to just sit there and wait till I come back down with your clothes?'

'How do you know Jed's home?'

'That's his car over there, isn't it?' he said, and pointed to the red Ferrari in the next row.

Paige nodded.

'Then he's home. Men who drive Ferraris don't use taxis.'

Antonio waited while she gnawed at her bottom lip for a full ten seconds. 'You won't let him anywhere near me, will you?'

She really was frightened. 'You have my word,' he assured her, and hardened his resolve to give Jed Waltham a taste of his own medicine. And right where it hurt most!

Paige scooped in a deep breath before letting it out with a shudder. 'Okay, then.'

He deposited her safely in his apartment, with instructions not to answer the door to anyone. He told her to make herself comfortable. There was whatever she might wish to drink behind the bar in the main living area, food or coffee in the kitchen, television, video and stereo in another smaller living room. He would be back, he said, as soon as possible.

'Be careful, Antonio,' were her last words.

His parting smile didn't seem to soothe her anxious face. But he couldn't let her natural female tendency for taking the line of least resistance sway him from doing what had to be done.

For a while Antonio thought Waltham *wasn't* home. But he answered his doorbell at long last, the considerable delay explained by his semi-naked state and frustrated expression. His chest and feet were bare, his trousers hanging around his hips, the zipper gaping. His lack of underwear was disgustingly obvious.

'Who the hell—?' he began aggressively, then stopped. 'Oh, it's you! Tony, isn't it?'

'Antonio,' came the cold correction. 'Antonio Scarlatti.'

'Really? You don't sound Italian.' Waltham started

doing up his trousers. 'Sorry about this. I was in the middle of something.' And, zipping up his fly with a pretty risky flourish, he threw Antonio one of those conspiratorial man-to-man grins.

Antonio just stared at him, his emotions wavering between distaste and disbelief. How could Paige have been taken in by this womanising creep, even for a moment?

The stockbroker wasn't at all fazed by Antonio's chilly expression, his own face still smirking. 'Is there something I can help you with, Tony? A cup of sugar? Packet of condoms?'

'I can't imagine you'd have any left,' Antonio drawled icily, and the man's smile finally began to fade.

'Honey, who is it?' A female voice drifted from the depths of the apartment. 'I'm getting cold in here. If you're much longer, I'm going to have to put some clothes on.'

'I'll just be a moment or two, sweetheart,' Waltham called over his shoulder. 'Go pop in the spa and keep it warm for me.'

Antonio's top lip curled with contempt at the sound of the female's empty-headed giggle. The stockbroker began eyeing his visitor with a more thoughtful expression. 'I take it this is not a social call?'

'You take it correctly,' Antonio returned. 'I've come to collect Miss Fortune's clothes.'

'Miss Fortune?' the creep repeated, frowning his confusion.

Antonio's temper was starting to seriously fray. The louse didn't even know Paige's surname.

'The lady's first name is Paige,' came his frosty elaboration. 'But you probably called her honey. Or sweetheart. Or babe.'

Now he got some reaction. Waltham's face darkened,

then tightened. 'Oh, I see. She ran along to you, did she? Probably told you a whole lot of bull about how I beat her up. Hell, it was only a little slap. If it had been any other guy she'd have gotten a lot more than that! Look, man, don't be fooled by the likes of her. She's nothing but a cheap, gold-digging little slut. And frigid to boot.'

Antonio tried not to look startled at this last highly unexpected announcement.

'Not that you would ever guess by looking at her,' Waltham raved on. 'That hot-looking body of hers promises more moves than a chess champion. I spent a damned fortune on taking her to the best restaurants and shows in town. But would she put out afterwards? Not even remotely! At first she said it was too soon, and then she said she just couldn't sleep with a man who didn't love her. She made me so crazy I told her I loved her. I even asked her to move in with me, to prove it. Which, of course, was her plan: to move in with some rich mug so she could claim half of everything they own. Usually I'm too smart for that caper, but I was so frustrated I wasn't thinking straight.

'I wouldn't have minded if she'd been good in bed, but, hell, anyone would think she was a virgin the way she carried on, crying afterwards and then saying she didn't want to do it again. I thought a bit of oral would get her going, but oh, no, she wouldn't have a bar of that, either. It was about then that I lost it and hit her. The silly little cow ran into the bathroom and locked herself in. She was in there so long I had a few drinks, then eventually passed out on the bed. I guess it was while I was asleep that she let herself out and went along to your place.'

Antonio was having difficulty keeping his hands off

the bastard. 'She didn't come along to my place,' he bit out.

'Oh? What happened, then? Did you run into her in the lift, was that it? Well, whatever, just watch it, buddy. She's bad news. A fruit loop. Toss her out before you get caught in the same trap I did. Meanwhile, don't believe a word she says about what happened last night.'

'The bruise on her face rather speaks for itself, don't you think?' Antonio said with cold fury. 'As for Miss Fortune being a gold-digging slut, I don't think what you described to me just now are the actions of a slut. Sluts, I've found, have no aversion to giving men like you whatever you want. As for her being a gold-digger, I would imagine most people would consider *you* the gold-digger for pursuing *her*.'

'Huh? What in hell are you talking about? The girl hasn't got a dime. She hasn't even got a job at the moment!'

'Paige might not personally have any money. But her father could buy your pathetic little stockbroking firm several times over without missing the money. Since Paige is Conrad Fortune's only child and heiress, some people might think she's a very desirable catch, whether she's good in bed or not!'

Antonio rather liked seeing Waltham's mouth flap open like a floundering fish.

'I gather you've heard of Conrad Fortune of Fortune Productions? Their television programmes win awards all over the world every year.'

The four-letter expletive which fell from those flapping lips expressed the stockbroker's situation pretty well, Antonio thought with savage satisfaction.

'I happen to be in Mr Fortune's employ,' he went on mercilessly. 'I see to his security and other personal needs. Italians are, by tradition, very good bodyguards. They don't shirk from doing what other men find…irksome.'

Antonio let his words sink in, with their implied threat. He gave private thanks to all those films which had painted every second Italian male—especially ones dressed in black—as potential killers.

'Recently, Mr Fortune gave me a different brief,' he continued, in the classically emotionless monotone of a movieland Mafia assassin. 'His daughter. I was charged with seeing no harm comes to her. So you see, Jed, I was concerned when it came to my attention that you'd raised your hand to her, then threatened her further.'

Antonio didn't know that Waltham *had* threatened Paige further, but it seemed likely, given her fear.

Waltham had gone a sickly ashen colour.

'You are fortunate that Miss Fortune wants your miserable hide spared. All she asks is the return of her clothes. So if you could get them, please, I'll be on my way.'

Now Waltham went dead white. 'I…I can't get her clothes.'

'Why not?'

'I…um…I burnt them,' he muttered, in the lowest of voices.

'You…burnt…them.'

'Look, when I woke up to find her gone, naturally I was angry,' he tried to explain.

'Naturally?' Antonio repeated coldly.

Waltham suddenly found some spirit. 'Damn it all, what did she expect? That I would calmly take what she dished out? I wanted to teach her a lesson. I'm a man, not a mouse!'

'I agree that you're not a mouse. But you're not a

man either. You're a louse! And it's *you* who's going to be taught the lesson.' The back of Antonio's left hand swiped hard across Waltham's face before the other man could even blink, snapping his head round as the blow landed forcibly on his cheekbone, pretty well in the same place Paige had been struck.

Antonio had no intention of leaving it at that. Taking the stunned man by the shoulders, he let his knee come up between Waltham's legs and crunch into the sleaze-bag's ill-protected equipment. Antonio stepped back and watched him sink to his knees, grasping his genitals as he groaned in agony.

'Don't worry, you'll live,' Antonio told the crouched form at his feet. 'You'll probably even get to be a pathetic lover again. But not tonight, I would imagine. Your ladyfriend will have to keep it warm for a few more days, I would think. Needless to say, if you ever bother Paige again...if you even *speak* to her...either personally or by telephone, you won't get off this lightly a second time. Do you get my drift?'

Waltham managed to nod.

'Smart man,' Antonio said, and walked off.

CHAPTER SEVEN

PAIGE couldn't settle to doing anything Antonio had suggested. Television was beyond her powers of concentration at that moment. She'd never been much of a drinker. And eating was the last thing she could manage. The revolving in her stomach would have rivalled that of a tumbledrier.

She paced up and down the spacious room, oblivious and uncaring of its luxury, her anxiety increasing with each passing minute. Logic suggested it would take Jed time to pack her clothes, but logic was not as strong as the intuitive feeling that something else was going on in the apartment next door besides clothes-packing. Her ears strained to detect any sounds of scuffling or shouting through the walls, but of course million-dollar penthouses were well insulated.

Agitated beyond belief, Paige found herself eventually making her way through the huge sliding glass doors and standing on the equally huge balcony. Again she strained to hear sounds, but nothing came to her ears but the faint sound of music from one of the opened windows below. Sighing her frustration, she leant against the curved steel railing and let the fresh sea breeze blow the heat from her face.

Distraction came in the form of the view of Sydney Harbour. It was magnificent, and very different from that at her own home, which was understandable. The two residences were on opposite sides of Port Jackson, for starters, and opposite sides of the bridge. Antonio's penthouse was also much higher, so that a larger body of water plus the whole of the inner city area was set out before her in one vast, hundred-and-eighty-degree panorama.

At that hour, and with the night sky perfectly clear of cloud, it was a sight to behold. The stars competed with the city lights to create a fairyland carpet out of the black waters of the harbour, a perfect foil for the bridge and the tall buildings beyond. In the distance, Darling Harbour glowed. No doubt its brand-new glitzy casino still buzzed with tourists and compulsive gamblers, but the rest of the city was pretty quiet. It was Monday night, after all, and those balmy summer evenings which brought Sydneysiders out onto the harbour in droves were still a few weeks off.

Paige shivered as a swirl of much stronger wind brought her out in goosebumps. Truly, it was too cool to be comfortable out here, and she turned to go inside. So much for Antonio's suggestion that they sit out on his balcony sipping coffee. He must have known it was out of the question. Which meant he'd probably never intended to bother with supper at all. Till this awkward business with Jed had cropped up, it probably would have been straight to the bedroom.

And she would have been with him all the way!

The thought annoyed her, and she slammed the glass door behind her. Why on earth was the infernal man taking so long?

The need for further distraction drove her to look around the place. Frankly, she was surprised and impressed. Although identical in floor-plan to Jed's penthouse, Antonio's was furnished in a more sophisticated and elegant style. The floors went from a grey granite in the foyer and hallways to a deep burgundy carpet in the living rooms, the furniture a mixture of lacquered black wood and the coolest of cream leathers.

Jed's place was over the top, with lots of dark studded leather, animal print furnishings and mirrors. Oh, yes, Jed liked mirrors!

Each place reflected the personality of its owner, Paige began to appreciate. Jed was a show pony, who needed pseudo-macho accessories to boost his self-image. Antonio didn't. His natural class and taste shone through in the things he'd chosen to surround himself with. This was the home of a man who knew what he was, and what he wanted out of life.

Antonio had obviously done very well for himself over the years, Paige realised as she wandered over to stare through the glass wall at the city skyline once more. A million-dollar view to go with the million-dollar penthouse. That Jag he'd been driving tonight wasn't cheap, either. And his clothes spoke for themselves. Still, her father was no fool. He would be paying Antonio a huge package to make sure no other company head-hunted him.

And, of course, Antonio had no dependants to drain away his finances. No doubt he meant to keep it that way, too. If a man meant to marry and have children he didn't leave it this late to start. Not that Paige knew exactly how old he was. But he had to be in his mid-thirties.

The sound of a key rattling in the front door lock propelled Paige back to the moment at hand and over to the foyer, her heart pounding as Antonio came in. Frantic blue eyes searched his face and hands for any evidence of a scuffle.

But there wasn't any.

Besides being unmarked, his hands were also empty.

'Jed wasn't in?' she asked, perplexed over what could have taken him so long if he hadn't been fighting or gathering up her clothes.

Antonio's smile was wry. 'He was in all right.'

'Oh? He wouldn't give you my clothes, then?'

'He *couldn't* give me your clothes.'

'Oh, my God, what did you do to him?' Paige burst out, frantic that Antonio might have done something really stupid. There was a wild glitter in his eyes which worried the life out of her.

'Nothing,' he denied, and, taking her arm, steered her back into the living room. 'Nothing much, anyway,' he muttered darkly.

'I think I need a drink,' he announced, and, leaving her in the middle of the room, he stalked over to the black-lacquered bar in the corner and poured himself a large whisky. 'You want something?'

'No, thanks. And what do you mean by *nothing much*?'

She watched agitatedly while Antonio took a deep swallow of whisky, then smiled a very rueful little smile. 'Let's say he'll be sporting a bruise bigger than yours tomorrow. And he won't be in a hurry to service the dolly-bird he had stashed in his bedroom. Other than that, he's fine.'

Paige didn't know whether to shout hooray or to cry. In the end, her dismay overrode her satisfaction that Antonio had indeed pulverised the man. 'Jed had a...a woman with him?' she choked out.

'Why do you think I hit him?'

Paige did not know what to say. Or think. She just stood there, her head and shoulders sagging. What a fool she'd been to have felt guilty over Jed even for a moment. His anger last night had not been the result of a broken heart, but a bruised ego.

'He couldn't give me your clothes,' Antonio added. 'Because he'd burnt them.'

'*Burnt* them!' she exclaimed, both startled and shocked. 'Why would he do such a terrible thing?'

'Men like him don't take rejection well,' Antonio stated drily. 'Not many men do, actually. I would say, when he woke and found out you were gone, he had to have something to destroy. Since you were no longer there in person, your clothes were his only option. After that, he went out and found another woman to bolster up his poor, pathetic male ego. He didn't love you, Paige. He *never* loved you.'

Paige could see that now. But it was still an upsetting situation. 'God, I'm an idiot,' she cried, and buried her face in her hands. Tears welled up in her eyes, tears of despair and self-pity. Her father was right about her. She had no idea about men. Jed had fooled her far too easily. Some smooth flattery. Some clever lies. And she'd simply believed him.

She shuddered at her gullibility.

Antonio's taking her gently into his arms seemed so natural, yet it brought a fresh well of emotion flooding her heart, and her eyes. With a strangled sob, she laid her head against his chest, tears spilling down her face.

'Poor Paige,' he crooned as he held her to him, one hand firmly around her waist, the other stroking her hair down her back.

Poor Paige indeed, she had to concede as she wept. Poor, silly, stupid Paige!

She'd actually thought she'd taken her life in hand this year. She'd done that course, got herself a new job, a new wardrobe *and*, she'd mistakenly thought, a new man, to banish Antonio from her mind and heart for ever.

Well, her new job was gone. So was her new man. Even her nice new clothes!

And now she was back, living at her despised home, and loving Antonio more than ever!

Her thoughts gradually brought her back to the reality of that very moment, which was that she was actually in Antonio's arms, and he was holding her to him very, very closely. So closely that she could feel his heartbeat under the palms of her hands, and a telling hardness pressing against her stomach.

This was what she'd been waiting for all her life, wasn't it? *Wasn't it?*

Her tears dried as the heat in her body rose, her own heart quickening. Her weeping stopped, and a tense silence gradually filled the air. Antonio's hand stilled on her back. She felt his pulse-rate pick up speed.

'I think, perhaps,' he said thickly, 'that I should take you home.' And he pushed her away to arm's length.

Paige's head lifted, her eyes wide upon his.

'You're upset,' he ground out, his own eyes like black coals upon hers.

If he'd looked at her with pity, she might have fled. But he didn't. His eyes reflected a passion which was intoxicating in its intensity.

'But I don't *want* to go home,' she told him huskily, and a storm of indecision filled his face.

'I doubt you have any idea what you want, Paige. You never have.'

'There's one thing I've always wanted, Antonio,' she insisted on a raw whisper. 'And that's you...'

'Like you thought you wanted Waltham?'

'I *never* wanted Jed the way I've always wanted you.'

His hands lifted from her shoulders to take her face and tip it upwards. 'Don't expect me to tell you I love you,' he said darkly, his impassioned gaze lancing hers.

'I don't,' she managed to say quite coolly, even though she was trembling inside.

'You told Waltham you only slept with men who loved you. Which was why he said he did.'

Paige was taken aback that Jed would admit such a thing, till she accepted that Antonio might have coerced the information out of him. 'What else did he tell you?'

'That last night was the first time you'd had sex together. Was that true?'

'Yes.'

'Did he use protection?'

'Yes.'

'Have all your other lovers always used protection?'

'What? Oh…oh, yes. Always.' Brad had been very careful about that.

'Good.'

His mouth began to descend, stopping only millimetres from hers. 'Once I kiss you,' he warned, 'there'll be no going back.'

'I won't want to go back.'

'I was talking to myself, Paige,' he muttered. 'Not you.' And his mouth closed the gap.

Antonio fought a deep self-disgust as he started to kiss her. He knew what he was doing was wrong. On all counts. Paige might sound sure about this, but she had to be especially vulnerable at this moment, distressed over what had happened the night before, and now tonight. Her confidence as a woman would be down, her self-esteem shaky. The classic scenario for a rebound affair. The perfect set-up for him to sweep her off her feet before she had time to think too clearly.

Her declaration that she'd always wanted him didn't mitigate Antonio's guilt. If anything, it made it worse, knowing he was taking advantage of that old teenage crush of hers even more cruelly than if he'd done so when she'd been seventeen.

His conscience demanded he not do this. His own self-respect demanded he tell Conrad to shove his black-mailing bargain and stick his job. He'd survive without Fortune Productions!

But would he survive without making love to Paige?

The chemistry which had always sparked between them was much stronger tonight, and dangerously out of hand. With her lips already softened and parting under his, Antonio's conscience was easily ignored, his earlier anger at being manipulated by Conrad totally abandoned. He no longer cared about anything but kissing the beautiful girl in his arms.

As his tongue dipped deep into her mouth, and she moaned softly, his last rational thought was to wonder if he had any condoms anywhere in the place. But then she moaned a second time, and that thought too was consigned to the same place as his conscience.

Paige's hands slid up his chest and around his neck, clasping her to him lest he somehow dematerialise.

'Antonio,' she whispered once, when his mouth lifted briefly. But then he was back, kissing her again, taking her breath away, making her see just why she'd waited so long, and why she hadn't been able to love any other man. She'd thought Jed would be an experienced and ardent lover, able to push Antonio out of her mind. Instead, he'd been quick, and crude. She'd hated every

second of their brief coupling, then shuddered with revulsion when he'd tried more intimate things with her
afterwards.

But when Antonio's mouth moved hotly and hungrily
over hers a wildly uninhibited passion began to burn
through her body, a passion which *demanded* intimacies.
She could not wait to touch him all over, to stroke his
skin and kiss his most private places. In turn, she wanted
his hands on her, stripping away all her clothes, exploring every inch of her naked flesh, searching out every
forbidden erotic zone. Her body was his to enjoy and to
use. She would give it to him.

Willingly.

Wantonly.

Lovingly.

They were both breathless by the time his hands fell
to her clothes. Paige helped him, undoing the small
pearly buttons between her breasts when he had trouble,
tugging the silky garment back off her shoulders and
letting it flutter to the floor, leaving her naked to the
waist.

Touch me, she begged him silently. Touch *them*. Oh,
please, Antonio. Please.

Antonio's breath sucked in sharply at the sight of Paige's
magnificent breasts, with their lush fullness and rose-
tipped peaks. They stood out in their arousal, taut and
tempting. But he didn't touch them, forcing himself to
wait till she was totally naked before him.

'Take off the rest,' he ordered thickly, and after the
briefest hesitation she obeyed him, swiftly, completely.
Dear God, what that did to him, seeing her eager compliance to his wishes, watching her quite stunning beauty
unfold before his eyes.

She was even more lovely than he'd imagined. A golden goddess. A temptress beyond description.

Paige's head swam as she stood there before him, watching his smouldering gaze move slowly over her totally nude body. She could not have been more turned on if he was actually touching her. Her stomach tightened. Her breasts swelled. Her thighs quivered.

'Don't move,' he ordered, and set to slowly undressing himself in front of her.

First his jacket. Then his top. Both discarded without a care. His eyes were solely on her, eating her up, telling her with every searing glance that he wanted her more than any man had ever wanted her.

His shoes were kicked off, his socks soon after. And then it was down to the nitty-gritty. His trousers and his underpants. Her mouth dried as he dropped the first, then stepped out of the second.

Her breath caught in her throat. Oh, yes…he wanted her more than any man had ever wanted her!

Paige stared down at him, then up into his face, and knew she was about to experience something very different from anything she'd ever experienced before. This would be nothing like Brad's gentle, easy-going style of lovemaking, or Jed's ghastly wham-bam-thank-you-ma'am brand of sex.

'Come here,' he commanded.

She felt as if she was in slow motion as she moved back into his arms, her lips gasping open at the feel of their naked bodies meeting, then melting together. She lifted her face to be kissed, but he didn't kiss her, just stared deep into her wide, dilated eyes.

'You do realise,' he warned in a strangled voice, 'that I can't wait a moment longer.'

'Neither can I,' she heard herself say, and he made a sound she would always remember. A raw, guttural groan which encapsulated everything and nothing of what she'd hoped he'd one day feel for her. Her own feelings were indescribable, her love for him momentarily abandoned in favour of sheer lust. She could never have dreamt of such urgency, or such a need. She simply *had* to have Antonio inside her, had to feel his flesh filling hers, stamping her body with his unique brand of sexuality.

'Just do it, Antonio,' she urged wildly. 'Do it!'

With another of those tortured groans, he pushed her legs apart and penetrated her then and there, filling her with a savage upward thrust which brought a stunned cry to her lips. She'd known he would be a passionate and primitive lover, known he would take her breath away. What she hadn't known was that she would thrill to such caveman treatment. When his large hands cupped her buttocks and hoisted her up off the floor she buried her face into his neck lest he see what was in her eyes.

But hiding her face from him was impossible when he carried her over and tipped her back across the high, wide leather arm of the sofa in the centre of the room. Her mouth opened on a gasp as her head and shoulders sank into the squashy cushions, her hair flying everywhere, her arms flopping up above her head. Her sex, however, remained firmly fused with Antonio's.

Stunned, she stared up at him from the depths of the sofa. She'd never experienced or imagined such a position. Yet it was surprisingly comfortable, especially after her legs snaked around his waist, her ankles linking. Her hips were well supported by the soft leather arm, her buttocks firmly clasped in Antonio's strong male hands.

It was also an incredibly erotic position, with their bodies so explicitly displayed for each other's eyes.

Paige thought Antonio looked magnificent, standing there with his long legs braced solidly apart, his broad shoulders and muscular arms having no trouble holding her to him like that. The years hadn't brought any flab to his stomach, though his tan was possibly more due to his Latin genes than time spent in the sun. His body hair seemed darker and more menacing than she remembered, or maybe that was because she hadn't seen that part which was now totally exposed, and closest to her wide-eyed gaze.

Dressed, Antonio always looked a handsome and elegant man. Nude, he was the primitive lover Paige had always pictured, and wanted.

His glittering black eyes took in every inch of her body with a slow and decidedly thorough survey, bringing a flush of heat to her cheeks and a squirming feeling to the pit of her stomach. Under his gaze her parched lips fell further apart, her nipples peaked harder, her belly tightened.

When his eyes reached that part of her which was as one with his he began to move, and to move *her*, his hands pulling her hard against him with each thrust of his hips.

'Oh, God,' she moaned, and simply had to close her eyes, her head twisting to one side, her helpless hands finding and grasping a cushion with frantic opening and closing movements of her fingers. It was impossible to think of anything but what he was doing to her body. How *he* felt. How *she* felt.

The blood was roaring in her head. Her heart was going faster and faster. Everything was spinning way, way out of control.

And just when Paige began to panic she shattered around him, crying out his name, her tortured face and wildly spasming body bringing hot tears to her eyes. For this was even worse than she'd feared. The pleasure. And the pain.

Because Antonio did not love her. He would *never* love her.

Just like Jed.

CHAPTER EIGHT

ANTONIO was stunned by the power of her orgasm, and the rush of elation it evoked within him.

Strange…he'd never been that kind of man before, whose ego needed stroking by the woman he was with. He'd never felt the urge to prove himself a greater lover than her last, never strived to impress in bed so that his partner thought he was the best thing since Casanova.

But it seemed that with Paige he *was*. His dark triumph at being able to give her such pleasure was only exceeded by the pleasure *he* was finding in *her* body. Maybe his memory was playing tricks on him, but he couldn't remember it feeling this good, even with Lauren. Or this wild!

Antonio had to admit that Conrad's daughter had been his sexual nemesis for a long time. But especially now, with her violent climax propelling him towards a climax of his own which was as compellingly irresistible as it was highly risky.

For he wasn't wearing a condom.

He'd meant to go and get one. There were surely some in his bathroom or in his bedside table drawer. Antonio always believed in being prepared.

But things had got out of hand. When she'd urged him to just do it, he'd totally lost his head.

Of course, he could still withdraw and get one.

Or he could just withdraw.

But he wasn't going to, was he?

Not because he was trying to get her pregnant.

Frankly, the thought of Paige conceiving would complicate things. How could he divorce the mother of his child?

The truth was he didn't want anything between his flesh and hers when he came. He wanted to keep feeling the heat of her, the tightness, the wetness. And he wanted to go on experiencing the indescribable ecstasy of what he was feeling at that moment.

Her contractions showed absolutely no sign of abating. It was unbelievable! Unbearable! If only he could last for ever. But then she called out his name again, and arched her back in one long, voluptuous movement, shifting the angle of her body, breaking what little was left of his control.

He came with a lightning flash of sensation, his cry as loud as a thunderclap. His fingers were digging into her flesh and his thighs trembling uncontrollably when the sudden urge for closer contact sent him bending over to scoop her up from the depths of the sofa, holding her tight against him while he shuddered deep within her.

At first she just clung to him, but then she started to cry, with deep, gasping sobs.

It rocked him, that gut-wrenching sobbing. Rocked and rattled him. Waltham had said something about her crying with him afterwards.

But surely this wasn't the same kind of crying! This couldn't be dismay or disappointment, or, God forbid, disgust. It had to be a reaction to the intensity of her release. He'd heard of such things happening, though hadn't come across it before.

He wanted to comfort her, to say something, *anything* to stop her heartbreaking weeping.

'Hush, honey, hush,' he found himself saying, his hands shaking slightly as they stroked her hair down her back. 'It's all right, Paige. It's all right. Please don't cry. Please, sweetheart…don't.'

She gradually stopped, and with one last hiccuping sob lifted luminescent blue eyes to his. They searched his face, looking for…what? he wondered.

And then she murmured something which rocked him even more than her crying.

'Make love to me, Antonio.'

He stared down at her. What did she think he'd *been* doing?

And then the penny dropped. The reason for the weeping. The disillusionment with Jed, and all her other lovers. Her distress over what had just happened between them. She didn't want just sex. She wanted love. She didn't want harsh reality. She wanted romance. It was as Conrad had said.

Just tell her you love her, said a voice in Antonio's head, and she'll be putty in your hands. Consolidate your declaration with some truly tender lovemaking, and marriage will be just around the corner.

He instinctively recoiled from such a cruel deception. She deserved better than a husband who didn't really love her, who would manipulate her like that. If he cared about her at all he would take her home right now and walk out of her life for ever.

And leave her for Brock Masters? His pragmatic side piped up again. Throw away everything you've worked for as well?

And what about your child? another voice inserted savagely. The one who might have been conceived here tonight? Who can say what Paige might do if she finds herself pregnant? Could you live with yourself if she does what Lauren did, not out of greed, but despair? You can see how vulnerable she is, man. Just *look* at her!

A whole host of emotions tore through Antonio. And while he tried to tell himself there were mitigating circumstances for what he'd done tonight, and what he was about to do, his main feeling was a raging guilt.

Oh, Paige, Paige, he agonised as he bent to cover her lovely mouth with his. Forgive me...

Paige could not believe the gentleness of his kiss. Or the way he looked down at her afterwards. With such sweet tenderness.

It brought tears to her eyes, and to her soul. Her parched, love-starved soul.

'Antonio,' she murmured, and held her hand against his cheek.

He didn't say a word as he carried her into the darkened bedroom; nor when he drew her down with him onto the huge bed; nor when he started making love to her again.

No matter. She didn't want words at that moment. Words would have spoiled the fantasy, the fantasy that Antonio loved her.

In the security of her silent dreamworld Paige could believe anything she chose. And she chose to believe there was more to Antonio's lovemaking than lust this time. It was there in the softness of his mouth and the gentleness of his touch. But most of all it was in the swift readiness of his body to give her pleasure and satisfaction once more.

No man, Paige enjoyed deluding herself, could want her again so quickly, unless she meant more to him than a one-night stand.

Not since her days at school had she enjoyed one of her fantasies so much, letting reality slip away as she sighed beneath her pretend love, sighed, then groaned, then gasped, her hips lifting to meet Antonio's as they came together one more amazing and marvellous time.

It was only afterwards, while Paige held him in her arms and felt him slip away into sleep, that reality resurfaced and she knew she could never bear to do this again.

Once was enough.

Once she could live with.

Twice would surely destroy her.

The only plus from tonight was that there was no possibility of a pregnancy to compound her stupidity. She'd started taking the pill a couple of years ago, after a near-date-rape scare one night, at the suggestion of a kindly doctor who'd said girls these days were always at risk, with sexual assault so rampant. Of course, she knew the pill wouldn't protect her from AIDS or other STDs. And once or twice she'd contemplated stopping. She was glad now that she hadn't.

Lord knows what Antonio had been thinking, however, when he'd gone ahead without protection. Had he presumed she was using some form of protection? Or did he believe she would think nothing of having an abortion if she fell pregnant?

She hated to think he would think that badly of her. Still, she supposed the responsibility for what had happened *was* mainly hers. *She'd* been the one to push the issue. She'd been the one who'd refused to go home, who'd told him to just do it, asked him to do it again. Fair enough if he assumed the worst.

He probably thought she was a big tart.

Not that it really mattered what he thought of her. All that mattered was that she extricate herself from his life as quickly as possible. Knowing men, he would probably want to keep her on tap for the rest of his fortnight's holiday. Heck, why not? He probably thought she was good for every which way he might like his sex. Kinky. Straight. Wild. Warm. He must have thought he'd won the sexual lottery!

Paige bit her bottom lip to stop herself from crying again, steeling herself inside with tough thoughts. She'd shed enough tears tonight. Frankly, she'd shed enough tears over Antonio to last a lifetime! Enough was enough. Time to take control of her wayward heart and weak flesh. Time to show him who was boss of her life.

She really could not allow herself to continue being a victim of her futile feelings.

She had to make a stand!

Sliding out from under him, she slipped from the bed, stopping only long enough to pick up the bottom of the quilt and throw it over his naked body. She could not bear to look at him like that, or to look at him at all for that matter. Not right now. Shortly, perhaps, when she'd washed the smell of him from her body and put something on to cover the evidence of his lovemaking. Maybe then she would be able to face him.

Antonio woke to a shake of his shoulder. He blinked a couple of times into the overhead light before focusing on the figure beside the bed.

Paige, he finally realised. Fully dressed. And with a slightly impatient expression on her face.

'Sorry to wake you,' she said briskly. 'But I really must be going home, and I didn't bring any money with me.'

Antonio's brain was still fuzzy from sleep. 'What do you need money for?'

'For a taxi, silly. You don't think I expect you to get up and drive me home, do you? You must be wrecked after your long day. Not to mention your pretty exhausting night.

'Not that I'm not grateful, mind,' she added, bending and giving him a peck on his startled mouth. 'You're as fantastic in bed as I always thought you'd be. And, frankly, after Jed, I needed my faith in male virility restored a little. But let's be honest, Antonio, you're not looking for a permanent female to share your life, whereas I'm reaching the stage where real commitment is what I'm looking for. Actually, one-night stands never did appeal to me. Why do you think I always lived with my boyfriends?'

She batted her eyelashes at him and smiled a sickly sweet smile. 'So, darling, as much as I fancy you enormously, I think we'll leave it right here. Oh, by the way, if you're worried there's a chance a little Scarlatti heir might have been produced tonight, then don't be. I'm on the pill. Not that I usually tell a man that. But you can know now that our sexual relationship is over.'

Antonio could find nothing to say to her. He supposed he should have felt relieved about the pill business. But he wasn't. Frankly, he was too taken aback by this whole unexpected turn of events to assemble his emotions—and thoughts—properly. Only one fact was sinking in, which was that despite Paige's verbal flattery over his performance in bed she wasn't nearly as vulnerable to him as he'd thought, or hoped.

'We really were both very silly tonight, weren't we?' she went on, in that faintly patronising tone. 'I guess I was upset over Jed, and you...well perhaps you've been working too hard, Antonio, and not getting enough regular sex. What you need is some desperate divorcee to satisfy your needs over the next fortnight, and I'll look for someone a little more suited to *my* needs. You get my drift?'

Antonio got her drift all right. Desperate divorcee indeed!

And there he'd been earlier, worrying about taking advantage of the girl, thinking she was a push-over. She was about as much of a push-over as her father!

But she'd shown her hand to him in more ways than one tonight. For one thing she wasn't in any way frigid, as Waltham had implied. That idiot must have been pretty terrible in bed. Paige liked her sex and she liked it a lot. She just preferred it with commitment.

Commitment, he mused, was the name of the game. Not love, so much. Or even romance.

Now commitment he could handle. Commitment he was familiar with. He'd been committed to Fortune Productions for years. All he had to do was do what he did at work when he went after a contract or a deal. Devote every breathing, waking moment to the challenge, and never take no for an answer!

'You don't *have* to go home, do you?' he said softly, and sat up, the quilt falling off his naked shoulders.

She turned away from him and stood up, laughing. 'Oh, yes, I do. No way am I going to waltz up home tomorrow morning after staying out all night with you, Antonio. A girl has her pride.'

'Pride?'

'Everyone around Fortune Hall knows you're the love 'em and leave 'em type. I have no intention of being added to your list of idle conquests. Bad enough that I once made a fool of myself over you. I don't intend to repeat the performance, or give Evelyn any opportunity to sneer down her nose at me. Not to mention my father! Good grief, the thought is too horrible for words. So you can either hop up and drive me home, or lend me some money for a taxi. It doesn't matter to me either way.'

Oh, it didn't, did it? Antonio began to fume. We'll just see about that, Miss Love 'em and Leave 'em yourself! I've got news for you. You won't be loving and leaving *me*, honey. You're going to be my wife, whether you want to be or not!

'I wouldn't dream of sending you home in a taxi,' he said with a smooth smile, and, throwing off the quilt, bounced naked from the bed. 'Just give me a minute...'

Paige groaned as she watched his gorgeous behind disappear into the *en suite* bathroom. That was *not* a sight which reinforced her decision to have done with the infernal man once and for all!

On top of that, Antonio himself didn't seem to want to leave things between them at a one-nighter. If he had, he would have taken up her suggestion of a taxi. He would not be rushing to escort her home.

Antonio had seemed genuinely taken aback by her decision not to see him again. No doubt he wasn't used to such rash treatment from women he'd just brought to rapture in his bed. Paige could not imagine many of his sexual partners not lining up eagerly for seconds. Or thirds.

But she wasn't one of his casual sexual partners, was she? She *loved* the man.

No! She would *not* weaken. She'd spoken her mind to him—and, in essence, it was the truth. She *did* want commitment. She'd had enough of loneliness, and heartache. She was fed up to her eye-teeth with men asking her out, then expecting her to jump into bed the very first night. She wanted someone who wanted what she wanted. She wanted someone whom she could love, and who would love her back. She wanted…the.impossible. She sighed.

The bathroom door opened and out strode Antonio, all wet and glistening from the shower, his still naked body just barely decent with a towel slung round his hips.

Paige tried not to look anything but amused. 'You going to drive me home like that, Antonio?'

His smile was wickedly attractive, and totally disarming. 'Would you like me to?'

Her face grew hot at the thought. 'Don't be ridiculous!' she snapped.

He shrugged. 'I guess I'll have to get dressed, then.' And he headed for the living room.

Paige made the mistake of following him and watching while he discarded the towel right in front of her and began to dress with irritating slowness, starting with his underpants and trousers. Once they were thankfully in place, he actually sat down on the sofa where he'd made love to her—if you could call that torrid encounter making love!—and took his time putting on his shoes and socks.

Such a sight and setting was not conducive to pure thoughts and brave resolves. Paige stared at Antonio's semi-naked body and started thinking of all the things she'd wanted to do with the man and hadn't. She hadn't even touched him all over. It had been all Antonio directing everything. Antonio doing the kissing and the caressing. Antonio choosing the positions.

A pity, Paige thought regretfully.

She'd once had this fantasy of giving a completely nude Antonio a long, sensual massage. She would relax him totally with the skill of her hands first, then slowly arouse him with her mouth till he was in a state of the

most acute arousal. Only when he begged her would she
slide over and down onto his aching flesh, where she—

'I'm ready,' Antonio drawled, and Paige was dragged
back to reality, her mouth snapping shut with a nasty
little lurch in her stomach.

For Antonio was watching her closely, and with a
slightly smug smile. Panic propelled her madly racing
heart into momentary arrest. What had he seen just now?
What had he guessed? Had he been aware of her staring
at him as he dressed? Had he seen the lust in her glazed
eyes?

Yes, of course he had! *He* might be an expert at wearing a poker face, but she wasn't quite so skilful over
hiding her feelings. He must have felt the hunger in her
glued gaze, then recognised the reason behind her far-
away expression, her parted lips, her flushed cheeks.

Somehow, she managed to school her face into a casual expression, but the damage had been done. Still, if
she were brutally honest with herself, the damage had
been done earlier tonight, when she'd responded to him
with such abandon, then begged him for more.

'Fine,' she said crisply. 'Let's go.'

She stalked off ahead of him towards the door, then
stood at a distance in the corridor while he locked up.
But Antonio was not to be so easily denied. The moment
they were alone together in the lift his hand found hers,
his fingers sliding between hers, then curling them over.

Her stomach curled over as well.

The automatic and involuntary response annoyed
Paige. But it underlined her vulnerability to the man.
Really, this was the last time she could allow herself to
be alone with him.

Meanwhile, she had to let him know that she had his measure.

Snatching her hand out of his would have seemed melodramatic, and panicky. So she left it there, pasted a wry little smile on her mouth and threw him a gently mocking glance.

The predatory gleam in his return gaze reaffirmed what she'd already suspected. Antonio wasn't going to give up easily. *He* was the one who wanted more now.

But only for the next fortnight.

Only a fool would think otherwise. Once his two-week break was over he'd be winging his way back to Europe, without Paige just a pleased smile on his handsome face.

The thought made her doubly determined not to let him seduce her again. She'd wasted enough of her life pining after this man. It was definitely time to move on.

The lift doors opened in the basement and she managed to free her fingers without making a fuss. He didn't appear disconcerted by her distancing herself a little as they walked to the car together, but she was sure she detected a slight stiffening of the muscles in his jawline, and in the set of his broad shoulders.

Antonio's earlier advice, to study his body language, not his face, did not bring Paige any comfort. Somehow, she didn't think her father's right-hand man had reached his present position in the company by being meek and mild, or by turning the other cheek. Although a quiet achiever, he was, nevertheless, an achiever. He would not be overly familiar with experiences such as failure, or rejection. What he wanted, he probably usually got. And that included women.

Paige had no illusions about Antonio in *that* regard.

Which meant she had to be extra careful, didn't she?

There would be no accepting any invitation from him, no matter how innocent-sounding it was. Or how desperate she was to get away from her father, or Evelyn, or whatever.

She had to be strong, not weak.
She had to be firm, not foolish.
She had to say *no*!

CHAPTER NINE

'WHAT are you doing tomorrow?'

Paige had been waiting for this, and it came at the first set of lights.

'Today, you mean,' she corrected.

'Don't be pedantic, Paige.'

'I'll be very busy,' she informed him, and he threw her a disbelieving glance.

'Doing what? You're unemployed at the moment.'

'Exactly. And I aim to get *un*-unemployed! Very quickly.'

'But there's not much you can do on a Tuesday. Any phone-in jobs from Saturday's *Herald* will have gone. The rest will require a resumé sent in, which can be done any day this week. The closing date is usually ages after the ad.'

'You've obviously forgotten my telling you, Antonio,' she pointed out firmly, feeling quite proud of herself, 'but I signed up with an agency. They have jobs on their books all the time, especially jobs for temps. If I phone them as soon as they open, I could be at an interview this very afternoon. My only problem is that I don't have any clothes to wear, except what I have on.'

'You don't have any other clothes at *all*?'

'Only what I wore home. A pair of blue jeans, a white shirt and a black jacket.'

'Nothing in your wardrobes at home?'

'A few things left behind from years ago. That's where this outfit came from. But you should see the rest.

Other than the odd bikini, shorts and T-shirt, the rest are dresses bought during my 'crush-on-Antonio' phase. No doubt you won't remember my coming down to dinner in them, but believe me when I tell you they are not dresses you'd wear to an interview. Not unless it's for a job up at the Cross,' she added, with a rueful laugh.

Antonio's laugh was just as rueful. 'Actually, I *do* remember you in a few of those dresses. And I know exactly what you mean. They fuelled a thousand X-rated fantasies for me back then.'

Paige stared helplessly over at him and he laughed again. 'You should see the look on your face. I told you I'd always been attracted to you. Didn't you believe me?'

'In a word? No!'

'Believe me, then,' he stated firmly as the lights turned green and the Jag roared off, heading towards the bridge.

Paige settled into a brooding silence in the passenger seat, angry at being rattled so easily by this declaration. But it had sounded so genuine!

He had to be just flattering her, surely. If he'd always found her so darned attractive, why hadn't he asked her out during any one of her many visits home? His excuse over her tender age had no longer held water then!

She felt Antonio's eyes flick her way as they slowed on their approach to the bridge toll, but she kept her own eyes steadfastly on the road ahead.

'Do you still have that red dress?' he asked. 'The one you wore to last year's Christmas party?'

'What?' Her head whipped round in shock. 'No...no, I don't,' she said sharply.

The irony of it was she'd thrown it in the gardener's

incinerator the following morning, and watched with a perverse satisfaction while it went up in smoke.

Recalling the incident brought some understanding of what Jed had done. There was something darkly cathartic about burning something which shouted failure at you.

'That's a shame,' Antonio said, and leant out to plop a coin in the automatic pay basket.

Her eyes followed, their expression a mixture of curiosity and cynicism. 'Oh? And why's that? It's hardly a suitable outfit for an interview, either.'

He didn't look at her while the electric window slid back up into place and the car moved off again, his attention returning to the road ahead. 'I was thinking you could wear it when I take you to dinner tonight,' he said casually.

Paige had to admire his persistence. But not his presumption. Or his arrogance. 'You'll have to be disappointed, then, won't you? I—'

'No matter,' he broke in, before she could tell him where he could stick his invitation to dinner. 'Wear one of those other little numbers you used to tease the hell out of me with. I distinctly recall a sparkly gold one, which had no back, a microscopic skirt and a halter neckline held together by the most devious, decadent little bow a designer ever created. I used to wonder what would happen if I came up behind you and tugged loose one of those teeny-tiny ties.'

Astonishment that he should recall any of those dresses, let alone one in such detail, sent Paige into a spin.

'So what *would* have happened?' he murmured, and slid those sexy black eyes over to her own startled gaze.

'Or should I just continue to let such a scene live on in my fantasies?'

Paige was totally speechless.

'I've embarrassed you,' he said. 'Sorry. I didn't mean to.'

'No it's all right,' Paige hastened to assure him. 'I'm just surprised, that's all. To be honest, I'm surprised about a lot of things tonight.'

You're not the only one, honey, Antonio thought savagely to himself. What had begun as Conrad's blackmailing bargain this morning had somehow developed into a personal challenge. He no longer cared about being blackmailed into marrying Paige. All he cared about was winning!

Antonio had always been a bit like a dog with a bone whenever someone told him he couldn't do something, or have something. It was a sure way to increase his determination to succeed at whatever project he had in mind, whether it be a business contract or, as in this case, a woman.

And Conrad's daughter was finally and definitely a woman. Quite an impressive woman, really, Antonio had to concede, with a surprisingly strong mind of her own.

He had underestimated her.

As had her father.

But he didn't underestimate her any longer. He understood her a lot better now as well. He appreciated the way her mind worked, not to mention her body.

That was the key to success where Paige was concerned, Antonio believed. That beautiful body of hers, and its uncontrollable cravings.

He'd seen the way she'd looked at him while he

dressed, seen the intensity of her desire smoke up her eyes.

He didn't know if it was him she wanted so much, or simply sex. All he knew was it was a pretty powerful need which had propelled her into his arms tonight, not once, but twice. He'd always suspected she was a hot little number. He just hadn't realised *how* hot.

If only he could get her alone with him again. Not for a night here and there, but for a considerable chunk of time. *Several* days and nights. *Then* she wouldn't be fobbing him off as she had that inadequate idiot, Waltham!

An idea came to Antonio, plus what he hoped was the right approach. At least he didn't have to lie. Or tell her he loved her.

'I don't know about you, Paige,' he said softly, 'but I thought tonight was pretty incredible. I can honestly say that I've never felt like that with any other woman in my life.'

Oh, damn, there it was again! That look! That totally vulnerable, frighteningly fearful, sweetly adoring look! Lord, but it tugged at his heartstrings.

The trouble was, his heartstrings didn't lead to a heart. He didn't *have* a heart. Didn't she know that yet?

He preferred Paige when she was tough, and just a touch cynical. He also preferred her naked and moaning. He definitely preferred her not doing anything to make him feel like a heel!

Paige tried not to react to such an outrageous statement, but it was impossible to stop that flood of fresh yet probably futile hope.

Because he could not mean it, surely. She couldn't have been that special to him, not Antonio, with all his other women.

Big blue eyes searched his darkly handsome face for any sign of sincerity, but only his mouth was smiling. His beautiful black eyes were, if anything, almost cold.

Her heart sank at the reality behind his words. He was just trying to con her back into his bed. Her own eyes grew cold and her laugh was dry. 'More special than the woman you were with at last year's Christmas party?' she scorned lightly. 'The one you were practically ravishing on the terrace?'

She watched his startled expression with a degree of vengeful satisfaction. 'Come now, Antonio,' she flung at him, 'I've heard all those lines before. You'll have to come up with something better than that if you want to go out with me again.'

Like, *I love you, Paige, and I want to marry you!*

'Actually, I've decided I don't want to go out with you again,' he returned coolly, and Paige's heart lurched.

'I want you to go away with me,' he added, and she stopped breathing altogether.

'I've rented this houseboat on the Hawkesbury River for ten days,' he went on, while her head whirled. 'I pick it up at Brooklyn this Wednesday. My plan was to just cruise around, fish, sunbake, read, listen to music. I always need to relax after a few months in that rat-race over in Europe. I was going to go alone...till tonight. Now, I suspect my mind won't rest for thinking about you. As for my body...it hasn't got a chance in Hades of resting, let alone relaxing. It will be suffering an agony of eternal frustration...'

His eyes lanced her with a look which was anything but cold this time. It smouldered and burned its way into every pore in her body, igniting her once more with longing for him.

'I'm not going to make false promises, Paige,' he continued, while she tried not to gape, 'but I too am reaching a stage—and an age—when I'm looking for someone steady in my life. So if you meant what you said about wanting commitment, if you still feel anything for me at all…then come away with me…

'Please.'

Was it that fervent *please* which swayed her? Or had she been a goner from the moment he'd looked at her as if she was everything he desired in this world?

Whatever, how could she pass up a chance to make her dreams come true, even if it *was* only a slim chance? Paige wasn't a complete fool. After her experience with Jed, she knew some men would say and do anything sometimes to get a girl into bed.

And to keep her there.

'If I come with you,' she said, 'what will I tell my father?'

'Is that a yes?'

She tried to keep her face nonchalant, knowing men responded better to uncertainty, strange, perverse creatures that they were. 'I guess so. As I said earlier tonight, I've always fancied you. I suspect you could make me fall in love with you, if I gave you the chance,' she added with considerable irony. 'But I'm not making any false promises, either, Antonio. I want more from a relationship than just great sex.'

'But of course,' he replied smoothly. 'As for what your father will say, when have you ever cared about what he thought? Still, if you're worried, don't tell him. Just leave with me on Wednesday while he's at work, and leave a note behind, saying you're going away with a friend for a brief holiday. That way, he won't have to know about us, unless something comes of all this.'

'But what if something does? A relationship with me

might affect your position in the company. Have you thought of that?'

Clearly he hadn't, by the shocked look on his face.

'I'm not sure how or why that would be.'

Paige wished she hadn't brought the subject up now. It might give Antonio second thoughts. But surely he must know how ruthless her father could be sometimes.

'You saw how he was tonight,' she pointed out unhappily. 'He wasn't too thrilled with our going out together. He also might be very annoyed if he thinks we've deceived him. You should know better than anyone that my father is not a man who likes to be crossed. He might take it into his head to fire you, or something horrible like that!'

Antonio's frown cleared, and he slanted her a reassuring smile. 'Don't you worry your pretty little head about my position in the company. I can guarantee your father won't fire me over any relationship I might have with you. In fact I think he'd be pleased as punch to see you with a man who wants more from you than the obvious.'

Her stomach contracted. 'Do you *really* want more from me than that, Antonio?'

'You have no idea how much more, darling Paige,' he murmured, those sexy black eyes of his flicking over her once more.

Her eyes widened while her heart flip-flopped.

Well, how *could* she have any idea? All this was as unexpected as it was beguiling.

Wednesday suddenly seemed an eternity away.

'Do…do you still want to take me to dinner tonight?' she asked breathlessly.

He didn't answer for a few seconds. Perhaps it was

the tricky intersection they were going through at the time, but Paige suspected it wasn't traffic on his mind.

'I think,' he said finally, 'since you're so worried about your father's reaction...we might give dinner tonight a miss.'

'Oh...' She could not keep the disappointment out of her voice, or her face.

'Yes, I feel the same, believe me. But the waiting will make our time together all the better. Be ready for me at nine Wednesday morning.'

His words evoked the perturbingly erotic thought that she would always be ready for him.

'Don't forget,' she said thickly, 'I...I don't have much in the way of clothes.'

'You won't need much. Those casual things you mentioned you had at home should do. The weather forecast is for warm sunny weather for the next few days, but bring your jeans and jacket just in case it turns nasty. What you're wearing would be perfect if we stop off for dinner any night at some riverside restaurant.'

Paige's mind went to that gold lamé dress Antonio seemed to remember so well. Would she dare wear that for him one night? And if she did...what would he do?

Exactly the same as he's planning on doing to you *every* night, darling, came a decidedly cynical voice. That's what this little boat trip is basically all about. Sex. Sex. And more sex. That line about his reaching an age where he's looking for commitment is probably nothing more than exactly that. A line.

And you fell for it, didn't you, you fool.

But it was too late now. She'd said yes. And, if she were honest, wild horses would not stop her going off with Antonio this Wednesday. Her earlier resolve not to ever be alone with him again had been swept away by the slimmest of hopes, and the strongest of desires. The truth was the thought of having him all to herself for ten days in the privacy of a houseboat was just too exciting to resist.

And, who knew? Maybe something *would* come of it. Maybe.

CHAPTER TEN

ANTONIO'S bedside phone rang at seven the following morning. It persisted, despite his attempts to ignore it. Only one person, he finally accepted, would be so rude, or so persistent.

He snatched up the receiver and put it to his ear. 'Conrad,' he said firmly, 'I'm on holiday.'

'Only in a manner of speaking,' his boss replied wryly. 'So what happened last night? Evelyn tells me Paige got in very late.'

Antonio bristled. 'Is that one of your housekeeper's duties? Spying for you?'

'She's an employee.'

'Which means she's expected to do your bidding, regardless,' he said sarcastically.

'She's a naturally observant woman.'

Antonio thought of the atmosphere between Paige and the housekeeper last night and found himself very much on Paige's side.

'Was it Evelyn who told Lew about the incident with Paige by the pool all those years ago?' he asked.

'I would imagine so. But what in hell has that got to do with anything?' Conrad snapped. 'I rang up to find out about here and now, not past history. Did you or did you not make love to my daughter last night? Is she or is she not going to marry you?'

'I have no intention of answering either of those questions, Conrad. Do you ask for a blow by blow description of how I go about getting you the best deals for your programmes?'

'Of course not. I know how competent you are at everything you do. I trust you implicitly.'

'Then trust me in this regard. Believe me, when Paige actually agrees to marry me you'll be the first to know.'

'You sound pretty confident she will.'

Antonio was hopeful, but not arrogantly smug. It would be dangerous to presume she was a sure thing. Paige was a far more complex creature than he'd ever imagined.

And far more intriguing.

Frankly, he could not wait for Wednesday to come.

'She's coming away with me tomorrow for a holiday together,' he said a little testily. 'Is that good enough for you?'

'Good God, but you're a fast worker! A holiday together, eh? Where?'

'That's my secret.'

'You like to play a close hand, don't you, Antonio?'

'I like to run my own race, Conrad. And I *don't* like being blackmailed.'

'I'll bet you liked it well enough last night,' his boss chuckled, and suddenly Antonio hated the man.

'That's my private and personal business,' he said frostily. 'Which reminds me. I don't want you making any leading remarks about last night to Paige. Or asking her any awkward questions about me. Ironically, your daughter is worried for my career if we become involved. After your disapproving father act last night, she thought you wouldn't like the idea of our having a relationship.'

'I told you my opposition would work in your favour. Obviously it did.'

'I have no idea if it did or it didn't. I only know that I don't want Paige upset.'

'My God, you really care about her, don't you?'

Antonio almost laughed. Men like Conrad had no conception of what real caring was all about. Real caring was *not* what he was doing with Paige. Though, to be honest, he liked her a darned sight more than her father.

'I'm simply looking after my best interests, Conrad,' he refuted. 'A distressed Paige is not going to make for an amenable companion.'

'Mum's the word, then, my boy.'

'I'm not your boy, Conrad.'

'You're right. You're not. You've always been your own man, Antonio, and I admire that about you. That's why you were my first choice for a son-in-law.'

'Really? Well, with Brock Masters as my understudy, you'd better damned well hope I'm successful!'

'I'm confident you will be.'

'Whether I am or not is entirely in Paige's hands.'

'I doubt that, Antonio. I would think it's very much in *your* hands.' And he hung up.

Antonio felt a moment of sheer fury and frustration before slamming the receiver down as well.

Only then did Evelyn quietly replace her extension, a nasty little smile on her face.

Paige was still sound asleep at eight, when Evelyn went into her room with a breakfast tray. The housekeeper looked down at the girl's exquisitely beautiful profile and felt a jab of jealousy so violent that she was momentarily consumed with the urge to tip the whole tray over her lovely face.

But she kept her temper, and lowered the tray carefully onto the dressing table.

She'd always hated the girl. Hated the beauty she took for granted and the inherited wealth she scorned. Evelyn especially hated the fact Paige didn't seem to care about either of those things.

But the girl cared about Antonio.

Oh, yes…she cared about Antonio very much indeed. She would be devastated when she learnt Antonio had married her not out of love but out of ambition.

And the silly little fool *would* agree to marry him. It was as sure as night followed day. She wouldn't be able to resist her handsome hero. Antonio would be slipping a wedding ring on her finger in no time flat, and walking away as the CEO of Fortune Productions.

And Evelyn would be there, waiting in the wings, waiting for just the right moment to let the beautiful bride know exactly why her sexy Italian husband had married her.

It would be *after* the wedding, of course. No way would she be telling Paige before the big event. Evelyn wanted Antonio to get what he deserved before she set her cat among the pigeons. He was one of *her* kind, was Antonio. Born poor, and having to struggle to get somewhere in life, having to work hard and put up with bastards like Conrad blackmailing him.

Not like Madam Muck, who'd been born with everything. Looks. Money. Sex appeal.

But none of that was going to bring the bitch any happiness. Oh, what pleasure she would savour at the look in those big blue eyes once Paige knew the truth! It would be almost as good as the day she'd come home from boarding school and found out that mongrel dog was dead.

Evelyn wasn't concerned for her own fate after she'd dropped her bombshell. She was getting tired of being at the beck and call of people she despised. She'd squir-relled away a nice little nest-egg over the years she'd been at Fortune Hall. She didn't need Conrad and his money any more.

Oh, yes…her day would come. And when it did, her satisfaction would last for a long, long time.

Evelyn's presence in the room woke Paige with a jolt, her eyes flying open to find the woman glaring down at her with so much hatred a shudder of terror ran all through Paige.

'Oh!' she cried out, before she could gather herself. But once she did Paige hid her involuntary reaction be-hind a covering smile, pushing her hair casually back from her face as she propped herself up on one elbow.

'You startled me, Evelyn,' she said, determined never to give the other woman the satisfaction of seeing her rattled.

Paige was taken aback by the speed the housekeeper masked her true feelings as well, the hard gleam in her gaze giving way to a bland expression.

'Sorry,' she said. 'Just following orders about your meals. I knocked, but you didn't answer.'

Paige doubted the other woman had knocked at all. 'I could just have easily come downstairs and made my own breakfast,' she pointed out politely. 'You know I don't expect to be waited on like this.'

Evelyn's pale, thin lips tightened. 'But I don't take my orders from you, dear, do I? Your father's the boss of Fortune Hall. And he told me you were to be made to eat up.'

Her pinched lips unexpectedly loosened into the trav-esty of a smile. 'Can't have you getting too skinny and unappealing, can we? Italian men actually like women with a bit of meat on their bones, you know,' she added as she turned and walked from the room, this time banging the door shut after her.

Paige just lay there for a moment, trying to get a grip on her galloping heart. That crack about Italian men had been pointed and nasty, but she couldn't really know anything. The woman was just trying to get a rise out of her. And to make her feel lousy and unattractive.

But she refused to rise to the bait.

She might have lost of a couple of pounds these last few days out of stress, but she felt confident she wasn't too skinny. Antonio certainly hadn't found anything unattractive in her body last night.

Sighing, Paige lay back and thought of Antonio, her beautiful, handsome Antonio. She hoped and prayed he wasn't playing her for a fool, like Jed had.

There again, he was nothing like Jed, was he? Except superficially. Ironically, it was his superficial likenesses to Antonio which had attracted her to Jed in the first place. Jed too was tall and darkly good-looking. He was sophisticated and successful, intelligent and charming.

But, when all was said and done, he didn't have Antonio's depth. Or his honesty. Or his sense of honour.

Paige frowned. Those last two thoughts were at total odds with her doubts about Antonio, weren't they? If he were so honest and honourable, then he would not lie to get her into bed with him, would he? To be fair, she had no evidence that he had ever lied to any woman in his life, not even the ones he'd bedded and swiftly abandoned. If he said he was now interested in commitment, then he probably was, wasn't he? If he claimed he'd always been attracted to her, then he *had*!

A huge smile blossomed on Paige's face. What a silly girl she was, worrying about Antonio's intentions.

Antonio wasn't a creep. Or a conman. He was a gentleman through and through.

Maybe he wasn't in love with her…yet. But that didn't mean he wasn't open to the experience.

Optimism burst through her like a thousand firecrackers and she sat up. She would *make* him fall in love with her. She would show him that life with her by his side would be so wonderful he would wonder how he'd coped without her. By the time those ten days were up, she was going to have him begging her to stay with him. He might even ask her to marry him!

CHAPTER ELEVEN

ANTONIO had barely brought the Jag to a halt outside the high security wall which hid Fortune Hall from the main road when Paige came running through a side gate, dressed in blue jeans and a black jacket, a large colourful sports bag clutched in her right hand and a roomy black handbag slung over her left shoulder.

His stomach tightened at the glorious sight of her long fair hair flying out behind her, glowing in the morning sun. Her lovely face looked young and fresh and free of make-up. But that was possibly an illusion, since the bruise on her cheek was almost invisible—no doubt the result of some clever concealer.

Still, she looked about sixteen, the image enhanced by the white shirt beneath the black jacket, a garment not dissimilar to the school blouse she'd been wearing the first day he'd seen her, getting off that train at Central.

Even then, Antonio recalled wryly, he hadn't been able to take his eyes off her. Nothing had changed, it seemed. The desires she evoked in him were just as dark, and just as distracting. What was it about her which could disarm him so, and deflect him from the mission at hand? Why did she make him feel so guilty all the time when all he was doing was giving her what she said she wanted? Great sex. And commitment.

Hell, he'd already changed his mind about divorcing her later on. Now that was *real* commitment, wasn't it? And if she wanted to have children, well, that was all right by him too. What more could she ask of a husband?

115

Antonio supposed the guilt came from that four-letter word which simply wasn't going to come into the equation.

Love.

He didn't love her, and be damned if he was going to tell her he did!

Plastering a welcoming smile on his face, he opened the car door and began to climb out.

Oh, God, he was just so gorgeous, Paige thought as Antonio climbed out from behind the wheel and walked round the front of the car, smiling at her.

Antonio didn't smile a lot. He wasn't that type of man. But when he did, and his almost forbidding seriousness was momentarily lightened, he looked even more handsome, if that were possible.

'I'll take that,' he said, and reached for her bag.

Paige mumbled a thank-you and did her best not to ogle.

For he was wearing jeans. She'd never seen him in jeans before. Never seen him looking so...accessible.

Up top, he was wearing a casual blue T-shirt beneath an equally casual navy jacket, the kind with a band around the hips and a zipper up the front. The zipper was undone and the sides flapped open as he walked, showing the broad muscles in his chest and the hip-hugging style of the jeans. His still damp hair looked extra black and glossy in the sunlight, and not slicked back as severely as usual. It looked as if he'd run an impatient hand through it instead of combing it properly. There were kinks and waves all over the place, which made her want to run her hands through it as well.

'This is pretty heavy,' Antonio commented as he

slung her bag into the boot. 'I told you you wouldn't need much.'

She flushed a little at the thought of some of the things she'd brought with her. That gold lamé dress was there, as well as that provocative little pink bikini she'd been wearing the day she'd thrown herself at Antonio. It had anchoring ties on the hips and between the breasts. With Antonio admitting his fascination for undoing ties on her, one could imagine what would happen if she dared wear it.

Paige had spent a couple of breathless hours last night fantasising over *that* little scenario!

'Oh, you know what girls are like,' she tossed back as they both climbed in the car and belted up. 'They can never make up their minds about what to wear, or what to pack. Or anything, really,' she added in a rather silly fashion.

When Antonio threw her a sharp glance, she knew she'd said the wrong thing. Lord, she must have sounded like some empty-headed twit!

'I hope you don't change your mind about being with me when we're miles up the river,' he said drily, and started up the engine.

Paige took a deep breath and set about redeeming herself. 'I won't, Antonio,' she said, in a far more serious tone, her eyes seeking out his and holding them. 'You have no idea how much I've been looking forward to seeing you again. And being with you again...'

His eyes warmed at her words. 'If you've been feeling anything like I've been feeling, my darling Paige,' he said wryly, 'then I would say I *do* have a very good idea.' His head swung back to the road and the car accelerated away from the kerb.

'Now, don't chat to me till we get through the city,

there's a good girl,' he added as he eased out into the line of cars. 'I'm not used to driving in morning traffic and I don't want anything to happen to stop us getting where we're going today. I'm already distracted enough by having you sit next to me. If you say things like you've just said, and look at me like you've just done, I'll run up the back of a truck in no time.'

Paige did as she was bid, hugging his flattering words to herself during the next twenty minutes, wallowing in the excitement and anticipation of the ten days ahead. Antonio bypassed the city centre and whizzed across the harbour via the tunnel, zooming up the other side with no time-consuming hold-ups.

Antonio was the first to speak, while the car was idling at a set of red lights around Chatswood.

'Did your father say anything to you yesterday?'

'About us, you mean?'

'Yes.'

'No. I didn't see him at all. He was gone by the time I got up in the morning, and he went out for dinner last night. This morning, I avoided going downstairs till he was gone. But I sent a fax to his office just before I snuck out to meet you.' No way had she been going to give Evelyn any letter to hand to her father. Paige didn't trust her not to steam it open.

The infernal woman had hovered all yesterday, clearly trying to work out what was going on. When she'd briefly gone out to do some shopping mid-morning, Paige had raced downstairs to her father's study, looked up Antonio's home number and given Antonio a short ring, telling him not to call her at home and ask for her, in case Evelyn answered the phone and recognised his voice. She was pleased Antonio hadn't thought her paranoid.

'What did you say in the fax?' he asked.

'That I was going away up the coast with a friend for ten days. That I would be coming back home afterwards, but only till I find a new place to live.' Going to Queensland was now out of the question. She would want to be in Sydney whenever Antonio was in town.

He shot her a sharp look. 'Is that really your plan?'

'Well...yes. You must know by now I can't stand living at home for long.' It was a bit too optimistic to think Antonio would ask her to accompany him back to Europe after only ten days.

'I see,' was all he said, and fell silent. The lights turned green and he drove on, a little more slowly than before, as though his mind was elsewhere and working overtime.

Paige wondered what he was thinking, then decided to find out. 'Don't you want me to?' she asked.

'That depends,' he said brusquely.

'On what?'

'On what kind of people you move in with, I guess. According to your father, you have a habit of always choosing male flatmates who invariably end up sharing your bedroom. On one occasion he was horrified to learn you were flatting with two men, and *both* boasted they knew you intimately.'

Paige laughed. She couldn't help it.

Antonio threw her a truly scandalised look, and Paige reluctantly decided it was time to clear the air where her past history with men were concerned. She didn't give a damn what her father thought of her. He could hardly stand in judgement of her sexual behaviour with all the mistresses he had stashed around the world.

But she didn't want Antonio believing she'd jumped into bed with every man she'd lived with, despite her having done nothing to dissuade him from this erroneous belief the other night.

But the situation had changed from that, hadn't it?

'I presume you're talking about Paul and Les?' she said.

'Don't recognise the names,' Antonio said stiffly. 'But if they're the two men you enjoyed a *ménage à trois* with, then, yes, I mean Paul and Les.'

Paige sighed. If she'd known her father was going to discuss his private investigator's findings in detail with Antonio, she'd never have let the creep get the wrong idea in the first place. But at the time she'd been so annoyed with her father she hadn't cared what *he* thought.

Clearly, Antonio carried a lot of misconceptions about her. She could only hope she could rectify some of them.

'Paul and Les were gay,' she said firmly. 'All my male flatmates over the past few years have been gay, Antonio. Gay men, I eventually learnt from hard-won experience, are nicer friends than girls, and safer than heterosexual males. If you must know, the only man I've actually lived with since leaving home is Brad. Till Jed, of course. I *was* going to live with him, but you know what happened there.'

She could feel his eyes upon her, disbelief and shock in his gaze.

'Better watch the road,' she advised drily when they began to drift towards the next lane, where a white taxi carrying two worried-looking passengers was coming alongside.

Antonio swore, but kept his eyes glued ahead after that. His knuckles, however, went white on the wheel and his shoulders bunched up. His straight black brows bunched up as well.

'Are you saying you encouraged your flatmates to lie to Lew about your relationships with them?' he growled.

'Well…yes,' she confessed. 'Sort of. I…er…always warned them Lew would be around, and told them to say whatever he wanted to hear. Paul and Les particularly enjoyed themselves, I think, pretending to be my live-in studs. Of course, they were very macho-looking guys—as are a lot of gay men. I often used them as cover when a guy was bothering me.'

Her explanation didn't entirely satisfy Antonio, judging by the lingering scowl on his face. 'So when you told me you always liked to live with your boyfriends you lied as well?'

'Actually…no, I didn't.'

'That doesn't make sense, Paige,' he said irritably. 'Not if by *boyfriend* you mean lover as well.'

'Yes, that's what I mean.'

'Oh, for pity's sake,' he exploded, the car shifting ground dangerously again when he lanced her with a savage look. 'You can't expect me to believe you've only slept with two men in your whole life, especially when one of those two was a oncer!'

'No,' she said coolly, her heart sinking at this open display of disdain and disbelief. 'I've actually slept with three. You're forgetting yourself, Antonio.'

He swore. Violently. Then fell silent once more.

'Don't you believe me?' she challenged into the highly charged atmosphere.

He shook his head frustratedly, then sighed a resigned sigh. 'I suppose I must, because I can't find a single, solitary reason for you to lie.'

'So why look for one?'

He stared grimly at the road ahead for a few seconds

before nodding up and down. 'Very well,' he decided aloud, and much to her relief. 'I won't!'

He glanced over at her, black eyes narrowed and thoughtful. 'You're a wicked little devil, do you know that? Fancy letting your father believe you lived with all those men. You worried the life out of him. Not to mention me...'

As much as she was pleased by his accepting her word, she couldn't believe that last statement! 'Oh, come now, Antonio, you never worried about me. Not really.'

'I was worried sick when you first ran away from home.'

Paige could not have been more stunned.

'I felt so lousy for hurting you the way I did. And for saying such thoughtlessly cruel things. When Lew found you, and Conrad sent me to bring you home, I happily went, hoping to have the opportunity to apologise and make things right. Admittedly, when I saw you weren't exactly suffering from a broken heart, my worries evaporated somewhat. Which reminds me. What happened between you and Brad? You never did tell anyone when you finally came home.'

'Nothing happened. We were very happy together.'

'So why did you leave him?'

'I didn't. He died.'

'Good God! How?'

'He had a surfing accident. Broke his neck.'

'And you didn't tell any of us? Not your father? Or me?'

'I didn't think either of you would care.'

'I see...' He threw her a puzzled look. 'And is that why you didn't become involved with anyone else for such a long time? Because you'd lost the love of your life?'

Paige opened her mouth to tell him the whole truth, but then closed it again. She sensed it was way too soon to tell Antonio something that heavy. He might run a mile under the burden of her unrequited love for him. Best keep things light.

'You could put it like that,' she said instead. 'But I'm well and truly over Brad's death now.'

'If you say so…' He sounded unconvinced.

'I say so,' she said, then smiled over at him.

His returning smile was slow in coming, but warm when it arrived. 'You're full of surprises, aren't you?'

'I hope so.'

'Why do you say that?'

'Because I wouldn't want to bore you. I have a feeling you're a man who's easily bored. Especially with a woman.'

'Is that so? And on what do you base that assumption?'

'On the passing parade of women in your life so far.'

'I'm not the heartless womaniser you think, Paige. The women I've had all knew the score. As I said…I don't make false promises. If you must know, I was in love once too. Not long before I came to work for your father. Lauren didn't die, but she let me down. Badly. She said she loved me, but she didn't. Frankly, I still feel pretty bitter over her betrayal.'

Paige heard the hard edge in his voice. This was something she hadn't envisaged, that Antonio had been suffering from a broken heart all these years.

The savagery of her resentment over this Lauren woman tore into her breast with a dark violence she had trouble hiding. It was as well Antonio was driving, with his eyes straight ahead, and couldn't see the fire burn momentarily in her own eyes.

'She must have been very beautiful,' she heard herself saying in a hard, flat little voice.

'She was,' he admitted curtly, then just dropped the subject.

Paige could not find the courage or the will to bring her up again. But Lauren's shadow moved into the car, drying up any further conversation and dampening Paige's earlier optimism.

It wasn't till the city was long left behind and the first glimpse of water came into view on the right that the depressive atmosphere lifted. And it was Antonio's doing.

'Nearly there now,' he announced, the brightness in his voice very welcome.

Paige responded with a blinding smile of relief. 'Tell me about this houseboat,' she urged.

'Seeing will be worth a thousand words.'

'You don't sound as though you know what to expect.'

'I do and I don't. They featured it briefly on a programme on television I saw once, but I've never actually seen one, or been on one before. Still, the man on the phone assured me ours was the latest in luxury, and easier to drive than a shopping trolley. The one I've hired is their one and only honeymoon houseboat.'

Paige's eyes rounded. 'He thinks we're on our honeymoon?'

'No. But the honeymoon houseboat is the most luxurious houseboat they own, and it's kitted out just for two. Why, would you like people to think we're on our honeymoon?'

'No. I don't like lies.'

'Neither do I. We're just lovers, then.'

'Illicit lovers,' she suggested mischievously. 'Sneaking off for a dirty ten days together.'

'Mmm. I like the sound of that,' he murmured, and gave her a look which melted every bone in her body. 'Is being provocative part of your plan not to bore me?'

'That's for me to know and you to find out.'

'I aim to find out everything there is to find out about you during the next ten days, Paige Fortune.'

'And I you, Antonio Scarlatti,' she countered, her heart going like a threshing machine.

He stared at her before switching his eyes back onto the road, and the bridge ahead. Once again, Paige was proving a vastly different person from the one he'd always imagined her to be. He'd glimpsed a hint of hidden depths the other night, but today was a real revelation!

What further shocks lay in store for him? What other preconceptions were going to be smashed?

He hadn't known that her first lover had been tragically killed; he had been taken aback by the news, then startled by the unexpected jab of jealousy which had accompanied Paige's confession that she'd been heartbroken over him all these years. Maybe that was the reason for her tears on the two occasions that she'd given herself sexually to another man. Maybe she was remembering what it had been like with the only man she'd ever really loved. Antonio conceded Brad must have been a fantastic lover to have taught her so well.

Again, this thought brought more jealousy. Or was it envy?

Envy, Antonio decided sensibly. Jealousy smacked of an emotional involvement, which simply wasn't the case. Clearly, he envied Paige the experience of making love to a person she'd loved and who'd loved her wholeheartedly in return. In hindsight, it was an experience which had eluded him. And would continue to do so, now that he was no longer capable of contributing his side of such an equation.

Not that he should be complaining. Sex with Paige had been great the other night, the greatest he'd ever had—even better than with Lauren. Frankly, Lauren had been a bit unimaginative in bed. And selfish.

Lauren...

He wished he hadn't brought the woman up in his mind. He hated thinking about her. When he did, he always felt like a failure. Antonio hated failure.

His eyes slid over to the beautiful, sexy girl sitting beside him and his resolve strengthened. He wasn't going to fail this time. He was determined to win, not only Paige's hand in marriage, but her heart as well. He was going to have it all this time. The job *and* the woman.

'You're not watching the road,' Paige chided.

'I can't help it,' came his rueful confession. 'I can't take my eyes off you.'

'Well, I suggest you do,' she pointed out drily. 'Because the turn-off to Brooklyn's coming up fast.'

Antonio swore, then expertly weaved his way over to take the turn-off, a surge of adrenalin kicking in, as well as a surge of something else.

'I hope you've brought that gold dress,' he said.

'What gold dress?'

His head whipped round to find she was laughing at him, those big blue eyes of hers dancing with devil lights.

Incredible eyes, those eyes. They could look oh, so innocent and vulnerable one moment, then oh, so sexy and knowing the next. At that moment they glittered and gleamed, taunting and teasing him with the promise of erotic delights he'd only glimpsed the other night.

He was almost grateful to dear old Brad. The man had obviously introduced her to sex with a joy and lack of inhibition which could only be praised in his absence. Even his untimely passing was a source of gratitude to Antonio, because it had kept Paige's natural sexuality bottled up for years in her grief, all the stronger now that it had been released. That idiot Waltham could have been Paige's sexual genie, but he'd been a fool. His failure had become Antonio's gain.

'Just you wait,' he told her with feigned displeasure. 'Teases get their comeuppance.'

'Promises, promises,' she said, with a toss of her gorgeous golden hair.

'No false promises from me, honey. When I say something, I mean it.'

'Really! So what form does a comeuppance take?'

'I think the word speaks for itself,' he quipped, enjoying himself enormously. 'When it comes up, you'll be the first to know!'

CHAPTER TWELVE

AN HOUR had passed after their arrival at the Marina at Brooklyn, and now they were ready to start cruising the river in the incredibly compact yet truly luxurious houseboat. Twenty minutes had been spent watching a how-to video, which had covered everything navigational and operational they might want to know, and the rest of the time had been taken in being shown through the houseboat itself, with all its fittings and fixtures, storage spaces and supplies. The controls had had to be explained, plus all the other simple yet important workings.

Finally, with their luggage aboard, and a brochure and map in Paige's hand, Antonio had started the incredibly quiet engine, and angled them safely away from the dock.

Paige could not believe the feeling of exhilaration which swept through her as they headed for open waters. Putting the map and brochure down, she went out on the front deck for a while, to admire the beauty and breadth of the river, before returning inside to where Antonio was standing at the wheel, one of those rare but truly happy smiles on his face.

'This is so much more fun than I thought it would be!' she exclaimed, combing her wind-blown hair back from her face with her fingers. 'I feel like we're going on an adventure together!'

Antonio was amazed to find he felt the same away. There again, going anywhere with Paige, he suspected, would be an adventure. She was so full of life and the unexpected. She was constantly surprising him.

The houseboat had surprised him as well. In all honesty, he hadn't expected to like it as much as he did. He'd come up with the houseboat idea on the spur of the moment, because he'd wanted to take Paige somewhere right away from everyone. He'd seen a programme on TV about cruising the Hawkesbury in various craft some time back, and been awed by the untamed majesty of the river, with its wide waterways, interesting inlets and large unspoiled surrounds.

Apparently, it hadn't changed much since the days of the early explorers, when aborigines had inhabited the caves in the rugged hills through which the river wound its leisurely way in scenic splendour. There were some houses dotted along the more habitable sections of riverbank, and the occasional restaurant and supply stop to cater for the holidaymakers, but on the whole the river remained as it had been for hundreds of years. With its proximity to Sydney another attractive facet—no plane flight necessary to get there—Antonio had filed it away in his mind as a possible idea for a relaxing holiday.

Once Paige had agreed to come, however, he'd had to set about making his proposed holiday real. He'd spent a good hour yesterday morning on the phone, negotiating. It had still cost him a small fortune, first to hire the honeymoon version, then to have the darned thing fully equipped with everything from food and wine to extra linen and towels. He'd had to offer a bonus to have it all done for him that same day.

Late last night he'd been thinking he could have taken Paige to the honeymoon suite in the most exclusive hotel in Sydney for the same price. But once he saw what he'd paid for—including Paige's reaction—he felt certain he'd done the right thing.

Her beautiful blue eyes had shone as brightly as the sky overhead, and she'd fairy gushed with delight over everything, from the weather to the river to the houseboat. *Especially* the houseboat. Antonio had been more than impressed himself, both by the furnishings and the design.

Divided into three living areas, it had a stylish sitting room up front, nautical in flavour to complement the wheel, a dining area in the middle, with rich pine cupboards and green granite tops, and a master bedroom at the back, all blue, complete with a cleverly compact *en suite* bathroom. The sky-blue quilted bed was very wide, and there were porthole windows above the built-in pine bedhead, and a massive skylight in the ceiling above. Outside, there was a sundeck up top, and decks front and back. A small dinghy was tied up at the back steps— useful, they'd been told, for rowing ashore, either for fresh supplies or maybe a picnic at any of the small coves and beaches which lined the river.

Antonio wasn't so sure about picnics, but he intended taking Paige to dinner to at least one of the excellent restaurants dotted along the river. He was looking forward to seeing her in that saucy little gold dress again.

And to seeing her *out* of it.

Such thinking sent his eyes sliding over to where Paige was standing at the viewing window, a metre or so away. She'd finally taken off that black jacket, but she'd pulled the white shirt out from her waist and it was hanging loosely over her hips, hiding her figure from his gaze.

Suddenly, he wanted her closer. Much closer.

'Come here,' he commanded softly, and took one hand off the wheel to beckon her to join him.

Paige only hesitated a second before moving into the gap he'd made between his body and the wheel, her back against his stomach and chest. His hand returned to the wheel, completing the circle his body created around her. With a contented sigh, she leant back against him, her eyes closing.

It wasn't a sexual moment for Paige—though perhaps Antonio might have thought differently. The feelings which flooded through her were ones of peace, not passion. It felt as if she'd finally come home, finally found where she belonged.

With Antonio.

'Better not relax too much,' he advised drily. 'You're supposed to be watching the waterways, as well as telling me things I'm already beginning to forget.'

'Such as what?' she murmured, her eyes half opening to glance upwards into his.

'Such as what side is port and what's starboard. And which side we were supposed to pass other craft on. You see, there's this big boat coming straight for us, and I think it's time for evasive action.'

She cried out in fright, her eyes snapping forward. There was indeed a huge yacht coming towards them, and it wasn't making any attempt to shift course. Fortunately, Paige had concentrated on that part of the video which explained the basic rules of right of way.

'Right!' she ordered. 'You must always pass on the right. And always give way to sail.'

'Aye-aye!' Antonio returned, already turning the wheel.

The yacht was finally doing the same, and they passed with plenty of room to spare.

'Congratulations,' Antonio praised, and bent to kiss the top of her head. 'You just passed your first test as first mate with flying colours.'

Ridiculous to feel so pleased. But she hadn't been on the end of much praise in her life.

'This is going to be such fun!'

'Mmm. Now that we're almost in the middle of the river, we have to make a vital decision. Should we turn left, and head up-river under the bridge? Or right, and go down-river towards Broken Bay?'

'I'll have to consult the map again,' Paige said. 'I left it over there on the coffee table. Excuse me. You'll have to let me out.'

'No, don't worry about it. I've decided to go down-river for today.' And he turned the wheel to the right.

'Why?'

'There's more water that way. And it doesn't look as crowded. I'd like to find us a nice private mooring as soon as possible and drop anchor for the afternoon. It's such a lovely day. We could have lunch, then loll round on the top deck for a while.'

Paige laughed. 'I can't imagine you lolling around anywhere.'

'I have to admit I haven't done a lot of lolling lately. Wow, now that's a tongue-twister! Still, I'm very much in need of some serious lolling. You know what they say. All work and no play makes Antonio a dull boy.'

'You? Dull? Never!'

'I have my dull moments, believe me,' he drawled. 'But now is not going to be one of them. So turn round and kiss me.'

'What?' Paige gasped.

'You heard what I said. Do as your captain tells you. Mutiny will not be tolerated. It requires the same punishment as teasing.'

Paige gulped, her peaceful, platonic pleasure giving way to passion with an astonishing speed. Her heart began to pound and a wild heat ignited deep inside her body, showing her how swiftly Antonio could change her mood from one of fun and friendship to one of wildly driven desire.

Slowly, she turned in his arms, fearful of seeming too easy, yet compelled to do whatever he wanted. Because *she* wanted it too. Instantly. Intensely.

Kiss me, he commanded. Oh, God...

Her eyes lifted at the same time as her body, widening as her lips moved closer, then squeezing tightly shut when contact was made.

She began kissing him, softly at first, then with more pressure, urging him to open his mouth, dying for the feel of his tongue.

She moaned when his lips remained firmly shut, her mouth finally lifting, her eyes fluttering open with dismay and reproach.

'I don't think this was a very wise idea,' was all he said, his own eyes narrowed and glittering.

Paige had a pretty good idea what he meant. She could *feel* it, pressing hard into her belly. Yet with her blood pounding and her head whirling she wasn't thinking about wisdom. She was wanting him far too much.

'I think perhaps you should go unpack,' he advised drily.

She didn't want to go anywhere. She wanted to stay here in his arms. But she gradually saw that that would be very cruel. It wasn't as though they could *do* anything right then and there, other than make the situation worse.

'I'll go change, shall I?' she said sensibly, but with a little sigh in her voice. 'Then see about putting something together for our lunch.' The kitchen cupboards were full of supplies, with fresh food in the gas-operated fridge.

'Good thinking,' he said crisply. 'Put a bottle of white wine in to chill as well. Oh, and hand me that map of the river before you go. I'll look for a suitable mooring.'

'Right,' she returned, just as crisply, and ducked under his arms. But as she handed him the map and hurried off Paige's main feeling was frustration. She hadn't wanted to go. She'd wanted to keep kissing him, wanted to touch him, wanted to...

Her face flushed as the thought hit, her stomach tightening as she realised Antonio could have asked her to do that, and she would have. When Jed had tried to force her head down there, she'd been so revolted she'd cried out like a banshee and flown from his bed.

It wasn't revulsion which flooded her when she thought of doing that to Antonio, but excitement.

Yet she was grateful he hadn't asked, in a way. It showed he respected her feelings, and that his interest in her wasn't solely sexual.

Paige threw her suitcase onto the high wide bed and began to unpack. When she came to the pink bikini, she didn't hesitate for long. As much as she liked Antonio feeling other things for her than sexual ones, she didn't want his taking this new respect *too* far.

Alone at the wheel, Antonio let out a long shuddering breath. What in hell had he thought he was doing, asking her to kiss him? He was in the middle of a damned river, steering a damned houseboat, hardly the best place for a romantic interlude.

Although it hadn't been romance he'd been thinking of once she'd kissed him so eagerly, had it? The moment her lips had met his, a black lust had invaded his veins with the speed of a lethal injection. Thank God he'd kept his stupid damned mouth shut, because if he hadn't all would have been lost!

Oh, he had no doubt he could have coerced Paige into ridding him of his instant and very painful erection. It had been obvious she was *very* turned on. But neither method which came to mind would have endeared him to her afterwards. There was a time and place for such selfishness, and this wasn't it. His mission over the next ten days wasn't solely sex and seduction, but the making of a real relationship.

'Remember this, Antonio?'

Her voice startled him, and the map he hadn't even begun to examine fluttered from his fingers onto the floor. Antonio knew, before he even glanced over his shoulder, that he was in trouble again. When he did, his muttered oath told it all.

Dear God, *more* bows! Two on her hips, a third between her luscious breasts, all three responsible for keeping that wretched excuse for a swimming costume from falling from her oh, so beautiful body.

Antonio had seen some provocative bikinis in his life, but this was something else. It always had been, but it seemed even more so, now that Paige's figure had matured.

Ironic that the colour was shocking pink. The colour almost matched the wild pink in its wearer's cheeks as she stood there before him in an obviously aroused state. Once again the temptation was there, to have her do things which his aching flesh craved.

'Now I know why I had trouble keeping my hands off you all those years ago,' he muttered darkly.

'Did you really?' she asked breathlessly, and actually began to walk towards him, movement doing things to those inadequately encased breasts which would have corrupted a saint.

'How can you doubt it? But let me warn you, Paige, if you keep coming over here, things will happen which we both might regret later. I can see the headlines now,' he added ruefully. '"Houseboat runs amok! Naked lovers found drowned in river!"'

Her approach was halted, not by his warning, but by another houseboat suddenly passing close on their port side. A man was behind the wheel and three teenage children were sitting on the sunlit upper deck, swinging their feet against the sides and watching the world go by. They spied Antonio and Paige through the wide front viewing window and waved. One of the two boys wolf-whistled. All of them stared.

Antonio lifted his hand to wave back. Paige stood rooted to the spot, blushing wildly.

Soon they were alone again.

'Well?' he said. 'What are you going to do?' He was no longer capable of resisting, if she insisted.

'I...I think I'll go cover up with some shorts and a proper top.'

His body didn't like the idea, but his brain did. 'Sensible girl.'

'Do you *want* me to be sensible, Antonio?'

'No.'

'Good,' she said, and with a smug little smile on her flushed face she whirled and left him.

He stared after her for a moment, then laughed.

'Just you wait till we're safely stopped somewhere!' he called after her.

She popped her head back into the sitting room, but only her head. 'Can I expect my first comeuppance?'

'You can depend on it.'

'Before or after lunch?'

'Both.'

'Oooh…' Her lips pursed into a provocative little circle.

'Yes, that too.'

'What too?'

'That's for me to know and you to find out. You see, I have a feeling you're the sort of girl who's easily bored with a man. Can't have that if we're to make a commitment to each other!'

Paige was on a sexual and emotional high for the forty minutes it took Antonio to find a mooring in a nice, quiet little cove. Her body burned for him, and her emotions soared.

He wanted her, plus he wanted to make a commitment to her. Her love for Antonio no longer had to be ignored, or hidden or even controlled! Her feelings could be allowed to fly, to reach the dizzying heights which she'd always known were possible.

She was just finishing making up two lunch plates of cold meat and salad when Antonio came inside from where he'd been securing the houseboat at the mooring. He stopped and just stood there, staring at her and saying nothing, a look of dark hunger in his hot black eyes.

'What?' she said, flattered and flustered at the same time.

'Have you still got that bikini on under those shorts and top?'

'Yes. Why?'

'Care to join me for a quick dip before we eat?'

'In the river? You have to be joking! It'll be freezing at this time of year.'

'That's the idea. Cool us off a bit so we can eat first.'

'Are you that hungry?'

'Mmm.' His eyes lanced hers, then raked down her body, seemingly stripping it as he went. Every nerve-ending in Paige's body began to vibrate, every erotic zone immediately went on alert. Surely he couldn't expect her to calmly eat lunch when all she wanted was him, not food.

'Yes,' he growled at last. 'Yes, I'm that hungry.'

'Oh…' Her dismay was as sharp as her disappointment. Her eyes slid away from his, confusion in her heart.

'So forget the damned salad and take them off.'

Her eyes whipped back to his, and widened. 'What?'

'The shorts and the top,' he ordered brusquely. 'Not the bikini. *I* want the pleasure of doing that.'

'H…here?'

'Right here. And right now.'

Her shorts had an elastic waist, and were easy to remove, but she still fumbled a little as she slipped them down over her hips. Letting them drop to the floor, she stepped very carefully out of them. Even then she swayed a little, and had to grab the cupboard-edge for support. The T-shirt had to be removed over her head. She felt as if she was doing it in slow motion, her breasts strangely heavy as the action of her arms lifted them upwards, pressing them together.

It was weird, that second or two when her face and eyes were hidden from his yet her body not. She could still feel his eyes upon her, feel the heatwaves of his desire hitting her like lightning bolts. They ignited a return desire so strong that nothing would be allowed to stand in the way of its consummation this time. Not even people passing by.

By the time she tossed the top aside and stood there, watching him watching her, she was his, totally, to do with as he willed.

'God help me,' was all he said as he visually coveted her curves.

'God help *me*, don't you mean?' she countered.

'Yes,' he rasped, nodding slowly. 'Yes, I would think that might be so. Now come here,' he commanded roughly.

She walked straight into his arms, and a kiss which bore no resemblance to the one she'd given him earlier. No tentativeness. Or tenderness. Just raw savagery, plundering her mouth and every misconception she'd ever had about lovemaking. And love.

For if this was love that she was feeling for this man, then it was the most dangerous emotion in the world. So violent in its intensity, and so powerful in its potential for self-destruction. Neither experience with Antonio the other night had prepared her for this...this darkly powerful and all-consuming passion.

She began kissing him back with an oral assault as brutal as his, raking her hands up into his hair, digging her nails into his scalp. He took her hair in return, winding it round one large hand and pulling her head backwards so that her mouth burst from his, her neck and back arching away from his body. With his free hand he tugged the bow between her breasts, Paige gasping when she felt the top part, then fall right away from her body.

Their eyes met for a moment, and then he kissed her again, snaking his free arm around her waist and yanking her hard against him. Her own arms wound tightly around his neck, her naked breasts and erect nipples rubbing against his chest.

She moaned under the thrust of his tongue, and the pressure of his penis against her stomach. It was so easy to imagine how it would feel, doing to *her* what his tongue was doing to her mouth.

Before she knew it her feet had been lifted slightly off the floor and he was carrying her with him into the bedroom, her body still clasped tightly to his. But, once there, he disengaged his mouth and laid her down across the bed, where she lay in a helpless state of dazed arousal while he stripped himself, then stripped her.

Stripping her proved amazingly quick, the bows on her hips as ineffective a barrier as the one between her breasts.

Paige's heart stopped when he tugged away the scrap of pink, her face heating when he just stared down at her for what felt like ages.

'You're so beautiful,' he said at last, and with unexpectedly gentle hands began caressing her where his eyes had been.

Paige moaned softly, then bit her bottom lip. When he replaced his hands with his lips and tongue she *did* cry out…with the sharpest, sweetest pleasure she had ever known.

Yet Jed's attempt to do the same had made her feel physically sick.

Antonio's mouth made her feel nothing but beautiful and sensual and loved. Oh, yes, there was love in his lips, and love in her heart for him.

'Antonio,' she groaned, when that love began reaching for a physical release.

'Antonio, please…'

When he stopped, and drove deep into her burning, throbbing flesh, she cried out his name again. It echoed through the houseboat, and possibly across the waters. And he answered her, calling out *her* name as they came together, telling her in that shatteringly intimate moment how special she was to him, how it was *her* he wanted to make love with, not just any woman.

'Oh, Antonio,' she murmured as she hugged him to her afterwards. 'That was wonderful. You were wonderful. Just wonderful...'

CHAPTER THIRTEEN

WONDERFUL.

She was the one who was wonderful, Antonio was to think many times over the next few days. A wonderful companion. A wonderful lover. And a wonderful listener. She made him want to confide in her, to share things which up till now he'd kept hidden from others for fear of being denigrated or laughed at.

A couple of days ago he'd actually found himself telling her all about his background, right back to his birth in a small village in the south of Italy, the illegitimate son of the black sheep daughter of his family. Named Gina, his mother had been a real disgrace, running round with lots of different men from the time she was fourteen. When she'd fallen pregnant, at eighteen, she hadn't even been able to point a definite finger at any man, though most of the males for miles had run for cover. The only clue to his father was that he must have been very tall, which had rather ruled out the men in the village. Possibly a tourist, the villagers had speculated. Gina had a penchant for tall men. And short men. Fat men. Rich men. Poor men.

Ashamed by the never-ending gossip, her peasant parents had finally thrown their notorious daughter and her bastard son out of the house. The man-mad Gina had gone to Rome, where she'd tried to raise Antonio herself, but it had been hard, and she'd finally turned to prostitution to make ends meet. Antonio recalled lying in a small bed against a thin cold wall, trying not to cry as he listened to the sounds of his mother being used or beaten, or both, in the next room. In the end, one night, when he was seven, she'd been bashed to death by a drunken client.

'Oh, you poor darling!' Paige had cried out at that point in his story, and had hugged him close. 'You poor, poor darling.'

He'd hugged her back and understood, perhaps for the first time, why he'd always reacted so badly to violence against women.

He'd had no trouble telling her the rest of his childhood story after that: how his grandparents had been forced to take him in, but how they'd felt ashamed of his existence. By the time he was twelve he'd been shipped off to distant relatives in Australia. They hadn't wanted him, either, but they'd tolerated his presence and at least sent him to school, where he'd put all his energies into learning languages, something he had a natural talent for. He'd left their home as soon as possible, much to their relief, and hadn't been in contact since. His elderly grandparents, he'd found out some time back, were long dead.

Paige had expressed sadness at this as well.

'Oh, what a shame! I'm sure they would have been so proud to learn of the success you've made of your life.'

Her sympathetic listening to his pretty sordid tale had touched him. She had a soft heart, a good heart. She would make a good mother, he'd realised at that point.

He'd asked her about her own mother as well. But she didn't know much more than he did. Just that the woman had been an orphan, brought up in foster homes. When she'd died she'd left behind no known relatives.

Poverty and emotional neglect, Antonio imagined, had

probably been responsible for making Paige's mother ruthlessly ambitious. And hard. And selfish.

Paige was nothing like her, thank heavens. Nothing like her father, either, except perhaps in her intelligence and lust for life.

Lust for other things as well.

Their main activity on the houseboat so far had been making love, in just about every place and position they could, except perhaps the top deck. Paige liked a degree of privacy for her passion.

Occasionally they felt guilty, and cruised a little before dropping anchor in another perfectly private little spot. He'd started one of the novels he'd brought with him, and done the odd spot of fishing. Paige spent quite a bit of time cooking. They hadn't been ashore for dinner as yet. They hadn't wanted to. Yet it was already Monday. The days were flying by.

Still, he'd rung and booked a table for the Wednesday night, since that was her birthday. And he had some special presents which he'd bought before they left Sydney, one of which he hoped would not be premature.

But by then time would really be running out, and he would have to make his move regardless.

Had she fallen in love with him as she'd said she might?

She never used the words, but once or twice he'd caught her looking at him with that wonderfully soft, almost adoring look in her eyes, and his stomach had flipped right over. There again, she had also sometimes looked at him with eyes empty of everything but a glazed desire. Perhaps all she felt for him *was* lust.

Surely not, he decided.

'You're doing it again!'

Antonio's head lifted from the towel he was lying on

to stare, first at her slender ankles, then at her shapely calves.

'Doing what?' he asked, shading his eyes from the sun with his hand as they worked their way higher.

'Nothing!'

His head lifted some more and he grinned up at her. She was wearing a pair of those short shorts of hers. Purple. And a purple and white striped midriff top which was an invitation in itself, being so bare that if she moved her arms slightly he was given tantalising glimpses of the undersides of her always bare breasts. Just looking at her excited him these days, which was awkward when he was only wearing a swimming costume. Fortunately, he was lying face-down on the top sundeck.

'That's why I came on this jaunt, isn't it?' he asked her. 'To do nothing?'

'Not all the time. What worthwhile activities have you got planned for the rest of today?'

'Well…later this afternoon, I aim to do some serious fishing. We're running out of supplies.'

'It's only one o'clock. The fish don't bite till dusk. There's a lot of time in between now and then.'

'In that case why don't you join me down here for some serious sunbaking? Pop off those clothes of yours and get yourself an all-over tan.'

She didn't exactly blush, but she looked scandalised at the idea, which rather amused him. Was this the same girl who, only last night, had prepared him dinner wearing nothing but an apron? Not the large barbecue kind of apron, either, which would have covered most of her. A saucy little tie-round-the-waist apron, with lace around the edges, which had left her naked from the waist up and totally nude at the back, except for the bow.

She'd burned the dinner in the end.

What *was* it about bows which turned him on so?

Damn it all, he shouldn't have started thinking about that now. Things were going from bad to worse in his nether region.

He glanced up at her again, and decided suffering of this kind really was masochistic when the girl of his dreams was standing right next to him.

'What's the problem?' he asked a mite testily. 'There's no one about to see you. A bit of nudity didn't bother you last night.'

'That was different,' she returned rather primly. 'That was night-time. Besides, I don't want to have skin cancer in ten years. It's all right for you Mediterranean born and bred people. You have heaps of melanin in your skin and go this lovely dark brown colour. We fair people get freckles, and melanomas.'

'I have some sunscreen here,' he suggested, determined not to give up. 'I could rub some on your back, and all those other hard to reach places,' he added suggestively.

'*That* stuff?' she scorned. 'It's downright dangerous. Mostly coconut oil and only sun factor four, and not worth spitting on.'

'Fair enough. But it does for me, so how about rubbing some on *my* back, then? I can't really reach.'

He lay back down and waited, and waited, for some movement, or an answer. When there was nothing but silence, he glanced up at her again to find her staring down at him with a frown on her face.

'What's the matter?' he asked, puzzled by her lack of response. It wasn't like her to turn down a chance of some action. Usually, she was insatiable!

'Nothing. I...oh, all right, then,' she said, and sighed.

A strange sigh, full of an oddly weary resignation, as if she was doing something she really didn't want to do, but would do it this once, *just* for him.

Paige knew she should not do this. This was something which should remain a fantasy in her mind. This was something which might lead to trouble.

Admittedly, she'd already touched him all over in the last few days. And kissed him all over. She'd even done *that*, up to a point. But this fantasy demanded much more. It demanded total sensuality and surrender to that sensuality. It demanded skill, and daring. It demanded total commitment. And total love.

The danger lay in the unexpected, and the unknown. What if she lost control and blurted out her love for him? What if the intensity of her emotions sent Antonio running a mile? Again.

He might want commitment. But not obsession.

No, no, she should not do this. Her common sense warned her against it. She was risking everything for the sake of physical pleasure.

But common sense had never been much of a match for the feelings Antonio could evoke. In the end, the temptation to bring that ultimate fantasy to life was too strong. And she was too weak...

Now Antonio sighed. With the anticipation of pleasure. For she'd squatted down and picked up the bottle of oil, and was now pouring some in the well of her right hand. His head was resting on his hands and turned to the side, his eyes slanted open just enough to see. He could not wait for her to lean over and start rubbing it into his back.

But then she did something which surprised him.

Instead of just leaning over him from where she was, she moved round to straddle his hips, her body settling onto his buttocks, pressing him hard down against the deck, producing a mad mixture of pleasure and pain.

Oh, hell!

Grimacing, he flexed every muscle he owned and gathered himself for the moment when her hands would find his skin...

Paige gave up trying to hold back the moment she touched him. If she was going to bring this fantasy to life, she was going to do it properly.

No stranger to massage, she let her fingers operate on automatic pilot for a while, kneading the tension out of Antonio's shoulders and shoulderblades, before working her way slowly down his spine.

'God, that feels good,' Antonio groaned when she reached the small of his back. 'You could do this for a living.'

'I had a lot of practice at it once.'

'What? Where?'

'In a massage parlour.'

His head snapped up and she pushed it back down. 'Only joking. I'll tell you later. I can't talk and do this at the same time.' Which was true. The feel of his flesh under her hands, plus the anticipation of what she was about to do, was turning her on so much she could hardly think.

'I'm just going to work on your legs,' she told him, her voice sounding like treacle as she lifted herself off his buttocks to kneel between his feet.

With painstaking and highly erotic thoroughness she massaged his thighs, then behind each knee, his calves, the soles of his feet, and finally each and every toe. By the time she worked her way back up his legs again Paige was beside herself with the most heart-pounding excitement. Antonio had long been reduced to silence, though he'd flinched and whimpered a few times when she'd been doing his toes.

'Turn over,' she ordered, after shifting to kneel beside him.

His eyes cracked open just enough to meet hers. 'I don't think that's such a good idea,' he told her thickly.

'But I do,' she insisted, and his eyes opened a little more.

With a shuddering sigh, he did as he was told.

'Mmm,' was all Paige could manage as she stared down at him.

Antonio stared back up at her for long moment, then thought, What the hell! Sitting up, he slipped off his togs, tossed them aside, then lay back down.

'Be gentle with me,' he murmured, his eyes closing.

She was. She was also incredibly sensual, incredibly imaginative and incredibly skilled. At some stage she divested herself of her own clothes as well, but would not let him touch her in any way.

'This is *my* fantasy,' she growled, and pushed his eager hands away to flog with impatient idleness beside his supine body once more.

Still, as much as he was dying to touch and taste her, *watching* Paige doing as much to him, with such a dark and decadent assertiveness, evoked its own wild excitement. No power on earth could have stopped him coming, yet she didn't seem to mind. She simply continued, rearousing him once more till he was totally erect again.

When she finally straddled him, and impaled herself upon his exquisitely tormented flesh, his head was practically lifting off. He could not take his eyes off her, watching her rise and fall upon him in a state of utter abandon, her breasts glistening from where she'd rubbed herself all over his oil-slicked body.

'Paige,' he cried out in warning, when he knew he was going to come once more.

He need not have worried. Because she was already there, her mouth gasping wide, her buttocks tensing as her spasms started. He groaned under the power of her contractions, then rushed to join her, their climaxes blending in one long scream of violent sensations. Afterwards, she collapsed forwards, her hair flying out then falling in a curtain over her face and his upper body. For a few minutes their chests continued to heave together but then they grew quiet, both of them spent forces.

Antonio lay there under her still, silent self, no longer in any doubt about Paige's feelings for him. He knew lust when he saw it.

His heart sank a little at the realisation, then hardened once he accepted the inevitability of the situation. She'd loved once, with a love which had stayed with her for years. Maybe she was no more capable of love now than he was.

But that didn't mean she wouldn't agree to marry him. Who knew? Maybe she wouldn't know the difference between love and lust, as Conrad had implied. She was still only young, and relatively inexperienced in life.

So he cuddled her to him, and told her how wonderful she was. She didn't say anything back, just buried her face into his chest, shuddering a little occasionally.

At least she didn't cry any more after they made love, he thought ruefully, though she was inevitably quiet, as though the experience had momentarily shattered her.

'So,' he said softly after a while, stroking her hair away from her face and eyes. 'Are you going to tell me where you learned to massage like that?'

Her chest rose as she scooped in a deep, deep breath. 'I learned watching the physio who used to do Brad,' she confessed on a long exhale. 'One day, when he couldn't afford a massage, I offered to try. After a while, I did it for him all the time.'

Antonio's gut crunched down hard at the thought that she'd done all those other things for him as well. Any gratitude he'd once felt for dear old Brad abruptly changed to a very black, very Latin jealousy.

'Really?' he drawled, and her head lifted abruptly.

'It's not what you're thinking. My giving Brad massages had nothing to do with sex. Whenever Brad needed a massage, sex was the furthest thing from his mind.' Her eyes grew quite frantic as they searched his cynical face. 'Believe me when I tell you I have never done what I just did for any man before, Antonio. You were the first. I'd been thinking about doing it with you, and finally I plucked the courage.'

Antonio savoured her confession, wallowing in a burst of sheer male ego. She'd saved that for him. *He* was the only one to have seen her like that. And to *feel* her like that.

He could almost be generous again towards her dead love.

'Why did Brad need massages?' he asked, his voice no longer carrying that hard, cynical edge. Now he was simply curious.

Sighing with what sounded like relief, she dropped her head to his chest and he cuddled her close again.

'He had arthritis. A very serious form. He'd had it

since he was a kid. But it was getting worse. That's why he moved north, to the warmer climate.'

'I see,' Antonio said. 'So how did you two come to meet in the first place?'

'Oh, I'd known Brad for years. He used to work in a take-away food place in the pavilion on Bondi Beach. He found it hard to work full-time with his arthritis. And surfing helped his arthritis. I've always been a bit of a beach addict. Anyway, he was nice to me one summer, when I was upset about something. After that, I would spend quite a bit of time with him during school holidays. He was always so easy to talk to. And he taught me to surf.'

'Did he make any passes at you?'

'No. Never.'

'But he must have found you attractive.'

'He told me later he did.'

'And you were attracted to him back?'

She hesitated at this question, and Antonio wondered why. 'I suppose so. He was good-looking, in a blond, surfie kind of way.'

'He was a lot older than you?'

'Yes, but he looked young for his age. And he was young at heart.'

'So how long did it take you to fall in love with him after me?' he asked, a bit confused by the time angle. 'Or did you think you were in love with both of us at the same time?'

Her head snapped up again, blue eyes indignant.

'No, of course not! We were just friends back then. Look, after what happened with you that day, I ran straight to Brad to pour my silly heart out. But he was packing to go north and didn't really have time to listen. He only let me go with him because he was worried I'd do something even more stupid. I wasn't living with him in that place when you came, Antonio. I used to sleep on the sofabed. We only became lovers…later…'

Antonio was truly taken aback at this news, and wasn't quite sure what to make of it. He was beginning to feel *really* confused.

'But you *did* fall in love with him?' he said, frowning.

'Not like it was with you,' she hedged. 'Though I did learn to love him. A lot.'

'And he loved you back?'

'In his way. Brad was a man who loved people, especially women. If it hadn't been me with him, it would have been some other woman. He was a pacifist, and a free spirit. He wasn't a jealous or possessive lover. I could have left him, if I'd wanted to, and he would not have tried to stop me.'

'That hardly sounds like the passion of the century!'

'I never said it was,' she said defensively, her body language showing distress.

Antonio decided to let the subject drop. He didn't think he was ever going to understand Paige's relationship with Brad. Or her brand of love. Everyone felt love differently, he supposed. He would always need passion on a grand scale. That was just the way he was. He'd been obsessed with Lauren, and nothing less would do.

He'd often thought what Paige wanted and needed was a father figure in a man, someone older and steadier who could make her feel safe and secure. Now that he knew more about her relationship with Brad, this thinking re-emerged. If she wanted some older man to take care of her, then he could fulfil that role, couldn't he? He could be lover and father at the same time.

'While we're talking,' he said quietly, 'tell me what kind of commitment you meant when you said you wanted it.'

*   *   *

Paige's heart jumped in her chest, then began to pound. Sitting up, she reached for her top and pulled it over her head. Then she dragged her shorts back on and stood up. Only then did she look down at Antonio, who was still disturbingly nude, his olive skin still shining, a stark reminder of all she'd done to him.

'What…what kind did *you* mean?' she countered, terrified of where this conversation was going. Had she ruined everything with that horribly revealing encounter? And then those revelations about Brad? What was Antonio thinking? What was he going to say?

'The usual kind,' he said matter-of-factly. 'Friendship at first, view to marriage and children.'

'Oh!' Paige exclaimed, her heart seizing up. 'Oh, I…I didn't think—I mean…I had no idea… That…that you'd want marriage and children, that is.'

He propped himself up on one elbow, his black eyes boring up into her. 'Don't *you*?'

Paige's heart galloped off wildly as everything she'd ever dreamt about suddenly seemed possible. 'Oh, yes. Yes, I do. Very much so.'

'When?'

Her runaway heart skidded to a halt again. 'What do you mean…*when*?'

'I mean when were you looking at getting married and having children? Soon? Or just some time in the mythical future? I do realise you're only young…'

How to answer that? I'd marry you tomorrow? I'd start having your baby tonight?

This last tempestuous thought swiftly turned into the most wicked temptation. But Paige steadfastly resisted it. She would not do such a thing to her child. Her child would have a father whom she was *certain* would want and love it.

'I don't think my age has much to do with it,' she told him. 'As long as you're *sure*.'

'Sure of what?'

'Of being truly wanted. And needed.'

He frowned. 'What about truly loved?'

'That would be nice too, of course. But sometimes that comes later, rather than sooner.' Oh, dear God, she hoped she was saying the right thing here. She knew he didn't love her. He'd virtually said as much. He hadn't gotten over that Lauren woman yet.

He was clearly thinking about what she'd said, but his eyes were irritatingly unreadable. 'Like it did with Brad?' he said at last.

'Yes. Sort of...'

'Sort of,' he repeated. 'So if I said I wanted you and needed you, it would be enough for now?'

'Is that what you're saying?'

'That's what I'm saying.'

Her eyes rounded. 'Are you seriously asking me to marry you?'

'I am indeed.'

She literally sank to her knees beside him. 'Oh, my God,' she choked out.

His smile looked almost amused. 'Is that a yes or a no?'

'Yes. No. Yes...'

His smile turned wry. 'I like a woman who knows her own mind.'

'But are you sure *you* mean it?' she said, her voice still strangled with emotion.

'Paige, darling...' Reaching up, he pulled her down on the towel beside him, smoothing her hair back from her face and kissing her lightly on her stunned mouth. 'I'm mad about you. *Marry* me. *Soon*.'

'How soon?'

'As soon as it can be arranged.'

Paige thought she would burst with joy. She didn't need words of love at that moment. Sometimes words could be very empty. But she hugged the loving look in his eyes and the unwavering strength in his voice to her heart. Love would come; she was sure. She had enough for the two of them.

'And her answer is?' he prompted.

'Whatever you want, Antonio,' she said, her hand shaking slightly as it reached to touch his cheek.

'I want you to be my wife,' he returned confidently, and Paige's heart turned over.

So dreams *did* come true. Who would have believed it?

CHAPTER FOURTEEN

'HAPPY birthday, darling.' Antonio lifted his glass of champagne in celebration, not just of Paige's birthday but his own success.

He'd won! And without having to feel a heel. Paige was happy. *He* was happy. Everything had worked out much better than he could ever have hoped.

As they clinked glasses across the table he gazed into the bright blue eyes of his beautiful bride-to-be and could not recall when he'd ever felt so exhilarated. He could not wait to see the look on Conrad's face when he told him his daughter had said yes to becoming Mrs Antonio Scarlatti as soon as a proper wedding could be arranged.

No way was he going to cheat Paige of a proper wedding. That wouldn't be right. This was for keeps!

Meanwhile, he had something he had to do.

'I have something for you,' he said.

Paige seemed taken aback. 'You've bought me a birthday present?'

'But of course.' And he began fishing around in his trouser pockets, smiling at her all the while.

Paige had never seen him looking as handsome as he did tonight. Their week's cruising had relaxed the tension lines around his eyes and mouth, and tanned his already olive skin to a rich bronze. He'd stopped slicking his hair straight back and allowed its natural wave free rein, giving him a dashing Latin look which she found sinfully sexy.

Tonight he was wearing cream trousers and an open-necked black silk shirt which revealed just enough dark chest hair to be tantalising. When they'd walked up the steps from the jetty which led into the restaurant half an hour earlier, all the women already seated at the elegantly set tables had simply stared, first at him with hunger, and then at her with envy.

She'd felt so proud of him, and so happy she could have burst.

'Ah, here it is,' he said, and, producing a long narrow box covered in royal blue velvet, slid it across the white linen tablecloth towards her.

Paige stared down at the gold insignia of a well-known Sydney jeweller, then frowned up at him. 'But you must have bought this before we came away?' She'd been imagining he might have picked her up some little thing from the riverside supply store they'd dropped in on that morning.

'I told you your father mentioned your birthday to me last week.'

'Yes, but I didn't expect a gift like this.'

'You know, that's a very endearing quality in a woman,' he mused. 'Not expecting gifts like this. I hope you keep that up when we're married.'

Paige pulled a face at him, then eagerly opened the box. Although it *had* to be jewellery of some sort she certainly hadn't anticipated the magnificence of the gold and diamond pendant necklace. 'My goodness!' she gasped.

'You like it?'

'Antonio, it's…it's too much. Really. It must have cost you a fortune!'

'Not quite. Why don't you put it on? It might take my mind off that bow at the back of your neck.'

Paige laughed. She was wearing the gold dress, as promised, and had mischievously put her hair up, just so that very bow would always be in view. Little did Antonio know that underneath the bow was a sneaky hook and eye. He could tug at the ties all he liked, but the dress wasn't going to come tumbling down.

'Want some help?' he offered drily as she fiddled a bit with the clasp at the back of her neck, just above the bow.

'No, thank you very much,' she retaliated swiftly. 'You stay right where you are till we're well out of public view, you wicked man.'

'Spoilsport,' he muttered.

The deep V neckline of the dress could have been made for the necklace, the main diamond in the centre of the pendant nestling into her cleavage.

'Perfect!' Antonio admired. 'Only one thing missing now.'

'Oh? What?'

'This…' And he brought out another box, this one ring-sized.

Paige could only stare.

'Aren't you going to open it?'

She just couldn't, so he did, flicking open the box with a flourish and holding it out towards her, the huge diamond sparkling under the candlelight.

'For the future Mrs Scarlatti,' he murmured softly, 'so that every man knows she's properly spoken for.'

Paige couldn't help it. Tears flooded her eyes.

Fortunately, she managed to sniffle pretty quietly, but Antonio still looked embarrassed. Or was he annoyed?

'Sorry,' she muttered, using her serviette as a handkerchief. 'Couldn't help it. This is just so...romantic.'

Antonio's sigh sounded relieved. 'Ah...I see. Shall we see if it fits?'

The fit was a little snug going over the knuckle, but she didn't complain. Once Antonio's ring was firmly on her finger, she wasn't about to take it off in a hurry.

'Shall we have another glass of champagne to celebrate our engagement?' he suggested. 'What about another bottle? This one's almost done.'

'Oh, yes, let's,' she agreed happily. 'It's not as though we have to drive the boat anywhere tonight. Or even row back.' They had safely dropped anchor a little way out from shore earlier that afternoon, and a man from the restaurant had collected them in a small power boat. He was also going to return them afterwards. A part of the service, he'd told them, to prevent any suitably sozzled patrons from drowning in the river after dinner.

'I'm going to get very tipsy!' Paige pronounced.

'I haven't been tipsy in years,' Antonio told her. 'Can't afford not to have a clear head when I'm doing business. And I'm always doing business,' he finished drily as he refilled Paige's glass, then ordered another bottle of champagne.

She picked up her glass and sipped while considering what Antonio had just said. 'You know, I don't know why you keep on working for my father. He's a tyrant. With your expertise and connections you could start up a production company of your own.'

'That's easy to say,' he said sharply, 'but starting up a new company in competition with those already established is fraught with more hazards than you could ever imagine. Besides, I've worked much too hard to get where I am to throw it all away now.'

'Sorry,' she said, feeling a bit chastened. 'Didn't mean to make waves. I know how hard you've worked. So where will we be living after we're married? Do you see yourself working in Europe for a long time?'

'Actually, no. I'll have to go back next week for a while, but when I come back at Christmas I'll be staying. I hope I'm not premature in mentioning this, but your father plans on retiring at the end of the year.'

'You're joking! Retiring? Father? I don't believe it!'

'I think you should. That's why I told you not to worry over our getting married. Your father needs me, Paige, to be the company's new CEO.'

'He's offered you the job?'

'We were working out the terms of the contract just last week.'

'But that's marvellous! Oh, congratulations, Antonio. You must be so pleased.'

'I am.'

'We should drink to it, don't you think?'

'I do indeed.' And they both raised their glasses.

'And now,' Antonio said after their toast, 'I think we should work out the plans for our wedding. I thought we could have it as soon as I get back, just before Christmas. Is that too soon for you? It won't give you very long to organise, only about six or seven weeks.'

Paige didn't care. All she wanted was to be Mrs Antonio Scarlatti.

'Of course,' Antonio added, 'it will have to be a church wedding. I don't believe in that other kind. I don't believe in divorce either, Paige.' And he eyed her with a wonderfully stern look.

Neither do I,' she reaffirmed happily. 'Shall we drink to a no-divorce clause in our marriage contract?'

Antonio looked startled. 'You want a marriage contract?'

'No, silly. I was just joking. But you do realise that if you marry me you'll one day be a very rich man. That's if Father doesn't cut me out of his will for marrying his right-hand man.'

Paige was gratified to see Antonio seemed truly taken aback by this. 'To be honest,' he said slowly, a dark frown gathering on his handsome face, 'I hadn't thought about that.'

His reaction worried her a little. 'It's not a *bad* thought, is it?'

He looked up at her, his beautiful black eyes troubled. 'No, no I guess not. But I would hate you to think I was marrying you for your money, because I'm not.'

'Oh, Antonio,' she said, smiling. 'Why would I think that? If you'd wanted to marry me for my money you'd have made a line for me years ago. No, my darling husband-to-be, I would never think that. Come on, let's drink to our never divorcing.'

Antonio raised his glass, but he didn't drink much then, or for the rest of the evening. He no longer felt like it. Oh, he tried to remain bright and happy for the rest of the meal, for Paige's sake, but a cloud had come over his earlier elation.

The truth was he felt like a heel again, a money-grubbing, cold-blooded heel, who had allowed himself to be blackmailed and manipulated for the sake of ambition and vengeance. Vengeance against life, and Lauren.

The trouble was he no longer gave a fig for Lauren. Paige was worth ten of her. As for life...blaming his ruthless behaviour on the circumstances of his childhood was, quite frankly, childish. Such thinking was beneath him. He was a grown man, successful because of his own hard work and basic honesty.

But where had that honesty gone to these past ten days? What would happen in the future if he allowed Conrad to think he could be bought?

Over coffee, Antonio came to a decision, and his inner mood lightened. Yes, he thought. Yes, that was what he had to do!

But he wouldn't say anything to Paige just yet. Best leave any such announcements till *after* the wedding. Best leave *Conrad* till after the wedding too, he decided. His boss could be vindictive when crossed. Hopefully, Conrad would not want to ruin his daughter's happiness by that stage. But he would have to be careful. Very damned careful.

'Didn't work,' Paige said as her empty coffee cup clattered into its saucer. 'I'm still quite drunk. You didn't drink your share of champagne, Antonio,' she said accusingly, her lovely face flushed, her eyes over-bright.

He thought he'd never seen her looking more desirable, with that naughty little gold dress barely covering her luscious body, and diamonds at her throat. 'Maybe that was my plan, to have my wicked way with you,' he drawled.

She giggled. 'Surely you've gathered you don't have to get me drunk to do that.'

Antonio laughed as he inspected the account which a waitress had discreetly placed by his elbow. Expensive, he saw. But worth every cent. He included a sizeable tip in the payment, and stood up.

'Come on, Princess Paige, let's get you back to the boat, and into bed.'

'With or without this gold dress,' she said, swaying as she rose.

He raced round to take her arm and lead her out of the restaurant, guiding her carefully down the steep stone steps, only then realising how smashed she was.

'My hero,' she murmured, and leant against him during the short ride out to the houseboat.

'I have to warn you,' she whispered to him once they were alone on the back deck. 'There's a hook and eye under the bow, and it's very tricky. Designed to fool men who want to have their wicked way with its wearer.'

'Thank you for telling me,' he returned, knowing full well that when and if he got her out of the damned dress it would only be to put her to bed. He didn't want her waking up the next morning with a hangover and no memory of his making love to her. 'But I won't be having my wicked way with you just yet,' he replied. 'I think you need a little sleep first.'

'No, no, I don't want to sleep. I'm too happy to sleep. I'll be okay soon. I'll just stay out here for a while and enjoy the fresh air and the full moon,' she insisted, disengaging herself from him to turn and grip the railing.

'But it's cold,' he argued when he saw the goose-bumps spring up on her arms. 'I'll get you a jacket, okay?'

'Okay.' She smiled one of those sweetly adoring smiles at him, and he melted in a way he'd never melted with a woman before.

Shaking his head, he hurried inside to get her jacket.

'I can see everything so clearly, Antonio,' she called after him. 'There's this man out in a small boat in the middle of the river. He's probably fishing. Oh, and he's got a dog. A lovely little dog. It's standing up on the bow. And— Oh, my God! Oh, how could he? Antonio! Antonio, he just threw the dog in the river!'

Paige's screeching, plus the sound of an outboard motor, sent Antonio dropping the jacket and racing out onto the deck. Paige immediately grabbed his arm and shook it violently.

'He just threw him in!' she was screaming. 'And he left him there. Went roaring off, laughing. The poor little thing's trying to swim after him. But the man's just getting further and further away. You have to do something, Antonio!'

'But Paige, if it's a dog, it won't drown.'

'It might. It's such a long way to shore from where it is. Look at it out there. It's so small. It's…oh, my God, I can't see it any more. *Do* something, Antonio!'

He hesitated, then shrugged resignedly. 'All right,' he said. 'Calm down. All right.' And he hurried to climb down into the dinghy. But it took time to untie the rope, then to put the oars into their slots.

'I can see it again, Antonio. Oh, it looks so small, and its poor little legs are thrashing away. It's going to get tired soon, I know. And then it'll sink and it'll drown. Oh, you're taking too long, Antonio! I'd be quicker swimming to him!'

'*No!*' he screamed, watching, horrified, as she kicked off her shoes, climbed up onto the railing and dived into the inky waters.

There was no hesitation this time. No taking off any shoes, either. Antonio simply stood up and dived in after her.

She had a good head start, and a cloud suddenly drifted over the moon, plunging the river into darkness. He called out her name as he swam, but she didn't answer. He thought he heard her just ahead, but it might have been the sound of his own swimming.

As much as he tried not to panic, it began to consume him. His head whirled with horrible thoughts. She was drunk. She would drown if he didn't reach her.

He swam harder and faster. Suddenly the moon came again and he spotted her, slightly off to the right, treading water and turning in circles, searching the river, looking for that stupid bloody dog. Antonio felt sick with relief. And angry. Angry that she'd risked her life so foolishly. Didn't she know that he couldn't stand life without her now?

A few more strokes and he was pulling her into his arms, feeling renewed fury when he saw how exhausted she was.

'You are a silly, silly woman!' he panted, holding her to him. 'You could have drowned.'

'Hey, there! You folks all right? You know, you shouldn't go swimming in the river at this time of night.'

Antonio spun in the water to see a small motor boat approaching them. Standing on the bow was a small wet dog, happily shaking himself.

'It…it's him!' Paige exclaimed breathlessly, pointing at the man, not the dog. 'You…you tried to drown your dog! I *saw* you!'

The man laughed, which didn't exactly endear him to Antonio. The boat slid to a halt beside them and the man bent to take Paige's hand first, pulling her easily out of the water. He was a huge man, with a grizzly grey beard and a weathered face.

'Couldn't drown Mitzy here if I tried,' he said. 'She could swim across the English Channel and back. As you can see, she's fine. Here, I think you'd better get out of there too, young fella. Swimming in the river at midnight is not such a good idea. Especially in your clothes,' he added drily.

Antonio let the old man help him into his boat as well, thinking he wished someone would throw *him* in the river at midnight. It was bloody freezing!

'But you *threw* your dog in the river!' Paige accused, teeth chattering.

The man produced a blanket and wrapped it round both of them. 'Yeah, well, the wife can't stand me bringing the dog in the house smelling of fish, so on the way home I always make sure Mitzy has a nice little dip. At night, she's not so keen to get in, so I have to give her a little hand.'

'My fiancée almost *drowned* trying to save your dog,' Antonio muttered through clenched teeth.

The man looked taken aback. 'Really? Geez, I'm sorry, mate. Thought you were just having a midnight dip.' He looked Paige up and down, then grinned at Antonio. 'I guess I was wrong. Not too many people go swimming in a party dress and diamonds! Still, she's all right now, ain't she? And you're one lucky man, marrying a brave little lady like that.'

'Yes,' Antonio said, clasping a sodden Paige to his side under the blanket. 'Yes, I surely am.'

'I'm sorry, Antonio,' Paige whispered as Antonio tucked her tight into bed. 'I spoiled our night, didn't I?'

He'd been so quiet since the fisherman had delivered them back to the houseboat. No doubt he thought her a fool. And she was, jumping in the river like that. She'd never have done such a silly thing if she'd been sober.

Antonio sat down on the side of the bed and stroked a stray strand of hair away from her face. His expression looked so serious that Paige's stomach tightened nervously.

'I have never felt so frightened in all my life,' he told her. 'I was so worried I might lose you...'

Paige's heart turned over with relief. He wasn't angry with her. He'd been worried. Taking his hand, which was now lying on the bed, she squeezed it tightly. 'You're never going to lose me, Antonio.'

Their eyes met, and she simply had to speak her heart. 'I love you, Antonio.'

His eyes widened, and she hesitated. Maybe admitting everything would lose *him*. But she had to take the risk. She could not keep silent any longer.

'I've always loved you,' she added, tears filling her eyes. 'Don't you know that? It's always been you, never anyone else. Brad was really just my friend, not my love. And Jed...Jed was an aberration of the moment, the result of my despair after seeing you with that woman at last year's Christmas party. I could not go on, I thought, wanting you, loving you, longing for you. So I tried to make a life for myself without you...'

He had her two hands in his by this point, and his eyes were stunned and sad at the same time. 'Oh, Paige...dearest Paige...I had no idea...'

'How could you? I never told you, except that one time by the pool.'

'When I broke your heart...'

'It's mended now. And it's yours, if you want it.'

'If I want it...' He lifted her hands to his mouth and kissed their fingertips. 'I can hardly express how much I want it. How much I want *you*, darling Paige. Because I love you too.'

She sat bolt upright, the blanket falling from her bare shoulders. 'You *do*?'

'I do indeed. I can't claim I always did, because I didn't. To be honest I didn't realise the depths of my feelings for you till just now, when I thought I might lose you. I'd practised being hard-hearted about women for so long that I just didn't recognise what I felt for you as love. True love this time, my darling. Not that immature, egotistical obsession I had for Lauren. What I feel for you is so much more, because you're so much more. Why, you're the most wonderful woman I've ever known, and I can't wait to marry you and have children by you.'

His dizzying words brought a level of joy to Paige which she'd never imagined she would ever feel.

'Well, you won't have to wait long,' she told him softly.

'What do you mean?'

'I'm going to stop taking the pill after my next period so that I'll be ready to have babies as soon as we're married. Oh, Antonio, wouldn't it be romantic if we conceived a baby on our wedding night?'

'You want to start a child straight away?'

'Yes, I do.'

'What about work?'

'The only job I want for a while, Antonio, is to be your wife, and the mother of your children.'

Antonio looked down at this incredible girl he loved and thanked God for women like her. Any last, lingering bitterness over Lauren was lost in Paige's arms that night, and finally Antonio was to experience the delight of making love to someone he truly loved, and who truly loved him in return.

She cried afterwards, this time, and Antonio finally realised the truth behind her tears at other times. She'd being crying for this…his love. The thought humbled him, and made him vow that he would make it up to her for everything she'd suffered because of him.

Nothing, Antonio reaffirmed the following morning, could ever be allowed to spoil things between himself and Paige. She was everything to him.

CHAPTER FIFTEEN

PAIGE woke on her wedding day to total happiness and the most delicious feeling of excitement and anticipation. Even the weather was kind, being warm and sunny.

But it was the personal warmth which had surrounded Paige during the last couple of months which continued to surprise and delight her. She could hardly believe how nice Evelyn had been since the announcement of her engagement to Antonio. And how helpful she'd been with the wedding arrangements.

As for her father…he was just over the moon, insisting that nothing was too much trouble, or too much expense. She was to have everything her little heart desired.

The truth was, however, that the only thing her little heart desired was Antonio. How she'd missed him these past few weeks! Phone calls were all very well, but nothing could compare with the real thing.

She could not wait to see Antonio again today. He'd flown in from London early yesterday morning, having had to work right up to the last minute to have everything tied up to his satisfaction before handing his job over to his second in command. He'd offered to come over straight away from the flight—he'd called her from the company car—but she'd been able to hear the exhaustion in his voice, so she'd told him to go home to bed for the day instead, and rest up for the wedding the following day. She would see him at the church, right on the dot of three. She'd promised faithfully not to be late.

They were to be married in the local Catholic Church, followed by a reception here at Fortune Hall. She'd tried to keep things small, but her father had insisted on giving her a big bash and inviting all his business cronies. She'd let him have his way, overcome by how sweet he was being to her. Perhaps he loved her after all!

Antonio had drawn the line, however, when she'd told him one night that her father wanted to buy them a house. He'd said he would buy his own house, thank you very much. He'd already auctioned the penthouse, and moved his furniture into storage. Several estate agencies were busy on the look-out for a house which fulfilled Paige's wish list.

Something not too large; she didn't want live-in staff. It was to be near the ocean, and with a large, enclosed yard which could keep children and a dog safe.

'Whatever you want, Paige,' Antonio had promised. 'Even the dog.'

A knock on the door interrupted her happy thoughts.

'Yes? Who is it?'

'Evelyn here, dear. I've brought you a special wedding breakfast. Can I come in?'

'You surely can. It's time I was up and about.'

Evelyn entered with a bright smile. 'Well, the big day is finally here!'

Paige smiled back as she bounced out of bed. 'I could hardly sleep for excitement,' she confessed.

'Same here, dear. Same here.'

Paige wasn't late for the wedding, but she was so nervous she could hardly remember a thing afterwards, except for how handsome Antonio looked in a dinner suit.

Her own appearance produced much oohs and aahs from the guests, though in reality her wedding dress was quite simple, with a fitted lace bodice, a full tulle skirt, and a matching tulle and lace veil. No trains. Nothing too fussy.

Her one bridesmaid—dressed in a cerise silk suit—was an old boarding school friend she'd kept in touch with, though not often. Antonio's best man was a fellow executive in the company, a nice enough man but a stranger to Paige. Having to scrape together a wedding party—even one so small—had been a telling indictment of their lives so far.

'The first thing we have to do once we're settled in our new house,' she told Antonio in the car on the way back from the church, 'is to start making some real friends of our own.'

He smiled and patted her hand. 'Don't worry, you'll have plenty of opportunity to do that.'

'How's that? I'll be at home, having babies.'

'Not all the time. An intelligent girl like you needs more than babies to stop you from being bored. I have a job proposition to put to you.'

'Really? What?' she asked excitedly, because in all honesty she'd been a bit worried about her impulsively romantic offer to give up work and stay home all the time. She was a people person. That was why she'd enjoyed waitressing and serving drinks, and even sitting at a reception desk.

'I'll tell you tonight.'

'Why not now?'

'I have to speak to your father first. And I don't want to speak to him till after the reception is well and truly over.'

'Is it something to do with Fortune Productions?'

'Yes.'

'Oh, goodie, I've always wanted to work there.'

He shot her a sharp look. 'Why's that?'

'Why not? I'll have you know I have some very good ideas for some new programmes. I believe I have my finger on the pulse of what people want to watch these days. Much more than Father has!'

'Mmm. I'm glad to hear that, darling.' And he leant over to kiss her on the cheek. 'We'll discuss your ideas at length tonight.'

'What? I'm not going to let you spend my wedding night talking business! You're going to be busy making babies.'

She just loved his look of mock disappointment. 'Must I?'

'You must! I positively insist!'

'Oh, well…'

They arrived at their reception, laughing.

Evelyn watched their joyous arrival, the feeling of pleasurable anticipation already building. She managed to control herself till the reception was drawing to an end and she saw Antonio leave his bride's side to speak to her father, both men leaving the room to go to Conrad's study. Clearly, Antonio was about to collect his contract. The deal was done, and about to be delivered!

Evelyn eavesdropped as a smiling Paige made her excuses as well, telling her bridesmaid that she was going up to change into her going-away outfit.

The happy couple were supposed to be going to some swanky Sydney hotel for the night before flying out for a honeymoon in Tasmania, then returning to Fortune Hall to stay for Christmas and the New Year.

Or so they thought!

Evelyn doubted there would be any honeymoon after what she had to tell the daughter of the house. Her dark excitement grew as she walked up the stairs towards Paige's bedroom. Her car was already packed and her letter of resignation in her hand, ready to be given to Conrad on her way out.

This time she didn't bother to knock on Paige's door but walked straight in, catching the blushing bride in nothing but a G-string. With her final moment of triumph at hand, Evelyn allowed her jealousy full rein, glaring her hatred at the girl's body, which had not a hint of fat, or a single physical flaw.

How good it was to see uncertainty cloud those far too beautiful blue eyes, so bright and happy a few seconds earlier, but now harbouring just a hint of worry.

'You could have knocked, Evelyn,' Paige said, snatching up a robe and hurriedly drawing it over her near nakedness.

'I suppose I could have,' Evelyn returned smugly, and swung the door shut behind her.

Everything inside Paige froze, a chill invading the room, and herself.

'What's wrong?' she asked, but deep inside she already knew. Evelyn had been pretending to be nice to her these past few weeks. It had all been an act.

But *why*?

'There's nothing wrong,' the hateful woman said, with a malicious gleam in her mean, beady eyes. 'Everything's absolutely perfect. I couldn't have planned it better if I tried. I've always thought you were a fool,' she sneered, 'but today you were played for the most prize fool of all!'

Paige did her best not to react, not to give this ghastly

creature the satisfaction of seeing her instant inner turmoil. 'I have no idea what you're talking about,' she managed to say in a surprisingly cool voice.

'Don't you now? Well, perhaps I can enlighten you. Your husband of a few hours doesn't love you, my dear. He didn't marry you because he wanted to, but because your father blackmailed him into it.'

Paige could feel herself staring at the woman, horror in her heart. It couldn't be true. Antonio *did* love her. She knew he did.

But Evelyn seemed to know differently…

'It was the morning after you came crawling home with your face a mess. Antonio had just flown in and Conrad had Jim bring him straight here. *Marry my daughter,* Conrad said, *and I will make you CEO of Fortune Productions.* At first, even with *that* carrot dangling, it was obvious Antonio wasn't keen. After all, who wants a slut and a fool for a wife? But your father isn't one to take no for an answer. *Don't marry Paige,* he added, *and I will offer the job to Brock Masters.* Naturally Antonio understood that the American's becoming CEO over him would mean the end of his career with the company altogether, so he reluctantly agreed.'

Even in her state of deep shock, Paige's mind still managed to go back to that night, when she'd walked downstairs and discovered Antonio there with her father, drinking champagne. What was it Antonio had said? They were celebrating a future merger…

That merger, she realised with growing horror, had been their marriage!

'Conrad wanted Antonio engaged to you before he went back to Europe,' Evelyn raved on. 'When he asked how he could convince you to marry him in such a short time, your father gave him some sound advice. *Seduce the little fool,* he said. *Tell her you love her. If all else fails, get her pregnant!'*

Paige thought of their first time together, and how Antonio hadn't used a condom. Not an act of uncontrollable desire, she realised wretchedly. But one of cold-blooded deliberation.

'But he didn't have to go that far, did he?' Evelyn jeered. 'You *wanted* to believe Antonio could love a little fool like you. You *wanted* to marry your handsome hero of a husband. But it wasn't you he wanted. It was the company! He's getting his contract as CEO right this minute, in Conrad's study, signed, sealed and delivered. Some hero *he* turned out to be!'

Paige could not take her eyes off the woman's ugly mouth. Neither could she say a word in Antonio's defence. Because she could see Evelyn was speaking the truth, the most ghastly, horrible, despicable truth!

'Knowing you,' the woman scorned, 'you probably won't have the guts to even tell him you know. You'd probably rather go on abasing yourself at his feet, and in his bed. Either way, it's going to be very hard, isn't it? Living with the truth, knowing your father was forced to buy you a bridegroom just to get you off his hands! People say beauty and wealth don't bring happiness. I can finally appreciate they're right. Happiness is feeling what I'm feeling at this moment!'

Paige wasn't sure afterwards how she managed not to fall apart right then and there. Somehow, she found the courage and the pride to keep the demons at bay and face her enemy with dignity, and disdain.

'Sorry to disappoint you, Evelyn,' she said scornfully, 'but you're not telling me anything I don't already know. Antonio revealed all about his bargain with Father when we were away together. He simply had to tell me once he actually fell in love with me. I'll have you know he also offered to give up being CEO of the company, but I begged him to take the job. So unfortunately, Evelyn, your happiness is short-lived, and you've lost *your* job here for nothing. Or have you already got your resignation ready?'

When the stunned woman glanced down at an envelope she was now crushing in her hands, Paige jumped to the right conclusion. 'Would you like to give it to me?' she asked, stretching out her hand and using every ounce of will she possessed to keep it steady. 'I'll hand it to Father myself. I do so hope, however, that you're not expecting references.'

There was satisfaction in seeing the woman thrown. She actually handed the envelope over before she rallied. Though it wasn't an over-confident rally. 'I…I don't believe you! You…you didn't know till I just told you now.'

'Like I didn't know about your killing my dog all those years ago?' Paige threw at her.

The woman's mouth dropped open.

'I'm not the fool you think I am, Evelyn. Yes, I wanted Antonio, and now I've married him. I don't give a damn who pushed him in my direction. Father did me a big favour, because I'm his wife now and I intend to stay that way. I suggest you get the hell out of here right now, because if you don't, Antonio will make you wish you had. You should have seen what he did to the man who dared to hit me once.'

Paige held her ground till the woman actually left. But the moment she was alone she sank slowly to the side of the bed, her emotions in tatters. In desperation, she tried to work out if anything she'd just said to Evelyn could possibly be true. Was there any hope Antonio *had* fallen in love with her? Or had it *all* been lies, right from the start? Was the charade going to be over now that he had what he wanted?

She was still sitting there, dazed and oddly dry-eyed, when Antonio came rushing into the room.

'Paige, come quickly! Your father! He's ill.'

She stayed where she was, and just stared up at him.

He frowned back. 'Didn't you hear what I said? It's your father. He's having a heart attack, I think. He collapsed, complaining of pains in his chest. I've called an ambulance and Jim is with him, ready to give CPR if needed. What on earth's wrong with you, Paige? Why are you sitting there staring at me like that? Are you in shock? Oh, God, I suppose you are. I forget sometimes how sweet you are. How...soft. Should I find Evelyn and send her up to help?'

His mentioning Evelyn's name finally snapped Paige out of it. 'No,' she said brusquely. 'No point. Evelyn's left.'

'What do you mean...left?'

'She quit. She was just here. Left her letter of resignation. And now she's gone. For good.'

'Why in hell would she do that, today of all days? Oh, who cares, anyway? You *don't*, do you?' he asked, shooting her a puzzled look.

'No,' Paige returned coldly. 'No, I certainly don't. You go back to Father,' she told him. 'I'll get dressed and come down straight away.' She stood up and turned away from her husband, feeling his hesitation and his slight bewilderment. But she could not bear to look at him. Not right at that moment.

'Go on,' she said sharply over her shoulder.

And he went.

Only when he was gone did her mind turn to her father. I hope you die, you unspeakable bastard! And I hope you rot in hell!

But even as she cursed him she knew she didn't really mean it. She wanted to hate him, wanted to hate them both! But she found she could not.

The tears came then, tears of confusion and humiliation and misery. Maybe Evelyn was right. Maybe she would *not* have the guts to confront them with their dastardly deeds. Because if she did there would be no future for her, and no children.

Not Antonio's, anyway.

But how could she live with this knowledge, and this pain?

Wretchedly, she pulled on the blue silk dress which she'd been going to wear to start her honeymoon, and carried her despair downstairs.

The ambulance had arrived and taken her father away before she could get to him. Antonio was waiting for her in the foyer, looking anxious. 'Are you all right, darling?' he asked as he took her arm and steered her through the already open front door. 'You look very pale. But the news is not too bad. The paramedic said it's probably only an angina attack.'

Jim was waiting at the bottom of the steps with the company limousine to follow the ambulance to the hospital.

'I had no idea he had a heart condition,' Antonio muttered as he helped Paige into the back seat, then joined her.

'But he didn't!' she protested. 'Did he?'

'Apparently so. He was advised to have a bypass, but he said he hated hospitals. And operations. That's why he was retiring. To take it easy. If he'd only told me the truth I would have done things differently.'

'What...what do you mean?'

His eyes carried worry as he looked at her. 'I hope this doesn't upset you, Paige, but I...I resigned from Fortune Productions today.'

'What?' Jim squawked from behind the wheel. 'Hell, Tone, you're the only decent guy in that damned company. What did you want to do that for?'

'Had to, Jim,' he said, and settled a searching gaze on his bride. 'I wanted to be my own man. Make my own life, with my new wife by my side. The woman I love more than anything else in the world. I couldn't do it working for her father, could I? People would have called any promotion I received nepotism of the worst kind. They would have lost respect for me. Respect is very important to Italians, you know. And to a husband,' he added, taking Paige's hands in his. 'I would never want to do anything to lose my wife's respect.'

Paige gulped. Oh, God, she was going to cry. All those things she'd said to Evelyn; all those made-up mad defences...they were true! Antonio might have been pushed into pursuing her, but once he had he'd really fallen in love with her. His love was so great, in fact, that he was prepared to give up what he'd worked for all his life!

Moved beyond belief, she searched for the right response.

What to do? Tell him she knew the truth?

No, no, she couldn't do that. He would believe it belittled him in her eyes. He would not be able to stand that. She had to keep it a secret, had to pretend she'd never been told.

'I think,' she said shakily, her eyes shimmering, 'that resigning was the right thing.'

'But I upset your father terribly.'

'Lots of things upset my father,' she said, still unwilling to forgive *his* part, no matter how it had turned out. 'He'll get over it. And he'll get well. You couldn't kill my father with a bus.'

'I know you probably won't believe this,' Antonio said, 'but your father loves you, Paige. I didn't believe it myself till just now. He told me how worried he'd been about you, and how guilty he felt over being such a rotten father. He blamed himself for what he saw as your restlessness. When he found out he might die soon, he wanted nothing more than to see you settled and happy with the right man. He told me that today was one of the happiest days of his life!'

Paige didn't believe that for a moment! His happiness was not so much for her, but for getting his own way. Look what happened as soon as he didn't! He had a damned heart attack. Still, if she was never going to reveal anything about this blackmailing business, then she supposed she would have to appear to believe Antonio.

'I suppose he *does* love me in his own warped way,' she admitted, the words sticking in her throat somewhat. 'And I suppose I love him back. He's my father, after all.'

'So you forgive me?' Antonio asked, with the most heartfelt emotion in his face.

'Forgive you for what?'

'For resigning. And for upsetting your father. I only hope I haven't killed him.'

Paige gave her husband's hand a comforting squeeze. 'There's no need for *you* to feel guilty,' she said firmly. 'Father will be just fine.'

Antonio's guilt lessened once he saw the man for himself again, plus the marked improvement in his colour and condition. Paige too seemed very relieved. She might not think she loved her father all that much, but she did. The last thing Antonio wanted was to feel responsible for his death.

'You worried the life out of me,' he said by Conrad's bedside.

'I worried the life out of myself. Think I might have that operation after all.'

'Good idea,' Paige chipped in. 'Then you can stop this retiring nonsense and look after your own company.'

Conrad smiled a wry smile at his daughter. 'Just look at her. Married less than a day and already telling her old man what to do. I still can't believe the change in you, missy. You're a different person. Just shows you what the right man can do. Speaking of the right man... I know you won't change your mind, Antonio, but would you stay on as caretaker CEO, just till I'm on my feet?'

'Can't Brock Masters do that?' Antonio asked, rather tongue-in-cheek.

'Brock Masters! You have to be joking. He's already been given his third warning. Damned fool's been taking drugs. He'll be out by Christmas.'

'Best move you ever made. And, no, Conrad, I won't be staying on as acting CEO. I told you my reasons for leaving today, and you have to appreciate they're very good ones.'

Conrad nodded resignedly, then smiled at both of them. Antonio smiled back. He might be a devious old devil, and what he'd done was very wrong, but Antonio would still always be grateful to his father-in-law for bringing him a happiness beyond anything he could have hoped for.

*   *   *

Beside him, Paige was slowly coming to the same thinking herself. No matter what her father's motives, he'd given her Antonio, hadn't he? Hard to hate a man who'd made her dearest dream come true.

Later that night, she snuggled into Antonio's arms after some very serious lovemaking and asked him a very important question.

'Would you like a boy or a girl first?'

It was a question which would consume them for the next nine months, especially after the doctor confirmed that Paige had indeed conceived, either on her wedding night or soon after. Antonio could not conceal his pleasure when the ultrasound at four months revealed a baby who was decidedly male.

By the time Julius Richard Scarlatti was born the following September, his ecstatic parents had moved into a nice four-bedroomed house on Maroubra Beach, painted the nursery green in case the next child was a girl, and bought a four-year-old black mongrel from the local dog pound who'd been on death row. They'd also completed production of the first series of an hourly programme called *The Romance Show*, which showed viewers romantic places, holidays, hotels, restaurants, clothes, lingerie, gifts and books. It had been Paige's idea.

In the year it went to air, everyone who watched the show quickly became addicted to its feel-good theme. Most agreed that the most romantic aspect of the show was the producers. The way they looked at each other sometimes, when they were shown, photographed in the newspaper. The way they laughed, and held hands. They looked so obviously in love with each other. So obviously happy together.

Which they were.

A SPANISH AFFAIR

HELEN BROOKS

CHAPTER ONE

'THINGS are really that bad? But why on earth didn't you tell me?' Georgie's sea-green eyes were wide with shock as she stared into her brother's troubled face. 'I could have helped in some way.'

'How?' Robert Millett shook his blond head slowly. 'You couldn't have done anything, Georgie, no one could, and there was still an element of hope before that last contract was pulled out from under our feet. Old man Sanderson really ducked and dived for that one. But, as he's so fond of saying, all's fair in love and war.'

Georgie's smooth brow wrinkled in an angry frown. Mike Sanderson was a mean old man and she wouldn't trust him as far as she could throw him, and as she was a tiny, slender five foot four to Mike's burly six foot that wouldn't be far! 'He's an out-and-out crook,' she stated tightly. 'I just don't know how he can sleep at night with some of the tricks he pulls.'

'Georgie, Georgie, Georgie.' Robert pulled his sister into his arms and hugged her for a moment before pushing her away and looking down into her flushed face. 'We both know Mike's not to blame for the mess I'm in. I had to make some choices over the last months when Sandra was so ill, and even now I know I made the right ones. I don't regret a thing. If the business fails, it fails.'

'Oh, Robert.' This was so *unfair*. When Robert had discovered his beloved wife, Sandra, was suffering from a rare blood disorder that meant she only had a few months to live, he had devoted himself to making her last days happy

5

ones, and taking care of their seven-year-old twins, David and Annie, and trying to shield them from as much pain as possible as their mother slowly faded away. Sandra and Robert had told no one the true state of affairs—not even Georgie had known Sandra's illness was terminal until four weeks before she had died.

That had been six months ago, and immediately she had understood what was happening. Georgie had packed her bags and left her wonderful, well-paid job in advertising and high-tailed it back to the family home to take some of Robert's burden in the last traumatic weeks of Sandra's illness.

She hadn't had to think twice about such a step—Robert and Sandra had opened their arms to her when, as a bewildered little girl of ten and newly orphaned, she had needed love and care. Now, thirteen years later, it was her turn to repay the tenderness and warmth they had lavished on her, which hadn't diminished a jot when their own children were born.

'What about the de Capistrano deal? They've already offered us the contract, haven't they? And the rewards would be brilliant.' Sandra had run the office side of Robert's building firm before she had become ill, and after a succession of temps had muddled through Georgie had had her work cut out the last few months to make sense of the paperwork. It didn't help that after the funeral Robert had retreated into a world of his own for some time, the strain of being Sandra's mainstay and support, as well as mother and father to the children, telling at last.

'De Capistrano?' Robert ran a tired hand through his thick hair, which immediately sprang back to its previous disorder.

Georgie noticed, with a little pang in her heart, that there were several strands of grey mixed with the honey-gold these days. But then that wasn't surprising after all her big brother had been through, she thought painfully. They were all of them—David, Annie and herself—missing Sandra like mad, but Sandra had been Robert's childhood sweetheart and her brother's grief was overwhelming.

'We'd need to take on more men and hire machinery to make it viable, and the bank's screaming blue murder already. I had relied on the profit from this other job to finance de Capistrano's.'

'But we can go and see them and ask at least?' Georgie's small chin stuck out aggressively, as though she was already doing battle with the pinstriped brigade. 'They aren't stupid. They'll be able to see the potential, surely?'

'I'd have thought you were dead against the de Capistrano deal after all your "green" rallies and such at uni?' Robert remarked quietly. 'Animal rights, save the hedgerows, Greenpeace... You were into them all, weren't you?'

Georgie stared at him, her heavily lashed eyes narrowing. Robert had been sixteen years of age when she was born, their parents having long since given up hope of ever having another child. Consequently his attitude had always been paternal, even before the car crash which had taken their parents, and she had often rebelled against his staid and—Georgie considered—prosaic views about a million and one subjects dear to her heart. But now was not the time to go into all that, she reminded herself, as she looked into the blue of his worried eyes.

'That's a separate issue,' she said very definitely. 'If it's a case of the de Capistrano contract or virtual bankruptcy for you, I'll take the contract.'

'If they could hear you now...' Robert summoned up something of a grin—his first one for days—which Georgie took as a good sign.

'They can't.' It was succinct. 'So, how about approaching the bank?'

'Useless.' It was clear all Robert's normal get up and go had got up and gone. 'I've got de Capistrano himself coming in later this morning and he won't be interested in a building firm that's on the rocks.'

Georgie searched her mind frantically. 'Well, what about asking de Capistrano to finance the men and machinery on a short-term basis?' she suggested brightly. 'Once we got going we could pay him back fairly quickly, and it's common knowledge he is something of an entrepreneur and filthy rich into the bargain.'

'Exactly, and he hasn't got that way by doing anyone any favours,' Robert said cynically. 'His reputation is as formidable as the man himself, so I understand, and de Capistrano is only interested in a fast turnover with huge profits. Face it, Georgie, he can go elsewhere and have no hassle. End of story.'

Her brother stretched his long, lanky body wearily in the big leather chair behind the desk strewn with the morning's post, his blue eyes dropping to the fateful letter open in front of him. It stated that Sandersons—not Milletts—had been successful in securing the contract for the town's new leisure complex. A contract which would have provided the profit margin to finance the extra men's wages and hiring of the machinery for de Capistrano's job.

'But, Robert—'

'No buts.' Robert raised his head to take in his sister's aggressive stance. 'De Capistrano is a Sanderson type, Georgie. He knows all the right angles and the right people. Look at the deal we were going to discuss this morning; he negotiated that prime piece of land for a song some years ago and he's been holding on to it until the time was right to build housing. He'll get his outlay back a hundred times over on the sort of yuppie estate he is planning.'

'Yes, well...' Georgie wrinkled the small straight nose she'd inherited from her mother in disgust, unable to hide her real opinion any longer. 'I'm sorry, but I have to say destroying that beautiful land *is* out-and-out sacrilege! People have enjoyed that ground as a park in the summer ever since I can remember and the wildlife is tremendous. Do you recall that rare butterfly being found there the year I started uni?'

'Butterflies aren't good business.' Robert shrugged philosophically. 'Neither are wild flowers and the like, come to that, or putting family first and being less than ruthless. Maybe if I'd been a bit more like the de Capistranos of this world my kids wouldn't be in danger of losing the roof over their heads.'

'Don't say that,' said Georgie fiercely, her eyes sparking green flames. 'You're the best father and husband and brother in the world. You've already admitted you've no regrets in putting Sandra first and it was absolutely the right thing to do. You're ten times the man—a hundred times— de Capistrano will ever be and—'

'*Have we met?*'

Two blonde heads shot round as though connected by a single wire and a pair of horrified green eyes and amazed blue surveyed the tall dark man standing in the doorway of the small brick building that was Robert's office. The voice had been icy, and even if the slight accent hadn't informed Georgie this was de Capistrano she would have known anyway. The impeccable designer suit and silk shirt and tie sat on the tall lean body in a way that positively screamed unlimited wealth, and the beautiful svelte woman standing just behind the commanding figure was equally well dressed. And equally annoyed if the look on the lovely face was anything to go by. His secretary? Or maybe his wife?

And then Georgie's racing thoughts were focused on the man alone as he said again, 'Have we met?' and this time the voice had all the softness of a razor-sharp scalpel.

'Mr de Capistrano?' Georgie's normally clear voice was more of a weak squeak, and as she cleared her throat nervously the black head nodded slowly, the deep, steel-grey eyes piercingly intent on her face. 'I'm sorry... I didn't know...' She took a hard pull of air before continuing more coherently, 'No, Mr de Capistrano, we haven't met, and I have no excuse for my rudeness.'

'So.' The furious anger in the frosty face hadn't diminished an iota.

'Mr de Capistrano.' Robert pulled himself together and strode across the room, extending his hand as he said, 'Please understand. What you overheard was less a comment on you than an endeavour to hearten me. There was nothing personal intended. I'm Robert Millett, by the way, and this is my sister, Georgie.'

There was a pause which seemed to last for ever to Georgie's tortured senses, and then the hand was accepted. 'Matt de Capistrano.' It was pithy. 'And my secretary, Pepita Vilaseca.'

Georgie had followed her brother across to the others and as the two men shook hands she proffered her own to the immaculate figure at the side of the illustrious Mr de Capistrano. This time the pause was even longer and the lovely face was cold as the tall slim secretary extended a languid hand to Georgie, extracting it almost immediately with a haughty glance which said more clearly than any words could that she had done Georgie the most enormous favour. Pepita. Georgie looked into the beautifully made-up ebony eyes that resembled polished onyx. Sounded like an indigestion remedy to her!

And then, as Robert moved to shake the secretary's hand, Georgie was forced to raise her eyes up to the dark gaze trained on her face, and acknowledge the reality of what she had imbibed seconds earlier. This was one amazingly…handsome? No, not handsome, her brain corrected in the next moment. Male. One amazingly *male* man. Overwhelmingly, aggressively male. The sort of man who exuded such a primal masculinity that the veneer of civilisation sat frighteningly lightly on his massive frame.

The leanly muscled body, the jet-black hair cropped uncompromisingly short, the hard good looks—

'Do you always…encourage your brother by doing a character assassination on complete strangers, Miss Millett?' Matt de Capistrano asked with arctic politeness, interrupting Georgie's line of thought and forcing her to realise she had been staring unashamedly.

She turned scarlet. Help, she breathed silently. Get me out of this, someone. He had held out his hand to her and as she made herself shake his, and felt her nervously cold fingers enclosed in his firm hard grip that sent frissons of warmth down to her toes in a most peculiar way, her mouth opened and shut like a goldfish in a bowl before she was able to say breathlessly, 'No, no, I don't. Of course I don't.'

'Then why today and why me?'

His voice was very deep and of an almost gravelly texture, the slight accent turning it into pure dynamite, Georgie thought inappropriately. 'I… You weren't supposed to hear that,' she said quickly, before she realised just how stupid that sounded.

'I'd worked that one out all on my own,' he said caustically.

Oh, how could she have been so unforgivably indiscreet?

Georgie's heart sank into her shoes. Her flat shoes. Which didn't help her confidence at all with this huge six-foot avenging angel towering over her measly five foot four inches—or perhaps angel was the wrong description. 'It was just an expression,' she said weakly. 'There was absolutely nothing personal in it, as Robert said.'

'That actually makes it worse, Miss Millett.' It was cutting. 'When—or should I say if?—anyone had the temerity to insult me I would expect it to be for a well-thought-out and valid reason.'

Well, hang on just a tick and I'm sure I can come up with several, Georgie thought darkly, forcing a respectful nod of her head as she said out loud, 'All I can do is to apologise again, Mr de Capistrano.' Which is exactly what you want, isn't it? Your full pound of flesh.

'You work here?'

Georgie thought frantically. If she said yes it might be the final death knell to any faint hope Robert had of persuading this man to finance the cost of the new machinery for a short time, but if she said no and the deal did go through he'd soon know she'd been economical with the truth!

'Temporarily,' she compromised hesitantly.

'Temporarily.' The lethal eyes demanded an explanation, but Robert—tired of being virtually ignored—cleared his throat at the side of them in a way that demanded attention. Matt de Capistrano paid him no attention at all. 'Does that mean you will be here for the foreseeable future, Miss Millett?'

Without your contract there isn't a future. It was that thought which enabled Georgie to draw herself up straight and say, as she met the icy grey gaze head-on, 'Not if you feel that would be inappropriate after what I've said, Mr de Capistrano.'

He blinked. Just once, but she saw she had surprised him. And then he swung round to face Robert, his dark aura releasing her as his piercing gaze left her hot face. 'I came here today to discuss a proposed business deal,' he said coldly, 'and I am a very busy man, Mr Millett. You have the financial details ready which my secretary asked you to prepare?'

Robert gulped. 'I do, Mr de Capistrano, but—'

'Then as we have already wasted several minutes of valuable time I suggest we get down to business,' Matt de Capistrano said tightly, cutting across Robert's stumbling voice.

What an arrogant, ignorant, overbearing, high and mighty—Georgie's furious adjectives came to a sudden halt as the grey eyes flicked her way again. 'I trust you have no objection to that, Miss Millett?' he asked softly, something in his face making it quite clear to Georgie he had known exactly what she was thinking. 'I take it you are your brother's…temporary secretary?'

Somehow, and she couldn't quite put a finger on it, but somehow he made it sound insulting. 'Yes, I am,' she responded tightly.

'How…convenient,' he drawled smoothly.

'Convenient?' It was wary.

'To have a ready-made job available like this rather than having to fight your way in the big bad world and prove yourself,' was the—to Georgie—shocking answer.

How dared he? How *dared* he make assumptions about her just because she had ruffled his wealthy, powerful feathers? That last remark was just plain nasty. Georgie reared up like a small tigress, all thoughts of appeasement flying out of the window as she bit out, 'I happen to be a very good secretary, Mr de Capistrano.' She had worked her socks off as a temp all through the university holidays in order to be less of a financial burden on Robert—one of her ten GCSEs being that of Typing and Computer Literacy before her A Levels in Business Studies, English and Art and Design—and every firm the temping agency had placed her with had wanted her back.

'Really?' Her obvious annoyance seemed to diminish his. 'You did a secretarial course at college?'

'Not exactly.' She glared at him angrily.

'My sister graduated from university two years ago with a First in Art and Design,' Robert cut in swiftly, sensing Georgie was ready to explode.

'Then why waste such admirable talents working for big brother?' He was speaking to her as though Robert and his secretary didn't exist, and apart from the content of his words hadn't acknowledged Robert had spoken. 'Lack of ambition? Contentment with the status quo? Laziness? What?'

Georgie couldn't believe her ears. 'Now look here, you—'

Robert cut in again, his face very straight now and his voice holding a harsh note as he said, 'Georgie left an excellent job a few months ago, Mr de Capistrano, in advertising—a job she was successful in obtaining over a host of other applicants, I might add. She did this purely for me and there is no question of it being a free ride here, if that is what you are suggesting. My wife used to run the office here but—'

'You don't have to explain to him.' Georgie was past caring about the contract or anything else she was so mad.

'But she died six months ago. Okay?' Robert finished more calmly.

There was a screaming silence for a full ten seconds and Georgie moved closer to Robert, putting her hand on his arm. She noticed the secretary had done the same thing to

Matt de Capistrano which seemed to suggest a certain closeness if nothing else.

'I'm not sure that an apology even begins to cover such insensitivity, Mr Millett, but I would be grateful if you would accept it,' the tall dark man in front of them said quietly. 'I had no idea of your circumstances, of course.'

'There was no reason why you should have.' Robert's voice was more resigned than anything now. He had the feeling Matt de Capistrano was itching to shake the dust of this particular building firm off his feet as quickly—and finally—as possible.

'Perhaps not, but I have inadvertently added to your pain at this difficult time and that is unforgivable.' The accent made the words almost quaint, but in view of the situation—and not least the big lean figure speaking them—there was nothing cosy about the scenario being played out in the small office.

'Forget it.' Robert waved a dismissive hand. 'But it is the case that I find myself in somewhat changed circumstances. We discovered this morning we had lost some vital work, work which I had assumed would finance the extra men and hire of machinery I need for your job, Mr de Capistrano.'

'Are you saying the estimate you supplied is no longer viable?' The deep voice was now utterly businesslike, and Georgie—standing to one side of the two men—suddenly felt invisible. It was not a pleasant feeling.

'Not exactly,' Robert replied cautiously. 'I can still do the job at the price I put forward, if my bank is prepared to finance the machinery and so on, but—'

'They won't,' Matt de Capistrano finished for him coolly. 'Are you telling me your business is in financial difficulties, Mr Millett?'

'I'm virtually bankrupt.'

Georgie couldn't stop the gasp of shock at hearing it put so baldly, and as the men's heads turned her way she said quickly, without thinking about it, 'Because he dedicated himself to his wife when she and the children needed him, Mr de Capistrano, *not* because he isn't a good builder. He's a great builder, the best you could get, and he never cuts corners like some I could mention. You can look at any of the work he's done in the past and—'

'Georgie, please.' Robert was scarlet with embarrassment. 'This is between me and Mr de Capistrano.'

'But you *are* a fine builder,' Georgie returned desperately. 'You know you are but you won't say so—'

'*Georgie.*' Robert's voice was not loud but the quality of his tone told her she had gone as far as she could go.

'I think it might be better if you waited in your office, Miss Millett,' Matt de Capistrano suggested smoothly, nodding his head at the door through which her small cubbyhole of a place was situated.

Georgie longed to defy him—she had never longed for anything so much in all her life—but something in Robert's eyes forced her to comply without another word.

For the first time since childhood she found herself biting her nails as she sat at her desk piled high with paperwork, the interconnecting door to Robert's office now firmly shut. She could just hear the low murmur of voices from within, but the actual conversation was indistinguishable, and as time slipped by her apprehension grew.

How long did it take to rip up a contract and say bye-bye? she thought painfully. Matt de Capistrano wasn't going to twist the knife in some way to pay her back for her rudeness, was he? Those few minutes in there had made it plain he'd never been spoken to like that before in his life, and a man like him didn't take such an insult lying down. Not that she had actually *spoken* to him when she'd insulted him, just about him. She groaned softly. Her and her big mouth. Oh, why, *why* had he had to come in at that precise moment and why had she left the door to her office open so he'd heard every word? And Robert. Why hadn't he *told* her how bad things were?

The abrupt opening of the door caught her by surprise and she raised anxious green eyes to see Matt de Capistrano looking straight at her, a hard, speculative gleam in the dark grey eyes. 'Daydreaming, Miss Millett?'

The tone of his voice could have indicated he was being friendly, lightly amusing in a pleasant teasing fashion, but Georgie was looking into his face—unlike the two behind him—and she knew different. 'Of course. What else do temporary secretaries do?' she answered sweetly, her green eyes narrowing as she stared her dislike.

He smiled, moving to stand by her desk as he said, 'I intend to phone your brother tonight from Scotland after certain enquiries have been made. The call will be of vital importance so can you make sure the line is free?'

'Certainly.' She knew exactly what he was implying and now added, 'I'll let all my friends and my hairdresser and beautician know not to call me then, shall I?' in helpful, dulcet tones.

His mouth tightened; it clearly wasn't often he was answered in like vein. 'Just so.' The harsh face could have been set in stone. 'I shall be working to a tight schedule so time is of the essence.'

'Absolutely, Mr de Capistrano.'

The grey gaze held her one more moment and then he swept past her, the secretary and Robert at his heels, and as the door closed behind them Georgie sank back in her seat and let out a big whoosh of a sigh. Horrible man! Horrible, horrible man! She ignored the faint odour of expensive aftershave and the way it was making her senses quiver and concentrated her mind on loathing him instead.

She could hear the sound of voices outside the building and surmised they must all be standing in the little yard, and, after rising from her chair, she peeped cautiously through the blind at the window.

Matt de Capistrano and his secretary were just getting into a chauffeur-driven silver Mercedes, and even from this distance he was intimidating. Not that he had intimidated *her*, Georgie told herself strongly in the next moment, not a bit of it, but he was one of those men who was uncomfortably, in-your-face male. There was a sort of dark power about him, an aggressive virility that was impossible to ignore, and it was...Georgie searched for the right word and found it. Disturbing. He was disturbing. But he was leaving now and with any luck she would never set eyes on him again.

And then she suddenly realised what she was thinking and offered up a quick urgent prayer of repentance. Robert's whole business, his livelihood, *everything* hung on Matt de Capistrano giving him this contract; how could she—for one second—wish he didn't get it? But she hadn't, she hadn't wished that, she reassured herself frantically the next moment, just that she wouldn't see Matt de Capistrano again. But if Robert got the job—by some miracle—of course she'd have to see him if she continued working here. *'Oh...'* She sighed again, loudly and irritably. The man had got her in such a state she didn't know what she was thinking!

'Well!' Robert opened the door and he was smiling. 'We might, we just might be back in business again.'

'Really?' Georgie forgot all about her dislike of Matt de Capistrano as the naked hope in her brother's face touched her heart. 'He's going to help?'

'Maybe.' Robert was clearly trying to keep a hold on his optimism but he couldn't disguise his relief as he said, 'He's not dismissed it out of hand anyway. It all depends on that phone call tonight and then we'll know one way or the other. He's going to make some enquiries. I can't blame him; I'd do the same in his shoes.'

'Enquiries?' Georgie raised fine arched eyebrows. 'With whom?'

'Anyone he damn well wants,' Robert answered drily. 'I've given him a host of names and numbers—the bank manager, my accountant, firms we've dealt with recently and so on—and told him I'll ring them and tell them to let him have any information he wants. This is my last hope, Georgie. If the man tells me to jump through hoops I'll turn cartwheels as well for good measure.'

'Oh, Robert.' She didn't want him to lose everything, she didn't, but to be rescued by Matt de Capistrano! And it was only in that moment she fully acknowledged the extent of the antagonism which had leapt into immediate life the moment she had laid eyes on the darkly handsome face. She didn't know him, she'd barely exchanged more than a dozen words with him, and yet she disliked him more intensely than anyone else she had ever met. Well, almost anyone. Her thoughts touched on Glen before she closed that particular door in her mind.

'So, cross your fingers and your toes and anything else it's physically possible to cross,' Robert said more quietly now, a nervous note creeping in as they stared at each other. 'If it's no we're down the pan, Georgie; even the house is mortgaged up to the hilt so the kids won't even have a roof over their heads.'

'They will.' Georgie's voice was fierce. 'We'll make sure of that and we'll all stay together too.' But a little grotty flat somewhere wouldn't be the same as Robert's pleasant semi with its big garden and the tree-house he had built for the children a couple of years ago. They had lost their mother and all the security she had embodied; were they going to have to lose their home too?

'Maybe.' And then as Georgie eyed him determinedly Robert smiled as he said, 'Definitely! But let's hope it won't come to uprooting the kids, Georgie. Look, get the bank on the phone for me first, would you? I need to put them and everyone else in the know and explain they'll be getting a call from de Capistrano's people. I don't want anyone else to tread on his very wealthy and powerful toes.'

Georgie looked sharply at Robert at that, and was relieved to see he was grinning at her. 'I'm sorry about what I said,' she said weakly. 'I didn't know he was there. I nearly died when I saw him.'

'You and me both.' Robert shook his head slowly. 'I'd forgotten there's never a dull moment around you, little sister.'

'Oh, you.'

The rest of the day sped by in a flurry of phone-calls, faxes and hastily typed letters, and by the end of the afternoon Georgie was sick of the very sound of Matt de Capistrano's name. Yesterday her life had been difficult—juggling her new role as surrogate mum, cook and housekeeper, Robert's secretary and shoulder to cry on wasn't easy—but today a tall, obnoxious stranger had made it downright impossible, she thought crossly just before five o'clock. Robert had been like a cat on a hot tin roof all day and neither of them had been able to eat any lunch.

One thing had solidified through the hectic afternoon, though. If Matt de Capistrano bailed them out she was leaving here as soon as she could fix up a good secretary for Robert. She could get heaps more money working at temping anyway, and every little bit would help the family budget for the time being. And temping meant she could be there for the children if either of them were ill, without worrying Robert would be struggling at the office, and she could pick and choose when she worked. She might even be able to do a little freelance advertising work if she took a few days out to tote her CV and examples of her artwork designs round the area.

Her previous job, as a designer working on tight deadlines and at high speed for an independent design studio situated north of Watford had been on the other side of London—Robert's house and business being in Sevenoaks—but there were other studios and other offices.

Whatever, she would remove herself from any chance of bumping into Matt de Capistrano. Georgie nodded to the thought, her hands pausing on the keyboard of her word processor as she gazed into space, only to jump violently as the telephone on her desk rang shrilly.

She glanced at her wristwatch as she reached for the receiver. Five o'clock. Exactly. It was him! She ignored the ridiculous churning in her stomach and breathed deeply, her voice steady and cool as she said, 'Millett's Builders. How can I help you?'

'Miss Millett?' The deep voice trickled over her taut nerves gently but with enough weight to make them twang slightly. 'Matt de Capistrano. Is your brother there?'

'Yes, Mr de Capistrano, he's been waiting for your call,' Georgie said briskly.

'Thank you.'

Boy, with a voice like that he'd be dynamite on the silver screen—Sean Connery eat your heart out! Georgie thought flusteredly as she buzzed Robert and put the call through. Deep and husky with the faint accent making it heart-racingly sexy— And then she caught her errant ramblings firmly, more than a little horrified at the way her mind had gone. He was a hateful man, despicable. End of story.

She heard the telephone go down in the other office and when, a moment later, the interconnecting door opened with a flourish she knew. Even before Robert spoke his beaming face told her what the outcome of Matt de Capistrano's enquiries had been. They were in business.

CHAPTER TWO

'WE MEET again, Miss Millett.' In spite of the fact that Georgie had been steeling herself all morning for this encounter, her head snapped up so sharply she felt a muscle in her neck twang.

A full week had elapsed since that day in Robert's office when she had first seen Matt de Capistrano, and it was now the first day of May and a beautiful sunny morning outside the building. Inside Georgie felt the temperature had just dropped about ten degrees as she met the icy grey eyes watching her so intently from the doorway.

'Good morning, Mr de Capistrano.' There was no designer suit today; he was dressed casually in black denim jeans and a pale cream shirt and if anything the dark aura surrounding him was enhanced tenfold. Georgie knew he and Robert were going on site for most of the day, along with Matt de Capistrano's architects and a whole host of other people, but she hadn't bargained for what the open-necked shirt and black jeans which sat snugly on lean male hips would do to her equilibrium. She wanted to swallow nervously but she just knew the grey gaze would pick up the action, and so she said, a little throatily, 'Robert is waiting for you if you'd like to go through?' as she indicated her brother's office with a wave of her hand.

'Thank you, but I wish to have a word with you first.'

Oh, help! He was going to come down on her like a ton of bricks for her rudeness a week ago. He held all the cards and he knew it. He could make their lives hell if he wanted. Georgie raised her small chin a fraction and her voice be-

23

trayed none of her inward agitation as she looked into the dark attractive face and said quietly, 'Yes, Mr de Capistrano?'

Her little cubby-hole, which was barely big enough to hold her desk and chair and the filing cabinet, and barely warranted the grand name of an office, was covered by one male stride, and then he was standing at the side of her as he said, 'Firstly, I do not think it appropriate we stand on ceremony with the Mr de Capistrano and Miss Millett now we are working together, yes?'

In spite of his perfect English he sounded very foreign. Georgie just had to take that swallow before she could say, 'If that's what you want, Mr de Capistrano.'

'It is,' he affirmed softly. 'And the name is Matt.'

The grey eyes were so dark as to be almost black, Georgie thought inconsequentially, and surrounded by such thick black lashes it seemed a shame to waste them on a man. And he seemed even bigger than she remembered. 'Then please call me Georgie,' she managed politely.

He inclined his head briefly. 'And the second thing is that I find myself in need of your assistance today, Georgie,' he continued smoothly. 'My secretary, Pepita, has unfortunately had a slight accident this morning and twisted her ankle. Perhaps you would take her place on site and take notes for me?'

Oh, no. No, no, no. She'd never survive a day in his company without making a fool of herself or something. She couldn't, she really couldn't do this! If nothing else this confirmed she was doing absolutely the right thing in trying to find a new secretary to take her place for Robert.

Georgie called on every bit of composure she could muster and said steadily, 'Perhaps you had better ask Robert about that. It would mean closing the office here, of course, which is not ideal. His men are finishing work on a shop we've been renovating and are expected to call in some time this afternoon, and there's the phone to answer and so on.'

'You have an answering machine?' Matt enquired pleasantly.

'Yes, but—'

'And your presence will only be required during the discussions with the architect and planner. After that you may return here and perhaps type up the notes for me,' he continued silkily.

Oh, hell! It would be today his precious secretary decided to twist her ankle, Georgie thought helplessly. She doubted if Matt de Capistrano would be around much in the normal run of things; a wealthy tycoon like him had his fingers in a hundred and one pies at any one time, and within a few weeks she would hopefully be out of here anyway. This was *just* the sort of situation she'd been trying to avoid when she'd decided to find a replacement secretary for Robert. 'Well, like I said, you'd best discuss this with Robert,' she said faintly.

'And if Robert agrees? I can tell him you have no objection, yes?' he persisted.

No, no and triple no. 'Of course, Mr—Matt,' Georgie said calmly.

'Thank you, Georgie.'

His accent gave her name emphasis on the last 'e' and lifted it into something quite different from the mundane, and she was just coping with what that did to her nerves when the hard gaze narrowed as he said conversationally, 'You do not like me, Georgie.'

It was a statement, not a question, but even if it had been otherwise Georgie would have been unable to answer him immediately such was the state of her surprise.

'This is not a problem,' he continued smoothly as she

stared at him wide-eyed. His gaze rested briefly on the dark gold of her hair, which hung to her shoulders in a silky bob, before he added, 'Unless you make it one, of course.'

'I... That is—' She was spluttering, she realised suddenly, and with the knowledge came a flood of angry adrenaline that strengthened her voice as her mind became clearer. If he thought she was some pathetic little doormat who would let him walk all over her just because he was bailing them out, he'd got another think coming! She was no one's whipping boy. 'I have no intention of making it one,' she answered smartly.

'This is good.'

Georgie's soft mouth tightened further as she caught what she was sure was the hint of laughter in the dark voice, although his face was betraying no amusement whatsoever, and she struggled to keep her tone even and cool as she said, 'In fact, I don't expect to be working for Robert much longer, actually. It's far better that he has someone else working for him here so that I can divide my time between looking after the children and temping work. So I doubt our paths will cross after that.'

To her absolute horror he sat down on a corner of the desk, his body warmth reaching into her air space as he said quietly, 'Ah, yes, the children. How old are they? Are they coping?'

That same expensive and utterly delicious smell she'd caught wafting off the hard tanned body before was doing wicked things to her hormones, but Georgie was pleased to note nothing of her inward turmoil showed in her voice as she answered evenly, 'The twins are seven, coming up for eight, and they are coping pretty well on the whole. They have lots of friends and their teacher at school at the moment is actually Sandra's—their mother's—best friend, so she is being an absolute brick.'

'And your brother?' he asked quietly, his head tilting as he moved a fraction closer which made her heartbeat quicken. 'How is he doing?'

Georgie cleared her throat. There were probably a million and one men who could sit on her desk all day if they so wished without her turning a hair and without one stray thought coming into her mind. Matt de Capistrano was not one of them.

'Robert is naturally devastated,' she said even more quietly than he had spoken. 'Sandra was his world. They'd known each other since they were children and after they married they even worked together, so their lives were intrinsically linked.'

'I see.' He nodded slowly, and Georgie wondered if he was aware of just how sexy he looked when he narrowed his eyes like that. 'Such devotion is unusual, one might even say exceptional in this day and age of supermarket marriage.'

'Supermarket marriage?' she asked bewilderedly.

'One samples one brand for a while before purchasing another and then another,' he drawled in cynical explanation. 'The lawyers get fatter than anyone, of course.'

'Not all marriages are like that,' Georgie objected steadily. 'Some people fall in love and it lasts a lifetime.'

The grey eyes fastened even more piercingly on her face and now the metallic glint was mocking. 'Don't tell me you are a romantic,' he said derisively.

She had been, once. 'No, I am not a romantic.' Her voice was cool now, and dismissive. 'But I know what Sandra and Robert had was real, that's all.'

She couldn't read the expression on his face now, but as he opened his mouth to speak Robert chose that moment to open the door of his office, his face breaking into a warm smile as he said, 'I thought I heard voices out here. Come on in, Matt. There's just a couple of points I'd like to discuss before we leave.'

Whew! As the door closed behind the two men Georgie slumped in her chair for a moment, one hand smoothing a wisp of silky hair from her flushed face. Something gave her the impression this was going to be one of those days!

She had been banking on using the time the office was quiet with Robert on site to organize the arrangements for the twins' birthday party. She and Robert had suddenly realised the night before that the children's birthday was only a couple of weeks away and neither of them had given it a thought. Sandra had always made a big deal of their birthday and Georgie wanted to keep everything as normal as she could in the circumstances, so—Robert being unable to face the thought of the house being invaded by family and friends and loads of screaming infants—she had thought of booking a hall somewhere and hiring a bouncy castle and a magician and the full works.

The buzzer on her desk interrupted further musing. 'Georgie?' Robert's voice sounded strained. 'Could you organise coffee, make it three cups, would you, and bring in your notebook? I want you to sit in on this.'

What now? Georgie thought as she quickly fetched out the best mugs and a packet of the delicious chocolate caramel biscuits her brother loved. He had lost a great deal of weight in the last months and she had been trying to feed him up since she'd come home.

Once the coffee was ready she straightened her pencil-slim skirt and demure, buttoned-up-to-the-collar blouse and steeled herself for the moment she faced those piercing grey eyes again. Since her first day of working for Robert she had always dressed well, bearing in mind that she was the first impression people received when they walked through the door, but today she had taken extra care and it was only in this moment she acknowledged the fact. And it irritated her. Irritated and annoyed her. She didn't *want* to care what Matt de Capistrano thought of her. He was just a brief fleeting shadow in her life, totally unimportant. *He was.*

The brief and totally unimportant shadow was sitting with one knee over the other and muscled arms stretched along the back of the big comfy visitor's seat in Robert's office when she entered, and immediately her body's reaction to the overt male pose forced her to recognise her own awareness of him. Georgie was even more ruffled when her innate honesty emphasised that his flagrant masculinity was all the more overwhelming for its casual unconsciousness, and after serving the men their coffee and offering them the plate of biscuits she sat down herself, folding her hands neatly in her lap after placing her own coffee within easy reach. She was not going to fidget or gabble or react in any way to Matt de Capistrano, not if it killed her.

'So...' Robert's voice was still strained. 'To recap, you feel Mains and Jenson will have to go?' he said to Matt, referring to the two elderly bricklayers who had been with Robert since he first started the firm fourteen years ago.

'What?' Georgie forgot all about the non-reaction as she reared up in her seat. 'George and Walter?' She had known the two men even before she had come under Robert's wing and they had always treated her like a favourite granddaughter, as had their wives. The first summer she had come to live with Robert and Sandra, when she'd been bitterly grieving for her parents, Walter and his wife had taken her away to France for two weeks to try and take her mind off her parents' untimely death and they had been utterly wonderful to her. 'You can't! You can't get rid of them.'

'Excuse me?' The steel-grey eyes had narrowed into slits of light and he was frowning.

'They're like family,' Georgie said passionately.

'Family's fine,' Matt said coolly. 'Inefficient employees are something else. Walter Jenson is well past retiring age and George Mains turned sixty-five a year ago.'

'They are excellent bricklayers!' Her green eyes were flashing sparks now.

'They are too slow,' he said dismissively, 'and this is not a charitable concern for geriatrics. Your brother must have lost thousands over the last few years by carrying men like Mains and Jenson. I've no doubt of their experience or the quality of their work, but Jenson was off sick more than he was at work over the last twelve months—severe arthritis, isn't it?' he asked in a brief aside to Robert, who nodded unhappily. 'And Mains's unfortunate stroke last year has slowed him up to the point where I believe he actually represents something of a danger to himself and others, especially when working on scaffolding. If you drop something from any sort of height you could kill or maim anyone beneath.'

'I don't believe this!' She glared at him angrily. 'They are craftsmen, the pair of them.'

'They are old craftsmen and it's time to let some young blood take over,' Matt said ruthlessly, 'however much it hurts.'

'And of course it really hurts you, doesn't it?' Georgie bit out furiously, ignoring Robert's frantic hand-signals as she jerked to her feet. 'Two dear ol—' She caught herself as the grey gaze sharpened. 'Two dear men who have been the rocks on which this business was built just thrown on to the scrap heap. What reward is that for all their faithfulness to Robert and this family? But faithfulness means nothing to men like you, does it? You've made your millions, you're sitting pretty, but you're still greedy for more and if more means men like Walter and George get sacrificed along the way then so be it.'

'Have you quite finished?' He was still sitting in the relaxed manner of earlier but the grey gaze was lethal and pointed straight at Georgie's flushed face. 'Then sit down, Miss Millett.'

'I don't think—'

'Sit down!'

The bark made her jump and in spite of herself Georgie felt her legs obey him.

'Firstly, your brother has made it clear just what he owes these two employees and they will be retired with a very generous package,' Matt ground out coldly. 'I think, as does Robert if he speaks the truth, that this will not come as a surprise to them; neither will it be wholly displeasing. Secondly, you talk of sacrifice when you are prepared to jeopardise the rest of your brother's employees' livelihoods for the sake of two elderly men who should have retired years ago?

'It is human nature for the rest of the men to tailor their speed to the slowest worker when there is a set wage at the end of each week. Your brother's workers have been underachieving for years and a week ago they were in danger of reaping their reward, every one of them. If Robert had gone bankrupt everyone would have been a loser. There is no place for weakness in industry; you should know that.'

'And kindness?' She continued to glare at him even though a tiny part of her brain was pressing her to recognise there was more than an element of truth in what he had said. 'What about kindness and gratitude? How do you think they'll feel at being told they're too old?'

'They know the dates on their birth certificates as well

as anyone,' he said icily, 'so I doubt it will come as the surprise you seem to foresee.'

He folded his arms over his chest, settling more comfortably in his seat as he studied her stiff body and tense face through narrowed eyes.

Georgie didn't respond immediately, more because she was biting back further hot words as the full portent of what she had yelled at him registered than because she was intimidated by his coldness. And then she said, her voice shaking slightly, 'I think what you are demanding Robert do is awful.'

'Then don't think.' He sat forward in his seat, draining his mug with one swallow and turning to Robert as he said, 'I'd suggest you take this opportunity to change the men over to piece work. With a set goal each week and good bonuses for extra achievement you'll soon sort out the wheat from the chaff, and you've limped on long enough.'

Georgie looked at her brother, willing him to stand up to this tyrant, but Robert merely nodded thoughtfully. 'I'd been thinking along the same lines myself,' he agreed quietly.

'Good, that's settled, then,' Matt said imperturbably. 'Now, if you'd like to get Georgie to note those few points that need checking on site we'll be on our way. Have you got any other shoes than those?' he added, looking at her wafer-thin high heels which she had never worn to the office before but which went perfectly with the charcoal skirt she was wearing. They also showed her legs—which Georgie considered her best feature, hating her small bust and too-slender hips—off to their best advantage, but she'd tried to excuse that thought all morning.

Georgie was still mentally reeling from the confrontation of the last few minutes, and a full ten seconds went by before she could say, her voice suitably cutting, 'I wasn't aware I was expected to go on site this morning, if you remember, so, no, I haven't any other shoes with me.'

'There's your wellies in the back of my car,' Robert put in helpfully. 'You remember we put all our boots in there when we took the kids down to the river for that walk at the weekend?'

Her brother probably had no idea why she glared at him the way she did, Georgie reflected, as she said, 'Thank you, Robert,' in a very flat voice. She was going to look just great, wasn't she? Expensive silk jade-green blouse, elegant skirt and great hefty black wellington boots. Wonderful. And that…that *swine* sitting there so complacently with his hateful grey eyes looking her up and down was to blame for this, and he was enjoying every minute of her discomfiture. She didn't have to look at him to know that; it was radiating out from the lean male figure in waves.

As it happened, by the time Georgie jumped out of Robert's old car at the site of the proposed new estate she wasn't thinking about her appearance.

Newbottle Meadow, as the site had always been called by all the children thereabouts, was old farmland and still surrounded by grazing cattle in the far distance. When Georgie had first come to live with her brother and his wife the area had been virtually country, but the swiftly encroaching urban advance had swallowed hundreds of acres and now Newbottle Meadow was on the edge of the town. But as yet it was still unspoilt and beautiful.

Georgie stood gazing at the rolling meadowland filled with pink-topped grasses and buttercups and butterflies and she wanted to cry. According to Robert, Matt de Capistrano had had the foresight to buy the land a decade ago when it had still officially been farmland. After several appeals he had managed to persuade the powers-that-be to grant his application for housing—as he had known would happen eventually—thereby guaranteeing a thousandfold profit as relatively inexpensive agricultural land became prime development ground. And then with the yuppie-style estate he was proposing to build...

Philistine! Georgie gulped in the mild May sunshine which turned the buttercups to luminescent gold and the grasses to pink feathers, and forced back the tears pricking the backs of her eyes. Badgers lived here, along with rabbits and foxes and butterflies galore. She and her friends had spent many happy hours marching out of the town to the meadow where they had camped for days on end and had a whale of a time. And now it was all going to be ripped up—mutilated—for filthy lucre. But it would be the saving of Robert's firm and ultimately her brother himself. The blow of losing his business as well as his wife would have been horrific.

Georgie bit hard on her lip as she turned to see Matt de Capistrano's red Lamborghini—obviously the Mercedes and the chauffeur were having a day off!—glide to a silky-smooth stop a few yards away. She had to think of Robert and the children in all of this, she told herself fiercely. Her ideals, the unspoilt meadow and all the wildlife, weren't as important as David and Annie and Robert.

'You could turn milk sour with that face.'

'What?' She was so startled by the softly drawled insult as Matt reached her side that she literally gaped at him.

'Forget Mains and Jenson; the decision has been made,' Matt said quietly, his eyes roaming to Robert, who had joined the other men waiting for them in the middle of the acres of meadowland.

'I wasn't thinking about George and Walter,' she returned without thinking.

'No?' He eyed her disbelievingly.

'No.''

''Then what?' he asked softly, turning to look into her heart-shaped face. 'Why the ferocious glare and wishing me six foot under?'

'I wasn't—' She stopped abruptly in the middle of the denial. Maybe she had been at that. But he would never understand in a million years, besides which she would be cutting off her nose—or Robert's nose—to spite her face if she did or said anything to stop Robert securing this contract. Matt de Capistrano would simply use another builder and the estate would become reality anyway. 'It doesn't matter,' she finished weakly.

'Georgie.' Before she could object he had turned her round, his hand lifting her chin as he looked down into the green of her eyes. 'Tell me. I'm a big boy. I can take it.'

It was the mockery that did it. He was laughing at her again and Georgie stiffened, her eyes slanting green fire as she fairly spat, 'You're going to spoil this beautiful land, desecrate it, and you just don't care, do you? You've got no soul.'

For a moment he just stared at her in amazement, and she observed—with a shred of satisfaction in all the pain and embarrassment—that she had managed to shock him. 'What?' he growled quietly.

'I used to play here as a child, camp out with my friends and have fun,' she said tightly. 'And this land is still one of the few places hereabouts which is truly wild and beautiful. People come here to *breathe*, don't you see? And you are going to destroy it, along with all the wildlife and the beauty—'

'People have been allowed to come here because I didn't stop them,' he said impatiently. 'I could have fenced it off but I didn't.'

'Because it was too much trouble,' she shot back quickly.

'For crying out loud!' He stared at her with very real incredulity. 'Is there no end to my crimes where you are concerned? Don't you want Robert to build this estate?'

'Of course I do.' She stared at him angrily. 'And I don't. Of course I don't! How could I when I look at all this and think that in a few months it will be covered with bulldozers and dirt and pretty little houses for people who think the latest designer label and a Mercedes are all that matters in life? But I don't want Robert to lose his chance of making good; I love him and he's worked so hard and been through so much. So of course I want him to have the contract.'

He shut his eyes for a moment in a way that said far more than any words could have done, and she resented him furiously for the unspoken criticism and the guilt it engendered. She was being ridiculous, illogical and totally unreasonable, but she couldn't help it. She just couldn't help it. This meadowland had healed something deep inside her in the terrible aftermath of her parents' death. The peace, the tranquillity, the overriding *continuing* of life here had meant so much. And now it was all going to be swept away.

It had welcomed her after the Glen episode in her life too, reaching out to her with comforting fingers as she had walked the childhood paths and let her fingers brush through grasses and wild flowers that had had an endless consistency about them in a world that had suddenly been turned upside down.

'I'm sorry.' Suddenly all the anger had seeped away and she felt she had shrunk down to a child again. 'This isn't your fault, not altogether.'

He said something in Spanish that she was sure was uncomplimentary, then said in English, 'Thank you, Georgie.

That makes me feel a whole lot better,' in tones of deep and biting sarcasm.

'You won't take the contract from Robert because you are angry with me?' she asked anxiously.

His mouth tightened still more and now the hand under her chin became a vice as he looked down into the emerald orbs staring up at him. 'I think I like it better when you are aware you are insulting me,' he said very softly.

Under the thin silk shirt she could see a dark shadow and guessed his chest was covered with body hair. He would probably be hairy all over. Somehow it went with the intoxicating male perfume of him, the overall *alienness* of Matt de Capistrano that was threatening and exciting at the same time. And she didn't want to be threatened or excited. She just wanted... What? She didn't know what she wanted any more.

'Georgie?'

She heard Robert calling through the buzzing in her ears as the warm hand under her chin held her for a second more, his gaze stroking over her bewildered face. And then he let her go, stepping away from her as he called in an unforgivably controlled voice, 'We are just coming, Robert, Georgie has been reminiscing about her childhood up here. It must have been fun.'

Philistine!

CHAPTER THREE

GEORGIE felt it wise to keep a very low profile during the rest of the morning, quietly taking notes on all that was said as she plodded after the men in her flapping wellington boots. She made sure she had no eye contact at all with Matt, even when he spoke directly to her as she found herself walking with him to the parked cars. 'Thank you, Georgie, that's your job here done for today,' he said easily. 'We are going to grab a spot of lunch before we finish off this afternoon. Would you care to join us?'

'I don't think so.' She looked somewhere in the middle of his tanned throat as she said quietly, 'I've things to do back at the office.' The last thing, the very last thing in all the world she wanted to do was to sit in a social atmosphere and make small talk with Matt de Capistrano.

'But surely you will have to eat?' he persisted softly.

'I've brought sandwiches which I'll eat at my desk.'

'How industrious of you.'

Sarcastic swine! 'Not really,' she answered tightly. 'I want to telephone a few places and set up the arrangements for Robert's children's birthday party. It's been pretty busy over the last few weeks and it's only just dawned on us they'll be eight in two weeks' time. We want to make their birthday as special as we can for them.'

He nodded as she forced herself to meet the grey eyes at last. 'What are you planning?' he asked, as though he were really interested.

Which she was sure he wasn't, Georgie thought cynically. Why would a multi-millionaire like Matt de

Capistrano care about two eight-year-olds' birthday party? 'A hall somewhere with a bouncy castle and so on,' she answered dismissively.

'Ah, yes, the bouncy castle.' He looked down at her, his piercing eyes glittering pewter in the sunshine. 'My nephews and nieces enjoy these things too.'

He was an uncle? Ridiculously she was absolutely amazed. Somehow she couldn't picture him as anything other than a cold business tycoon, but of course he would have a family. Robert had mentioned in passing some days ago that Matt de Capistrano was not married, but that didn't stop him being a son or a brother. She brought her racing thoughts under control and said quietly, 'Children are the same everywhere.'

'So it would seem.' He looked at her for a second more before turning to glance at Robert in the distance, who was still deep in conversation with the chief architect. 'I will take you back to the office while the others finish off here and meet them at the pub,' he said expressionlessly.

'No.' It was too quick and too instinctive and they both recognised it. Georgie felt her cheeks begin to burn and said feverishly, 'I mean, I wouldn't want to put you to any trouble and Robert won't mind. Or, better still, I could take his car and he can go with you—'

'It is no trouble, Georgie.' The words themselves were nothing; the manner in which they were said told her all too clearly she had annoyed him again and he was now determined to have his own way. As usual.

Could she refuse to ride with him? Georgie's eyes flickered to Robert's animated face and her brother's excitement was the answer. No, she couldn't. 'If you're sure you don't mind,' she said weakly, striving to act as if this was a perfectly normal conversation instead of one as potentially explosive as a loaded gun.

'Not at all.' He bent close enough for her to scent his male warmth as he said softly but perfectly seriously, 'The pleasure will be all mine.' And he allowed just a long enough pause before he added, 'As we both know.'

This time Georgie couldn't think of a single thing to say, and so she stood meekly at his side as he called to Robert and informed him he would see them all at the White Knight after he had taken Georgie back to the office. Her eyes moved to the red Lamborghini crouching at the side of the road. She had never ridden in a Lamborghini before; in fact she hadn't seen one this close up before either. Perhaps at a different time with a different driver the experience would be one to be savoured, but the car was too like its master to be anything else but acutely disturbing.

It was even more overwhelming when she found herself in the passenger seat and Matt shut the door gently behind her. She felt as though she was cocooned in leather and metal—which she supposed she was—and the car was so low she felt she was sitting on a level with the ground. However, those sensations were nothing to the ones which seized her senses once Matt slid in beside her.

The riot in her stomach was flushing her face, she just knew it was, but she couldn't do a thing about it, and when Matt turned to her and said quietly, but with a throb of amusement in his voice, 'Would you like to take those off?' as he nodded at her boots which were almost reaching her chin she stiffened tensely. How like him to point out she looked ridiculous, she told herself silently. He couldn't have made it more clear he found her totally unattractive. But that was fine; in fact it was great. *Really* great. Because that was exactly how she viewed him.

'No.' She forced herself to glance haughtily his way and then wished with all her heart she hadn't. He was much, much too close.

'I can come round and slip them off for you if it's difficult with that tight skirt?' he offered helpfully.

Georgie felt more trapped than ever. 'No, I'm fine,' she said tightly, staring resolutely out of the windscreen.

'Georgie, it is the middle of the day and I am giving you a lift back to the office,' he said evenly. 'Can't you let yourself relax in my company for just a minute or two? I promise you I have no intention of diverting to a deserted lane somewhere and having my wicked way with you, even if you do view me as a cross between the Marquis de Sade and Adolf Hitler.'

Shocked into looking at him again, she said quickly, 'I didn't think you were and of course I don't think you're like either of those two men!'

'No?' It reeked of disbelief.

'No.' This was awful, terrible. She should never have got into this car.

He raised his eyebrows at her but then to her intense relief he turned, starting the engine, which purred into life with instant obedience.

She turned back to the windscreen, but not before she had noticed the lingering amusement curling the hard mouth. He was obviously enjoying her discomfiture and, more to show him she was completely in control of herself than anything else, Georgie said primly, 'This is a very nice car.'

'Nice?' He reacted as though she had said something unforgivable. 'Georgie, family saloons are *nice*, along with sweet old maiden aunts and visits to the zoo and a whole host of other unremarkable things in this world of ours. A Lamborghini—' he paused just long enough to make his point '—is not in that category.'

She'd annoyed him. Good. It felt great to have got under that inch-thick skin. 'Well, that's how I see it,' she said sweetly. 'A car is just a car, after all, a lump of metal to get you quickly from A to B. A functional necessity.'

'I'm not even going to reply to that.'

She saw him glance down at the leather steering wheel and the beautiful dashboard as though to reassure himself that his pride and joy was still as fabulous as he thought it was, and she repressed a smile. Okay, she was probably being mean but, as he'd said earlier, he was a big boy; he could take it. 'I'm sorry if I've offended you,' she lied quietly.

'Sure you are.' The husky, smoky voice caught at her nerve-ends and she allowed herself another brief peek at the hard profile. He had rolled the sleeves of his shirt up at some point during the morning and his muscled arms, liberally covered with a dusting of black silky hair, swam into view. His shirt collar was open and several buttons undone and his shoulders were very broad. His body had an aggressive, top-heavy maleness that was impossible for any female to ignore.

The incredible car, the man driving it so effortlessly, the bright May sunshine slanting through the trees lining the road down which they were travelling—it was all the stuff dreams were made of, Georgie thought to herself a touch hysterically. He was altogether larger than life, Matt de Capistrano, and he was totally unaware of it.

'Are both the Mercedes and this car yours?' she asked carefully after a full minute had crept by in a screaming silence that had become more uncomfortable second by second.

'Would that be a further nail in my coffin?'

The very English phrase, spoken in the dark accented voice and without a glance at her, caused Georgie to stiffen slightly. 'I don't know what you mean,' she said flatly.

'I think you do,' he returned just as flatly.

'Now, look—' Whatever she had been about to say ended in a squeak as he pulled the car into the side of the road and cut the engine. 'What are you doing?' she asked nervously.

'I want to look at you while I talk to you,' he said softly, 'that is all, so do not panic, little English mouse.'

'Mouse?' He couldn't have said anything worse, and then, as she jerked to face him and saw the smile twisting the firm lips, she knew he was teasing her.

And then the smile faded as he said, 'I think we need to get a few things out into the open, Georgie.'

'Do we?' She didn't think so. She *really* didn't think so. And certainly not here, in this sumptuous car with him about an inch away and with nowhere to run to. She should never have antagonised him, she acknowledged much too late.

'You look on me as the enemy and this is not the case at all,' Matt said softly. 'If your brother fails, I fail. If he makes good, it's good news for me too.'

The hostility which had flared into life the minute she had set eyes on him, and which showed no signs of abating, was nothing to do with Robert and all to do with her, Georgie thought as she stared into the metallic grey eyes narrowed against the sunlight. But she could hardly say that, could she? So instead she managed fairly calmly, 'I think that's stretching credulity a little far. This business is everything Robert has; your interest here is just a tiny drop in the vast ocean of your business empire. It would hardly dent your coffers if this whole project went belly up.'

'I have never had a business venture go "belly up", as you so charmingly put it, and I do not intend for your brother's to be the first,' Matt returned smoothly. 'Besides which...'

He paused, and Georgie said, 'Yes?'

'Besides which, you underestimate his assets,' Matt said quietly.

'I can assure you I do not,' Georgie objected. 'Robert has no secrets from me and—'

'I wasn't talking about financial assets, Georgie.'

'Then what?' She stared at him, her clear sea-green eyes reflecting her bewilderment.

He had stretched one arm along the back of her seat as he turned to face her after switching off the engine, and she was so aware of every little inch of him that she was as tense as piano wire. It wasn't that she expected him to jump on her—Robert had told her it was common knowledge Matt de Capistrano had women, beautiful, gorgeous women, chasing after him all the time and that he could afford to pick and choose—more that she didn't trust herself around him. She seemed destined to meet him head-on and usually ended up making a fool of herself in the process. He was such an *unsettling* individual.

'What do you mean?' she repeated after a moment or two when he continued to look at her, his eyes with their strange dark-silver hue holding her own until everything else around them was lost in the intensity of his gaze.

'He has you.' It was soft and silky, and Georgie floundered.

'Me?' She tried for a laugh to lighten what had become a painfully protracted conversation but it turned into more of a squeak.

'Yes, you.' He wasn't touching her, in fact he hadn't moved a muscle, but suddenly he had taken her into an intimacy that was absorbing and Georgie found herself thinking, If he can make me feel like this, here, in the middle of the day and without any desire on his part, what on earth is he like with those women he does desire? No wonder they flock round him. As a lover he must be pure dynamite.

And that shocked her into saying, 'Sometimes I'm more of a liability than an asset, as you well know,' her voice over-bright.

'I know nothing of the sort. How can honesty and idealism be viewed in that way?' he returned quietly.

She wished he would stop looking at her. She wished he would start the car again. She wished she had never agreed to have this lift with him in the first place! 'You don't agree with me about Newbottle Meadow for a start.' She forced an aggressiveness she didn't really feel as an instinctive protection against her body's response to his closeness.

'I don't have to agree with you to admire certain qualities inherent in your make-up,' he returned softly.

'No, I suppose not,' she agreed faintly, deciding if she went along with him he would be satisfied he had made his point—whatever that was—and they could be on their way again.

He gave her a hard look. 'Don't patronise me, Georgie.'

'Patronise you?' She bristled instantly. 'I wouldn't dream of patronising you!'

The frown beetling his eyebrows faded into a quizzical ruffle. 'But you enjoy challenging me, don't you?' he murmured in a softly provoking voice that stiffened Georgie's back. 'Do you know why you like doing that?' he added in a tone that stated quite clearly he knew exactly what motivated her.

Because you are an egotistical, unfeeling, condescending—

He interrupted her thoughts, his voice silky smooth. 'Because you are sexually attracted to me and you're fighting it in a manner as old as time,' he stated with unforgivable coolness.

For a moment she couldn't believe he had actually said what she thought he had said, and then she shut her mouth, which had fallen open, before opening it again to snap, 'It might be hard for you to accept, Mr de Capistrano, but not every female you look at feels the need to swoon at your feet!' as she glared at him hotly.

'I can accept that perfectly well,' he returned easily, 'but I'm talking about you, not anyone else.' His expression was totally impassive, which made their conversation even more incredible in Georgie's eyes. The colossal *ego* of the man, she thought wildly. 'And I know I'm right because I feel the same way; I want you more than I've wanted a woman in a long time. For however long it lasted it would be good between us.'

Georgie fumbled with the door handle. 'I'm not listening to this rubbish a second longer,' she ground out through clenched teeth, more to stop her voice shaking than anything else.

'You are going to look slightly...unusual walking through town with your present attire, are you not?' Matt asked evenly as he glanced at the acres of rubber adorning her feet. 'And there is no need to be embarrassed, Georgie. You want me, I want you—it is the most natural thing in the world. There's even a rumour it's what makes it go round. It doesn't have to be complicated.'

The amusement in the dark face was the last straw. She turned on him like a small green-eyed cat, her eyes spitting sparks as she shouted, 'You are actually daring to proposition me? In cold blood?'

'Oh, is that what the matter is?' His expression was hard to read now but she thought it was cynicism twisting the ruthless mouth. 'You wanted a bouquet of red roses and promises of undying love and for everness? Sorry, but I don't believe in either.'

'I didn't want anything!'

'Then why are you so upset?' he asked reasonably. 'You could just tell me I've got it wrong without the melodrama, surely? It's not the most dreadful thing in the world to be told you are desirable by a member of the opposite sex.'

Desirable. Matt de Capistrano thought she was desirable and, if she hadn't got all this horribly wrong, he had been suggesting they have an affair. Georgie felt a churning in her stomach that wasn't all fury, and it was only in that moment she acknowledged Matt knew her better than she knew herself. But she would die before she let him know that, she added with deadly resolve.

'There are ways and ways of being told something,' she said tightly, hearing the prim-sounding words with something of a mental wince.

'I thought you appreciated honesty.'

'I do!' She glared at him, furiously angry that he was trying to make her feel bad about objecting to his stark proposal.

'Let's just test that statement, shall we?' he suggested silkily, and before she could object she found herself in his arms. The kiss was as devastating as ever she had imagined—and she *had* imagined what it would be like to be held in his arms like this, she admitted silently. It was sweet and knowing and erotic, and the feel of him, the intoxicating exhilaration which was inflaming her senses and making her head spin, was irresistible.

Matt was breathing hard, his muscled body rigid as he held her to him in the narrow confines of the car, and the gentle eroticism was a conscious assault on her senses. Georgie knew that. But somehow—and this was even more frightening than the sensations his lovemaking was calling forth—somehow she couldn't find the strength to resist him.

If he had used his superior strength and tried to force her, even slightly, she might have objected. But he was a brilliant strategist. Even that thought was without power compared to the tumultuous emotions flooding her from the top of her head to the soles of her feet.

He was holding her lightly but firmly, one hand tilting her chin to give his mouth greater access to hers, and slowly but subtly his mouth and tongue were growing more insistent. She didn't want to kiss him back and she knew she mustn't, but somehow that was exactly what she was doing. Which didn't make any sense, her struggling thoughts told her feverishly. But then what did sense have to do with Matt de Capistrano?

Everything! Now her mind was screaming the warning. Everything, and she forgot it at her peril. A man like him wouldn't be interested in a girl like her for more than two minutes. She had sparked his attention because she had stood up to him—insulted him, actually—and that was all. It would be a fleeting episode in the life of a very busy man; remembered one moment and then forgotten for ever. *But she wouldn't be able to forget it.*

When she jerked away from him he made no effort at all to restrain her, which to Georgie was further proof of the strength of his interest. He saw her as a brief dalliance, she thought wildly. Wham, bam and thank you, ma'am, while this project was on the go and he had to be around now and again, and then he would be off to pastures new without a second thought.

'I don't want to do this,' she said feverishly, straining back against the passenger door as she stared into the dark face and the piercingly grey eyes fixed on her flushed face.

He said nothing for a moment, his expression unreadable, and then he settled back in his own seat and started the engine again, drawing out on to the road before he said quietly, 'Yes, you do, but you are frightened of the consequences. You needn't be. It would simply be a case of two relative strangers getting to know each other a little better with no strings attached and no heavy commitment.'

Oh, yes, and pigs might fly. However nicely he put it, he wanted her in his bed, and whilst he might be able to engage in sex with 'no strings attached' she could not. She simply wasn't made that way. She breathed in deeply and then out again, calling on her considerable will-power to enable her voice to be calm and steady. 'I don't want to get to know anyone right at the moment, Matt,' she said firmly. 'I have more than enough on my plate with Robert and the children. I neither want nor could cope with anything else.'

'Rubbish.' It was brisk and irritatingly self-assured, and had the effect on Georgie of making her want to lean across and bop him on his arrogant nose.

'It's not rubbish,' she said tightly. 'And we don't even *like* each other, for goodness' sake!' She glanced at him as she spoke, and saw the black brows rise. 'Well, we don't,' she reiterated strongly.

'I like you, Georgie,' he said very evenly.

Okay, plain speaking time! 'You want me in your bed,' she corrected bravely. She heard him draw a quick breath, and added hurriedly, 'And that is something quite different.'

'I can assure you I would not take a woman into my bed whom I did not like,' Matt said calmly. 'All right?'

She wasn't going to win this one. Georgie forced herself not to argue with him and said instead, 'There is no question of my having a relationship with you, Matt, however free-floating.'

They had drawn well into the suburbs now, and as the Lamborghini purred down a main residential street an elegant young woman, complete with obligatory designer shopping bags, stepped straight in front of the car. Matt swore loudly as he braked violently, coming to a halt a foot or so away from the voluptuous redhead, whereupon he wound down the window and asked her, in no uncertain terms, what exactly she was playing at.

Georgie watched as the beautifully made-up face turned his way and a pair of slanted blue eyes surveyed first the car, and then Matt, and she wasn't surprised at the gushing apology which followed, or the suggestion that if there was anything, *anything* she could do to make amends for giving him such a fright he must say.

To be fair Matt didn't appear to notice either the red-head's beauty or her eagerness to make atonement, but no doubt if he had been alone in the car that would have been a different matter, Georgie told herself as they drove on. And this sort of thing would happen a hundred times over, in various forms, to someone like Matt de Capistrano. There would always be a redhead somewhere—or a blonde or brunette—who would let him know they were ready and available.

He was a wealthy, powerful and good-looking man, and the first two attributes made the third literally irresistible to some women. Not that it was just women who were drawn to members of the opposite sex who could guarantee them a life of wealth and ease... Her soft mouth tightened at the thought.

And Matt was a sensual man, dynamic and definitely dangerous. He was as much out of her league as the man in the moon.

'You haven't said a word in five minutes.' The deep cool voice at the side of her made her jump. 'I'll have to kiss you more often if it turns you into a sweet, submissive-type female.'

'I said all there was to say,' she bit back immediately, bristling instantly at the covert suggestion his lovemaking had rendered her weak and fluttery.

'You didn't say anything.' They had just reached the set of traffic lights before they turned into the street in which Robert's premises were situated, and as the lights glowed red Matt brought the car to a halt and glanced at her, his eyes narrowed and disturbingly perceptive. 'Someone has hurt you, haven't they, Georgie?'

She blinked just once, but other than that slight reaction she forced herself to remain absolutely still and keep her expression as deadpan as she could. Nevertheless it was some seconds before she trusted herself to say, with a suitably mocking note in her voice, 'You assume I've been hurt because I don't want to jump into bed with you? Now who's being melodramatic?'

And then the lights changed and the lasers drilling into her brain returned to the windscreen as he drove on. She wanted to sink back in the seat but she kept herself straight, willing herself to think about nothing but exiting from the car in as dignified a manner as possible.

Her lips were still tingling from his kiss, and now she was berating herself for not responding more vigorously to his audacity in thinking he could come on to her like that. She should have made it clear that she considered his effrontery impertinent at the very least, she told herself silently, not entered into a discussion on the pros and cons of having an affair with him! She'd handled this all wrong. But ever since she had got into this sex machine on wheels she had felt intensely vulnerable and more aware of Matt than ever.

They drew up outside Robert's small brick building after Matt had negotiated the Lamborghini carefully into the untidy yard, strewn with all manner of building materials, and before she could move he had opened his door and was walking round the sleek bonnet to hers.

'Thank you.' Emerging gracefully from a Lamborghini clad in the original seven-league boots was not an option, and Georgie was pink-cheeked by the time she was standing. 'I'll type those notes ready for you to collect later,' she said stiffly.

'I've no intention of giving up, Georgie.'

'I beg your pardon?'

He looked down at her from his vantage point of six foot plus, his eyes wandering over her small heart-shaped face and corn-coloured hair, and he brushed one silky strand from her cheek as he said, 'I want you...very much.'

'That...that doesn't mean anything. There must be a hundred and one women out there who are more than willing to jump into bed with you,' she said quickly through the sudden tightness in her chest.

'You've got some sort of fixation about me and bed, haven't you?' It was thoughtful. 'I wonder what Freud would make of that?'

'Now, look, Matt—'

'But I don't mind,' he said kindly. 'You can fantasise about it all you want, but I can assure you when it happens it will be outside all your wildest imaginings.'

'I've told you, it is *not* going to happen!'

She was talking to the air. He had already disappeared round the bonnet of the car and slid into the driver's seat, letting the growling engine have its head as he roared out of the yard with scant regard for other road users.

Georgie stood for some minutes as the dust slowly settled in the golden sunshine and the mild May breeze ruffled her hair with gentle fingers. He frightened her. The thought was there before she could reject it but immediately she rebelled. He didn't. Of course he didn't! Maybe her own reactions to him frightened her, but that was different. She could control them. *She could.* And she would. This time the affirmation in her head was even stronger. Oh, yes, she would all right. She'd had enough of love and romance to last her a lifetime. Once Robert and the children were over the worst, perhaps in a few months, she would put all her energy into the career she had begun on leaving university two years ago, and she would work until she reached every goal she set herself. Autonomous. That was how she wanted to be.

She turned sharply, entering the office and kicking off the boots as though they were the source of all her present troubles. She had the notes to type up and the children's party venue to arrange; she had to get working immediately. The thought was there but still she stood staring out of the window, the incident with Matt evoking a whole host of memories she normally kept under lock and key.

Glen Williams. If she closed her eyes she could picture him easily: tall lean frame, a shock of light brown hair that always fell over his brow in a lopsided quiff, bright blue eyes and a determined square chin. His parents had lived next door to Robert and Sandra and she had met Glen, who was two years older than her, on the first day she had come to live with them, along with his two sisters, one of whom was her age and the other a year younger.

She had immediately become great friends with the two girls, which had been just what she needed at the time, being heartsore and tearful at the loss of her parents, and for the first few years Glen had treated her in the same way he had his kid sisters—teasingly and with some disdain. And then, on her fourteenth birthday, something had changed.

She had dressed up for her birthday disco and had had her waist-length hair cut into a short sleek bob earlier in the day, and from the moment Glen had walked in with a bunch of his pals he had monopolised her. Not that she had minded—she had been consumed with a schoolgirl crush on him for ages. And from that evening they had been inseparable and very much an official 'item' in their group of friends.

Glen had not been academic but had always had a passion for motor cars. After failing every one of his A levels, he had used his considerable charm and got taken on at a local car supermarket-type garage in the town as a trainee mechanic.

That same year she had achieved mostly As in her GCSEs, and had gone on to attain two As and a B in her A levels two years later. During those years they had spent every spare moment they could together and had had some wonderful times, even though they hadn't had two pennies to rub together.

Georgie continued to stare out of the window but now she was blind and deaf to anything but the memories swamping her consciousness.

Glen had been so encouraging when she had tentatively discussed embarking on an Art and Design degree. She would come home weekends—he'd come and fetch her himself—and with him doing so well at the garage and Georgie sure to qualify well and get a great job, they'd be set up for the future. Nice house with a garden, holidays abroad and later the requisite two point four children. They'd got it all worked out—or so she had thought.

And so she had happily trotted off to university with Glen's ring on the third finger of her left hand—he had proposed the night before she had left—and for the first little while everything had seemed fine. He had arrived to collect her each weekend and they had planned a small register office wedding—all they could afford—at

Christmas. She would be nearly nineteen then and Glen had just had his twenty-first birthday. His parents had offered to convert Glen's big double bedroom into a little bedsit by adding a two-seater sofa, small fridge and microwave to the three-quarter-size bed, TV and video and wardrobe the room already contained, as their wedding present, and Robert and Sandra's gift had been a proposed two-week holiday in the sun. They would be together every weekend in their snug little nest and once she had finished her degree and got a job they would think about looking for a house. Life had been cut and dried.

It had been round about the end of November she'd really noticed the change in him. The last couple of weekends she had felt he was distant, cool even, but he had just been promoted at work and she had put his remoteness down to the added responsibility and pressure. The problem had been work all right—but the owner's daughter, not Glen's new position.

Harold Bloomsbury owned a string of garages across London and the south east and his only daughter was the original pampered darling. Julia had made up her mind she wanted Glen—Georgie had later found out she had been flirting with him for ages on and off, but when Glen had got engaged Julia's pursuit had become serious—and although she was plump and plain the Bloomsburys' lifestyle was anything but Spartan. Magnificent townhouse and a villa in Tuscany and another in Barbados, along with a yacht and fast cars and all the trimmings of wealth—Julia's husband would be guaranteed a life of comfort and ease by daddy-in-law.

Glen had weighed all that on the one side and love in a tiny bedsit in his parents' house on the other, and three weeks before they were due to get married had told her the wedding was off. He hadn't said a word about Julia;

Georgie had found out about the other girl through a friend
of a friend a few days later. They were too young to settle
down, he had lied, and he'd felt it was being terribly unfair
to her to get married whilst she was doing her degree. They
had lived in each other's pockets for five years—perhaps it
was time for a break to see how they both felt? Maybe at
Easter they could meet and review the situation and go
from there?

She had been stunned and bewildered, Georgie remembered now as she turned abruptly from the window and
gazed at her desk piled high with paperwork. She had cried
and—this made her stomach curl in recollection—had
begged Glen to reconsider. He'd been her life for years;
she hadn't been able to imagine a world in which he didn't
have pre-eminence.

For a week she had been sunk in misery and unable to
eat or sleep, and then she'd found out about Bloomsbury's
daughter and her ex-fiancé and strangely from that moment
she had begun to claw back her sanity and self-esteem.
Hating him had helped, along with the bitter contempt
she'd felt for a man who could be bought. The one small
comfort she'd had was that she hadn't slept with Glen,
however tempted she'd felt when their petting had got
heated. She'd had a romantic vision of their wedding night
being special. Special! Her lip curled as she sat down. But
at least it had saved her from making the mistake of giving
her virginity to that undeserving rat.

He'd married Julia the following May, and it had been
a relief when, six months later, Glen's parents had moved
to a small bungalow on the coast, their daughters now living in the centre of London in a student flat. Glen's parents
hadn't liked Julia and had frequently reported she was making their son's life a misery, but Georgie hadn't wanted to
know. The Glen chapter of her life was a closed book. But

it had left deep scars, how deep she hadn't fully acknowledged until she had come face to face with Matt de Capistrano.

He was fabulously wealthy and arrogant and ruthless—just like Julia Bloomsbury. He thought he only had to want something for it to happen, that everything—people, values, morals—could be bent to his will just because he could buy and sell the average Mr Joe Bloggs a hundred times over. Well, he was in for a surprise. Her green eyes flashed like glittering emeralds and the last lingering sensation induced by his kiss was burnt away.

People like Julia Bloomsbury and Matt had no conscience, no soul; they rode roughshod over people and didn't even notice they were trampling them into the ground. Money was their god, it bought them what they wanted and that was all that mattered. And the meadow, Newbottle Meadow, was a perfect example of that. She hated him. Her chin rose and her shoulders straightened as a little inner voice asked nastily why she was so adamant about convincing herself of the fact.

'I do, I hate him.' She said it out loud, opening the drawer of her desk and fishing out her wilting sandwiches as she did so. 'And the sooner he accepts that the better it'll be for both of us.'

And then she grimaced at the foolishness of talking to herself, bit into her chicken and mayonnaise sandwich and determined to put all further thoughts of Matt de Capistrano out of her mind.

CHAPTER FOUR

AFTER eating her lunch Georgie was on the phone for more than an hour searching for a venue for the children's party. She drew a blank at all the community and church halls in the district, and the prices one or two of them wanted to charge were exorbitant anyway for someone in Robert's current position. She then decided Robert would have to allow her to hold the twins' party at home and he could disappear for the afternoon, after he had helped her set up, but trying to hire a bouncy castle for that particular day proved just as fruitless.

Eventually she put all thoughts of the party on hold and decided to type up the notes from the morning before attacking the rest of her workload.

She worked like a beaver all afternoon, clearing a vast mountain of paperwork and dealing with the men's wages when they called in later in the day. There was still no sign of Robert at four o'clock and then at ten past she heard the door open and looked up expectantly. 'Where have you been—?' She stopped abruptly. Instead of Robert's pleasant face Matt de Capistrano was looking at her, his eyes molten as they roved over her creamy skin and golden hair.

She tried to make a casual comment, to look away and busy herself with the papers on her desk, but she could not. She felt transfixed, hypnotised, and as her heart began to pound at the expression on the dark face she told herself to open her mouth, to say *anything*. 'I thought you were Robert,' she managed weakly.

'But as you see I am not,' he returned coolly.

'No...' Oh, what an inane conversation, she told herself angrily. Say something sensible, for goodness' sake! 'Do you know where he is?'

'We had a few hitches on site after lunch, potential drainage and so on, so we've been pretty tied up all afternoon,' Matt said quietly. 'He should be here in a few minutes; he was leaving just after me.'

She nodded in what she hoped was a brisk secretarial fashion. 'Your notes are all ready.' She wrenched her gaze from his and pointed at the large white envelope on one side of the desk. 'I hope I got everything down and—'

'You're incredibly lovely,' he said slowly. 'And without artifice. Most women of my acquaintance put on the war paint before they even get out of bed in the morning.'

And no doubt you speak from experience, she thought tartly. 'Really?' she managed a polite smile. 'Now, regarding the west part of the site, where the architect said—'

'Damn the architect.' He had moved to stand in front of her and now, as her surprised eyes met his, he said softly, 'Have dinner with me tonight?'

Was he mad? She stared at him, her cheeks flushing rosy pink as her eyes fell on to the V below his throat where his shirt buttons were undone to expose a tantalisingly small amount of tanned skin and the beginnings of dark body hair. She snapped her eyes upwards but it was too late; her body was already tingling. As much in answer to her own traitorous response to his maleness she said very stiffly, 'That is quite out of the question, as I thought I made perfectly clear this morning.'

'Would it help if I kissed you again?' he asked contemplatively.

Just you try it! You'll soon know what it feels like to have a word processor on top of your head. She glared at him and her face must have spoken for itself because he nodded thoughtfully. 'Perhaps not,' he acknowledged drily.

He was enjoying this! It was just a game to him, a diversion! 'I have plenty of work to do if you've quite finished,' she snapped angrily.

'Finished? I haven't even started.' And his smile was a crocodile smile.

'Wrong.' Georgie's gaze was sharp. 'I haven't got time to bandy words with you, Matt.'

'Then cut out the necessity and have dinner with me,' he responded immediately.

What did it take to get it into that thick skull of his that she would rather dine with Hannibal Lecter? 'No.' It was final. 'I like to get dinner while I listen to the children tell me about their day and then we all dine together. They need that sort of reassurance in their lives at the moment.'

'And you don't ever have an evening off?'

'No.'

'Then I will pick you up about nine, yes? Once they are in bed,' he drawled silkily, his accent very strong as he stared down at her, his hands thrust into the pockets of his jeans and a shaft of sunlight from the window turning his hair blue-black.

'For the last time, I am not going to have dinner with you!'

It was unfortunate that Robert chose that precise moment to walk into the building. Georgie saw him stop dead, his eyes flashing from her pink face to Matt's coolly undisturbed one, before he said, 'Problems?'

'Not at all,' Matt said easily. 'I asked Georgie to have dinner with me tonight but she informs me she feels the children need her at the moment and she has to stay at home.'

'Georgie, you don't have to do that—'

'I want to, Robert.' She cut off her brother's protest abruptly.

'Well if you're at a loose end tonight why don't you join *us* for dinner?' Robert asked Matt in the next moment, much to Georgie's horror. 'It's not exactly restful, so I warn you before you say yea or nay. The kids are always pretty hyper at the end of the day, but you're welcome.'

'Great, I'd love to.' It was immediate and Matt didn't look at Georgie.

'Good. Problem solved.' Robert smiled happily at them both and for the first time since Sandra's death Georgie felt the urge to kick him. It had happened fairly frequently through her growing up years, but never as strongly as now.

'But...' Matt turned to Georgie as he spoke and she just knew the tentative expression on his face wasn't genuine. 'Will there be enough for an extra mouth at such short notice?'

She would have loved to have said no, because she knew as well as he did that she had been manoeuvred into a corner, but she gritted her teeth for a second and then said brightly, 'If you like pot roast?'

'Love it.'

'Oh, good.'

And then she ducked her head to hide the acid resurgence of bitterness that had gripped her. Manipulating, cunning, Machiavellian, underhand—

'White wine or red?'

'What?'

Robert had walked through into his office but Matt had paused at the interconnecting doorway. 'I said, white wine or red?' he said easily, the gleam of amusement in the grey eyes telling Georgie all too clearly he had known exactly what she was thinking.

'Whatever,' she growled ungratefully.

'Right.' And then he had the audacity to add—purely for Robert's benefit, she was sure, 'It's been a long time since I've enjoyed a family evening round a pot roast; I really appreciate the kindness.'

Add hypocritical and two-faced to the other list, Georgie thought balefully as the door closed and she was alone, her teeth clamped together so hard they were aching.

Matt was only ensconced with Robert for some five minutes before he emerged again, stopping by her desk and picking up the envelope as he said, 'When and how do you want me?'

'What?' The ghastly sexual awareness that took her over whenever she was within six feet of this man made her voice breathless.

'Dinner?' He smiled innocently. 'What time and how do I dress? Formal or informal?'

Impossible man! She kept her voice very prim and proper as she said, 'Half-past six. I don't like the twins to eat too late as their bedtime is eight o'clock. And informal, very. The children might even be in their pyjamas if there's a programme on TV they want to watch after dinner and they've finished any homework they have.'

'Homework?' He wrinkled his aristocratic nose. 'Poor little things. Why are children not allowed to be children these days? There is enough time for the homework and other such restrictions when they are a little older.'

She agreed with him absolutely but she wasn't about to tell him that. 'They have to learn a certain amount of discipline,' she said evenly as her stomach churned at the thought of the forthcoming evening.

'How stern you sound.' His voice made it very clear he didn't rate her as an aunty and it rankled—unbearably. She hadn't been cast in the role of Wicked Witch of the West before. 'Half-past six it is, then. Robert's given me the address.'

Georgie waited until she was sure Matt's Lamborghini had left and then knocked on Robert's door before she popped her head round to say, 'There's a couple of things I need to get for dinner so I'll see you at home later, okay?'

'Georgie?' As she made to withdraw, Robert's voice called her back. 'You didn't mind me inviting him, did you? I didn't think at the time, but you're doing enough looking after me and the kids without me asking along any Tom, Dick or Harry.'

Matt de Capistrano was definitely not your average Tom, Dick or Harry, Georgie thought wryly, but as she looked into her brother's eyes—the lines of strain and grief all too evident on Robert's countenance—she said brightly, 'Of course not; it pays to keep him sweet at the moment, doesn't it? And the kids will like a guest for a change. Just don't make a habit of it, eh?'

'You're a brick, and take the car. I'll get a taxi later.'

A brick she might be, but this particular brick was going to have to vamp up a boring old pot roast into something great, and she only had a couple of hours to do that, clean the house, make the children presentable and a hundred and one other things that were *absolutely* imperative if Matt de Capistrano was going to set foot across the threshold of their home.

After buying two very extravagant desserts, flowers for the table, a packet of wildly expensive coffee and a good bottle of brandy, Georgie drove home at breakneck speed to find the children involved in building a castle of Lego with the middle-aged 'grandmother' from next door who came in to sit with them each day when they got home from school.

Five minutes later—with Mrs Jarvis happily toddling

home after her customary little chat—the house was a scene of feverish activity. Once the sitting room was cleared of every piece of Lego, Georgie organised David vaccing downstairs and Annie dusting, whilst she dressed up the pot roast with cream and wine and quickly prepared more vegetables and a pot of new potatoes to add to the roast potatoes she had peeled that morning.

That done, she marshalled the children upstairs to bath and change into their clean pyjamas, whilst she set the table in the dining room with the best crockery and cutlery and arranged the flowers she had bought earlier.

The children downstairs again, looking demure and sweet as they sat on the sofa in front of their favourite video, Georgie flew upstairs to shower and change after spraying the house with air freshener and lighting scented candles in the dining room.

She heard Robert arrive home as she stepped out of the shower, and shouted for him to check the vegetables before she dived into the bedroom she shared with Annie and pulled on a pair of casually smart trousers and a little fig-ure-hugging top in bubblegum-pink cashmere.

Too dressed up. She looked at herself in the mirror and gave a flustered groan. Definitely. The children would be sure to make some comment and then she would just die.

She whipped off the trousers and replaced them with a pair of old and well-washed jeans. Better. She stood for a moment contemplating her reflection. Yes, that was just the right note and this top *was* gorgeous; she couldn't consign it the same way as the trousers.

Her hair only took a minute or two to dry, courtesy of her hairdryer, falling in a soft silky veil about her face, and apart from her usual touch of mascara on her fair eyelashes she didn't bother with any make-up. She had just fixed her big silver hoops in her ears when she heard the doorbell ring, and her stomach turned right over.

'Calm, girl, calm.' She shut her eyes tightly before opening them and gazing into the mirror. 'This is nothing. You've had guests for dinner in the past, for goodness' sake, and that is all Matt de Capistrano is. Get it into perspective.'

The faltering perspective received a death blow when she walked into the sitting room a few moments later. The two men were standing with a glass of wine in their hands and Matt's hard profile was towards her as he listened to something Annie was telling him. He was giving the child his full attention and was not yet aware of her, but as Georgie looked at his impressively male body clothed in black trousers and an open-necked charcoal shirt her breath caught in her throat. *He was gorgeous.* It was the last thing she either needed or wanted to think. And dangerous. Infinitely dangerous.

And then he turned towards her and she was caught in the light of his eyes, and she had never felt so vulnerable or unprepared. 'Hallo, Matt.'

'Hallo, Georgie,' he murmured softly, her name a caress as his accent gave it a sensuality that made her innermost core vibrate.

'I'll…I'll just see to the dinner.' She fled into the kitchen and then stood for a moment or two just staring helplessly around her. What was she going to do? *What was she going to do?* And then the panic subsided as cold reason said, Nothing. You are going to do nothing but play the hostess. This is one night in a lifetime and once it is over you can have a quiet word with Robert and make sure he doesn't repeat the invitation. Simple.

By the time they all walked through to the dining room it was clear Annie was in love and David had a severe case of hero worship. Georgie had drunk two glasses of wine on an empty stomach, however, and her Dutch courage was high as she watched the children hang on Matt's every word.

'And you *really* have some horses in Spain and here as well?' Annie was asking as Georgie brought in the last of the dishes. Annie was horse-mad and had been having riding lessons for the last year. 'What are they like?'

'Beautiful.' Matt's eyes stroked over Georgie's face for the briefest of moments as he said the word, and then his gaze returned to the animated child. 'You could perhaps come and see them some time if your father wishes it?'

'Really?' It was said on a whoop of delight. 'You mean it?'

'I never say anything I do not mean.' And again Georgie felt the glittering gaze pass over her, although she was intent on removing the lids of the steaming dishes. 'Of course I mean the ones in England,' he added teasingly. 'Spain would be rather a long way to go to see a horse, would it not?'

'I wouldn't mind.' Annie's tone made it clear she would go to the end of the earth if Matt was there and Georgie gave a wry smile to herself. Any age and they'd go down before that dark charm like ninepins. He had a magnetism that was fascinating if you were foolish enough to forget the ruthless and cold mind behind it.

'That's very good of you, Matt.' It was obvious Robert was a little taken aback and not at all sure if this was a social pleasantry said lightly but without real intent.

And then Matt disabused him of that idea when he said, 'Why not this weekend, if you aren't doing anything? You and the children and Georgie could come for the day and have a look round the estate. It would be a distraction for the little ones.' This last was said in an undertone to Robert, and then Matt added to David, 'And bring your swimming trunks, yes? I have a pool and you can practise your breast stroke.'

So David had told him he and Annie were learning to swim at the local baths at some point when she had been busy in the kitchen? And Matt, being Matt, hadn't missed a trick. Horses and a pool—he really was the man who had everything. But not as far as she was concerned.

Georgie kept her voice light and pleasant as she said, 'Tuck in, everyone, and I'm sure the children would love a day out. Unfortunately I shan't be able to make it this weekend as I'm meeting an old university friend who is down in London for a few days, but you and the children must go, Robert.'

'Your friend is very welcome to come along too,' Matt said just as pleasantly.

'Thank you, but I think we'll leave it as it is.' Georgie offered him the dish of roast potatoes as she spoke and as their fingers touched she felt an electric shock shoot right down to her toes.

'Your friend doesn't like horses?' She'd seen the awareness in his eyes and knew the physical contact had registered on him too.

'I don't know.'

'You could ask her.'

Enough was enough. He could try his big-brother tactics on everyone else but she was not having any of it. 'Simon is the quiet type.' She saw the name connect in the dark eyes and assumed a smiling mask to cover up the apprehension his narrowed gaze was causing. 'He doesn't like crowds.'

'He would consider six a crowd?' The mocking voice carried an edge of steel which said only too plainly such a man would be an out-and-out wimp.

Georgie shrugged dismissively. She didn't trust herself to speak without telling him exactly what she thought of him, and that was not an option with the twins present; neither did she think it opportune to mention that Simon was engaged to be married to her best friend from her university days, and that he'd asked her to help in selecting a piece of jewellery to give to his bride as a surprise wedding present.

'I'm going to be eight soon.' Annie cut into the awkward moment and Georgie could have kissed her niece. 'So is David 'cos we're twins.'

'Right.' Matt nodded as he smiled into the little girl's openly admiring face.

'I think I should have been eight ages ago,' Annie continued firmly. 'Stuart Miller is nearly nine and he can't spell yet. Can he, David?'

David had his mouth full of pot roast and merely shook his head in agreement.

'And me and David know really big words.' Annie's massive blue eyes were fixed on the object of her adoration. 'Have you got any children at home?'

Georgie choked on a piece of potato. Never let it be said that Annie was backward in coming forward! However, by the end of the meal Georgie had discovered plenty about Matt de Capistrano through Annie's innocent chattering. He was the product of an English mother and Spanish father and had one sibling, a sister, who had produced a quiverful of children. His father had died several years ago and his mother continued to reside in her own home in Spain, where Matt also had business interests. He had homes in both countries and divided his time equally between them, and he liked horses and dogs and cats. This last was important to Annie, who had decided she wanted to be a vet when she grew up. And his favourite colour was green.

This last question was answered along with a glance at Georgie and the grey eyes smiled mockingly.

Oh, yes, she just bet, Georgie thought silently as she returned the smile politely without giving anything away. And with a blue-eyed blonde it would be blue, and a brown-eyed brunette brown and so on.

Once dinner was over Georgie shooed everyone into the sitting room and retired to the sanctuary of the kitchen, refusing any offers of help, where she dallied until the children's bedtime. She spent longer than normal upstairs with them and then when they were both asleep and it became impossible to delay the moment a second longer, she made her way downstairs, glancing at her watch as she did so. Half-past nine. In another half an hour or so, once she had made them all more coffee, she could gracefully retire and leave the two men to talk. This evening might not be as bad as she had feared.

She realised her mistake as soon as she entered the sitting room. 'Georgie, did you find anywhere to have the kids' party?' Robert asked before she had even shut the door behind her.

'The party?' She was desperately aware of the dark figure sitting to one side of the open French windows on the perimeter of her vision but she kept her eyes on Robert. 'No, no, I didn't, as it happens. I'll try again tomorrow and—'

'Don't worry, Matt's had the most brilliant idea,' Robert interrupted her.

'He has?' She darted one quick wary glance Matt's way and saw the dark face was totally expressionless. It was not reassuring.

'As you can't make this weekend he's offered for us all to go over the next and have the kids' party at his place.'

Robert imparted this news as though it wasn't the most horrendous thing he could have said.

For a moment Georgie was too astounded to say anything, but then reason came back in a hot flood. 'We couldn't possibly,' she protested quickly. 'It's very kind, of course, but they will want their schoolfriends to their party. It's far better we leave things as they are.'

'I meant for their friends to be invited.' Matt was sitting on the large oak chest used to store the children's huge collection of Lego and now he folded his arms over his chest, settling more comfortably on the wood as he surveyed her flushed face with an air of cool determination. 'I bought an old farm some time ago and had the place gutted and rebuilt, and there's plenty of land for the children to enjoy themselves in. The pool is indoors and heated, so they can let off some steam in there, and we can have that bouncy castle on the lawn outside the house if it's fine or in one of the old barns if the weather is inclement. And all kids love a barbecue.'

'I…I couldn't get a bouncy castle,' Georgie said weakly. 'There's not one for hire.'

'There will be if I want one,' Matt said smoothly. 'I've suggested to Robert you have a run over to my place now so you can satisfy yourself it would be okay; it's only half-an-hour's drive.'

This was going from bad to worse. 'I don't think—'

'We can make a day of it,' Matt continued evenly, 'and any parents who want to stay for the day are welcome, or if they just want to come back for the barbecue in the evening that's fine too. My staff are used to large social gatherings and there's a very good catering firm my housekeeper uses at such times.'

His *staff*?

'So it could be a morning by the pool and a buffet lunch,

followed by the bouncy castle and a magician and so on in the afternoon with an evening barbecue,' he continued seamlessly.

'Matt—'

'Do you think David and Annie would enjoy that?' he added with innocent deadly intent. It was the clincher and they both knew it.

How could she deprive David and Annie of such a treat? Georgie asked herself silently. She couldn't. And this master strategist had played her like a virtuoso playing a violin. But he was mad; he had to be. To do all this just because she had refused to have a date with him? This was megalomania at its worst.

'That's settled, then.' Robert appeared to be quite unaware of the electric undercurrents in the room as he nodded from one to the other of them. 'I'll get the coffee on, Georgie. You sit down for a while; you've not stopped all day.'

Before she could stop him Robert had bustled out of the room. Georgie, still coping with her shock, sank down on to the sofa before she realised she should have chosen the single safety of a chair, and the fact was emphasised when Matt sat down beside her in the next moment, slanting a look at her from under half-closed lids.

'I'd genuinely like to give the twins a treat after what they have been through, Georgie,' he said quietly. 'They're nice children, both of them.'

His thigh was touching hers and she had never been so aware of another human being's body in her life, and it took a moment or two before she could say, forcing sarcasm into her voice, 'And that's why you offered to accommodate hordes of screaming infants for the day? Pure magnanimity?'

'Ah, now that's a different question.' He shifted slightly

on the sofa and her senses went into overdrive. He was half turned towards her, one arm along the back of the sofa behind her, and she felt positively enclosed by his dark aura, enclosed and held. 'I've never pretended to be "pure" anything.'

He was doing it again. Laughing at her in that dark smoky voice of his, although there was no trace of amusement on the hard male face. She had made the mistake of raising her eyes to his and now she found it impossible to look away.

'Will you come with me tonight?' The words themselves were nothing, but the way he said them sent a shiver of something hot and sensual down her spine.

'I...I can't.' She gestured helplessly towards the dusky twilight outside the window. 'It's dark now, and late. And...and Robert's getting the coffee.' There was no way—*no way*—she was leaving here with Matt de Capistrano tonight, not with him looking and smelling like the best thing since sliced bread, Georgie thought feverishly. She needed time to distance herself again, get her emotions under control and let cold reason take the place of sexual attraction. But how long—the nasty little voice that was forever making itself known these days asked—how long would that take? An hour? A day? A month?

'Okay.' His voice was soft, silky soft. 'It's probably better you see it in the light anyway. Tomorrow, then. I will call in the office and drive you out there before you come home.'

'I don't need to see your home, Matt, I'm sure it's fine,' she had the presence of mind to say fairly firmly.

'I insist.' It was firmer still.

'But—'

'And then if there is anything you are not happy with—matters of safety, that sort of thing—we can sort it before the party. You'll be quite safe,' he added mockingly as he lifted her small chin and gazed down into the sea-green eyes with a cynical smile. 'My housekeeper and her husband, who oversees the gardens for me, live in, and my groom has his own purpose-built flat above the stables so there are always people about.'

His thick black lashes turned his eyes into bottomless pools, Georgie thought weakly. And then she took a hold of herself, straightening slightly as she removed her chin from his fingers with a flick of her head. 'I didn't think my safety was in question,' she said stiffly, and then was mortified when he laughed softly.

'Little liar.'

His smoky amusement made her face flame. 'No, really—'

'You were worried I would do this...' He put his mouth to hers and stroked her sealed lips lightly, the scent of him heady in her nostrils. He wasn't touching her now except by their joined mouths, but he might as well have been because Georgie was utterly unable to move.

The kiss was sweet, even chaste for a few moments, and then the hand on the back of the sofa slipped down into the small of her back and she found herself drawn into the hard steel of his body as her lips opened beneath his. And he was ready for her, plunging swiftly into the secret contours of her mouth as his tongue and his lips created such a wild rush of sensation she moaned softly, trembling slightly.

His other hand was lightly cupping one breast now through the baby-soft wool, and as he began a slow erotic rhythm on the hardening peak that caused little tremors of passion to shiver in ever-increasing waves Georgie felt drugged with passion.

He was good. He was so good at this. The acknowledgement of his expertise was on the edge of her consciousness and didn't affect the tumultuous emotions which had taken hold.

She could feel the solid pounding of his heart under the thin charcoal silk and as he pulled her even closer his body told her he was as aroused as she was. And it felt so good, *wonderful* to know she could affect him in this way, Georgie admitted fiercely.

Her hands had been curled against the solid wall of his muscled chest, but now they moved up to the powerful shoulders as she moaned softly in her throat and he answered the unspoken need with a guttural sound of his own.

He had turned her into the soft back of the sofa at some point as his body covered hers, and now, as the trembling in her body was reflected in his, he raised his head, his eyes glittering in the semi-light of the standard lamp Robert had switched on earlier. 'You see?' he murmured softly. 'You want me as much as I want you, Georgie. The chemistry is red-hot.'

She was breathing hard now his lips had left hers, and although part of her was crying out in mute protest at the declaration, she was having to fight the urge to reach up for his mouth again. And she mustn't, she mustn't. He had already stormed her defences and caused an abandonment that was only fully dawning on her now his mouth had left hers.

She stared at him, her eyes huge. 'This…this is just sex,' she whispered shakily.

'I know.' He smiled, a sexy quirk of his firm mouth. 'Great, is it not?'

'It isn't enough, not for me.' She pushed at him and he immediately released her, his hand returning to the back of the sofa as he still continued to lean over her without touching her now. His retreat gave her the courage to say more firmly, 'I mean it, Matt. I don't want this.' She drew in a deep breath and added, 'All I want is for you to leave me alone. That's not too much to ask, is it?'

'Much too much,' he said with quiet finality. 'I have tasted you twice now and I want more, much more. But I can be patient, believe it or not.'

'All the patience in the world won't alter my mind.'

'And I never back down from a challenge,' he warned softly.

So she had been right; he saw her as a challenge because she hadn't immediately fallen gratefully into his arms, Georgie thought hotly, her anger banishing the last remnants of his lovemaking and putting iron in her limbs. 'I have absolutely no intention of having a relationship with you,' she stated very coldly, 'or anyone else for that matter. Robert and the twins are my prime concern at the moment, but even if they weren't around I wouldn't sleep with you. Is that clear enough?'

'Abundantly.'

At least he wasn't smiling now, she thought a trifle hysterically, before she said, 'Good. I'm glad you've seen sense at last.'

He muttered something dark and Spanish and—Georgie was certain—uncomplimentary under his breath, and had just opened his mouth to reply when Robert called from outside the door, 'Georgie? Open the door, would you? I've a tray in my hands,' and she leapt up and fairly flew across the room.

It was another twenty minutes before Matt stood up to leave and Georgie was amazed at his acting ability. If it wasn't for the steely glint in his eyes when he glanced her way she might have been convinced she had imagined the whole episode from the way he was smiling and conversing with Robert.

'That was a wonderful dinner, Georgie.' As the three of them stood on the doorstep his voice was the epitome of a satisfied guest thanking his hostess. 'You certainly know the way to a man's heart,' he added smoothly.

Sarcastic so-and-so! Georgie smiled sweetly. 'So it has been said,' she agreed demurely.

She saw the grey eyes spark and then narrow, and reminded herself to go carefully. Matt de Capistrano was not a man it was wise to annoy, but he made her so *mad*.

The telephone had started to ring in the sitting room. Robert said, 'I'm sorry, Matt, do you mind if I get that?'

Matt was already shaking his head and saying, 'No, you go and I'll see you tomorrow.'

'Goodnight, Matt.'

The two of them were alone now, and in answer to her dismissive voice he smiled. 'Walk me to my car.'

She didn't have time to agree or disagree before he took her arm and whisked her down the shadowed drive.

'Let go of me!' Her voice was on the edge of hostility but she was desperately trying to remain calm; Matt *was* Robert's bread and butter, after all.

'I like you better when you are soft and breathless in my arms than spitting rocks,' he drawled with mocking composure.

Her face bloomed with colour and Georgie was desperately glad of the scented darkness which hid her blushes as she breathed, 'I *told* you to forget all that.'

'Have there been many?' he asked with sudden seriousness, his hand still on her arm.

'What?' She stared at him, bewildered by the abrupt change.

'Men who have complimented you on your dinners,' he said with silky innuendo.

'That's my business.' She was shocked and it showed. How *dared* he question her about her love life? Not that she had one at the moment, and the last three years hadn't been anything to write home about, either, if she was being honest. She had had the occasional date after Glen, of course, but after a time she had begun to wonder why she was bothering to make the effort when there wasn't anyone she remotely fancied. She knew she didn't want to get involved with anyone again—certainly not for a long, long time anyway, if at all—and even when she made it perfectly clear the date was on a purely friends basis, the man in question always had to try and paw her about at the end of the evening. And so she had made up her mind that unless that magical 'something' was there she was content to be single. And it hadn't been. Until now. She shuddered as the last two words hit.

'You're cold.' He enfolded her into his arms as he spoke, but loosely, his fingertips brushing her lower ribs and the palms of his hands cupping her sides. 'You should be wearing something more than that pink thing out here.'

The warm fragrance of him was all about her and the harnessed strength in the big male body caused a fluttering inside that Georgie recognised with a stab of disgust at her own weakness. 'I didn't plan to be out here, if you remember,' she said as tartly as she could, considering her legs were like jelly. 'And the "pink thing", as you call it, is a very expensive cashmere top that cost me an arm and a leg.'

'Which arm and which leg?' He drew her closer, so they were thigh to thigh and breast to breast. 'They all feel like the real thing.'

She tried to push away but it was like pushing against solid steel. 'Matt, please.'

'Yes, Georgie?' His eyes moved to the soft gold of her hair for a moment.

'I…I have to go in.' It wasn't as firm as she would have liked.

'Okay.' He didn't relax his hold an iota. 'But first you repeat after me: I will be ready and waiting when you arrive to pick me up tomorrow night, Matt.'

'But I told you I don't need to see your house; I'm sure it's quite suitable and—'

'No, that was not right. I will be ready and waiting when you arrive to pick me up tomorrow night, Matt,' he repeated softly, his dark body merging into the shadows like a creature of the night.

'Matt!' She wriggled but it was useless. 'Robert will see us.'

'Good.'

'I'll scream.'

Georgie looked at him steadily and saw he was vastly amused. Oh, this was ridiculous! What must they look like? But he wasn't going to give in; she could read it in the dark, aggressively attractive face looking down at her. Well, one quick visit to his house wouldn't hurt, would it? She could make it clear she had to be back in time to get the children's dinner and so on, she comforted herself silently. 'I will be ready and waiting when you arrive to pick me up tomorrow night, Matt.'

'That wasn't so bad, was it?' Grey eyes softened to warm charcoal. 'I'll be at the office for five, yes?'

'And I must be home to get the twins' tea.'

'Cinderella, twenty-first century,' he murmured softly. 'But first you shall go to the ball.' And he kissed her, long and hard until she was breathless, and then put her aside and slid into the Lamborghini seemingly in one fluid movement.

She was still standing exactly as he had placed her, one hand touching her tingling bruised lips, when he roared out of the drive into the street in a flash of gleaming metal. And then he was gone.

CHAPTER FIVE

GEORGIE didn't sleep much that night. She spent most of the long silent hours trying to sort out her feelings, but by the time a pale, pink-edged dawn crept stealthily over the morning sky she'd given it up as hopeless. This was disturbing and outside her understanding, or more to the point Matt de Capistrano was disturbing and outside her understanding! She corrected herself wryly. And she didn't want to feel like this; it horrified her.

For the last few years she had been in control. Once she had recovered from the caustic fall-out of Glen's rejection she had changed her mindset and her goals. She had known exactly what she was doing, where she was going and what she was aiming for. And now...now she wasn't sure about anything and it terrified her; in fact it was totally unacceptable.

For some reason Matt's dark face seemed to be printed on the screen of her mind. She didn't want it there, in fact she would give anything to have it wiped clean, but somehow there it stayed.

She was sitting in front of the bedroom window, Annie asleep in her small single bed in one corner of the room, and as the small child stirred and then settled down to sleep again Georgie's eyes remained on her. It was true what she had said to Matt, she told herself fiercely. She had more than enough to do to cope with the twins and Robert. If he couldn't understand that then it was tough.

She turned and looked outside again to where an adolescent song thrush was sitting in the copper beech outside the bedroom window. Its bright black eyes surveyed her for one moment and it seemed to hesitate before rising up into the sky in a glorious swoop of freedom, the earth and all its dangers and difficulties forgotten in the wonder of being alive. She mustn't hesitate either. She nodded to the thought as though it had been spoken out loud. Matt had made it quite clear he wanted her for one thing and one thing only, and if she didn't put him behind her and escape—like that bird into the sky—he would clip her wings in a way Glen would never have been able to do. She had recovered from Glen; she had a feeling Matt de Capistrano was the sort of man you never recovered from.

At five o'clock she was in the shower and by six she was dressed and downstairs, preparing breakfast for everyone and four packed lunches. She paused in the middle of spreading mashed egg and salad cream on to buttered bread, glancing round the small homely kitchen as she did so. What had Matt thought of this home? His lifestyle was so different as to be another world away. He had staff to cater to his wants, to serve him breakfast and anticipate his every need. And in his love life she was sure there were plenty of willing women to supply everything he needed there too! He was rich, ruthless, selfish and shallow. *He was.* She reiterated it in her mind and didn't question why she needed to convince herself of his failings. She saw it clearly now, she reassured herself as the pile of sandwiches grew. Crystal-clear.

The crystalline certainty continued until the moment she saw Matt.

He arrived prompt at five and drove her away from the office after a word or two with Robert in private, and when the Lamborghini entered a winding drive some twenty-five minutes later, after a sign which said, 'Private. El Dorado'. She turned to him with questioning eyes.

'It means the golden land,' he answered her softly, 'a country full of gold and gems.'

'And have you filled your El Dorado with gems?' she asked a little cynically. No doubt the house would be a monument to his success and full of all the trappings of wealth. Which was fine, of course it was, if that was what he wanted. It fitted the image.

'In a manner of speaking,' he answered somewhat cryptically.

She opened her mouth to ask him what he meant, but the words hovering on her tongue were never voiced as in that same moment the car turned a corner in the drive and the sort of sprawling thatched farmhouse that belonged in fairy stories came into view.

'Oh, wow…' It wasn't particularly articulate but the look on her enchanted face must have satisfied Matt because he smiled slowly after bringing the car to a halt on the end of the horseshoe-shaped drive.

'Come and have a look round inside first,' he suggested quietly, 'and then I'll show you where we could have the barbecue if it is wet, and of course the bouncy castle.'

His accent lent a quaintness to the last two words that made her heart twang slightly, and as they walked up the massive stone steps towards the big oak door she said, aiming to keep the conversation practical and mundane, 'This is very nice; did you have to do much work to get it to this point?'

'The place was almost derelict when I purchased it,' he said, taking her arm as he opened the front door to reveal a large hall panelled in mellow oak that was golden in the sunlight slanting in from several narrow windows above them. 'An old lady, the unmarried daughter of the original farmer, had lived here for years alone, getting more and more into debt as the house fell down about her ears.'

'What a shame.' As Matt closed the front door Georgie stared at the curving staircase a few yards away which was a beautiful thing all on its own. 'Why did she decide to sell in the end?'

'She became too arthritic to continue,' he said shortly.

'Poor thing,' Georgie sympathised absently, her eyes on a fine painting on the far wall. 'She must have hated leaving her home.'

'Not so much the house, more the animals she had here,' Matt said quietly. 'She needed to go into a nursing home for proper care, but she had used the house and the grounds almost as a sanctuary for the remainder of her father's farm animals and the pets she had accumulated, who had grown old with her.'

Something in his voice caused her eyes to focus on him. If the person speaking had been other than Matt de Capistrano, ruthless tycoon and entrepreneur extraordinaire, she would have sworn there was tenderness colouring his words when he'd spoken of the old lady.

'What happened to them? To the animals?' Georgie asked softly.

Now his voice was expressionless, brisk even, when he said, 'You can meet a few, if you wish.' He had been leading her down the sun-kissed hall, which had bowls of fresh flowers on several occasional tables, and as they reached the far end he opened another door which led on to a large, white-washed passageway.

The opening of this last door caused a bell to tinkle somewhere, and in the next moment a big—very big—red-cheeked woman appeared from a doorway at the end of the passage, several dogs spilling out in front of her with a medley of barks and woofs.

'You kept them?' Georgie stopped abruptly and stared into his dead-pan face before she bent to fuss the excited animals who were now jumping round their feet. 'You kept the old lady's pets?'

'Aye, that he did, lass.' The woman—Matt's house-keeper, Georgie assumed—had now reached them and began shooing the dogs back into the room they had come from, continuing to say as she did so, 'We've more geriatrics here than in the nursing home where poor Miss Barnes is, bless her.' And then she straightened, holding out her hand as she said, 'I'm Rosie, by the way, Mr de Capistrano's housekeeper, and I'm very pleased to meet you, lass.'

She must have replied in like because everything continued quite normally for the next few minutes, but as Matt led her after Rosie, who had walked back into the massive farmhouse kitchen at the back of the house, Georgie's head was spinning. She was conscious of an overwhelming desire to take to her heels and run. This was danger—this place, the man at the side of her, all of it. He wouldn't stay in the niche she had made for him in her mind and it was imperative he did so.

This feeling continued as, after a tour of the farmhouse, which Matt had turned into a fabulous place, he took her outside into the surrounding grounds.

She had met what Rosie called 'the inside pests'—five dogs and several assorted cats—but now in the fields directly behind the house and to one side of the stable block she saw there was a small flock of ten or so sheep, two donkeys and several ancient horses meandering around along with one or two bony bovines.

'They took all her savings, most of her furniture and certainly her health,' Matt said quietly at the side of her as Georgie looked across at the animals pottering about in the sunshine. 'But she loved them more passionately than most people love their children. What could I do but agree they could live out their time quietly and peacefully here?'

'I suppose to her they *were* her children.' Georgie kept her voice even and steady although inside she felt as though she were drowning.

'Come and see my other gems,' Matt said lightly, seemingly unaware of the body blow he had wrought her. 'These are the 24-carat kind.'

She followed him into the stable block, where Matt's groom was working, and the young man joined them as Matt introduced her to his two thoroughbred Arab stallions and a dappled mare and young colt.

Okay, so he was kind to old ladies and animals, Georgie told herself silently as she listened to the two men talk about the merits of a new feed on the market. But she was neither, and she forgot that at her peril. He had already made it quite clear how he viewed an affair with her. It was a thing of the body, not of the mind, and the sexual attraction he felt for her would eventually burn itself out. And in view of her inexpertise in the bed department that might be a darn sight quicker than he had bargained for!

She was not a *femme fatale*, like his secretary or the women he normally associated with socially, and his world was as alien to her as—she searched her mind for an appropriate simile—as fish and chips out of a paper bag would be to him!

She ran her fingers over the raw silk coat of one of the stallions. The advertisement for a replacement secretary for Robert should be appearing in the paper tomorrow; hopefully she would soon be out of Matt's sphere and it wouldn't take long for a man like him to forget her.

'Magnificent, isn't he?' The warmth in Matt's voice brought her eyes from the horse to his face, and he turned to glance at her in the same moment. 'Do you ride?' he asked quietly.

'No.' There hadn't been any spare cash for anything so frivolous as riding lessons when she had been younger, and even now she knew Robert was struggling to pay for Annie's lessons.

'Would you like to?'

She shrugged, turning away from the stable and the horse's velvet nose which was twitching enquiringly over the half door. 'Annie's the horsewoman,' she said lightly. 'She'll go ape over this place.'

'Ape?'

'She'll love it,' Georgie explained as Matt fell into step beside her. 'She's crazy about animals although Robert and Sandra never wanted any. Your menagerie will be heaven on earth to her.'

'So I will be a means of satisfaction to at least one Millett female?' he enquired with silky mockery.

She ignored that, turning at the entrance into the stable block and waving to the young groom as she called her goodbyes.

Once outside in the mild May air she glanced about her as she said, 'You were going to show me where we could have the barbecue and bouncy castle if it is wet?'

'So I was. Please come this way, ma'am.' He imitated her brisk, no-nonsense voice with dark amusement and Georgie wanted to kick him, hard.

From the outside the large building some fifty yards to the left of the farmhouse looked like a big barn—but as Matt opened the huge wooden doors and they stepped inside Georgie saw it had been converted into what was basically a massive hall. A row of windows ran right round three walls at first-floor level and there was a stage at the far end where she presumed a band could play. To the side of the stage was a well-equipped bar, and a host of tables with chairs piled on them stood all along the right wall.

'Would this do?' Matt asked with suspicious meekness.

She nodded stiffly, suddenly vitally aware of the height and breadth of him beside her. 'It's very nice,' she said flatly.

'And the pool met your requirements?'

The pool had been terrific, more in keeping with a leisure centre than a private home, and being joined to the main house by means of a covered way off the well-equipped games room at the back of the house it was just as consumer-friendly in the winter as the summer. 'Everything's lovely,' she said reluctantly.

'Why don't we have a dip before dinner?' he suggested softly.

'I haven't got a swimming cos—' She stopped abruptly. 'Before *dinner*?'

He shut his eyes briefly at the shrill note and said patiently, 'People do, Georgie; it is quite a civilised way to live. I have a changing room full of suitable swimwear.'

And he knew exactly where he could stick it! She glared at him, berating herself for being so foolish as to trust him. 'You promised me you would take me straight home,' she said frostily. 'I need to look after the twins.'

'No, you do not,' he stated evenly. 'Robert might be just a mere man but he is more than able to take them out for a burger and then tuck them up in bed later. He is their father when all is said and done. Besides which...'

He hesitated, and Georgie eyed him with blazing green eyes as she clipped, 'Yes?'

'They need to bond, the three of them, and you are in danger of getting in the way,' he stated with unforgivable clarity.

'What?' Georgie couldn't believe her ears.

'You're pushing Robert out and swamping the twins with an over-indulgence of love in the process,' Matt stated quietly. 'Before long you'll have two brats on your hands if you aren't careful.'

Nothing in the world could have stopped her hand connecting with the hard tanned skin of his face. The slap echoed round the barn for some moments as they both stood stock still, looking at each other, Matt with a face of stone and Georgie wide-eyed and shaking. 'How dare you, how *dare* you say that when you have only met David and Annie once?' Georgie said painfully, her face reflecting her shock and hurt. 'They are wonderful kids, the pair of them.'

'I know that; I'm talking about what could happen in the future,' he grated tightly.

She called him a name that made his eyes widen and which surprised the pair of them. 'I want to go home right now,' she bit out furiously, her anger masking the horror that was now dawning as she saw her red handprint etched on the skin of his face.

'No way.' His eyes narrowed and she knew he meant it. 'You are going to stay here and have dinner with me whether you like it or not, and if you'd just take a little time to think about what I have said you might see there is some truth in it.'

'So you're saying I'm ruining the twins and stopping my brother from seeing his children?' Georgie asked wildly.

'*I am saying*—' He paused, moderating his tone before he continued more quietly, 'I am saying you need to let the three of them have some time together now and again, that is all. When was the last time Robert took David to the swimming baths or Annie to her riding lesson? When does he put them to bed and listen to what has happened in their day? When, Georgie?'

She stared at him, stunned and silent.

'David needs his father to go and see him when he has a football match now and again.' The dark husky voice was relentless. 'It is necessary and healthy.'

'Robert has had enough to do to cope with Sandra's death,' Georgie said fiercely.

'Initially, yes.' He allowed another brief pause before he said, 'But it has been six months, Georgie, and that is a long time in the life of a child. Robert has slipped into the habit of letting you be mother *and* father to the twins and I feel his wife, Sandra, would not have wanted this.'

'You didn't know her!'

'This is true.' The grey eyes were fixed on her stricken face. 'And this is why I can speak with impartiality. Sometimes it takes an outsider to see what is happening, and I do not doubt your love for your brother and his children but you cannot be their mother, Georgie. You are their aunty—precious, no doubt. But you will burn yourself out if you continue to try to be everything to everyone.'

Where had the shallow philanderer gone? She couldn't see him in this man who spoke with quiet but determined force and it scared her to death. And it was in challenge to that thought that she flung out, her voice scathing, 'All this talk about Robert and the twins when you know full well what you really want! You don't care about them; you're using them to get your own way. You are just the same as all the others!'

He was angry. Really, really angry. A muscle had knotted in his cheek and his grey eyes were steely, but his voice was even and controlled when he said, 'I'll ignore that because it is not worthy of a reply. You are a young woman of twenty-three and yet you act like a matron several decades older. When do you ever go out and enjoy yourself, Georgie? Have fun? Let your hair down?'

'With men, you mean?' she bit out with open hostility.

'We don't all need to sleep around to think we're having a good time. I like my life, as it happens.'

'I have it on good authority you have barely left the house in six months except to escort the children to and fro and go to work,' Matt returned harshly. 'That is not a life; that is an existence. Even this Simon is not what you led me to believe.'

'Excuse me?' He could only have got all this from Robert and she couldn't believe her brother had betrayed her in this way. Only it wouldn't have been like that, she reasoned in the next milli-second. Matt knew just how to word a question to get the maximum response and Robert would have been quite unaware he was being pumped for information. 'I did not "lead" you to believe anything!' she protested with outraged dignity.

'That is a matter of opinion.' He stared into her furious face, his own as angry, and then after a moment she saw him take a deep breath and visibly relax as he raked back his hair in a gesture that carried both irritation and frustration in it. 'Damn it, I did not want it to be like this,' he growled tightly.

She could believe that! Oh, yes, she could believe that all right. She knew quite well what he had had in mind. He had made sure of that himself—no strings attached and no heavy commitment was how he had termed it. He didn't believe in love or for everness. Well, if she was absolutely truthful, she wasn't quite sure what she believed in, but one thing she did know—when she made love with a man it would have to be believing there was at least a strong chance they would have some sort of a future together. It was just the way she was made and she wasn't going to apologise for that or anything else about herself either.

She drew herself up to her full five foot four inches and glared at him before turning out of the barn, but she had only gone a few steps when he caught at her arm, turning her round to face him. 'Would it help if I said if I was the twins' age you would be my ideal as a surrogate mother?' he asked with exaggerated humbleness.

'No,' she snapped hotly.

'Or that I think Robert is the luckiest brother in the world and that you have steered the good ship Millett through turbulent waters wonderfully well?'

'No again.'

In truth she was having a job not to cry, but she would rather die than let him know that. Maybe she *had* been a touch obsessional in trying to be everything the twins needed, but she could still remember how she had felt at ten years old when she had lost her parents and her world had disintegrated about her. But...but it *was* different for David and Annie. Her innate honesty was forcing the recognition in spite of herself. They still had their father, for a start, along with each other and the security of their home and all their friends. She had been whipped out of the environment she'd always known and placed with Robert and Sandra, and although they'd been wonderful, *marvellous*, it had been a terribly tough time. She *had* been overcompensating without realising it and in the process encouraging Robert to sit and brood rather than take his share of responsibility with the twins. *Oh, hell!*

'Georgie?' As she raised stricken eyes to Matt's face she saw he was watching her very closely. 'It is not criminal to have the kind heart,' he said softly. 'Better an excess of indulgence and pampering at this time than for them to feel cast adrift.'

If he had continued with the home truths in that cool relentless voice she could have coped, even the slightly mocking teasing attitude after he had caught her arm had kept the adrenaline running hot and strong, but this last was too much.

'I...I want to go home.' Her voice wobbled alarmingly over the declaration but she continued to fight the tears until the moment he pulled her into his arms, holding her against the solid warmth of his body. And then she just bawled her eyes out, in an unladylike display of wailing and choking sobs and a runny nose that was all out of proportion to anything which had gone before.

She couldn't have explained that her tears were as much for the lost little ten-year-old she had been as for Robert and Annie and David, for Glen's cruel cavalier treatment, for the humiliation and desperation she had felt at that time, and for Sandra. Poor, poor Sandra. Everything was all mixed up together and she cried as she hadn't done in years, not since her parents' death in fact.

Matt let her cry for long, long minutes, making no effort to ask any questions as he held her pressed against his chest and made soothing noises above her blonde head. And then, as the flood reduced to hiccuping sobs, and then valiant sniffs and splutters against his damp shirt-front, Georgie was overcome with embarrassment at her ignominious tears. How could she, how *could* she have lost control like that, and in front of Matt de Capistrano of all people? What must he be thinking? And then she found out.

'At a guess I would say that has been held in for far too long.' His voice was low and soft, his hands warm and soothing as they stroked her slender back. 'Am I right?'

Georgie stiffened slightly. This was a very astute and clever man in the normal run of things, and she had just given him a heaven-sent opportunity that even the thickest of individuals would capitalise on.

'I didn't mean to make you cry,' he continued quietly. 'You know that, don't you?'

'It wasn't you.' Her face was burning now, she could feel it, but she couldn't stay pressed against his chest for ever and so she pushed away from him, only to find he wasn't ready to let her go. She rubbed her pink nose, knowing she must look like something the cat had dragged in. 'Have you a hanky I can borrow?'

'In a moment.' He continued to look down into her tear-smudged face, into the startlingly green eyes that were so incredibly beautiful. 'If it was not my clumsy remarks, then what?'

'I...I don't know. Lots of things.' She heard her shaking voice with a dart of very real irritation at herself. She had to be strong and on her guard around Matt; trembling femininity was not an option. 'It's been a stressful time for everyone.'

'And you have been very brave.'

Oh, hell; if he kept this up she was going to blub all over him again, Georgie thought feverishly, as tears pricked at the back of her eyes again. After not crying for years it now seemed she couldn't stop!

'Not really.' She shrugged, trying to move out of his arms but not quite able to break free. 'I suppose the twins' situation is so close to the one I endured as a child that it makes it difficult to separate the two in my mind. The feelings I had then tend to get in the way sometimes.'

'Explain.' He let go of her long enough to delve into his pocket for a crisp white handkerchief, but after he had handed it to her and she was mopping at her face the strong arms enclosed her again, but lightly now, a few inches between them.

Not that it made much difference, Georgie thought a trifle hysterically. The big hard body, the delicious and literally intoxicating smell of him was all around her and it made her head spin. She had never in her wildest dreams believed that sexual attraction could be so strong or so physical, but it was making her legs weak.

She drew a deep breath, the handkerchief still clutched in one hand, and began to explain about the circumstances that had placed her in Robert's home.

He listened without interrupting until she had finished. 'So tiny and so ethereal.' There was what sounded like a note of disconcertment in the deep male voice. 'You appear at first sight to be...'

'The original dumb blonde?' she finished for him with a slight edge to her voice now, the memory of their first meeting suddenly very vivid. He had thought she was the type of female who spent all her time on the phone talking to other dumb females, then!

'Delicate and breakable,' he corrected evenly. 'But in truth you are—'

'As tough as old boots?' She did it on purpose, as much to annoy him and thereby shatter the intimate mood he'd created so effortlessly as to assure herself she was *not* going to be fooled by this new side of him.

'A very strong and courageous woman.' He tilted his head. 'You still haven't told me his name, Georgie.'

'Whose?' She had tried to hide the instinctive start she'd given at his ruthless strategy, but she knew the piercingly intent gaze had registered it.

'The man who has caused you to build this shell around yourself,' he said silkily.

He was not going to have this all his own way! She stared up at him, wondering why God had given him such a sexy mouth on top of all his other attributes, and said steadily, 'I could ask you the same question, Matt. You've told me you don't believe in love and for everness; there has to be a reason for that.'

He drew back and stared into her face, not able to hide

his surprise. And then his eyes narrowed and his hands fell from around her waist, and she knew she had hit a nerve. It was disturbing that it didn't give her the satisfaction she'd expected.

'*Touché*, Miss Millett.' His voice was cool, withdrawn, and in spite of herself she felt the loss of the warmth that had been there previously with a physical ache. 'So we are both…realistic; is that what you are saying?'

It wasn't at all what she had said and he knew it. She scrubbed at her face one last time and then offered him back the handkerchief. She could probe but, as she wasn't prepared to talk about Glen, it wouldn't be wise. She had said far too much already when she thought about it, all that about her childhood and so on. She wished now she had kept quiet.

'Come.' He held out his hand, his grey eyes unfathomable as he stared down into her heart-shaped face. 'I know just the thing to relax you and make you feel better,' he added with a touch of dark amusement.

Her imagination running rampant, Georgie peered up at him suspiciously. 'What's that?' she asked flatly.

'A swim, what else?' His smile was definitely of the wicked kind. 'As I said, I have many costumes in one of the changing rooms and you will find something suitable I am sure. We can swim a little, have a cocktail or two, and then change for dinner later.'

'I told you I'm not staying for dinner.'

'And I told you you are,' he said pleasantly. 'If nothing else, Rosie would be very upset to think you do not wish to partake of the meal she has been preparing most of the day.'

Georgie flushed. He was making her feel crass and it was so *unfair*. 'That's emotional blackmail,' she said tightly.

Matt shrugged and the gesture was very Latin. 'It is the truth.' And then his attitude changed somewhat as he added, 'I want to give you an evening off duty for once, Georgie; is that really such a crime? And Robert was in full agreement when I suggested this to him. "Very kind" was how he termed it, I think.'

Her flush deepened, and now the grey eyes were definitely laughing when he said, 'I promise to be a good boy at all times; does that help? I will treat you as I would treat my maiden aunt.'

He was standing in front of her, tall and lithe, his arms crossed over his broad chest and his shirt open at the bronze of his neck. He looked very masculine and dark and good enough to eat. Georgie swallowed hard. Impossible man. Impossible situation! 'All right.' She heard herself say the words with a faint feeling of despair. 'But just dinner, no swim.' Clothed, she could just about cope, but half-naked?

'You cannot swim?' he asked evenly. One dark eyebrow had slanted provocatively and she just *knew* he was sure of her answer.

'Yes.' It was reluctant.

'Then this is what we will do,' he stated firmly. 'Already Rosie will have taken the cocktails out to the pool area and I have had it heated warmer than usual so it will be quite pleasant. I have a swim before dinner each evening. It is very good for the circulation.'

Maybe, but the thought of Matt in next to nothing was playing havoc with her blood pressure.

And then he stretched out his hand again, this time taking one of hers as though he had a perfect right to touch her whenever he pleased, and she found herself walking alongside him as they made their way back to the house. She was all out of arguments.

CHAPTER SIX

AN HOUR later, as Georgie lay on a thickly cushioned lounger at the side of the pool sipping an exotic pink cocktail, she had to admit to herself she was having a whale of a time.

Admittedly there had been several sticky moments. Firstly, when she had stood in the changing room used by Matt's female guests and looked at the vast row of minuscule bikinis and wraps, she had panicked big time. The tiny scraps of material all bore designer labels, and all seemed indecent to her fevered gaze, but eventually she had managed to find a one-piece among all the wisps which, although cut away at the sides and with a frighteningly plunging neckline, was a size eight and a little more decorous than the rest.

She had ignored the dozen or so diaphanous wraps, all gossamer-thin and quite beautiful in a rainbow of different colours, and regretfully reached for one of the towelling robes, which she had slipped on over the swimming costume and tied tightly round her waist.

She had glanced into the huge mirror which took up all of one wall at her reflection. The only thing showing were her feet and hands! She'd cope with the moment when she must find the nerve to disrobe later; this concealed almost every inch of her, and it had given her the courage to leave her hidey-hole with her head held high and her back straight.

Her cucumber-cool resolve had faltered somewhat when she'd emerged to find Matt climbing out of the pool, obviously having swum a few lengths while he was waiting for her.

He was wearing a pair of brief black swimming trunks which left nothing—absolutely nothing—to the imagination, and his thickly muscled torso had gleamed like oiled silk, the body hair on his chest a mass of tight black curls. She had known he would be magnificent unclothed, but the reality of the powerful male body, which didn't carry a morsel of fat and was primed to lean perfection, had been something else. Something dangerous and threatening and utterly mind-blowing.

She had forced herself to pad across towards him as he'd raised a casual hand in welcome, her mouth dry and the palms of her hands damp, but thankfully he had bent to pour out their drinks at her approach, and by the time she'd reached him she had pulled herself together.

'To the most beautiful maiden aunt anyone could wish to have,' he drawled mockingly as he placed one glass in her hand, raising his in a salute. 'And to a pleasant evening getting to know each other a little better.'

Georgie found it almost impossible to concentrate on anything else but the acres of hard tanned flesh in front of her, but somehow she found the strength to say, in a voice that could have passed for normal, 'To a nice evening,' as she raised her glass too. 'Mmm, that's gorgeous.' The cocktail tasted wonderful. 'What's in it?'

'Sloe gin, banana liqueur, crushed raspberries, white wine…and a couple of other things which are my secret,' Matt returned softly. 'I invented this cocktail a few years ago and there's many who would love to know the ingredients.'

'What's it called?' She took another gulp, needing something to distract her from the flagrant maleness in front of her, the taut belly and hard male thighs.

'Passionate Beginnings.' He was totally straight-faced.

She eyed him severely. 'You just made that up,' she accused uncertainly.

'Would I?' His voice was even softer now, and she shivered in spite of the hothouse warmth.

'You're not cold?' he asked in surprise.

'No, not cold exactly.' Her oxygen supply was in severe danger of running out and she felt weak at the knees, but just at this moment a lack of warmth was not one of her problems!

'Good.' He smiled, utterly at ease with himself in spite of practically being in the nude. 'Then finish that and come and have a swim.'

Apart from the acute discomfort she felt when she first slipped off the robe and sensed Matt's eyes on her—she didn't dare to look at him—the time that followed was full of laughter and fun. Matt was like a kid again in the water, splashing her and grabbing her ankles until she was forced to pay him back in kind, and they had a time of clowning around as well as some serious swimming.

Georgie was not a particularly strong swimmer, but even if she had been she realised quite quickly she wouldn't have been able to compete with Matt. He cut through the water with incredible speed, an automaton clothed in flesh and blood and sinew.

After half an hour or so she climbed out of the pool and sipped her drink again, lying on one of the sun loungers as she watched him cover length after length with effortless ease.

It was another ten minutes before he joined her, and Georgie's stomach muscles clenched as he pulled himself out of the water and strolled over to the lounger at the side of hers. It was one thing lying here supposedly relaxed and cool, sipping elegantly at a drink, when that powerful male body was in the water; quite another when it was a foot or so away.

She had debated whether to clothe herself from head to foot in the robe again when she had first sat down, but with the temperature in the pool area being what it was had decided that would be too ridiculous. And she was a grown woman, she told herself firmly, not some adolescent green behind the ears. Two adults in swimwear was not a prelude to an orgy, even if one of them *was* Matt de Capistrano.

And so she topped up his barely touched drink with a smile when he sat down, exchanged a little small talk and then settled herself back and shut her eyes, commenting this was the most restful evening she had had in a long, long time. She was surprised how well she lied.

She didn't know what she expected in the minutes that followed her declaration, but after a little while she dared to open her eyes enough to slant a quick glance at the side of her.

Matt was lying back on his lounger too, apparently perfectly relaxed, his eyes shut and the big body stretched out and still damp from the water. Georgie frowned. He hadn't made a move on her at all, hadn't even tried to kiss her. And then she felt her face flame at her own inconsistency. She didn't want him to! Of course she didn't. What on earth was the matter with her anyway?

'David and Annie will have the best birthday party ever here,' she said quietly as she sat up and reached for her glass.

'Good.' He didn't move or open his eyes.

'It's really very kind of you to allow your home to be invaded by a host of strangers, especially as most of them will be screaming infants.'

'My pleasure.'

What was the matter with him, for goodness' sake?

Georgie's irritation was totally unfair and she knew it, which made it all the more aggravating. Suddenly the desire to talk, to find out more about the enigmatic individual at the side of her was strong. There was a whole host of questions burning in her brain, and all of them much too personal. She brushed back a strand of silky blonde hair from her cheek and swallowed hard, before she compromised with, 'Do you manage to spend much time at your home in Spain?'

He opened his eyes then, the piercing gaze focusing on her for a moment before he sat up and reached for his own glass, draining the last of the pink liquid before he said, 'Not as much as I would like. My sister's last child is three months old and I have seen him only twice, although this last period has been a particularly difficult one business-wise, with a complicated takeover here in England. Fortunately the Spanish side of things is flowing easily at the moment, and with my brother-in-law at the helm out there I know I have someone I can trust to oversee things for me.'

'Do you have any family from your mother's side here in England?' she asked carefully.

'An uncle.' He swung his legs over the side of the lounger to face her and her senses went into hyperdrive. 'He and my father started the English side of the business with my English grandparents, who are now dead, although my uncle chooses to do less and less these days. He prefers to travel and as he never married and has no ties he is something of a free spirit.' It was wry, and Georgie got the impression not wholly acceptable.

She wanted to ask about Pepita; why he didn't have an English secretary here in England for a start. She had sensed a closeness between Matt and the beautiful Spanish woman that went beyond the bounds of a working relationship, although she could be wrong. But she didn't think so. She hesitated, not knowing how to put it. 'Is…is Pepita's ankle any better?' she asked lamely.

'Yes, I think so.'

It was dismissive and perversely made Georgie all the more determined to continue.

'Does she travel with you back and forwards to Spain?' she asked in as neutral a voice as she could manage, just as a door at the far end of the huge room opened and Rosie called out, 'Dinner in fifteen minutes, Mr de Capistrano.'

'Thank you, Rosie.' He rose as he spoke, holding out a hand to Georgie as he said quietly, 'No doubt you will want to shower before dinner; you should find all you need in the changing room.'

Had he purposely not answered her, or had the question been lost in Rosie's ill-timed interruption? Georgie wasn't sure but the moment had gone anyway. She looked up at him, but before she could take his hand he said, his voice silky smooth now, 'I do not bite, Georgie,' as he bent down and pulled her to her feet.

For a heart-stopping moment she was held against his muscled chest, her hair tousled and her cheeks pink; and she knew he was going to kiss her. So it came as a drenching shock when she was put firmly to one side and Matt's voice said coolly, 'You'll find the towels to one side of the shower cubicle.'

The *towels*? She tried with all her might to show no reaction at all when she said politely, 'Thank you,' before she scurried away, grabbing the robe as she went.

Had he known she expected him to kiss her? Probably. She groaned softly as she stood under the deliciously warm water in the shower after lathering herself with an expensive-smelling body shampoo. Very probably. He was an experienced man of the world; reading a woman's body signals was as natural to him as breathing. But he had shown her he didn't kiss a woman because she indicated she was available, only when he was ready to do so.

She groaned again before taking herself in hand. But she wasn't available, she *wasn't*. She might have suffered a momentary aberration but that was all it had been.

She lathered her hair with the shampoo quickly before rinsing down and drying herself with one of the huge fluffy bath sheets. On the wooden shelf which ran under the mirror along one wall there was every available cream and lotion known to man, along with a display unit holding a vast array of cosmetics, including nail varnish, combs and brushes in unopened packages, lipsticks and anything else a beautician might need.

Georgie ignored it all, drying her hair quickly before she slipped on her own clothes and surveyed herself in the mirror. Without even her customary touch of mascara she looked about sixteen, but that suited her! She scowled at the small slim figure staring back at her. She couldn't compete with the sort of glamorous, dazzling women he was used to and she didn't intend to try, she told herself fiercely, as a beautiful face with slanted ebony eyes flashed across the screen of her mind.

Matt was waiting outside for her when she stepped out of the changing room, looking dark and foreign against the light surroundings. His eyes roamed over her freshly scrubbed face for a moment and then he seemed to echo her previous thoughts when he said softly, 'Sweet sixteen and never been kissed. Although you have, haven't you? Been kissed. Did you respond to him like you respond to me, Georgie?'

'Who?' His previous attitude had lulled her into a false sense of security, she realised now, which was probably what this master strategist had had in mind.

'This man you will not talk about,' he answered with gross unfairness, considering he had closed up like a clam about his own past.

She stared at him for a moment, feeling out of her depth, and then tossed her head slightly as a surge of anger swept away the weakness. She opened her mouth to tell him to mind his own business but he was too quick for her, bending swiftly as his arms went about her and he started to kiss her.

'Let me go, Matt.' She struggled but only briefly, her movements accentuating the softness of her shape against the hard angles of his body, that supremely male body she had had to fight not to ogle for the last hour.

'Why?' He lifted his head but only after he had clasped her face and kissed her until she was gasping.

'Because you said you'd be good,' she managed breathlessly.

'Oh, I am good, Georgie, I promise,' he said with a wicked twist of his lips. 'If nothing else I'm good.'

'You know what I mean.' She was flushed and excited and desperately trying to hide the evidence of her own arousal.

That she'd failed miserably became obvious when he brushed a tantalising finger down the soft slope of one breast and up again. She was swollen and aching, the nipple hard and tender, and as her breath caught in her throat he smiled again. 'You're going to continue to fight me?' he murmured mockingly. 'Why, when you know this can only have one conclusion?'

The Julia Bloomsbury philosophy again. I want therefore I must have. The grating quality of the thought stiffened her back and gave her the strength to jerk away from him, her voice holding a harsh note as she said, 'Matt, there is no way—*no way*—I would sleep with a man I've only known for a few days. I'm not made that way.'

'How long would you have to know a man, my innocent?' he asked smoothly, watching her with gleaming eyes.

Oh, this was crazy; she was getting in deeper and deeper here.

'I don't know.' She shrugged, her face straight and her eyes unhappy. 'A long time.'

'Time is relative.' His mouth was tilting with amusement. And then suddenly his attitude changed, his head nodding as he said, soberly now, 'But I like this in a woman, the ability to hold herself with some value. This is good.'

'It is?' She eyed him uncertainly. She didn't trust him an inch.

'But yes.' His hand reached out and lifted a lock of her hair, allowing it to fall back into place strand by strand as it fanned her face with silky gold. 'Man is the hunter. Did you not know this?'

'Maybe long ago before we became civilised,' she agreed warily.

'I am not civilised, Georgie.'

He didn't appear to be joking and she wasn't altogether sure she disagreed with the statement anyway. The veneer of civilisation sat very lightly on Matt's dark frame; he was dangerous and alien and had more than a little of the barbarian about him.

And then he flung back his head and laughed, the first real laugh she had heard from him, before he said as he met her eyes again, 'You frown at me when I try and make love to you and you frown at me when I agree I must not. What can I do to please you?'

He was laughing at her again and the mockery enabled her to say, her voice very cool, 'Why not try to be a friend first and foremost, or is that too radical a concept for you to take on board?'

'You want friendship from me?' he asked, his eyes on her full soft lips.

'That's beyond your capabilities?' she mocked tauntingly.

'With your brother, no.' He let his gaze take in her creamy skin, the small firm breasts and slender waist, and his voice was dry when he added, 'But you are not a six-foot male, Georgie.'

'It's friendship or nothing.' She sounded much firmer than she felt, she thought with some satisfaction, considering inside she was a quivering mess. She didn't have the first idea what made Matt tick, but she did know it would be emotional suicide to have an affair with him. She would be leaving Robert's office soon but, Matt being Matt, he would still arrange things so he could see her, at least while Robert was involved businesswise with him. This way, with certain ground rules in place, she would have some protection—whether from Matt or her own desire she wasn't sure. Whatever, she needed something!

'Then I agree.' His capitulation was too quick and too easy to be believable.

'Just friends,' she reiterated distrustfully.

'If this is what you want, Georgie.' The way he said her name never failed to set the juices flowing.

Her heart squeezed a little and her voice was all the more firm when she said, 'It is.'

'Then let us go into dinner and celebrate finding each other—as friends,' he murmured silkily. 'Yes?'

She nodded doubtfully. How was it, she asked herself silently, that instead of a victory this felt more like a defeat?

*   *   *

The dinner was absolutely wonderful, and Georgie found in spite of her racing heart—which just wouldn't behave itself—she enjoyed every mouthful. Goat's cheese, pepper, radicchio and pine nut salad for starters, followed by ravioli of lobster with a red pimento sauce and then chocolate and pear roulade. As she finished the last mouthful of dessert she looked at Matt, seated opposite her across a table resplendent with crystal and silver cutlery in a dining room which was all wood beams and antique furniture and flowing white silk voile curtains, and said, her tone awestruck, 'Do you always eat like this?'

He grinned at her. 'If I was trying to get you into my bed—which now of course I am not,' he clarified meekly, 'I would say, yes, of course, Georgie. As it is...' He allowed a moment or two to elapse. 'You are my friend, yes? And friends do not embroider the truth. So I have to say that I asked Rosie to make something of an effort tonight, although she is an excellent cook and always feeds me well.'

Georgie was still reeling from the grin, which had mellowed the hard face and made him appear years younger, and it took her a moment or two to smile back and make a light comment. He was *dangerous* and never more so than when he was pretending not to be, like now. Or was he pretending? As the evening continued and they had coffee in the exquisitely furnished room Matt had had turned into a drawing room and which overlooked the rolling landscaped gardens at the front of the house, she wasn't sure.

He was relaxed and amusing and the perfect host, and he didn't put a foot—or a hand—wrong. When she made noises about going home just after eleven o'clock he jumped up immediately without any ploys to detain her, and the drive home was uneventful. He saw her to Robert's door, lifted her chin and kissed her fleetingly on the tip of her nose and returned to the car without demur, leaving her standing on the doorstep long after the Lamborghini had disappeared into the night.

Whether it was the wine she had imbibed alone at dinner—Matt had been drinking mineral water after the one cocktail he had allowed himself, due to the fact he intended to drive her home—or the fact that it was the end of an emotionally exhausting day, Georgie didn't know, but she suddenly felt utterly drained.

It was an effort to mount the stairs and get into bed, and she fell asleep as soon as her head touched the pillow, but after a few hours' deep sleep she awoke, knowing Matt had been in her dreams. She lay quietly in the room she shared with Annie, her mind going over all she and Matt had said and done, and she couldn't even think of going back to sleep.

He was in her mind, in her head... She stared into the shadows caused by the burgeoning morning light as her heart thudded at the thought of all that had happened in such short a time, and again the sense of danger enveloped her. And it warned her—more effectively than any spoken words could have done—that she had to be very careful not to let him into her heart too.

Georgie had cause to think, over the next few weeks, that she had grossly exaggerated everything that morning after she had first had dinner with Matt.

As the days passed—the twins' party being the sort of success that would be talked about for years afterwards by their envious friends—and May merged into a blazing hot June, Matt seemed to have inveigled himself into the position of family friend with very little effort.

In spite of there being some sort of hiccup with regard to the starting date of his contract with Robert, he had insisted on financing the hire of extra men and machinery for another job which Robert had won in the meantime and which he would have been unable to accept but for Matt's magnanimity. The two men seemed to have more in common than Georgie would have thought, and it wasn't uncommon for Matt to call round for a coffee or a meal once or twice a week now, when he was always greeted rapturously by Annie and David.

Georgie had left Robert's employ as she'd planned and was now working for a temping agency at double the money Robert could afford, with the knowledge she could take time off in the children's school holidays without feeling she was putting pressure on Robert in his office. Consequently she was not privy to the ins and outs of what was happening with his business, but Robert himself had assured her that the very tasty contract with Matt was still on but just delayed a while due to a few problems with the planners.

'Couldn't have worked out better, actually,' Robert had said when he'd first broken the news in the middle of May. 'This way, with Matt agreeing to lend me the money to finance the Portabello job, we can do that through the next two or three months and then have Matt's job round about September onwards when it's often slack. We've never been busier, Georgie.'

And that was helping him come to terms with Sandra's loss. Georgie nodded to the thought as she fixed the children's breakfasts one baking hot Saturday morning towards the end of June. Which was good, very good. And he was taking more time out to be with the twins in spite of being so busy, and that was even better. He was on an even keel again, Annie and David too, and she had to admit all this was due in no small part to Matt de Capistrano. So why, knowing all this, and accepting Matt now seemed to have done exactly what she had asked and relegated her to friend status and nothing more, was she becoming increasingly dissatisfied and on edge with the status quo?

Did he see other women? She paused for a long moment, staring blindly out of the kitchen window at the sun-scorched grass, before shaking herself mentally and going to the door, whereupon she called the twins, who had been playing in their tree-house since first light, due to the muggy heat in the bedrooms which made sleep difficult. Of course he would.

She dished up the pancakes loaded with lemon and sugar which were the twins' treat every Saturday morning when there was a little more time for a leisurely breakfast, and after going to the foot of the stairs called Robert down too.

He'd be bound to carry on with his social life as normal, she told herself, her mind functioning quite independently of her mouth as she joined in the small talk between Robert and the twins now and again. He had certainly made no attempt to seduce her! Friends she had said and friends they were—he probably viewed her as a female Robert. She glanced at her brother's big square face and sighed inwardly. Perhaps she needed a holiday?

After cooking more pancakes for the other three and serving gallons of freshly squeezed orange juice, Georgie eventually had the house to herself after Robert carted the twins off to their swimming lesson.

She glanced at the kitchen table loaded with dirty dishes and the huge bowl on the worktop which still held some pancake mixture and sighed again. Once she had cleared up in here, the house was waiting for its weekend cleaning session, and there were the beds to change and the fridge to defrost… Life seemed a never-ending cycle of work and more work these days. She grimaced at the maudlin self-pity even as she reiterated, I'm twenty-three, not eighty-three. I want to enjoy life, feel free again, have some fun!

'*Oh, stop it!*' Her voice was harsh and she was suddenly horrified at her selfishness. 'Think of Robert and the kids, for goodness' sake. What's the matter with you?'

'I have it on good authority that it is the first sign of madness to talk to yourself.'

Georgie jumped so violently as the deep male voice sounded from the doorway behind her that the last of her orange juice shot up in an arc over the table.

'Matt!' She spun round, her hand to her breast, to see him standing big and dark behind her. 'You scared me to death,' she accused breathlessly.

He looked good, very good, but then he always did, she thought ruefully. But today, clothed in light grey cotton trousers and an opened-necked cream shirt, he looked especially good. Or perhaps she was just especially pleased to see him? That thought was too dangerous to pursue, and so she said, forcing a cross note into her voice. 'Why do you creep up on folk like that?'

'I wasn't aware I *was* creeping,' he said with amiable good humour. 'I met Robert and the children on the drive and Robert opened the door for me. He called to you.'

'Did he?' She had been so lost in her own dismal thoughts it would have taken more than her brother's voice to rouse her. 'Well, what do you want?' she asked ungraciously, suddenly aware of how sticky and hot she had got bending over a hot hob.

They looked at each other for a second, his grey eyes pinning her as they darkened and narrowed, and Georgie found she was holding her breath without knowing why.

'A pancake?' His gaze moved to the remaining mixture in the bowl.

A pancake? She found she was staring at the dark profile

stupidly and had to swallow hard before she could say, 'I'm sure Rosie has given you breakfast.'

'As it happens she has not,' he answered almost triumphantly. 'She has gone with her husband to visit relatives in Newcastle for the weekend. I had some toast and coffee earlier but I was in the pool at five this morning and it has given me the appetite.'

It wasn't often he made a mistake in his excellent English and on the rare occasions he had Georgie hadn't liked what it had done to her heart. She didn't like it now, and to cover the flood of tenderness she said abruptly, 'Sit down, then.' He sat, and, chastened by his obedience, she added, 'I suppose the heat made you unable to sleep?'

He didn't answer immediately, and as she turned to look at him she read the look in his eyes and flushed hotly as he said, very drily, 'This...friend thing carries certain penalties, does it not?'

'I wouldn't know,' she lied firmly.

He slanted a look at her from under half-closed lids and her colour rivalled that of a tomato. 'I'll see to the pancakes,' she snapped tightly.

'Thank you, Georgie.' It was meek and most un-Mattish.

Fifteen minutes later Matt had demolished three pancakes, a further two rounds of toast and two pint mugs of black coffee, and Georgie was trying to fight the immense satisfaction she felt in seeing him sitting at her kitchen table.

'You have given me breakfast; I intend to give you lunch.' She had been washing the dishes at the sink and as he turned her round to face him she kept her wet hands stretched out at the side of her as she said, 'Matt, please, I have to finish these and then start upstairs. I've masses to do and—'

'No.' He put a reproving finger on her lips. 'You're hav-

ing a break. I've already told Robert you won't be back
until later tonight.'

'Excuse *me*!' She glared at him. 'You can't just muscle
in and tell me what to do. I need to see to the bedrooms.'

'I could tell you exactly what you need to see to in the
bedroom of one particular individual who isn't a million
miles away, but we won't go into that now,' Matt said
smoothly.

'Matt—'

'I know, I know…friends.'

The sexual knowledge in the dark grey eyes was in danger of stripping away all her carefully erected defences and
exposing her deepest desires, and Georgie felt mesmerised
as she stood before him. Why could he always *do* this? she
asked herself crossly. It wasn't fair.

He was holding her lightly on the shoulders, his fingertips warm through the thin material of the old cotton top
she had pulled on first thing, and, in spite of everything she
had said to Matt and to herself, at this very moment in time
Georgie knew she wanted him to respond to her secret
need. This wanting him had got worse through the last
weeks, not better. It was with her every minute she was
awake and it haunted her sleep to the point where she felt
exhausted every morning.

She didn't know where an affair with Matt would take
her; certainly he wouldn't be content with the fumbling
petting she had allowed with Glen. It would be all or nothing with Matt. The only trouble was, 'all' in his case meant
full physical intimacy and little else; 'all' in her case would
be a giving of her heart and her soul as well as her body.

The thought freed her locked limbs and gave her the
strength to step back away from him as she said, her voice
very even and controlled despite the turmoil within, 'What
did you have in mind for today?'

'A drive into the country, lunch at a little pub I know and then an afternoon relaxing at home by the pool. Rosie has left dinner for us; she's decided you are far too thin and need feeding up,' he added provocatively.

'*Too thin?*'

'I, on the other hand, think you are just right,' he said softly. 'For me, that is.'

Yes, well, she wasn't in a fit mental state to pursue that particular avenue. 'I'll have to shower and change.'

'I can wait.' There was a hungry fullness to his mouth that stirred her senses. 'I'm getting quite good at it,' he added drily.

'I won't be long.'

'Take all the time you want, Georgie.' He was wearing a sharp lemony aftershave that turned into something incredible on his tanned skin, and her heart went into hyperdrive when he added silkily, 'You are worth waiting for.'

Oh, boy, he was one of his own! Georgie didn't know if she was annoyed or amused as she hurried up to the room she shared with Annie and stripped off her sticky clothes. She didn't linger under the shower and her hair only took a few minutes to blowdry into a silky veil to her shoulders, so it couldn't have been more than a quarter of an hour before she had dressed again in a light white top and flimsy summer skirt, applying just a touch of mascara to her thick eyelashes before she made her way downstairs again.

However, the man who was sitting waiting for her at the kitchen table looked to have aged about ten years.

'Matt?' She was horrified at the change in him. 'What's the matter?'

'I've just had a phone call.' He gestured vacantly at his mobile phone which was lying in front of him on the table. 'It's my mother.'

'Your mother?' Oh, no, no.

'My sister...my sister's with her now, at the hospital. She found her collapsed and virtually unconscious, doubled up with pain.'

'Oh, Matt.' She didn't know what to do or say. His voice had been raw, and in the last few minutes worry and anxiety had scored deep lines in his face. Appalled, she murmured, 'You must go to her of course. What can I do to help?'

'What?'

He was clearly in shock, and Georgie saw his hands were trembling. She couldn't believe how it made her feel and it was in that second—totally inappropriate in the circumstances, she thought afterwards—that she realised how much she loved him. And it was love. Deep, abiding, once-in-a-lifetime love. As different from the puppy love she had felt for Glen as chalk from cheese. But she couldn't dwell on this catastrophe now.

She watched Matt take a deep breath and straighten his shoulders, and his voice was more normal when he said, 'I had better phone the airport. And my uncle, I need to let him know, and he'll have to hold the fort here.'

'I'll come with you.' She didn't even think about it; it was the natural thing to do somehow.

'To the airport? There's no need, really—'

'To Spain,' she cut in calmly. 'You need company at a time like this and we're friends, aren't we? Friends make time for each other.'

'To Spain?' There was a moment of silence and she saw he was struggling to take in what she had said. 'But your work, the twins—'

'I'm temping, so work is not a consideration. As for the twins; they have their father.' She eyed him steadily. 'And each other.' She was repeating the words he had said to her weeks earlier but neither of them were aware of it.

'You would do this? Come to Spain with me?' he asked somewhat bewilderedly.

Spain. The ends of the earth. Planet Zog! 'Of course.'

'Why?'

Because I love you with all my heart and all my soul and all my mind and all my strength. 'Because it might make things a little easier to have a friendly face with you,' she said quietly, 'and you have been terrific to the twins, Robert too, and I've never really said thank you.'

He raked back his hair in a confused gesture that tore at her heart. 'I...I do not know what to say, Georgie.'

At another time, in different circumstances and without the awful possibility of his mother being seriously ill, Georgie would have made plenty of that. The great Matt de Capistrano, silky-smooth operator and master of the silver tongue, at a loss for words? Never!

As it was she lifted up her hand and touched his cheek, careful to keep her eyes veiled so she gave nothing away as she said softly, 'You would do the same for me, Matt, for any of your friends.' And she did believe that, she affirmed silently. He was not a mean-minded man or ungenerous, far from it, and he would go the extra mile without counting the cost. The trouble was, common sense added ruefully, the masculine, ruthless side of him would keep his feelings beautifully under control the whole time. Whereas she...

'If you want to speak to your uncle and make any necessary arrangements, I can phone the airport if you like?' Georgie's voice was brisk now, but then it faltered as he took her hand in his own, holding it against his heart for a moment as he looked down into the deep green of her eyes before he raised the delicate fingers to his lips.

For several moments, moments when the world was quite still and frozen on its axis, she held his gaze. The air itself was shivering with intimacy and the trembling in her stomach threatened to communicate itself to her voice when she murmured, 'It will be all right, Matt, I'm sure of it.'

'Thank you,' he said huskily. He cupped her face in his big hands, kissing her parted lips with a tenderness she would have thought him incapable of. It hurt. Ridiculously, when he was being so nice, it hurt terribly because she wanted it so badly—she wanted *him*. But not just for a few weeks or months, even a year or two. She wanted him for ever, and for everness was an alien concept to him. Oh, what a mess, what a gargantuan mess.

'You're beautiful, Georgie.' His voice caught on her name in the way it always did, making it poignantly sweet. 'Whoever he was, he was a fool. You know that, do you not?'

She nodded. Glen had hurt her terribly at the time, but she knew now he would have hurt her more if she had married him because sooner or later he would have let her down. And it would have been worse, much worse, after they were married, perhaps even with children. He hadn't loved her enough; maybe he wasn't capable of loving anyone enough. Perhaps Julia sensed this and that was why they weren't happy? Whatever, she knew now she hadn't loved Glen enough either. Life with Glen would have been like wearing comfortable old clothes: no highs, no lows, mundane and ordinary. Millions of people the world over settled for just that, admittedly, but she wouldn't be able to do that again. Not now. Not after Matt.

He kissed her once more, and but for the circumstances and the fact that his mother was lying in a hospital bed halfway across the world Georgie was sure she would have leapt on him and ravished him on the kitchen table. As it was she called on every ounce of resolve and carefully removed herself from his hands, her voice a little shaky as she said, 'I'd better phone Robert and let him know what's happening.'

'Wait until I have spoken to the airport. It may be quicker to take a private plane,' Matt said quickly, with a return of his normal authority and command. 'We can land at La Coruna and I will arrange to have a car waiting.'

Georgie nodded silently. She would cope with this—the knowledge that she loved him—she would. As long as he didn't know, everything would be all right. Nothing had changed, not really.

'I'll go and sort out my passport and a few clothes,' she said quietly, scurrying up to the room she shared with Annie. Once in the sunlit room, however, she sank down on the bed for a few moments, staring blankly across the room.

She was committed to being with him for the next few days now, for good or ill, and however things worked out she wasn't sorry she'd offered to go with him. She wanted to see where he had been born, understand that other part of his life and see further glimpses of his complex person-ality which would be bound to unravel with his family and friends. Had he taken many women to his home town?

Her soft mouth drooped unknowingly for a few seconds and then she raised her head high, narrowing her eyes as she thought, If nothing else, *if nothing else* she would make sure he remembered her a little differently from all the rest. Friendship might not be what she would have chosen, but it singled her out from the crowd!

CHAPTER SEVEN

IT WAS just three o'clock in the afternoon when the private plane Matt had hired landed at La Coruna, northern Spain, where Matt's brother-in-law was waiting for them.

Carlos Molina turned out to be a small man who was as round as he was tall, but he had soft melting eyes, a mouth which looked as though it smiled a lot—but which was strained and tight today—and a shock of unruly curly hair. Georgie liked him immediately.

Matt's influence—and no doubt his wealth—had swept them through Customs in minutes, and once the introductions were over the two men conversed swiftly in Spanish for a few moments before Matt turned to Georgie and said quietly, 'I'm sorry, but Carlos's English is not good and I need to know the details of my mother's collapse.'

'How is she?' Georgie asked softly. They had said little on the journey but when she had taken his hand shortly after departure in a gesture of comfort he had held on to it like a lifeline.

'There is talk of an operation; gall bladder, Carlos thinks.'

'*Sí, sí.*' Carlos had been trying to follow their conversation, nodding his black head the while. 'You come now the car, she is waiting.'

Georgie hadn't known what she was expecting to see when they left the air-conditioned building, but she supposed her mind had veered towards scorched landscapes and baking hot skies. However, as the silver-blue Mercedes

Carlos was driving ate up the miles she was breathless at the scenic beauty unfolding before her eyes.

It was hot, but only as hot as an English summer at its best, and as the car made its way south-west from the airport she had an endlessly changing view of mountains and little villages set in pine-clad hills, traditional-style whitewashed villas set among orange and lemon groves, fields of almond, olive and fig trees separated by ancient mellow walls, and houses of golden stone perched on rocky outcrops.

The quality of the light and intensity of colour was totally different from England and overwhemingly beautiful, and they had just passed a village square festooned with market stalls overflowing with produce into the cobbled streets beyond, when Matt said softly at the side of her, 'You like the country of my heart?'

'Like it?' She turned to him impulsively, her face alight. 'It's wonderful, Matt. How can you ever bear to leave it and stay in England for so long every year?'

He smiled slowly. 'England, too, is beautiful,' he said quietly. 'Although I look on Spain as my home I consider myself as English as Spanish, unlike my sister, Francisca. Perhaps it is the names, eh? I was christened after my maternal grandfather Matthew, whilst Francisca took our parental grandmother's first name. Whatever, Francisca is Spanish from the top of her head to the soles of her feet. Is that not right, Carlos?' he said to the man in front of them.

'Sí, sí.' It was very enthusiastic and obviously approving.

Matt turned back to her, his voice dry. 'Carlos is one of the old school,' he said mockingly. 'He likes his woman barefoot and pregnant.'

The way he said the words, in his husky, smoky voice, made Georgie think it wouldn't be such a bad thing after all—if you were Matt's woman, that was—but she forced an indignant note into her voice as she said, 'I'm sure Carlos thinks nothing of the sort. How many children have you got, Carlos?'

He answered in Spanish, and when Georgie glanced enquiringly at Matt, the hard mouth was twisted in a smile as he said softly, 'Hold on to your hat, Georgie. It was eight at the last count.'

'Eight?' She was truly shocked.

'But yes.' He shifted in his seat and as his thigh briefly brushed Georgie's it took all her will-power not to react. 'Spanish men are very virile,' he murmured, straight-faced now. 'Did you not know this?'

She decided not to pursue that path. 'And Francisca wants a big family too?' she asked instead, her cheeks pink but her voice prim.

His smile this time was merely a twitch. 'Of course.'

'That's ideal, then, isn't it?' She turned from him to look out of the window. They were passing a small family, the man leading a plump little donkey which had two curly-haired tots sitting on its furry back and the woman in a long red skirt with a big straw hat on her head, and something about the scene caught at her heart. The children waved to the car and Georgie waved back. They all looked so happy, so relaxed, so *alive*. Life was simple to them, a joy.

And then she caught herself sharply. No. No thinking, no cogitating. One minute, one hour at a time—that was what she'd decided earlier and that was what would see her through the next few days. If she allowed her heart to rule her head and became one of his women it would end badly, for her. As long as she kept that to the forefront of her mind she would be all right.

A few miles further on they passed a crystalline lake,

tranquil under the turquoise sky, and within minutes the Mercedes turned into a narrow twisting lane off the main road on which they had been travelling. 'It is better I visit the hospital with Carlos now,' Matt said quietly, 'and you must rest and take some refreshments. My housekeeper will take care of you.'

Even as he was speaking they passed through wide open, massive iron gates and into a shadow-blotched drive, huge evergreen oaks forming a natural arch beyond which Georgie caught a glimpse of magnificent grounds stretching away into the distance.

'This is your home?' she asked softly.

He nodded. 'Mi Oasis. My Oasis. It has always been named such and I saw no reason to change it when I bought the place ten years ago.'

The car had been climbing a slight incline, and now the drive opened up to reveal an enormous house some hundred yards in front of them. Unlike most of the houses she had seen on the journey this one was not whitewashed but built of mellow, honey-coloured stone and bedecked with ornate balconies bursting with a profusion of purple, white and scarlet bougainvillaea, geraniums and pink begonia, and surrounded by more oak trees. The windows were many and large, with small leaded squares of glass that twinkled in the sunlight, and in the middle of the drive in front of the house a magnificent fountain complete with cherubs riding prancing horses cascaded into a small stone pool.

'Does this place get a wow, too?' He was smiling as he spoke, his voice faintly mocking but warm, and Georgie wrenched her eyes away from the beautiful old house as she said, 'A double wow, actually.'

'Once you have eaten and bathed you must have a walk in the gardens at the rear of the house,' Matt said quietly, his eyes on the front door of the house which had just opened to reveal a small uniformed maid. 'Pilar will accompany you if you wish.'

'I'd rather explore on my own, thank you,' she said quickly. His voice had been slightly distant and she sensed his mind was focused on his mother now, although his innate good manners had not revealed his impatience to get to the hospital. 'You go, Matt. I'll be fine here until you get back.'

Matt insisted on introducing her to his Spanish housekeeper, Flora, who had appeared beside Pilar within moments, and then escorting her personally to her rooms on the second floor of the three-storey building before leaving, however. 'You will be all right until I return, Georgie?' He touched her cheek as he spoke. 'I have told Flora to bring you a tray in half an hour, once you have had time to shower and change.'

'Thank you.' This wasn't the time to be reflecting on how incredibly sexy he was, and she hated herself for it, but here, in Spain, he seemed ten times more foreign and a hundred times more dangerous. 'And please don't worry about me, Matt. I'll love exploring. The whole point of my coming with you was to be a help, not a hindrance.' And then she forced herself to add, 'That's what friendship is all about, isn't it?'

His thick black lashes hid the expression in his eyes as he responded, after a pause, 'Just so, *pequeña*. Just so.' He bent and touched one flushed cheek with his lips as he spoke, and such was her rush of sexual awareness that Georgie couldn't form the words to ask him what *pequeña* meant before he smiled one last time and closed the door behind him.

'Whew...' She stood exactly where he'd left her for a full minute before she trusted her legs to carry her across the room, whereupon she opened the windows on to the balcony and stepped outside after kicking off her shoes and flexing her aching toes.

The sun-warmed tiles were smooth beneath her bare feet and the ornate iron on the balcony sides was covered in bougainvillaea and lemon-scented verbenas, but it was the scent from the wonderful gardens below, bursting with tropical trees and shrubs and flowers, that flooded her senses. Acres and acres of grounds stretched before her in a dazzling display of colour, and after soaking up the sight for more than five minutes she turned reluctantly into the room behind her. And what a room, what a *suite* of rooms, she thought dazedly.

She was standing in the sitting room, which was the size of Robert's lounge back in England, and the dull rose furnishings embodied two two-seater plump soft sofas, a pine bookcase and a small writing desk and chair, a TV and video and a cocktail cabinet which enclosed a small fridge. The floor was pine and the drapes at the window the same dull rose as the sofas, and this colour scheme was reflected in the big double bedroom which led off the sitting room, although the main colour in there was cream. The bathroom was an elaborate affair in cream marble, and again the towels were in dull rose and gold.

When she had asked, Matt had told her this suite was one of four on this floor, with another four on the floor above. The east wing was given over to the servants' quarters with garages below and an extensive stable block, and the west wing was Matt's private domain which he had promised to show her later.

On the ground floor, which she had not yet seen apart from the baronial hall and huge curving open staircase, there was apparently a drawing room, a sitting room, two other reception rooms, the dining room and breakfast room, and the kitchens.

It was palatial opulence at its best, Georgie thought faintly. Luxurious, grandiose and undeniably stunning. And with more newly built stables behind the west wing, an Olympic-size swimming pool and tennis courts in the grounds... Her mind trailed to a halt. *What was she doing here?* Her, little Georgina Millett from Sevenoaks? This was Rothschild league!

She stood still, her fists pressed to her chest as she panicked big time. The house in England was gorgeous, but this...this was something else. She hadn't realised just how wealthy and powerful Matt was.

After a minute or so of silent hysteria she took a hold of herself. Matt was still Matt. He had been Matt before she had seen this place and he was still Matt. Okay, so he was richer than she'd ever dreamed. She took a deep breath and then gulped hard. But he was the same man who had sat and laughed and joked with the kids in Robert's little dining room over the last weeks, who had taken on a menagerie of decrepit animals to please a frail old lady, who was worried sick about his mother...

And then she gave in to the storm of weeping which had been threatening for the last minutes, had a good howl and dried her eyes. She loved him. She couldn't do anything about it even if every hour that passed emphasised how hopeless it was. Matt was no ordinary man, and she wasn't talking about his wealth now. If he had been dirt-poor he would still have been different, commanding, magnetic. Matt de Capistrano was...well, Matt de Capistrano, she finished weakly. And that said it all. And she'd had to go and fall in love with him...

By the time she had stood under the warm silky water for five minutes Georgie felt refreshed and calmer.

She was still in the big towelling robe which had been hanging in the bathroom when Pilar knocked on the outside door a little while later, and after calling for the little maid to enter she walked into the sitting room and took the tray from her.

There were enough slices of cold beef, pork and ham, green salad, savoury pastries, chopped egg and tomatoes to feed a small army, and Georgie looked at the tray askance, before she raised her eyes to Pilar and said quickly, 'This is lovely but I'll never be able to eat it all.'

'*Perdón, señorita?*'

Georgie repeated herself more slowly, and the little Spanish girl's puzzled frown vanished as she smiled and said, '*Sí, sí.* Do not worry, *señorita*. Señora Flora, she always give b-i-g *raciones*, big—how you say—big snacks, *sí*? Señor de Capistrano, he have the big appetite.'

Georgie nodded thankfully. 'As long as she won't be offended if I leave quite a bit.'

After dressing quickly in a sleeveless ice-blue jersey top and white wide-legged linen trousers Georgie ate a little of the food on the vast tray, washing it down with the glass of red wine that had accompanied the food, before making her way downstairs.

She met Pilar as she reached the bottom of the massive staircase and from the look on the Spanish girl's face Georgie assumed, rightly, she had committed an unforgivable *faux pas* in bringing the tray down herself. She deposited it into Pilar's hands with a smile and told her she was going for a walk in the lovely grounds at the back of the house, and departed swiftly. Her first gaffe and she didn't doubt there would be others. Clearly she didn't know the right way to behave! Unlike Matt's other women, no doubt.

Once in the gardens she paused to look back at the house again. It was so, so beautiful, she thought wonderingly. The decorative iron fretwork, the different shades of the mellow stone, the vivid splashes of crimson, mauve and white from the balconies—she couldn't quite believe she was here!

She explored for a long time, wandering through the grounds and saying hallo to the couple of gardeners she met who had clearly been alerted to her arrival as they greeted her by name.

She was sitting on an ancient wooden seat overlooking an orchard of peach, orange, lemon and cherry trees when she heard her name called, and looked round to see Matt approaching. He hadn't been out of her thoughts for a minute and now she looked anxiously into his dark face. 'Your mother?' she called across the space separating them.

'Brighter than I had expected.' He reached her in a few strides and before she had realised what he was about to do he had pulled her into him, his strong arms slipping round her waist as he moulded her into his hard, firm body, and his chin resting on the top of her head as he nuzzled the warm silkiness of her hair. 'You smell like all the summers I have ever known,' he murmured huskily. 'So fresh, so good.'

How did she answer that? And she wasn't at all sure this embrace could qualify as one of friendship! She rested against him for a moment, simply because she couldn't resist doing so, and then moved back in his arms to say, 'What did the doctors say? Is she going to be all right, Matt?'

'*Sí, sí.*' He shook his head, his voice very smoky as he said, 'Excuse me, Georgie. I have been speaking Spanish all day. Yes, she will be all right I am sure, but she will need the operation. I'm having a specialist flown in from the States tonight and he will operate tomorrow.'

'You are?' How money talked.

'He is a friend of mine and an excellent doctor. My

mother knows and trusts him and it is important she is confident and tranquil.'

Georgie nodded. He looked impossibly handsome and darkly masculine, and the subtle, delicious smell of him was undermining her resolve.

'She would like to meet you.' He was still holding her and didn't seem to notice her attempts to break free.

'She would?' This wouldn't do, she would have to manage more than two words every time she opened her mouth. 'You told her about me then?'

'Yes, I told her about you, Georgie.' His eyes were almost black slits as they narrowed against the evening light which was still very bright. 'I told her you were Robert's sister and that we were friends. This is right, yes?'

'Of course.' And as anguish streaked through her soul she told herself sharply, This is the only way and you know it. You *know* it.

'But I think maybe she guesses it is hard for me to be friends,' Matt continued softly. He traced the outline of her mouth with one finger as he looked down into her face, and when the kiss came it was hot and potent, a raging fire that devoured with dangerous intensity. She had shifted in his arms, momentarily with protest but almost immediately succumbing, even as a little voice in her head berated her for the weakness. After all she had resolved, all she'd determined, he only had to touch her and she was his. The voice was insistent but it couldn't compete with what his mouth and hands were doing, and what she wanted. She loved him so much, so very much.

He was muttering her name and somehow they had come to be lying on the thick grass which was threaded with daisies and forget-me-nots and other bell-like wild flowers. She could feel every muscle, every male contour of his hard shape as intimately as if they were naked, and he wanted her. His body was telling her that all too blatantly.

The heady rush of sensation which had exploded within her was sending waves of pleasure into every nerve and sinew, and his hands were moving erotically and with experienced purpose as they caused her to moan softly in her throat.

Their mouths were joined in a fusion that was a kind of consummation in itself, his tongue thrusting as it invaded her body. His thighs were locked over hers, his hands lifting her buttocks forward to acknowledge his arousal and his heart slamming against his ribcage so hard she could feel it in her own body.

She was returning kiss for kiss, embrace for embrace with an uninhibitedness which would have horrified her if she'd been capable of conscious thought, but it was some minutes before she realised the restraint Matt was showing. He had made no attempt to take their lovemaking to its natural conclusion, indeed she felt he had withdrawn in some way, and this seemed to be borne out when she twisted away and looked into his face, and he let her go immediately. 'What's the matter?' she asked shakily.

'Nothing is the matter except that I cannot trust myself where you are concerned, *pequeña*,' he said ruefully. 'If I had not stopped it would have been impossible to do so in another minute. You understand me?'

'But...I thought...' She didn't know how to go on as the realisation dawned that she had offered herself on a plate to him and *he* had been the one to call a halt.

'That I would take advantage of you at the earliest opportunity?' he asked silkily, his voice losing its softness. 'You came here with me because your heart was moved with sympathy, yes?'

She nodded weakly, because it was all she was capable

of with his big lean body stretched out at the side of her and the taste of him making her head spin.

'And this same sympathy has lowered your defences and made you wish to give me comfort,' he continued quietly. 'This is good, I like this, but when we make love properly, Georgie, it will be for one reason and one reason only. Because you want me as much as I want you and it is the only thing filling your mind and your heart. Not pity or a wish to comfort, not even that the evening is soft with the scent of flowers and there is romance in the air like now.'

Was he *crazy*? Didn't he know how much she wanted him? Not through pity or anything else except good old earthy desire, made all the more powerful because she loved him.

Georgie opened her mouth to tell him of his mistake and then shut it again with a little snap. It wasn't Matt who was crazy, it was her, she told herself silently as cold reason stepped in. She knew in her heart of hearts he would eat her up and spit her out and go on his own sweet way sooner or later, so why on earth was she playing with fire?

'Come.' He rose to his feet with the sinuous grace which characterised all his movements, and held out his hand to help her up. 'We will wander back to the house and have cocktails before dinner. Then we will eat and talk and laugh, and later see the moon rise like a queen in the sky. Yes?'

She took his hand, scrambling to her feet with none of his panache. He had told her he didn't believe in true love and for everness and he was thirty-six years old, not a raw callow youth who didn't know his own mind. But what had made him that way? There had to be something, surely? People didn't just wake up one morning and decide to be that cynical. Would her experience with Glen have sent her down that path if she hadn't met Matt before she had become hardened? Well, she'd never know now, would she? Because she *had* met him.

She smoothed down her rumpled clothes, her cheeks flaming as she fumbled with the tiny mother-of-pearl buttons on her top, several of which were undone.

Matt, on the other hand, appeared perfectly cool and relaxed, as controlled and in charge as ever. There were times, Georgie told herself with silent savagery, when she hated him as much as she loved him, and this was definitely one of those times!

He drew her arm through his as they strolled back to the house through the perfumed warm air, every bird in the world—or so it seemed to Georgie's feverish senses—singing a love song. Matt was chatting easily, filling her in on everything that had happened at the hospital that afternoon and reiterating his mother was bright and cheerful. Which was great, fantastic, Georgie thought ruefully, but how he could think about anything else except what had nearly happened out there, she just didn't know! But then it was just a sexual thing with him, a hunger that required sating. You ate when you were hungry, drank when you were thirsty and bedded a woman when you wanted sexual release. Matt's philosophy on life in a nutshell.

They entered the house though the open French doors of the stately drawing room, which was clearly the way Matt had exited, although Georgie had left the house by the less exalted exit by the kitchens, and he kept hold of her as they walked through the high-ceilinged, cathedral-type splendour into the hall beyond.

'Do you use the drawing room often?' she asked a little weakly. The exquisite furnishings—most of which looked to be priceless antiques—were a little daunting.

'High days and holidays; isn't that what you English say?'

His voice had held a mocking note and now Georgie's was a touch indignant when she said, 'You're English, too.'

'Half-English,' he corrected softly. 'And this makes a difference, yes?'

Oh, yes. She almost missed her footing, although there was nothing to trip over but her own sinful thoughts.

Matt glanced at his watch. 'There's plenty of time before we need to change for dinner for you to come and see my home within my home,' he offered, adding with a mocking twist of his lips, 'And you must consider yourself highly honoured to be asked. It is only by invitation anyone passes into the inner sanctum.'

Georgie didn't return the smile and stared at him steadily. 'Is that true?' she asked quietly.

The teasing look vanished, and Matt answered just as quietly, 'Yes, it is true. And I am chary with the invitations. I value my privacy.'

She could believe that. He might entertain lavishly and have a wide group of friends and acquaintances, but she had learnt Matt de Capistrano was a man who revealed only a little of himself to anyone, and then even that little was jealously monitored.

Georgie walked with him down the hall and watched as he opened the heavy wood door leading to his separate wing. Matt waved her past him, and she found herself in what appeared to be another smaller hall complete with a beautifully worked wrought-iron spiral staircase.

'Come.' He took her hand in his. 'The downstairs first, I think.'

The downstairs first. That meant he intended to show her the upstairs next. And upstairs meant his bedroom.

The hall floor was again wood—honey-coloured oak— and the painted walls reflected this colour but in a much paler hue. Instead of the fine paintings which adorned the main hall, these walls had continuous sheets of bronze-tinted mirror from waist height, and in the last of the day's sunlight slanting in the tall narrow windows on the right-hand side of the hall the space became a place of pure golden light.

Matt opened the door on his left and again stood back for her to precede him.

'Oh, Matt.' Surprised into looking at him, she saw the dark grey eyes had been waiting for her reaction. They were standing looking out over a wonderful indoor swimming pool, beyond which, at the far end of the pool, there were huge palms and plants enclosing several big upholstered loungers and a table and chairs. The end wall consisted mostly of glass, with two large patio doors which opened out onto a walled garden full of flowers and shrubs and trees.

'My gym.' He had been leading her to a door halfway along the pool and now opened it to reveal a well-equipped gymnasium and sauna, complete with showers and toilet facilities.

'It's wonderful.' As he closed the door to the gym again Georgie glanced around her, quite overwhelmed. 'Did you have all this done?'

He nodded. 'I prefer to swim and exercise in the nude,' he stated, without appearing to notice the effect of his words on the colour of Georgie's skin, 'and this would not be...appropriate outside on certain occasions.'

Georgie nodded in what she hoped was a cool, cosmopolitan kind of way and forced the X-rated pictures flashing across the screen of her mind back under lock and key. 'It's very nice,' she said primly, 'and very private.'

'Just so.'

Was he laughing at her? As they walked back into the hall she glanced at his dark face out of the corner of her eye but his expression was deadpan. Not that that meant anything. Not with Matt de Capistrano, she thought resentfully.

'Up you go.' As she climbed the spiral staircase she was terribly aware of Matt just behind her and almost stumbled as she stepped out into the open plan bedroom. She hadn't been expecting his bedroom to be next—she'd assumed that would be at the top of the house—and she certainly hadn't expected it to be so…so— She gave up trying to find suitable adjectives and gazed warily about her.

Again the end wall was all glass, and the huge, soft, round billowy bed, which was easily two and a half metres in diameter, was only slightly raised off the wooden floor, positioned so the occupant had a scenic view across tree tops and the vast expanse of light-washed sky. The lefthand wall was mirrored like the hall had been but this time in a smoky glass to five feet high, at which point shelves holding books, magazines and tapes reached to ceiling height.

A TV was fixed on the right hand wall, next to which the doors of the walk-in wardrobe were open to reveal neatly stacked shelves and racks of suits and other masculine clothing.

A large plump three-seater sofa was standing at the opposite end of the room from the bed, by the side of which was a fridge and a low table holding a coffee machine and cups. On the other side of the sofa there looked to be a well-stocked cocktail cabinet.

The sofa and the duvet, along with the floating voile curtains at the windows, were in a light cream, but the numerous pillows and massive cushions piled on the bed, along with the stack of cushions scattered on the sofa were in unrelenting black cotton.

Altogether it was an uncompromisingly masculine room,

devoid of colour and any feminine frills, and this was re-flected in the *en suite* bathroom when Matt opened the door next to the wardrobe to reveal a bathroom of black marble and silver fittings without one plant or feathery fern to soften its elegant, stark beauty.

Georgie stared inside, the subdued lights which had come on automatically when the door was opened, and which were hidden for the most part, emphasising the voyeuristic nature of the gleaming marble and inevitable mirrored wall rising up behind the black marble bath.

Georgie couldn't think of a single coherent thing to say. She was still struggling to come to terms with that incred-ible bed, which just had to have been built inside the room to Matt's specification, and now to be presented with such unashamed lasciviousness...

She swallowed hard, her throat dry. This was one unre-pentant bachelor, she told herself fiercely, everything she had seen this far screamed it, and she ignored it at her peril.

'You do not like these rooms?' He closed the door to the bathroom as he spoke and she was forced to meet the dark piercing gaze trained on her face.

'Like them?' How did she answer that? They were beau-tiful, magnificent, but they carried their own warning and it was like a slap in the face. But the rooms themselves were out of this world. 'Yes, of course I like them,' she answered after a moment, her voice very even. 'They're extraordinary; the whole house is stunning.'

He surveyed her unblinkingly. 'Never play poker, *pe-queña*.'

'What?' She pretended not to know what he meant, to give herself time to get her brain in gear.

He smiled, but it was just a movement of his lips and didn't reach the steel-grey eyes. 'Come and see the top floor,' he said easily, as though he wasn't in the least bothered by what he imagined she was thinking. Which he probably wasn't, Georgie affirmed miserably.

And then she flushed furiously when, instead of moving towards the staircase, he paused for a moment, brushing his lips across her forehead as he murmured, 'The top floor is safer, I promise.'

'Safer?' She tried to ignore what his closeness was doing to her hormones and injected a note of annoyed surprise into her voice. 'I don't know what you are talking about.'

'Sure you don't.' Now the hard, faintly stern mouth was wolfish.

'Matt, I'm telling you—'

And then her voice was cut off and her stomach muscles contracted when his hand followed the curve of her cheek down to her throat. He wasn't holding her, he was barely touching her, and yet his fingers were fire against her skin and she had to stiffen herself against his touch.

'This is what I'm talking about,' he said very softly, 'the chemical reaction that happens whenever we're in ten feet of each other.'

His gaze dropped to her mouth and her lips parted instinctively, as though her body had a mind of its own. She could feel warmth pulsing through her and sensed the tension that was holding his big muscled body taut, and she knew she had to break the moment. That bed, that wonderful, marvellous, voluptuous bed, was too close...

'I'm ready to see upstairs now,' she said in a staccato voice. Chemical reaction he'd said. Just chemical reaction. *What was she going to do?*

CHAPTER EIGHT

THE top floor of Matt's wing was another surprise. A large part of it was given over to a frighteningly well-equipped study, with all the latest technology in use, but behind this area, at the far end of the room, an extended enclosed balcony in the form of a small sitting room gave a bird's eye view stretching into infinity.

Beyond Matt's estate there were rolling hills and countryside and small villages, a dramatic vista which was awe-inspiring.

'Sit down. I'll fix us a drink.'

Georgie nodded her acquiescence, wandering over to the full-length semicircle of windows. 'I don't think I've ever seen a view to match this one,' she said slowly without turning to look at him.

She heard the chink of ice against glass and then was conscious of him just behind her. 'Incredible, isn't it?' he murmured softly.

'Surely all this part of the house didn't have such huge windows when you bought it?' she asked quickly, the scent of his male warmth surrounding her and telling her she had to keep talking.

There was a brief pause and then he said, 'No, it didn't. I had this wing changed to suit my requirements. I like space and light.'

It wasn't what he said but something in his voice, the merest inflexion, which sent pinpricks of awareness flickering down her spine. The almost obsessive demand for spaciousness, the mirrors, the huge windows... 'You're

137

claustrophobic?' She turned to him but it wasn't really a question. And as his eyes narrowed, she reiterated, 'You are, aren't you?'

He shrugged. 'A little.'

A lot, she bet. 'Have you always been so?'

'No, not always.' His voice was dismissive and he made it clear he didn't intend to respond further to the curiosity in her voice when he took her arm and drew her down on to the sofa, handing her a glass of white wine as he said, 'Relax and enjoy the view, Georgie.'

Easier said than done.

She sat, her knees tightly together and her back straight, staring rigidly out across the rolling hills and countryside which merged to a dusky faint mauve on the far horizon. So he had a small chink of weakness in that formidable armour he wore—claustrophobia. And it was indicative of the inner strength of the man that she had known him for many weeks now and had never guessed. She found that thought incredibly depressing.

'Are you ready to tell me about him yet?'

'What?' She had jerked away like a skittish colt before she could collect herself.

'Did he break your heart, Georgie?' he asked gruffly.

This was so *unfair*! He revealed nothing—*nothing*—of himself and yet he expected her to spill everything. She stiffened and then raised her small chin. 'His name was Glen,' she said steadily. 'What was her name?'

'Her?' His eyes went flat and cold.

'Yes, her. There must have been a her.' She was guessing, but everything about his body language told her she'd hit gold. Or ashes, depending on how you looked at it.

'Kiss and tell?' he said harshly.

She blanched at his tone, but she wasn't going to back down now. She was tired of going round in circles, and since the first moment she had laid eyes on Matt she felt that was what she'd been doing. 'Exactly,' she challenged bravely. 'Or aren't you up for it yourself? You just expect me to tell you all, is that it?'

He stared back at her for a long moment as something worked in his hard face which she couldn't read. 'I didn't mean—' He stopped abruptly, dark colour slashing his cheekbones. 'Or maybe I did. Hell, I don't know what I mean.'

The momentary loss of composure pleased her more than words could say. It was a start. If nothing else it was a start, wasn't it?

He drew air in between his teeth in a low hiss, his glittering eyes narrowed on her pale face, and then said coldly, 'You won't like what you hear and it will serve no useful purpose.'

'I'd prefer to be the judge of that,' she said, speaking evenly, not wanting him to guess that part of her was terrified. 'I haven't lied to you, Matt, I've been totally honest since we met.' Her conscience twanged here but she brushed aside the still small voice which questioned why she hadn't told him she loved him. That was different, quite different. It was. 'I've always made it clear I'm not in the market for a casual affair; I don't live my life like that. I know you but I don't know you, and you offer nothing of yourself, not really.'

'Charming.'

'Oh, you've been great to Robert and the twins, don't get me wrong, and you're amazingly generous, but that's just money, isn't it?' she said, looking him straight in the eyes and trying not to dwell on how darkly handsome he looked sitting there, a touch away.

'Which of course is nothing,' he drawled sarcastically.

'No, it's not,' she agreed tersely, suddenly furiously angry with him too. 'Money is great if you've got it and it certainly smoothes the way, but Sandra and Robert had something no amount of cash could buy. And, having seen them, having seen what they had, I would never be content with anything less.'

'It's dangerous to put a relationship on a pedestal like that and rather arrogant to assume you know what their marriage was really like.' It was expressionless and cold. 'You could find yourself following some sort of illusion for the rest of your life and end up with nothing.'

'I saw their ups and downs and know how hard they worked at their marriage to make it the success it was,' Georgie answered tightly, 'and I didn't view it through rose-coloured spectacles, if that's what you're insinuating.'

He stared at her, his black brows drawn together in an angry scowl. 'How are we arguing when I meant this to be—?' He stopped abruptly.

'Cosy and intimate?' she suggested with acid sweetness.

'Relaxing and beneficial.'

Relaxing and beneficial? Yeah, sure! She glared at him, her green eyes stormy, and took a long gulp at the wine to prevent herself from throwing it at him.

From rage he was suddenly grinning and it had the effect of leaving her in no man's land, especially when he said, his voice husky, 'You're a formidable opponent, Miss Millett.'

'Opponent?' She wasn't ready to melt yet. 'I thought we were supposed to be friends, and friends should be able to have healthy disagreements.'

'Right.' He nodded, his mouth quirking at the haughty note in her voice. 'What else are friends allowed to do?'

'Do you mean to tell me you've never had any women friends?' she answered stiffly.

'Not ones with eyes the colour of pure jade and hair of

raw silk,' he murmured softly. 'You've bewitched me, do you know that? You fill my thoughts and you invade my dreams, and all I think about is you.'

It was an unexpected confession and Georgie couldn't quite believe it was real.

'I mean it.' As always he read her face.

He probably did. For now. But now would turn into yesterday and then what would she do? She knew, even without looking too deeply inside herself, that once she gave Matt everything she would never recover from it.

'Her name was Begonia.'

'What?'

He tilted her face towards him, his fingers gentle, and said again, 'You asked her name. It was Begonia.'

She didn't want to know her name. She didn't want to know anything about this woman he had known and cared for. And she wanted to know everything.

'I met her at university, here in Spain,' he said quietly. 'We were together for eighteen months and then it finished.'

Was she beautiful? Had he loved her with all his heart? Had Matt finished it? Where was she now?

'And Glen?' he asked without a change of tone. 'Who was Glen?'

Glen was nothing. Georgie took a deep breath. 'Glen was the original boy next door,' she said carefully. 'I grew up with him once I went to live with Robert and Sandra; his sisters were my best friends for a while. We got engaged and he broke it off a few weeks before the wedding.'

'Why?'

'He found someone else.' He was still holding her face and now she broke the hold, turning away slightly and taking another gulp of wine before she added, 'He went off with his boss's daughter; she was very wealthy or, rather, her father was. They got married a few months later.'

'He was a fool.' It was tender.

'Yes, he was.' She was trying very hard to keep any emotion out of her voice. 'But I realised later—' once I had met you and realised what love was all about '—it would have been a huge mistake.'

'Do you mean that?'

There was a note in his voice she couldn't quite place, and now she raised her eyes to meet the piercing gaze trained on her face and said quietly, 'Oh, yes, it's not bravado. I had hero-worshipped him when we were younger and he could do no wrong in my eyes, so it was an awful shock when he unceremoniously dumped me, but after a while I realised I'd built him up in my head as someone completely different to who he really was. Puppy love, I suppose; certainly blind infatuation. Marriage to Glen would have been a disaster.'

She swallowed hard. She wanted to ask more about this Begonia and now was the time, she might never have another opportunity like this, but could she bear hearing it?

And then the decision was taken out of her hands when the telephone at the side of the sofa began to ring. Matt swore softly as he picked up the receiver, his voice sharp as he said, '*Sí?*'

Georgie could hear it was a woman's voice on the other end of the line and as her senses prickled she wasn't surprised to hear him say, '*Sí*, Pepita,' followed by more Spanish. And his voice was not sharp now.

She rose to her feet, wandering across to the windows with her back towards him and looking out on to the view as her ears strained for every inflexion of his voice.

'I am sorry, Georgie.' As Matt replaced the receiver she turned round slowly, her face showing nothing but polite enquiry. 'That was Pepita. She was anxious for news of my mother.'

'She knows her, then?' She was amazed how calm and matter-of-fact her voice was when the screen of her mind was replaying a picture of the other woman's elegant, red-taloned hand resting intimately on his arm.

He nodded. 'Pepita has been with me for many years,' he said absently. 'She knew my mother well; they are great friends.'

Yes, they would be, because Pepita would have made sure of it. She wanted Matt. Georgie suddenly realised the knowledge had been there in her head from the first morning. Pepita was in love with him. Was he aware of it?

'She was phoning from her car; she is on her way here with some flowers for my mother.'

Right. She wasn't taking them to the hospital or arranging for them to be delivered. She was bringing them here, to Matt's home. 'I wasn't aware Pepita was in Spain,' Georgie said pleasantly. And now she asked the question she had asked once before in England, and never received an answer to, 'Does she travel backwards and forwards with you between England and Spain?'

'Most of the time.' There was the faintest note of mild irritation, as though he didn't want to talk about his beautiful secretary. 'My uncle in England has his own secretary, of course, and the office there is efficient, but I prefer to have Pepita with me for any confidential work.'

He preferred to have Pepita with him. Georgie put the half-full glass of wine down on a small occasional table and gestured at her clothes as she said, 'I'll think I'll go and freshen up before dinner, if that's all right?'

'Of course.'

Yes, it would be 'of course' now Pepita was on her way here. And then Georgie caught at the thought, self-disgust strong. She loathed the destructive emotion of jealousy and she had never been subject to it before. She had to get a handle on this. Matt was a free agent; he could sleep with a hundred women, including his secretary, and she had absolutely no right to object. No right at all…

Georgie hadn't known what clothes to bring with her when she had hastily packed her suitcase earlier that morning in England, but now, standing in her bra and panties in front of the open wardrobe in her room, she blessed the impulse that had made her grab two or three dressy outfits at the last moment. She would bet her life on the fact that Pepita was not going to arrive in anything less than designer perfection, and although her salary couldn't run to Versace or Armani her jade-green silk dress with an asymmetric hemline, the off-the-shoulder three-quarter length pastel cashmere dress and, lastly but not least, the viscose-crêpe minidress in soft charcoal would all hold their own with a designer label.

Her green eyes narrowed on the minidress. The wafer-thin straps on the shoulders and touch of embroidery which followed the neckline took the dress to another dimension once it was on, and her strappy sandals in dark pewter toned perfectly. It wasn't quite so dressy as the other two but that was perfect; she didn't want Pepita to think she had tried too hard. And the material and colour were misty and chimerical, bringing out the colour of her hair and eyes and accentuating the honey tone of her skin.

She had a thick braided bracelet and necklace in silver that she'd worn with the dress at the dinner dance she'd originally bought it for, and apart from two sets of earrings they were the only pieces of jewellery she had brought with her. Fate? She reached for the dress as she nodded at the reflection in the mirror.

She brushed her hair until it hung either side of her face like raw silk, but apart from darkening her thick eyelashes with mascara and applying the lightest touch of peach-coloured lipstick to her mouth she titivated no more, in spite of the picture of a beautifully made-up face and exquisitely enhanced ebony eyes which kept getting between her and the fresh-faced girl in the mirror. She wasn't used to wearing much make-up and she wasn't about to make herself feel uncomfortable. She wasn't a *femme fatale* and there was no point in trying to look like one.

Once she was ready she glanced one more time in the mirror. The three-inch heels gave her slender five feet four inches a boost, but she would never be model material, she decided resignedly. And Pepita must be five foot ten if she was an inch.

But that didn't matter. She frowned the admonition. She was here to give moral support to Matt through a difficult time by way of thanks for all he had done for Robert and the twins. That was all. *That was all.*

She picked her way carefully down the wide curving staircase once she had left her suite of rooms, vitally aware that the last thing she needed was to trip over the unaccustomed high heels and go sprawling from top to bottom. Once in the shadowy hall she came to a halt, however, uncertain of which room Matt would be in.

'*Señorita?*' A uniformed angel in the shape of Pilar appeared from the direction of the kitchens. 'You want the señor, *sí*?'

Oh, yes. Georgie nodded, her hair shimmering as she moved her head. 'I wasn't sure if he was in the drawing room or not,' she preferred tentatively.

'No, no, *señorita*. Is blue room, I think.'

Pilar led the way to one of the other reception rooms, opening the ornately carved door for Georgie and standing to one side for her to enter. And in the split second it took for Georgie to look into the room beyond she saw the couple standing by the window draw apart, Matt turning to face her as he said coolly, 'Georgie, we have been waiting for you. Come and have a cocktail.'

They had been embracing. Georgie tried to think of something to say and failed utterly, so she merely walked into the beautiful room which was furnished in shades of blue with as much aplomb as she could muster, forcing herself to smile as Pepita extended a languidly limp hand and said flatly, 'It is nice to see you again. I hope your brother is well?'

'Hallo, Pepita. Yes, Robert's fine.' Her voice was steady and even friendly, but she felt as though she had just received a heavy blow in the solar plexus. *They had been embracing*; Pepita's hands resting against the cloth of his dinner jacket and her head lifted up to meet Matt's downward bent one. Had they actually kissed? It was a pose which suggested they had but she hadn't seen that. Whatever, this wasn't your average working relationship!

Matt was pouring her a drink, and as he handed her the fluted glass his eyes roamed hungrily all over her for a few vital seconds, but his voice was contained when he said, 'You look lovely tonight, Georgie.'

'Thank you.' She smiled and took the drink as though she hadn't a care in the world, but even though she wasn't looking directly at Pepita now the image of the beautiful Spanish woman was imprinted on her mind.

As she'd suspected, Pepita was dressed to kill. The sleeveless silk dress with a deep V neck in dark scarlet was the ultimate in clingy sultriness and Pepita's figure was amazing; the high red sandals with studded ankle straps she was wearing showed her long slim legs off to perfection.

Had Pepita known she was staying with Matt? Georgie

rather suspected not. She also had a sneaking suspicion her presence was as welcome as an old flame at a wedding.

It soon became clear Matt had invited Pepita to stay for dinner and Georgie supposed—if she was being honest—he could have done little else, but it was a terrible evening as far as Georgie was concerned.

Pepita had obviously decided to sparkle, and she accomplished this with a brittle effervescence that had Georgie wanting to punch the other woman on the nose for most of the time. Pepita was never actually rude, but she managed to introduce people and situations Georgie had never heard of into the conversation, constantly emphasising Georgie was the odd one out. It was annoying, it was very annoying, but other than cause a scene Georgie could do little about it, and a scene was quite out of the question with Matt's mother lying ill in hospital with a forthcoming operation looming.

The food Flora had prepared was wonderful and the dining room was like something out of a Hollywood movie, but Georgie could have been eating cardboard for all it registered. Matt himself said little—it was difficult for anyone other than Pepita to get a word in, and Georgie could see how the other woman kept her slim figure because she never stopped talking long enough to swallow anything—and Georgie got the impression once or twice he was almost bored. Or perhaps he was regretting bringing her with him now Pepita had turned up?

This thought occupied her all through Flora's wonderful dessert of strawberry granita with a liqueur muscat chantilly. When she thought about it, Georgie reflected she had left him no choice but to let her tag along. She had *announced* she was accompanying him rather than asking him. Other than being blatantly rude, she hadn't left him with any option, had she? Her ears began to burn with embarrassment and her mouth went dry with panic.

She should never have come. This had been a huge, huge mistake and Pepita's presence confirmed it. Probably the Spanish woman spent most of her evenings with him here when they were both in Spain? And Pepita was only one of many glamorous women who would vie to be noticed by him. What on earth had she been thinking of to push herself on him the way she had? What must he be thinking?

She suddenly felt very naïve and stupid, all the confidence the lovely dress had given her evaporating away, but in the next instant she raised her chin a fraction, her eyes narrowing slightly. She was blowed if she would give Pepita the satisfaction of even an inkling of what she was thinking. Cool, calm and collected—that was her mask for the evening and she would wear it even if it killed her, and to the bitter end too. No slinking away or pleading a headache, even if that was in actual fact a reality. But then Pepita's chatter was enough to give a deaf man a headache! It continued all through their after-dinner coffees and brandy. By the time eleven o'clock chimed Georgie was just thinking she couldn't survive another minute without screaming, when Pepita rose to her feet, her movements slow and languid.

'Thank you so much for a lovely dinner, Matt.' She smiled and touched his arm as she spoke—he had risen with her—and Georgie reflected, with a painful squeeze of her heart how good they looked together. 'Do give your mother my love along with the flowers? And if there is anything, *anything* I can do you know you only have to ask.'

'Thank you, Pepita.' He turned to Georgie, holding out his hand and pulling her to her feet whereupon he drew her into the side of him as he said easily. 'We'll see you out.'

Georgie knew she had turned lobster-red but she couldn't help it; there had been an intimacy about both the gesture and the words she was sure Matt hadn't meant, but certainly it had hit Pepita on the raw if the stone-hard glint in the other woman's onyx eyes as she met Georgie's was anything to go by.

Matt kept hold of her as they all walked into the hall, and once he had opened the front door and they all stepped outside he didn't seem to notice her subtle attempts to disentangle herself.

Pepita was driving a bright red Porsche—which somehow seemed to sum up the evening as far as Georgie was concerned—and whether by design or accident showed a great deal of smooth tanned leg as she slid into the driver's seat. And then the car was pulling away with a flamboyant hoot of the horn and within a moment or two they were alone.

'Nice car.' Georgie had finally managed to extricate herself by pretending to fiddle with the strap of her sandal a moment before, and now she straightened, her voice cool.

'Yes, it is.' His face was in shadow and she couldn't see the expression in his eyes.

'Does she live near?' She had hoped her voice would sound polite and conversational and heard the edge to it with a feeling of despair.

'Quite near.'

'That's very convenient.' The black brows rose and she added quickly, 'For work purposes, I mean.'

'Of course,' he agreed pleasantly. There was a second's silence and then he horrified her by saying evenly, 'There is no need to be jealous, Georgie.'

'*Jealous?*' Matt was the second person she wanted to hit on the nose that evening and her response shocked her because she was normally a very non-violent person. 'I think you flatter yourself, Matt,' she bit out with caustic venom.

'Possibly.'

'And I can assure you I don't have a jealous bone in my body!'

'A very delectable body too.'

She glared at him, so angry she didn't trust herself to speak for a moment. How dared he suggest she was jealous of Pepita? she asked herself furiously, ignoring how she had felt for the last few hours. The ego of the man was colossal! No doubt he'd thoroughly enjoyed the thought he had two women panting after him all evening! Well, he could go and take a running jump, the arrogant so-and-so.

'Pepita's mother—when she was alive; she died three years ago—was my mother's closest friend,' Matt said from behind her as they turned into the house. 'I was ten years of age when Pepita was born and I have watched her grow from an infant.'

How cosy. And that explained the hungry look in Pepita's ebony eyes, did it? Who did he think he was kidding? 'You don't have to explain anything to me,' Georgie said tightly.

'I am not doing it because I have to,' he said softly, catching her arm and turning her round once he had shut the door, 'but because I want to. I do not wish any misunderstanding between us.'

She stared at him in the dimly lit hall, her green eyes huge with doubt.

'Pepita is like family,' Matt said quietly, 'that is all.'

She wanted to believe him, and the fervency of the wanting carried its own warning. He was pure enigma; she didn't understand him at all and she never would. For the moment she was someone he wanted, a passing obsession, but he was used to women who were content to have fun with him for however long it took for the affair to burn itself out and then leave his life as gracefully as they had entered. And she didn't have it in her to be like that. She'd leave wailing her head off and clinging hold of his legs! She loved him.

'Like I said, Matt, you don't have to explain anything to me,' she said steadily, her voice quiet now. 'I came here because I thought it might help to have a friend with you at a difficult time. That's all.' Which was probably the most stupid thing she had done in her life.

'You are very good to your friends, Georgie.' He had bent and wrapped his arms around her before she realised what was happening, his lips seeking hers hungrily, possessive and devouring.

If someone had told her just two or three minutes before that she would be kissing him back she would have laughed at them, but that was exactly what she was doing as a flood of passion engulfed her. Her arms had wound round his neck and her body was pressed close to his, and she could no more have stopped her response to him than ceased breathing.

He didn't draw away until she was trembling and weak in his arms, and then his voice carried a smoky mocking note when he murmured, 'Very good.'

This was just a game to him. It gave her the strength to take a step backwards and say determinedly, 'Goodnight, Matt.'

'Goodnight, Georgie.'

She had half expected him to try and detain her but he didn't move as she walked to the staircase, and she was halfway up the stairs when his voice arrested her. 'I would like you to come with me to the hospital tomorrow and meet my mother.'

She remained perfectly still for the split second it took

to compose her face, and then she turned, one hand holding the smooth carved handrail as she said lightly, 'I'd like to meet her.'

It didn't mean anything, she warned herself firmly as she continued up the stairs. Not a thing. He obviously felt obliged to introduce her after she had come all the way from England, and no doubt his mother would think it odd if he didn't. Nevertheless the misery of the evening spent in Pepita's company was suddenly all gone and she all but floated along to her suite, walking through the sitting room and straight into the bedroom where she stood and looked at the bright-eyed girl in the mirror. 'Careful, Georgie.' She touched her lips, which were moist and swollen from his kisses, with the tip of one finger. 'He hasn't made any promises except that he doesn't believe in love or commitment.'

She stood at the mirror for a moment more, her eyes searching her flushed face as though the answer to all her confusion was there, and then sighed deeply, turning away and kicking off the sandals before making her way into the bathroom.

She would run herself a warm bath and lie and soak for half an hour at least; she was far too het-up to go to sleep yet. And she would not think of Matt at all. She wouldn't. These few days were a brief step out of time and that was the way she had to look at them. Pepita, the love affair that had gone wrong for him at university, his other women— she would go mad if she tried to sort it all out in her head tonight. He was one of those men whose dark aura engulfed everyone and everything it came into contact with, and she couldn't trust herself any more than she could trust him.

She walked back into the bedroom thoughtfully once the bath was running, taking off her clothes and donning a towelling robe before wiping off her mascara with her eye-make-up removing pads.

She must phone Robert tomorrow and assure him everything was all right; he had sounded worried when she'd said she was going to Spain with Matt although he had calmed down once she had explained about his mother. But she knew her brother had still been unhappy about the situation when she had put down the phone. Had he guessed how she felt about Matt? No, not Robert. Intuition wasn't his strong point. Perhaps he just wanted to warn her from getting involved, let her know that men like Matt de Capistrano were not the roses round the door type. Well, she knew that.

She narrowed her eyes as she padded back into the bathroom and turned off the taps. Yes, she knew that all right—in her head. So why was her heart still hoping for something different?

CHAPTER NINE

WHETHER it was the warm bath or the fact that Georgie had expelled enough nervous energy in the last twenty-four hours to exhaust ten women, she didn't know, but she awoke the next morning after a deep refreshing sleep that had—as far as she could recall—been dreamless. It was Pilar who woke her, placing a steaming cup of coffee on the bedside cabinet as she said gently, '*Señorita*, you sleep well, *sí*? You wake now.'

'What time is it?' Georgie sat up and sank back against the pillows as she watched the little maid draw back the drapes and let bright sunlight flood into the bedroom.

'Is ten o'clock, *señorita*.' And at Georgie's gasp of dismay, Pilar added, 'Is no problem. The *señor*, he have his swim an' he say for you to come to the breakfast, *sí*? In...' Pilar held up her fingers.

'Ten minutes?' Georgie suggested.

'*Sí, sí, señorita*. The ten minutes. Okay?'

'Okay.'

Once Pilar had left the room Georgie let the coffee cool a little while she had a quick shower, gulping it down as she partly blowdried her hair and then pulled it up in a loose ponytail on top of her head, although more strands fell about her face than stayed in the band.

She pulled on a pair of jeans and a skinny midnight-blue top and glanced at her watch. Ten minutes exactly. She'd better get downstairs.

She felt quite in control as she walked into the breakfast room but her aplomb was blown to pieces in the next moment. Matt was already sitting at the breakfast table casually reading a newspaper, and it was clear he had just showered, probably after his swim.

It was also clear he didn't believe in formal attire at the breakfast table. The black silk robe was open to the waist and the muscled hairy chest was the stuff dreams were made of. That, and the way his damp hair curled slightly over his forehead, softening the hard features and giving them a touch of dynamite, robbed Georgie of the power to respond immediately to his easy, 'Good morning.'

She lost the power to know how to walk as she tottered across the room towards the table, almost falling over her own feet, and by the time she sank gratefully into a chair her cheeks were scarlet.

'Did you sleep well?' Matt asked gravely, apparently not noticing he was sharing breakfast with a beetroot.

'Fine, thank you.' She cleared her throat twice. 'Have you rung the hospital yet? How's your mother?'

'She had a good night and my friend is with her now. He said they will operate first thing tomorrow, when he's had a chance to do some necessary tests.'

Georgie nodded in what she hoped was a calm, informed sort of way.

'Coffee?' He was already pouring her a cup as he spoke and the movement of the big male body sent her hormones spiralling.

'Thank you.' She took the cup from him and hurriedly gulped at it, burning the inside of her mouth and trying to pretend her eyes weren't watering with pain.

'Help yourself to cereal and fruit and croissants,' Matt said nonchalantly. 'Flora will be bringing in a cooked breakfast in a little while and she gets hurt if you don't clear the plate.'

'Does she?' Georgie was alarmed. She had seen the

amount of food Matt seemed able to tuck away with seemingly little effort, and the loaded tray Pillar had brought to her room when she had arrived the day before was in the forefront of her mind.

'I told her just a little for you,' Matt said soothingly. 'You don't eat much, do you?'

'I eat loads.' It was indignant. 'Don't forget I'm eight or nine inches smaller than you and probably weigh half as much. Women are built differently to men.'

It probably wasn't the cleverest thing she had ever said. She watched the dark eyes turn smoky as he murmured, 'I'm aware of that, Georgie.'

She dragged her eyes away from his face and the acres of bare flesh beneath it, and concentrated on the array of cereals, fruits, toast, croissants and preserves in the middle of the table, hastily reaching for a ripe peach and beginning to slice it on her plate. If she was having a cooked breakfast she wouldn't be able to manage anything more.

Matt demolished a bowl of muesli to which he added a sliced banana and peach, followed by two croissants heaped with blackcurrant preserve, before Flora appeared wheeling in the heated trolley holding their plates.

Georgie was eternally grateful that Flora had heeded Matt's advice where her plate was concerned, but she stared fascinated at the contents of Matt's plate.

'I'm a growing boy.' He had noticed her rapt contemplation and his voice was amused. 'I have to keep my strength up in hope of…'

'In hope of what?' she asked absently, her mind still occupied with the half a pound of sausages and bacon, three eggs, mushrooms, tomatoes, fried potatoes and onions adorning Matt's plate. And then, as the silence lengthened, she raised her eyes to his face and he said gravely, 'Just in hope.'

An image of that wickedly voluptuous bed flashed across her mind and she quickly lowered her eyes to her plate. He was too sexy and flagrantly male clothed, but partly clothed... She bit into a sausage and prayed for composure. What did he have on under that robe? A piece of mushroom went down the wrong way and she coughed and spluttered, her agitation not helped at all when Matt left his seat to come and pat her back and offer her a glass of water.

'I'm fine, really,' she mumbled, sniffing loudly and trying to ignore the muscled legs at the side of her. He could at least have put on some pyjama bottoms or something after his swim if he didn't want to get dressed, she told herself self-righteously. But perhaps he didn't wear pyjamas?

'Here.' He bent down, dabbing at her wet eyes with a napkin, and she caught the full impact of the smell of expensive body shampoo on clean male skin before he strolled round the table again.

She finished her breakfast without further mishap but with every nerve and muscle in her body as taut as piano wire and conscious of the slightest movement from the big male body opposite. Matt, on the other hand, appeared supremely relaxed, enjoying a leisurely breakfast with obvious enjoyment.

As well he might, Georgie thought feverishly. *She* wasn't the one flaunting herself! Although, to be fair, Matt didn't appear to be aware he was flaunting himself, she admitted silently. He was a man who was very much at ease with his own body, as his comment the day before about his preference for swimming and exercising in the nude proved. She didn't dare dwell on that thought.

'So...'

She raised her eyes as she forked the last mouthful of

food from the plate into her mouth, and saw Matt was look-ing at her with unfathomable eyes. 'Yes?' she asked warily.

'We will visit the hospital this afternoon after an early lunch,' Matt said decisively. 'What would you like to do this morning?'

The aggressive sexuality that was as frightening as it was exciting made her voice slightly shaky as she said, 'Any-thing, I don't mind.'

'If only...' He gave a small laugh, low in his throat, at her expression. 'Well, as it is no good my suggesting a lazy morn-ing in bed, and you did your exploring of the gardens yes-terday, perhaps it would be good to show you a little of the surrounding area, yes? And we can maybe stop for something to eat close to the hospital rather than come back here.'

'Whatever you think.'

'How submissive.'

She stared at him, not sure if he was being nasty or not, and suddenly his expression cleared and he smiled ruefully. 'There is something of the spoilt brat in every man, *pe-queña*, and I have found since I met you I am like every man. I do not like this; I had thought myself above such ignoble behaviour, but it would seem you bring out the worst in me. Of course, if we were lovers all this tension would be dealt with and life would be sweeter for both of us.'

'Life is quite sweet enough, thanks,' she said tartly.

'Liar.' It was slightly taunting but said with a smile which Georgie found it difficult to return. He was such a *disturbing* man, she told herself resentfully. The last weeks she had felt she was living on a knife's edge all the time, and it was exhausting. The very air seemed to crackle with electricity when Matt was about and these moments of hon-esty he seemed to indulge in made things worse.

'Come.' He rose from the table, holding out his hand as

he walked round to her chair. 'If you feel the need to persist in this ridiculous wish to deny us both I can only be patient until you accept the error of your ways.'

'Matt—' Her voice was cut off as he pulled her to her feet and his mouth caught hers with an urgency that was thrilling. He kissed her long and deeply, draining her of sweetness before his lips moved to her ears and throat causing convulsive shivers of ecstasy.

Her fingertips slipped under the silk at his shoulders, roaming over the leanly muscled flesh beneath the robe before they tangled in the pleasing roughness of the hair on his broad chest and then up again to his hard neck.

He was all male and unbelievable sexy, and Georgie allowed herself another moment or two of heaven before she pulled firmly away.

'I know, you are not that sort of girl,' he murmured, not quite letting go of her as he looked down with smouldering eyes.

'What sort?' she asked with a trembling attempt at lightness.

'The sort who makes love on the floor of the breakfast room.'

If he loved her as she loved him it could be the breakfast room table and she wouldn't care! 'I think Pilar might be just a little surprised,' she managed fairly blandly. 'Don't you?' She removed herself from his hold, stepping back a pace as she said evenly, 'What time do you want to leave?'

'Half an hour?' he suggested softly. 'It will give me time to take a shower.'

'I though you had showered,' she said, surprised.

'A cold shower, Georgie.'

When Georgie stepped outside into the scented warmth of a hot Spanish day half an hour later, Matt was waiting for her. He was sitting at the wheel of a Mercedes-Benz SL convertible and the beautiful silver car purred gently to life as she slid into the passenger seat. 'Another boy's toy?' she asked lightly, partly to hide what the sight of him—clothed in black shirt and trousers—had done to her equilibrium.

'Just so.' He smiled, his teeth flashing white in the tanned skin of his face.

She enjoyed seeing more of the country of his birth nearly as much as she enjoyed being with him. They ate lunch in a shadow-blotched plaza in a small cobbled town, the tall tower of a brown church in the distance with a great bell outlined against the blue sky. It was heaven. Or, rather, being with Matt was heaven. And dangerous. And perilous. And a hundred other adjectives that described jeopardy.

When they arrived at the hospital Georgie found she was nervous. Excruciatingly nervous. Matt's mother was his nearest and dearest and although he had never said so in so many words she knew he loved his mother deeply. And his mother was a friend of Pepita's.

The hospital was luxurious, and obviously not run of the mill, and Matt seemed to be something of an icon. They were practically bowed along the thickly carpeted corridor to his mother's room, although the sister in charge left them at the door at Matt's quietly polite request.

'Just be yourself.' She wasn't sure if he had sensed her agitation but his voice was distinctly soothing. 'You'll get on like a house on fire.'

No pressure! But before she could say a word he had knocked and opened the door, his voice warm as he said, 'Visitors for Señora de Capistrano?'

'Matt...' The voice was English but perfumed with a melodious sweetness that suggested years in a warm climate as it said, 'I have been waiting for you and Georgie.'

Georgie wasn't aware she had been ushered into the room; all her senses were tied up with Matt's mother.

Señora de Capistrano was one of those women whose age was immaterial compared to her beauty. She must have been over fifty—Matt was thirty-six after all—but the blonde-haired woman lying in the bed could have been any age from forty upwards. Her blonde hair was threaded with silver, which only seemed to add a luminescence to her faintly lined, creamy skin, and her blue eyes were of a deep violet shade that was truly riveting.

She was beautiful, outstandingly beautiful, and she was smiling a sweet, warm smile that took Georgie completely by surprise. She didn't know what she had been expecting—perhaps a strong reserve, even hostility in view of the fact that Pepita was a friend—but Matt's mother was either an incredible actress or genuinely pleased to see her.

'Georgie, this is my mother.' Matt's voice was tender. 'Mother, Georgie.'

'Come and sit down, dear.' One pale slim hand indicated the chair at the side of the bed, and as Matt went to draw another from across the room his mother said quickly, 'I understand the doctor, your friend Jeff Eddleston, wants a word, dear. He was most insistent you see him as soon as you arrived. I think he wants to go to his hotel and go to bed as soon as he can.' The violet gaze included Georgie as Matt's mother said, her voice indulgent now, 'My son summoned poor Mr Eddleston from halfway across the world in the middle of the night, and he came. That is true friendship, don't you think?'

Georgie was of the opinion that Matt could summon almost anyone without a refusal—he was that sort of man—but she simply smiled and left it at that.

'Now?' Matt was clearly loath to leave.

'Now.' Señora de Capistrano smiled gently. 'He's a brilliant doctor, so I understand? Everyone is in awe of him here.'

Matt's expression said very clearly that he was not. 'I won't be long.'

'Take all the time you need, dear. Georgie and I will get to know each other a little.'

When the door had closed behind her son, Señor de Capistrano turned her violet gaze on Georgie and looked at her for a long moment. 'So you are the one,' she said softly.

'I'm sorry?' Georgie stared at her bewilderly.

'Matt has spoken of his English "friend" more than once lately, but I did not think it would be in these surroundings that we met.' It was a touch rueful.

'You're feeling a bit better, I understand?' Georgie said carefully.

'Yes, yes.' It was impatient, and for the first time Georgie could see Matt in the beautiful woman in front of her. There was a moment's pause, and then Matt's mother said, 'My name is Julia, Georgie. I would like us to be friends.'

'So would I.' Georgie was out of her depth and it showed.

'Can I talk to you confidentially?' The lovely eyes were piercing. 'You know I am to have an operation tomorrow?' Georgie nodded. 'Then I am claiming that as my reason for putting aside all politeness and convention and coming straight to the kernel in the nut,' Julia continued urgently. 'I love my son, Georgie. I want the very best for him; he deserves it.'

It could have been unfriendly but it wasn't, neither was it inimical. Georgie sat and waited, knowing it was a time to be silent.

'When I met my husband and we fell in love there was

great opposition from his family.' It wasn't what Georgie had expected to hear and her eyes opened wide for a moment, but Julia continued, 'We weathered the storm until we came into calmer waters, and that only happened after Matthew was born. I was accepted then. I had given my husband a son so all was well, and it didn't matter I was English. As far as Matthew's father and I were concerned it hadn't mattered anyway. We loved each other, deeply. If we had been childless all our lives we would still have been together, loving each other.'

'You were very fortunate,' Georgie said softly. 'My brother and his wife were like that.'

The silver-blonde head nodded in acknowledgement. 'Matthew was brought up in a loving home,' Julia said quietly, 'but he also has the genes from his father's people in his blood. My husband was a wonderful man, kind and gentle, but not so his parents or their parents. They were very proud and hard, one could say cruel even.'

'I don't understand?' Georgie said quietly.

'They were the kind of people who never forgot an insult or a harm done to them,' Julia said softly. 'Vendettas, blood feuds, honour. This was the language they talked and lived. My son is not like his father, Georgie, but neither is he all his grandparents either. There is a little of both in my Matt, I think, and life will shape which takes pre-eminence. Life...or a woman.'

Georgie looked at the woman in front of her, her eyes wide with sudden understanding. But Julia had got it all wrong, she thought feverishly. Matt didn't love her; she had no sway over him except that he wanted her body for a brief time. But how could she say that to his mother?

'When such a person as my son is hurt or betrayed it goes deep.' Julia was no longer looking at Georgie but had turned to gaze out of the big picture window opposite the bed, where the tops of green trees could be seen beneath a cloudless blue sky. 'And it takes an equally deep feeling to cauterise the pain and bring about healing.'

'Julia?' Georgie didn't know what to say but she had to say something to stop this terrible misunderstanding. 'If you are saying what I think you're saying, that I am the one to bring about the healing from some incident in Matt's past, you've got it all wrong. He doesn't love me; he has already told me he doesn't believe in love or commitment.'

'Honour and pride.' It was said on a sigh.

She had to say it, crass though it might sound. Georgie took a deep breath and said quietly, 'He wants an affair, that's all. A brief interlude. He…he is interested because I haven't immediately fallen into bed with him.'

Julia's amazing eyes fastened on Georgie's flushed face, and they stayed there for what seemed like an endless time. And then Matt's mother said quietly, 'He needs you, Georgie, but how do you feel? Do you care for him? Really care for him?'

It took more strength than Julia was aware of for Georgie to strip off the armour and say steadily, 'Yes, I do, but I'd prefer him not to know.'

'I can understand that, and I promise you he will not learn it from me. But in return for that confidence I want to tell you something. Something very private and something I have not spoken of before, not to anyone. But you, you I want to tell.'

Georgie stared into the beautiful face and she felt a shiver run down her spine. This had been far from a cosy chat and she had the feeling it was about to get worse.

'When Matthew went to university he was a bright, strong boy with a zest for life that was unquenchable and a warmth that was very much like his father's,' Julia began slowly. 'When he graduated the brightness and strength was still there, but the zest for life had been turned into a desire to take it by the throat and the warmth was quite gone. This...' Julia hesitated, her hand moving to her throat. 'This was due to a girl.'

'Begonia.'

'He has spoken to you of Begonia?' It was sharp and Julia's face was amazed.

'No. Well, yes. At least...' Georgie tried to pull her thoughts together. 'He said he knew her for eighteen months and then it finished,' she said quickly.

Julia looked at her for another moment before nodding. 'It is not as simple as that, but then knowing my son you would not have expected it to be. He was in love with Begonia and she betrayed him,' she said flatly. 'But not in the normal sense. They were together for a year—you know?'

Georgie nodded painfully. Yes, she knew.

'And then something dreadful happened. We received a phone call from the university to say that Matt was missing and that the police were involved. Then came a ransom note. It stated Matt was being held until we delivered a certain amount of money to a designated pick-up point. We delivered. Matt was released from the tiny underground room he had been held in for five days and left in the middle of nowhere. But my son is no fool, Georgie.

'He had taken a note of sounds and driving distances, even though he was blindfolded and cuffed, and eventually the police found the street and then the actual cellar. Then it got worse. I won't bore you with the details, but suffice to say he had been held by supposed friends who needed money for their drug addiction.'

The claustrophobia. Georgie stared at Matt's mother in horror. 'Begonia was one of them?' she whispered weakly.

Julia nodded. 'Matt did not know about her drug habit;

perhaps he would have helped her if he did. Anyway, need-less to say, the abduction affected him deeply. He...he was not the same afterwards. He became very cynical and cold.'

Georgie nodded. She could understand that. 'And Begonia?' she asked quietly.

'Begonia and the others received a severe prison sen-tence. The parents of one of the boys involved got a clever lawyer, who insisted it was just an ill-advised practical joke which had gone wrong, but in view of the sum of money involved this argument was not acceptable. It transpired Begonia had been sharing her favours with this boy as well as Matt.'

Georgie shook her head slowly, her hair brushing her cheeks in a shimmering veil. For a first love to go wrong was bad enough, but in those circumstances...

'Matt has had women companions since then, of course, but he has chosen only those who were beautiful enough and shallow enough to fit into his lifestyle. Francisca calls them dolls and she is right. Matt only smiles when his sister says this, but when he spoke of you... He did not smile. No, he did not smile.'

'Julia—' Georgie squirmed on the upholstered seat. 'He doesn't *love* me. Whatever he feels, he's made it clear it's not love.'

'Then he is a fool,' Matt's mother said very softly, her eyes gentle on the lovely face in front of her.

'That's what Matt called Glen,' Georgie said ruefully. 'My ex. He...he let me down rather badly.'

'And Matt called him a fool? Well, well.' Julia lay back against the plump pillows behind her and surveyed Georgie afresh. 'Don't give up on him, Georgie. Not yet. It takes time to climb out of the darkness into the light, especially when that darkness is the only protection you have against a giant step that makes Neil Armstrong's look easy. I know my son. I know what is of his father. My husband loved me utterly and absolutely, and that is the way Matt will love when he finds the right woman.'

And if she wasn't the right woman? Where did that leave her? Georgie's green eyes were cloudy. Matt's mother loved him and that was right and proper, but it coloured her viewpoint to look at things for Matt's good. What about *her* good?

Matt could have any woman he wanted and he couldn't fail to recognise the fact by the number which pursued him. He was handsome and wealthy and powerful, and she was an ordinary girl from a little town in England he had happened to meet, and who didn't tell him exactly what he wanted to hear. That had interested him, intrigued him even. But what happened when the chase stopped and the hunter got his quarry?

'I think you're mistaken about me,' Georgie said quietly, 'about how Matt feels, but thank you for telling me about what happened in his past anyway. It…it explains a lot.'

Julia nodded. 'It does, doesn't it?' she agreed softly. 'But as to my being mistaken… Well, time will tell, Georgie.'

Time. Would it be friend or foe? She wished she could believe for the former but cold reason told her it would be the latter.

And then the door opened and Matt was back, and in spite of all her fears Georgie's heart leapt as she looked at him.

They spent over an hour at the hospital and by the time they left Georgie knew she could love Matt's mother. Julia was so sweet, so warm; she could understand what had attracted Matt's father to his English bride after being brought up in a home which, by the sound of it, although palatial, had been devoid of much love and laughter.

'You'll come again before you leave?' As Georgie made her goodbyes, Julia's voice was insistent.

'If you want me to.'

'I do.'

It was very definite, and once outside in the corridor Matt took her arm, drawing her round to face him as he said softly, 'I told you you two would like each other.'

And it was ridiculous, really ridiculous, and probably just because her emotions had been oversensitised during the talk with Julia, but somehow Georgie got the strangest feeling he wasn't altogether pleased at how things had gone. The grey eyes looked down at her, their expression hidden behind congeniality, and then they were walking down the corridor again and the moment was lost as they enjoyed the rest of the day together.

Julia's operation went well the next morning, and after Matt had visited the hospital he returned before lunch and found Georgie in the gardens, his voice light and easy as he said, 'Grab a swimming costume and a towel, I'm taking you to a beach I know where we can swim and laze the afternoon away.'

'But lunch?'

'Flora's packing a picnic hamper,' he said smoothly. 'We'll eat on the way; I know a spot, and I prefer it to having sand in my food.'

She nodded, but her smile was faintly wary. He had been different since their visit to see his mother the day before. The rest of the afternoon and evening spent sightseeing had been lovely, and the small restaurant at which they had eaten—surrounded by fragrant almond groves—had been magical, but there had been a distance, a coolness in Matt she was sure she hadn't imagined. Or maybe she had. She didn't know where she was when she was within six feet of him!

She had had the foresight to bring her own swimming costume with her from England—a somewhat uninteresting one-piece in dark blue so after picking up a bath towel from her bathroom Georgie joined Matt on the drive outside where he was just putting the picnic basket into the car.

He surveyed her slim shape clothed in three-quarter length jeans and a figure-hugging top in bright poppy-red silently for a moment, before he said quietly, 'Youth personified.'

'Hardly.' Georgie pushed back a strand of silky hair, tucking it behind her ear, as she said, 'I am twenty-three, Matt.'

'Ancient,' he agreed drily.

She stared at him, uncertain of his mood but knowing there was something she didn't like in his tone, and then slid into the car silently. If he wanted an argument he could argue with himself; she only had a few days here with him and they were going to have to provide a lifetime of memories.

Once they were on their way, however, the brief unease was lulled by the ever-changing vista outside the car. Sugar-white houses with balconies of iron covered in morning glory, flowered walled gardens adjoining small orchards, simple granite churches and quiet lanes hedged with hibiscus and jacaranda—Georgie drank in the rich tapestry of views and scents and began to relax.

She had vowed she would live life minute by minute with Matt, expecting nothing, and she wasn't going to spoil today by thinking too much, she decided, just after the car passed two small bare-footed children. The tiny tots were leading a bewhiskered nanny goat along the dusty road by means of a piece of frayed rope tied round its furry neck.

She had to stop examining everything his mother had said, she told herself firmly, and hoping for a miracle.

'Here.' Beyond the small village they had just passed stretched green meadows, and now Matt turned the car off the road and on to an unmade track winding away into the distance. 'I know the perfect spot for a picnic.'

After some two hundred yards or so he stopped the car. 'Look over there,' he said quietly. 'My mother and father used to bring Francisca and myself here before we went on to the beach, and my sister liked it better than the sea. She was frightened of the waves, you see, but this was safe to paddle in.'

Georgie looked. The grass sloped down to a small, crystal-clear stream fringed with pebbles, the water running with gurgling purpose over smooth mounds of polished rock. It was an enchanting little dell and she could just imagine the delight of two small children eating a picnic by the side of the stream.

Had he brought other women to this idyllic haven of days gone by? Days when he had been carefree and happy? She didn't dare ask. Instead she said, her voice very even, 'Does Francisca bring her children here?'

'That tribe of monkeys?' Dark eyes crinkled as he smiled and Georgie's heart was rent with love. 'She would never round them all up again if she let them loose in the open.'

'I'm sure they're not as bad as all that?' Georgie said reprovingly.

'Worse than you could imagine,' he returned drily as he opened his car door, walking round the bonnet and helping her to alight before he reached for the picnic basket and blanket in the back of the car. 'If I ever needed anything to convince me that marriage and children and settling down is not for me, a visit to my sister's house would do it. Bedlam. All the time.'

It was too softly vehement. Georgie watched him as he carried the hamper down to the stream, but it was some moments before she moved herself. If that hadn't been a warning, or at least a reminder, of all he had said in the past she didn't know what was! How dared he? How *dared* he warn her off like that? And then a terrible thought struck—had his mother told him what she had admitted yesterday, that she loved him? But no, no, she trusted Julia. This was just Matt being Matt.

Her stomach was churning as she sat down on the blanket he had spread out on the grass, but his remark had brought her up with a jolt. Which was probably exactly what she had needed, she admitted ruefully.

The picnic was definitely a de Capistrano one, and therefore in a different league from anything masquerading under that name which Georgie had enjoyed in the past. Wine, Flora's delicious home-made lemonade, slices of ham, turkey, beef and pork, crusty bread and little pats of butter, ripe red tomatoes, crisp salad, hard-boiled eggs, pâté, little savoury pastries, tiny tubs of fondant potatoes, goat's cheese, olives; the list went on and on, and that was before they looked at the various individual portions of mouth-watering desserts Flora had included.

'How many people did Flora think were coming on this picnic?' Georgie asked after they had eaten hungrily in companionable silence for some minutes.

'Just you and I, *pequeña*.' Matt had had one glass of the fruity red wine Flora had included before refilling his glass with lemonade, but now he poured more of the rich black-currant liquid into her glass before lying back on the blanket and shutting his eyes against the glare of the sun.

Georgie looked at him at the side of her, the big lean body stretched out like a relaxed panther but with all the inherent dangerousness of the big cat merely harnessed for the moment. A small pulse was beating at the base of his tanned throat and she had an overwhelming urge to place her lips to it before she took hold of herself firmly.

Matt had perfect control of his emotions. Why couldn't she feel the same? She drank the wine in a few hasty gulps, the warmth of it comforting after the bleakness of her thoughts, and then lay back on the sunwarmed blanket herself. He could pick her up or put her down seemingly just as he pleased whereas her head, her mind, her soul were all filled with him twenty-four hours a day. But then her heart was involved, not just her body. Unlike his.

The sun was warm on her face, a gentle breeze caressing her skin idly as it wafted the scent of a hundred wild flowers against the background music of the gurgling water. She must have slept, because when she became aware of the mouth brushing her lips it seemed part of the dream she had been having. An erotic, disturbing dream.

She opened dazed green eyes and looked into Matt's face above her and for a long moment they were both immobile, drowning in each other's eyes. Then with a muffled sound which came deep from his throat he pulled her into him, turning so that she was lying across his hard chest, her racing pulse echoing the slam of his heart.

The kiss was achingly sweet, his mouth pleasuring them both as it explored hers. A deep languorous warmth was filling her, moving into every little crevice and nerve and causing her body to throb as the ache inside her slowly ripened.

And then he lifted her from him, his voice none too steady as he said, 'Time to go, I think, or we will never have that swim.'

She didn't care about that, about the beach! She just wanted to stay here for ever, in this little place away from the real world and reality. She watched him sit up, his back tense under the black cloth of his shirt, but when he turned to face her he was composed again, the lover of a few moments ago gone.

'It is not far.' He offered her his hand as he rose to his feet and she accepted it with a smile that was forced. 'And the sea is perfect today, calm and tranquil.'

Unlike her! Georgie shut her eyes for a second as he gathered the hamper together, and then opened them to watch him pack the basket with expert precision. But then he did everything perfectly, she thought with a moment's bitterness. That was the trouble.

It was just after three o'clock and the sun was high when Matt drove the car out of the long winding lane they had been following for the last five minutes, and out on to the tough springy grass beyond which stretched the sort of beach Georgie had only seen in advertisements on the TV.

The secluded bay was set against a dramatic backdrop of pine-clad hills and in the far distance blue-mauve mountains. The dazzling white beach was strewn with delicate rose-pink and mother-of-pearl shells beyond which lapped vivid turquoise-blue water.

Matt had stopped the car and Georgie was aware of him watching her face, but it was some moments before she could drag her eyes away from the enchantment in front of her and say softly, 'It's the most beautiful place in the world, Matt. Thank you for showing it to me.'

Something worked in his face as she spoke but his voice was restrained when he said, 'My pleasure, Miss Millett.'

'Matt—' She stopped abruptly, not knowing how to continue but conscious of his pain beneath the composed mask he wore. There had been something in his expression, almost an acceptance, that had sent a chill flickering down her spine. His will was iron-like, the intensity of the spirit deep inside the man frightening. She could never reach him, never get through to the hurt individual behind the mask. She just didn't know *how*.

'Yes?'

'It doesn't matter.'

By the time Georgie had struggled into her swimming costume under the towel Matt was already in the clear blue water, and he waved to her from where he was swimming in the slight swell of the waves.

The sand was hot beneath her feet as she ran down to the water's edge, but at least she felt *herself* in her own swimming costume, she told herself bracingly.

In spite of the warmth of the sun the water was icy cold, and she gasped as she waded further and further towards Matt, although once she was swimming she didn't notice the cold any more. The water was silky, wonderful, and the small turquoise waves were totally non-threatening.

She lost sight of Matt just when she thought she was close to him, and then squealed in surprise—taking in a mouthful of salt water in the process—as he emerged just in front of her like a genie from the depths of a bottle.

'You did that on purpose!' she glared at him, but then, as he gathered her to him and kissed her thoroughly, the pair of them sinking under the clear water, she forgot to be angry. This was paradise; it was, it was paradise, and she would never feel so alive, so *aware* in the whole of her life.

They spent a crazy half-hour in the water, acting like two kids let out of school for the day, before Georgie, utterly exhausted, made for the shore. Matt had indicated he wanted to do some serious swimming before he came in, and after she had collapsed on the blanket he had brought from the car Georgie watched him for a few minutes.

The hard lean body cut through the water with military

precision, and she found herself wondering at the ruthless determination which drove him to push himself to the limit. Most people found swimming therapeutic, but she had the idea that to Matt it was just another area in which he had to prove to himself he could do it alone—beat the elements. It saddened her, taking some of the joy out of the time they had shared, and she lay back on the blanket, suddenly weary.

The air was warm and salty, the lapping of the tiny waves on the beach a soothing background music, but she couldn't really relax. After a little while she became aware the sun was too hot to ignore and sat up, wrapping the towel round her cocoon-fashion as she continued to watch Matt in the water.

And then he came out. He might just as well have been nude for all the tiny black briefs concealed.

Georgie watched, fascinated, as the lithe, tanned body strolled up the beach towards her. The hair on his powerful chest narrowed to a thin line bisecting his flat belly, and the smooth-muscled hips and long strong legs were magnificent. *He* was magnificent, every perfectly honed inch of him.

She couldn't tear her eyes away from him as he came nearer, even though she knew he must be aware she was ogling him, and it was only when he was within a few yards of her that she found the strength to lower her eyes and pretend to fiddle with the towel.

'Enjoy yourself?'

'What?' For an awful minute Georgie thought he was referring to her brazen gawping.

'The sea is so much better than even the best swimming pool, don't you think?' he said.

She forced herself to say, 'Definitely. Oh, definitely.'

'Fancy a drink?'

'What?' Oh, she had to stop saying that, she thought a trifle desperately.

'A drink?' he reiterated patiently. 'I'll bring the picnic basket down.'

'Great.'

Great, great, great! Please put some clothes on! She watched him pad towards the car and she watched him return, and she wondered if he was aware of how woefully inadequate the small piece of cloth round his hips was. But if he was, he didn't care. She shut her eyes tightly for a second as he threw himself down beside her on the blanket, and then opened them wide when he said coolly, 'Wine or lemonade?'

She didn't need anything to heat her blood further! 'Lemonade, please.'

He poured her a glass, and then himself, downing his in a few swallows before lying back on the blanket contentedly. 'This is very good.'

Speak for yourself. 'Yes, it's very nice,' she said faintly.

'Few people know of this bay; it is usually deserted.'

That wasn't actually much comfort right at this moment. She glanced at him warily. 'You must be exhausted after all that swimming,' she said carefully. 'You were in the water for more than an hour.'

'No, I am not tired, Georgie.'

She knew what was coming. She had known from the moment they had walked on to this beach what he had in mind, but as he rolled over and took her into his arms she made no attempt to push him away. She wanted him. The rights and wrongs of it suddenly didn't matter any more. She needed him in a way she had never imagined she could need anyone.

His lips were first coaxingly seductive, and then, when she met his kiss for kiss, fiercely erotic. He penetrated the softness of her mouth with his tongue, producing flickers of sensual awareness from the tips of her toes to the top of her head, his increasingly urgent caresses reflecting the fine tremors shivering across his muscled body.

'You taste and feel so good,' he murmured huskily. 'Deliciously salty-sweet and incredibly soft. Hell, Georgie, do you know what you do to me?'

The question was rhetorical, the leashed power of his arousal all too evident. It brought a fiercely primitive response from the depths of her, a wild satisfaction that his body couldn't deny his need of her. She could feel his shudders of pleasure and she exulted in them, in his strength, his maleness.

She loved him. She wanted to know what it would be like to make love with him. It was as simple as that in the end.

His hands were moving over the silky soft material of her swimsuit with slow, tantalising sureness, causing her body to spring to life beneath his fingers. Her nipples were erect and hard under their cover, her whole being gripped by quivering sexual tension.

She opened her eyes, which had been shut, so she could see his face, and his eyes looked back at her, hot and dark and glittering. But he wasn't rushing her. She was aware of this. His hands and mouth were moving with seductive insistence and creating rivulets of fire wherever they touched and teased, but this was no swift animal mating but rather one of calculated finesse. He was making her liquid with desire and he knew it; knew every single response he drew forth before she did.

She was responding to his expert mastery with instinctive passion and desire born of her love for him, and just for a moment she felt a vague sense of loss that it wasn't that way for him. He wasn't being swept along by love for her, he merely wanted her. It was just sex for him. But then he moved in a certain way, his hard chest creating a tight, exquisite pressure over her aching breasts and she forgot to think, forgot everything in the sensation after sensation washing over her body.

'Georgie, say it. Say you want me.' He was murmuring against her hot skin, his voice a low growl. 'Say you want me like I want you.'

He raised himself slightly, looking down into her dazed face as his hands cupped her cheeks.

'Say you want me to undress you, to take you here on the sands with the sky above us. Tell me.'

She stared up at him with drowning green eyes, gasping slightly as his hands moved to her breasts, shaping their full roundness through the fabric of her swimming costume. And she said the only words that were in her heart, 'I love you, so much,' as her head moved from side to side in a feverish agony of need, her eyes closing.

'No, say it as it is. No pretence, Georgie, not between us.'

For a moment she didn't understand, lost as she was in a spinning world of sensation and light, and then as his fingers traced a path into the soft hollow of her breasts before he began to peel the swimming costume away she understood what he was demanding. This had to be on his terms; he wanted her to tell him she was inviting him into her body, that she wanted and needed him, but she wasn't allowed to say love. *But she did love him.*

'I love you.' This time it wasn't said with frenzied desire but was a statement of fact, and Matt recognised it as such, his hands freezing on her body.

She lay very still, looking up at him, allowing him to see the truth in her eyes, and as she saw the shock on his face slowly being absorbed by the coldness spreading over it she knew she would remember this moment all of her life.

'No, no, you do not.'

'Yes, I do.' As his hands left her she sat up quickly, adjusting the swimming costume and drawing the towel round her shoulders. Suddenly, in spite of the heat of the sun, she felt cold. 'You might not like it,' she said with painful dignity as he sat, half turned away from her, his profile hard and stunned, 'but nevertheless that's how it is. You asked for no pretence between us, Matt, after all. And you might as well know the rest of it now. I wanted to make love with you *because* I love you, and there has never been anyone else in that way.'

'You're telling me you didn't sleep with Glen?' Although his voice was very flat she sensed the shock.

'No, I didn't. It just didn't seem right, somehow, but until I met you I hadn't realised why. But I didn't love him, not as you're supposed to love the person you want to be with for the rest of your life.' There, she'd said it. It would do no good, she knew that, but she couldn't have gone the rest of the life wondering whether if he knew it would have touched something deep inside. It was scant comfort when she looked at his rigid face, but at least he had heard it as it really was. The ball was well and truly in his court.

'I never made you any promises, Georgie.' His voice was cold now, his accent strong, and he still didn't look at her. 'You knew how it was all along, how I feel about the sort of commitment you are talking about. I am not cut out for togetherness; I do not want it.'

'Why are you so frightened to say the word?' she asked quietly. 'Because love goes hand in hand with the possibility of betrayal and loss?'

He did look at her then, his grey eyes as sharp as cut slate.

'This Begonia you told me about, the girl at university, she hurt you badly, didn't she?' His mother had said she'd never talked about it to anyone and Georgie had the feeling Matt hadn't, either. 'What happened, Matt?' she prompted softly, hoping her voice didn't betray the way she was shaking inside with the enormity of the confrontation. If he would just tell her, open up a little...

He drew in a deep hard breath. 'It will accomplish nothing to talk about it,' he said gratingly. 'The past is the past.'

'But it isn't the past for you, not really,' she countered steadily. 'And until it is you'll never be able to reach out for the future.'

'Save me the trite platitudes, Georgie!'

'You want to row with me, don't you?' she said, struggling for composure in the face of his anger. 'Attack is the best defence and all that. And it's just to cover up the fact that you are scared stiff to take a chance and trust someone!'

'You want to hear about Begonia?' he rasped bitterly. 'Then I will tell you! Every little sordid detail.' And he did. He told her it all, his voice sinisterly quiet now and very cold.

Georgie stared at him the whole time. He was right; this had accomplished nothing, she realised miserably, except to make him hate her. She had expected he would feel some relief in the telling, but instead, in revealing what he saw as his humiliation and defeat, she had made him hate her. He was a proud man, obsessively so. He would never forgive her for this.

'She was sick, Matt.' When he had finished talking and the silence became painful Georgie's voice was a whisper. 'Sick in mind and body, and someone like that can't love anything or anyone. Love is not like that—'

'And what makes you the expert?' As he swung to face her again his voice was savage.

'How I feel about you.'

He flinched visibly, but almost immediately rose to his feet, his face icy-cold. 'You are talking about sexual attraction,' he said stonily, 'although you have dressed it up to appear as something else to placate the conscience years and years of civilisation has bred. You are fooling yourself, Georgie. The emotion you are talking about does not exist in the pure form. A biological urge to mate, a wish for a nest and procreation, a need for protection or warmth, security—all those are facets of this thing you call love. It is totally unnatural to expect two people to live together for the rest of their lives. Man is not a monogamous animal.'

She had lost him. Or perhaps you had to have something in the first place to lose it, and she had never had Matt. 'I don't believe that and I don't think you do, not in your deepest heart of hearts.' Her voice *was* shaking now, she could hear it. 'There *is* a kind of love that lasts for ever, a kind that wants and needs intimacy and commitment and all that embraces. My brother and his wife had it, and I think your parents did too.'

'You know nothing about my parents,' he said cuttingly, 'so do not presume to lecture me.'

She had stood to her feet as he had been talking, and now her head jerked back as his arrogance hit a nerve. For the first time since they had been talking raw anger flooded her and she didn't try to quench it. She needed its fortifying heat to combat the agony inside. 'Lecture you?' she said with acidic mockery. 'Lecture *you*, the great Matt de Capistrano? I wouldn't dare! How could a mere mortal like me dare to disagree or venture a opinion in such exalted presence?'

'Do not be childish.'

'I might be childish but I'd rather be that than a block of stone like you,' she shot back furiously, his coldness serving to inflame her more. 'At least I'm alive, Matt! I feel, I ache, I cry—I do all the normal things that human beings do. Sure, life can make us wish we'd never been born on occasion, but real people fight back. You have let Begonia destroy you, do you realise that? They might have released you from that hole in the ground but you've dug yourself a deeper and more terrible one. You're not a man; you're a dead thing.'

'Have you quite finished?' It was thunderous.

'Oh, yes, I've finished all right. With you, with this ridiculous farce, with this country! I want to go home.' The last five words came out in a wail which wasn't at all the impression she wanted to give after he'd labelled her childish.

'I promise you you will be on the first available flight to England tomorrow,' he bit out caustically.

'Careful, Matt.' She might be devastated but he wasn't going to crush her completely! 'Promises aren't your thing.'

The drive home was the sort of nightmare Georgie wouldn't have inflicted on her worst enemy.

Matt's face could have been cut in stone and he didn't look at her or speak to her once. Georgie sat, huddled on her seat with her side pressed up against the car, as her mind reiterated all the harsh words she had thrown at him. And they had been harsh, she told herself with utter misery. She loved him, she loved him with all her heart, and all she had done was to call him names. She should have been understanding, kind, loving, showed him that true love turned the other cheek and that it didn't matter to her how he was, she still adored him.

But he was so arrogant, so infuriating, so altogether impossible! She had never even considered she'd got a temper before she'd met Matt, and then, boy, had it come to the fore! But all she'd said... She shut her eyes tightly and then opened them again, staring blankly through the windscreen without seeing a thing. She dared bet no one had ever spoken to him like that in his life. How could he make her say things like that when she loved him so much? She'd give the world to be able to heal the wounds Begonia and his so-called friends had inflicted.

When they drew up outside the house Matt left the car and opened her door—courteous to the last, Georgie thought with agonising black humour—but he didn't say a word until they were standing in the hall. 'You must be tired after such an exhausting day,' he bit out tightly, his grey eyes granite-hard as they looked down at her. 'I will see that Flora sends a tray up to your room after you have bathed and got ready for bed.'

In other words he didn't want to see her again until she left for England tomorrow. Georgie nodded stiffly, raising her small chin and calling on every scrap of tattered dignity she had left as she said, 'Thank you, but I am not hungry.'

'Nevertheless a tray will be brought to you.'

Do what you want; you always do anyway. She inclined her head before turning away and walking towards the staircase on legs that trembled. He was an unfeeling monster, that was what he was.

Once in her bedroom Georgie sat on the bed for long minutes before she could persuade her legs to carry her into the bathroom.

She wanted to cry, needed the relief of tears, but deep inside there only seemed to be dry ashes, which was making her feel worse.

After a warm bath she washed her hair and pulled on her towelling robe, wandering out into the sitting room and walking on to the balcony where the scented twilight was heavy with the last rays of the sun. She lifted her face to the sultry air, hearing the birds twittering and calling as they began to settle down for the night, and wondered how she could still walk and talk when her heart had been torn out by its roots. But this was just the beginning; she was going to have to learn to deal with this pain for the rest of her life—a life without Matt.

Flora brought her the tray ten minutes later, but although she thanked Matt's housekeeper, and smiled fairly normally, she knew she wouldn't be able to eat a thing and didn't even bother to uncover the dishes, although she took the large glass of white wine the tray held out on to the balcony with her. She sat down in the cushioned wicker chair it held, sipping the wine as her eyes wandered over the magnificent view.

She didn't regret saying everything she'd said, not really, she decided after a long while. She just wished she'd said it differently, that was all. Not in anger.

The dusk was falling rapidly now, the sky pouring flaming rivulets of scarlet, gold and orange across its wide expanse of light-washed blue. It was beautiful, magnificent, but tonight its beauty didn't touch her soul with joy and that frightened her. She felt as dead inside as she had accused Matt of being, and something of this feeling was reflected in her voice when she heard Flora behind her.

'The tray's on the little table, Flora,' she said dully without turning round. 'I'm sorry I couldn't eat anything but I think I've probably had too much sun today.'

'Forgive me, Georgie.'

She heard the voice almost without it registering for a stunned moment, and then she shot round, spilling the wine and with her hand to her throat as she saw Matt just behind her.

He looked terrible, awful. And wonderful. Her heart gave a mighty jolt and began to race like a greyhound, and she knew she wasn't dead inside after all as the pain hit. 'What...what do you want?'

'For you to keep on loving me.' He made no attempt to come any nearer.

'You don't believe in love,' she said, her face awash with the tears she'd thought she couldn't cry.

'If what I feel for you isn't love, then all the poets have got it wrong,' he said with grating pain. 'From the first moment I saw you it was there, Georgie. I tried to tell myself it was a million other things—sexual attraction, desire—but you've heard all that. I...I can't let you leave me, Georgie. I will die if you leave me. I haven't recognised myself the last few weeks and it has terrified me.'

The last was said with a kind of angry bewilderment which would have been funny in any other circumstances.

'You...you wouldn't die. What about Pepita and all the others?' She hadn't realised until she had said the name how much the other woman's presence in his life still rankled.

'Pepita?' He made an irritable, disdainful movement with his hand, and the meaning behind it almost made Georgie feel sorry for the beautiful Spanish woman. Almost. 'Pepita is like a sister to me; I have told you this. And there are no others. There will never be any others now I have met you. You have done this; you have ruined me for anyone else.'

'You said...' Georgie took a great gulp of air, trying to control her quivering bottom lip. 'You said—'

'I know what I said.' His voice was a deep hard groan. 'I said you were fooling yourself, all the time knowing it was I who was in that state of mind, not you. You challenged me that I was frightened of speaking the word love because of all it entailed, and this is true. This was true.'

'So what's changed?' she asked, seeing him through a mist of tears. 'What's changed your mind?'

'The thought of losing you, my love.'

It was the endearment she had never thought to hear from him and Georgie found she couldn't take it in. 'You wanted an affair,' she accused tremulously.

'I still do. An affair that lasts the rest of our lives and beyond, a real love affair. I want *you*, Georgie. Not just a warm body in my bed. I want us to be everything to each other; wife and husband, lovers, friends, and, yes, I admit that still terrifies me, but not as much as living life without you. When you confessed your love for me today I knew this. You know the land I bought? Where the butterflies live?' he asked suddenly.

'The butterflies?' And then she caught her thoughts. 'Oh, yes, Newbottle Meadow.'

'It will not be built on,' he said softly. 'I have already purchased new land, an old factory site that is *very* ugly, and this will be Robert's new undertaking. I have informed the authorities that I will be turning the land into a wildlife sanctuary and a place for people to walk, and will be donating an annual sum for its upkeep and so on.'

'When did you do that?' she asked dazedly.

'When I met the girl I had been waiting for all my life,' he said simply. 'Weeks ago. It will be called ''Georgie's Meadow'' from now on.'

For a moment Georgie stared blankly at him. 'Me?' she said.

'You.' And now he took her in his arms, kissing her long and hard until she was breathless. 'My love, for ever.'

'I want babies,' she warned ecstatically, wondering how a kiss could wipe away all the agony of the last hours.

'So do I, *pequeña*, hundreds.'

'They might be like Francisca's children!'

'They will be perfect. How could they be anything else when they have a perfect mother?' he said tenderly, picking her up as though she weighed nothing at all and sitting down with her in the chair, before kissing her again until she was weak and trembling in his arms.

'Matt?' When she finally managed to pull away to look at him, her eyes were bright and her mouth full and ravished.

'Yes, my love?'

'I'm not perfect,' she said with absolute seriousness.

'Yes, you are. For me, that is.'

And that was the way it continued to be.

Unlimited access to all your favourite Mills & Boon romances!

Start your free trial now

with MILLS & BOON

Available at
weloveromance.com